"The story grabs you and doesn't let go till you find out who wins—if anyone."
Paul D. Marks, Shamus Award-winning author of *White Heat* and *The Blues Don't Care*

"*Code Four* is a body slam to traditional procedurals with a taut line of suspense and an unblinking look at the inner workings of a major police department. A truthful tour de force of *real* police work."
Gray Basnight, *Madness of the Q*

"A more than worthy finale to an outstanding series. Like all great endings, I put down the book with the idea these people's lives were continuing, but I wasn't going to get to see them anymore."
Dana King, two-time Shamus Award nominee and author of the Penns River novels

"A fitting finale to Conway and Zafiro's series of incisive police procedurals, *Code Four* pulls you in from the first page. It is both timely and terrifying in its portrayal of police brutality and corruption."
Richie Narvaez, author of *Noiryorican*

"*Code Four* is a hard-hitting, complex, and unsettling read."
Cynthia Kuhn, author of the Agatha Award-winning Lila Maclean Academic Mysteries

"Relentless and compelling, *Code Four* grabs your heart and batters it with a powerful, disturbing and headline-real story of crime and police work, public and private politics and pure procedural mystery. Conway and Zafiro are the best cop writers on duty today. *Code Four* hits with the shock and brutality of a brick through your windshield. A violent and unforgettable tale of the pull of corruption and the power of truth."

Mark Bergin, author of *Apprehension*

"This terrific police procedural explores what lies beneath the surface. An intriguing wrap-up to a suspenseful series."

John Shepphird, Shamus Award-winning author

"*Code Four* is a book about cops, written by two former cops who know all about that job. The writing is seamless, tight, tense and clean. The characters are so well developed you swear you know them. Like the book title, Zafiro and Conway have everything under control and they're in charge of the situation."

Jim J. Wilsky, author of *Sort 'Em Out Later*

"*Code Four* is another stellar ride-along with real world police work. This series shines a mag light beyond headlines and into the day to day lives of a department on the edge. Tense, taut and rushing toward the conclusion, this is a great capper to a great series."

Eric Beetner, author of *All the Way Down*

ACCLAIM FOR *CODE FOUR*

"Frank Zafiro knows cops and he knows the streets—especially my streets. With *Code Four*, he and Colin Conway have written a timely and compelling crime novel."
**Jess Walter, Edgar Award-winning author
of *Citizen Vince* and *The Cold Millions***

"For those who like their mystery/thrillers filled with plenty of action and intrigue and a realistic edge (reminiscent of Joseph Wambaugh police-procedurals), look no further than Conway and Zafiro. These two write with authority, because they actually worked the job."
**Robin Burcell, *New York Times* bestselling author of
The Last Good Place and *Wrath of Poseidon***

"Top-notch crime fiction…a realistic tale of murder, corruption, politics, and greed. But at its heart *Code Four* is a personal and brutally honest look at the men and women of law enforcement. Those who walk a razor edge between right and wrong and risk everything for justice."
**Bruce Robert Coffin, award-winning author
of the Detective Byron mysteries**

"*Code Four* is a tightly written procedural laying bare the infectious reach of corruption when officers believe the ends justify the means. Loaded with authentic detail, Zafiro and Conway deliver a thrilling, and heart-pounding conclusion to the Charlie-316 series."
James L'Etoile, *At What Cost* and *Bury the Past*

"The real deal. Emphasis on real."
Colin Campbell, author of the Jim Grant thrillers

"*Code Four* is a must-read in the canon of modern police procedurals. From personal vendettas to consent decrees, Conway and Zafiro don't shy from the inherent paradox to police work—that justice isn't so cut and dry as we'd like to believe. We humans may be the only species that writes and enforces laws, but we're not immune to savagery or misjudgment or corruption. *Code Four* is an authentic look at people who are cops...not cops masquerading as people."
Matt Phillips, *Countdown* and *Accidental Outlaws*

"*Code Four* is a riveting tale of an unsanctioned police investigation into one of its own. Simmering suspense builds to a thrilling climax that will keep crime fiction fans on edge and reading long into the night. A timely and recommended read."

**Brenda Chapman, author of
the Stonechild and Rouleau series**

"Conway and Zafiro have capped their gritty police procedural Charlie-316 series the only way they could have: with booming escalation. All at once engaging, authentic and driving, they give the reader insight into the reality of cops' lives with the added extremity of the series' drama. See what comes from guys who've done the job and are now writing about the most riveting parts of it."
Ryan Sayles, *Together They Were Crimson*

CODE FOUR

a Charlie-316 novel

Colin Conway | Frank Zafiro

Code Four: A Charlie-316 Novel

Cover design by Zach McCain

ISBN: 978-1-7371120-0-6

Original Ink Press, an imprint of High Speed Creative, LLC
1521 N. Argonne Road, #C-205
Spokane Valley, WA 99212

This one is for Brad Hallock,
the man responsible for our friendship.

CODE FOUR

Code Four: a radio code issued by police officers to indicate everything is under control and officers are now in charge of the situation they were dispatched to.

NIGHT

There was no moon out.

Not that it mattered in this neighborhood.

At the west end of the block sat a McDonald's, its interior dark and quiet. A couple of hours had passed since the last burger was sold for the evening. A rusty pickup remained in the parking lot, but no employee was inside the building. Overhead lights encircled the property and bathed it in a bright, sickly white.

Across the street to the south was a vacant lot. Standing in the middle of the property, a real estate skid sign leaned from a broken support. Had it been in another neighborhood, this land might have been dark. However, the McDonald's provided enough illumination for two parcels.

The Burger King immediately next door furnished even more light. Newly constructed with modern finishes and updated logos, the establishment proudly announced its presence with brightly illuminated signs and even more energy-efficient parking lot lights than its competitor.

It didn't matter that both fast-food restaurants were on Division Street, the most heavily trafficked corridor and busiest retail strip in Spokane, Washington. It also didn't matter that both restaurants were now closed, and the gleaming parking lights were only to deter criminal activity and promote public safety.

What really mattered was that there was no physical barrier from the rear of either establishment before the start of the nearby neighborhood filled with post-World War II houses. A row of trees at full bloom would have been a welcome relief to the residents of the small, mostly rental homes. Much like the light pollution, the trees were probably an afterthought. Which meant that the nearby tiny houses with postage-stamp yards were lit up every night almost as severely as a prison yard.

Almost, but not quite.

At least, that's what Tyler Garrett supposed.

Even though he'd been a police officer for more than a decade, he had never been inside a prison. Not that this was any kind of anomaly, since most cops had never seen the inside of a prison. For that fact, most had never been inside a local jail. Oh, they would have seen the booking area, of course, and probably even the in-processing station, but that was about as far as most officers would take any curiosity into the correctional system.

Garrett, however, had actually seen the inside of a jail cell. He'd been in there after he was in-processed, escorted to a cell, the lock was secured, and a jailer walked away. It had occurred a couple of years ago, but that was in the rearview mirror now. And if he was honest with himself, which he was nothing but these days, it wasn't as bad as everyone made it out to be.

The jailers couldn't get inside his head any more than others outside those concrete walls could. If that was the case—if his mind could remain his own—then he was free to be himself. A game was still a game and the pieces had to be moved.

Who cared where the board was?

Garrett checked his watch to find that it was shortly after two. He needed to get some sleep soon or tomorrow's shift would be a bear. For almost an hour now, he'd sat off the little tan house, the one directly behind the vacant lot, the one awash in light from both the McDonald's and the Burger King. This was the last known residence of Veryl Wooley.

Veryl.

It was a redneck name, for sure, but the man had been a

good earner. Smart and loyal, too. At least, that was what Earl Ellis had told him. Garrett never had direct contact with Wooley, so he had to go with Earl's feedback.

It had been a few days that he'd sought the man. Garrett knew where he lived and what he drove. Well, where he *supposedly* lived and what he *supposedly* drove. Garrett observed this house at various times and never saw a 2012 Mazda 3 in front. The little house didn't have a driveway and, therefore, didn't have a garage.

Perhaps Wooley had moved. Maybe he was staying with a girlfriend. Or he could have taken a trip to see a family member. Hell, his car might be in the shop. There was an endless list of reasons for the car to not be there. The same could be said for Veryl Wooley.

Garrett could give himself a headache thinking about the reasons.

Hunting Wooley might be a fool's errand. That didn't panic him, though. Besides, why should he worry? He knew what risks faced him now and he'd done his best to contain them. He minimized those few he couldn't control by compartmentalizing them—they couldn't hurt him if they couldn't get close to him. Therefore, worrying now was a waste of energy and imagination. His energy. His imagination.

The only thing that truly bothered him at that moment was getting enough sleep. The new day shift assignment was a crimp in his lifestyle. It wouldn't stop him from doing what needed to be done, but it still sucked.

With a resigned sigh, Garrett reached for the ignition switch. He felt its tension against his gloved fingers as it waited for the opportunity to fire the engine to life. In mid-turn, he froze, stopping before the engine could alert anyone of his presence. His fingers now returned the ignition switch to its resting place.

The front door to the little tan house had opened. Even though no light came from inside the house, nor a porch light, the figure who emerged was illuminated by the neighboring parking lot lights.

A short, skinny white man now stood on the concrete steps of the tan house.

Even from this distance, Garrett was sure it was him—Veryl Wooley. He'd seen his booking photo on the department's computers.

Wooley wore loose-fitting jeans, an over-sized shirt, and a baseball cap turned backwards. He glanced up and down Heroy Avenue once, then twice. He reached back and pulled the door closed before looking down the block again. Satisfied he was alone, the man bounded down the stairs. He held his unbelted jeans around his waist as he did so.

"Typical," Garrett muttered.

Wooley either didn't have the Mazda anymore or it was parked elsewhere. Once on the sidewalk, he headed west toward Division Street. It was too late to catch a bus—they stopped operating shortly before midnight—so either he was going to the nearby convenience store or he was meeting someone.

If Veryl decided to bolt across the busy arterial, there was no way for Garrett to cross the concrete median in his car. He would lose the man as well as alert him that he was being followed. It was a sucker's play to do that.

Garrett slipped out of his car. His hand touched the gun holstered in the small of his back to ensure it was secured. He wore a long-sleeved black T-shirt, black jeans, and ankle-high black patrol boots.

At Division Street, Wooley paused for the three lanes of northbound traffic. Even at this hour, the flow was sporadic enough with the late-night bar crowd heading home to make caution worthwhile. Wooley took an unnecessary look north to ensure no traffic was heading the wrong way then stole another glance south. Something in that second glance must have caught his eye because he looked back from where he came.

Garrett was only a few feet away when Wooley's eyes widened, and he stepped into the road.

A northbound Mustang slammed on its brakes and skidded. Its squealing tires sounded extremely loud at this late hour. The Ford's horn pierced the night.

"Stop!" Garrett yelled. It was a foolish command, especially since he wasn't in uniform.

Veryl Wooley sprinted across the northbound lanes of Division Street over the concrete median then the southbound lanes. Garrett was on his heels, albeit a bit slower as he heeded caution to avoid oncoming cars.

Maybe it was instinctual or maybe that's where he had planned to go all along, but once Wooley made it to the safety of the well-illuminated Office Depot parking lot, he turned north and ran toward the gas station at the corner.

Garrett sprinted after him. He was faster than his quarry. Some of this was physics since he was a bigger and stronger man. Some of this had to be training, since Wooley was not the type to have spent any time in or around a gym.

As he neared the man, Garrett yelled, "Veryl!"

Hearing his name, Wooley glanced over his shoulder and saw Garrett within arm's reach. The man panicked and turned deeper into the parking lot, forsaking the convenience store.

This move surprised Garrett and when he planted his foot to turn, it slipped out from underneath him. He slammed to the asphalt. He grunted as his shoulder and hip hit the ground at the same time. Without hesitation, he scrambled back to his feet and ran.

When Wooley made it to the darkened alley behind the office supply store, he turned southbound. A neighborhood abutted the corridor.

Garrett leaned forward and pushed himself harder. The rubber soles of his boots slapped the asphalt. When he entered the rocky, uneven terrain of the backstreet, the rhythmic slap of his soles changed to a crunching beat.

The short stretch of alley was dark but in the distance was light from the next road several hundred feet away. He couldn't remember the street's name, but—

Garrett suddenly slowed. *Where did Wooley go?*

The alley was empty and there was no way that the shorter man could have run the entire length of the shopping center to turn back into the front of parking lot. Garrett's trot slowed to a walk. Blood pounded in his ears as he inhaled deeply through his nose. He held the breath for several seconds before pushing it out in a long, slow exhale.

Did he jump a fence into a nearby yard?

That's what I would have done.

But Wooley hadn't done anything Garrett might have considered.

First, Tyler Garrett would never have left the safety of the lit Office Depot parking lot.

Second, he would have continued toward the sanctuary of the convenience store where there was more than likely an employee working. That meant a witness.

Third, he would have stayed at the lit intersection where the heavy traffic would have provided additional witnesses.

But Garrett had to give the man credit for something. Against all the things Garrett wouldn't had done, Veryl Wooley unexpectedly broke left toward the darkened alley and got away.

So where will he go now? Home?

That seemed the natural play. It might take some time, but he would eventually go there.

Garrett turned around to head back the way he came and suddenly stopped. It was hard to place over the traffic sounds on the nearby arterial and the blood still pulsating in his ears, but he thought he'd heard something.

His eyes strained to see in the low light. Trash cans lined the length of fence that separated the houses from the alley.

There it is again.

The sound he first heard—a faint wheeze followed by a ragged gasp of air.

He hunched as he hurried through the alley. This time, though, he searched along the fence line. He checked behind a couple of large, rectangular trash cans. Long, sticky weeds protruding from the fences grabbed at his pants. The alley smelled like feces and garbage.

As he moved toward the next set of trash cans, they rocked suddenly. A darkened figured burst from a hiding place behind them. Veryl Wooley managed one step before Garrett grabbed him with both hands. They pirouetted together for a moment until Garrett tossed the smaller man into the nearby fence line. He bounced off and knocked over a trash can.

The smaller man exhaled loudly, "Oof!" then fell over the can. His knees struck the ground and his chest flopped onto the side of the can.

Garrett stepped behind him and punched down onto a kidney, compressing it between his fist and the hard plastic of the trash can.

Wooley straightened and squealed. His guttural cry was that of a wounded animal.

Garrett punched again, but this time into the opposite kidney. Veryl Wooley rolled away and tucked himself into a fetal position against the fence. He hollered, "I give! I give!"

A light came on at the back of the house nearest them. The back door squeaked opened, and an elderly man poked his head out. "The hell is going on out there?" he yelled.

"Police!" Garrett shouted. "Caught a prowler out here."

Wooley shouted, "He's not—" but Garrett kicked him to cut off his protest.

"Need some help?" the elderly man asked. His voice, although clearly aged, was not frail. "I can grab my gun and come out."

An armed citizen was the last thing Garrett needed. "My partner is on the way. Please stay inside."

Garrett kicked Wooley again for good measure. The smaller man whispered, "I didn't say nothin'."

The back door started to close then it squeaked open again. "If you're gonna give 'em hell, will you keep it down? I gotta get some sleep."

The door squeaked closed, but the rear light remained on.

Garrett bent down then and whispered, "Where's Earl?"

"Who?"

Garrett punched Wooley in the midsection. He didn't connect with anything important as the man was turtled up with his arms crossed over his belly, but the simple act of hitting the man was part of the process.

"Earl Ellis. Where is he?"

"How would I know?"

Garrett kicked him.

"I don't know! I don't know!"

"Keep it down," Garrett ordered. "We don't want to wake the old man again."

"Then stop hitting me," Wooley whined.

He knelt. "I won't hit you if you tell me where Earl went."

"But I—"

Garrett faked as if to strike Wooley in the face. The smaller man cowered in response and covered his head with his arms. Garrett punched his exposed belly.

Spittle flew from Wooley's mouth, and he coughed several times. When he finally recovered enough breath to speak, he rasped, "If I knew where he was, I'd tell you. I promise, man. I wouldn't hold out. I *promise*."

Garrett studied Wooley for a moment. The two men remained motionless in the quiet of the foul-smelling alley. Finally, Garrett nodded and patted Wooley's leg. "I believe you."

The smaller man visibly relaxed. "You do?"

Garrett reached behind his back and slowly withdrew his gun. When he pointed it at Wooley, the cowering man whined, "Ah, man."

"Shut up and listen. You see or hear from Ellis, you tell him to get in touch."

"I will," Wooley said, his voice laced with fear. "In touch with who?"

"He'll know." Garrett cocked his head slightly. "Do you know who I am?"

Wooley's eyes widened and he started to nod his head.

Garrett extended the gun.

"No." Wooley exaggeratedly shook his head side to side. "I have absolutely no clue who you are."

Garrett slipped his gun back into his holster and stood. "And the next time you see me, don't run. It just makes me mad."

"For sure, man. I won't—"

Garrett kicked him a final time. This time was in the shin, which elicited a howl of pain as Wooley grabbed his leg. He left the man moaning and rolling in the alley.

As he walked back to his car, Garrett's thoughts drifted away from Veryl Wooley and the missing Earl Ellis to the thing that worried him the most right now.

He checked his watch. It was almost quarter of three now.

If he didn't get some sleep soon, tomorrow would be rough.

MONDAY

In the end, your integrity is all you've got.
—Jack Welch, CEO

Chapter 1

"Thirty damn minutes," Chief Robert Baumgartner muttered as he slammed the telephone receiver into its cradle.

His friend and confidante, Captain Tom Farrell, froze. The captain remained halfway lowered into the chair opposite Baumgartner. The two men were meeting in the chief's office to talk about budgeting concerns, but that topic was suddenly low priority.

"What happens in thirty minutes?"

"It all hits the fan," Baumgartner growled.

The captain dropped into his chair. "I'm not following."

Baumgartner smacked his desk and bellowed, "Damn it!"

Farrell instinctively flinched, regained his composure, and crossed one leg over the other. He lay his elbows on the arms of the chair and watched quietly as the chief collected himself.

Baumgartner hated when his emotions slipped out like that, especially in front of members of his staff. He frowned as a sting radiated outward from his palm and he shook his hand in response. His face warmed in embarrassment and he knew his cheeks would soon redden.

He'd gotten close with Tom Farrell by going to his house for dinners and having him out to his for the same. Dropping his guard in front of him was probably a natural consequence. He wondered how often he did that.

Baumgartner pushed those thoughts away and leaned back in his chair. He stared at the now silent and observant captain. Farrell waited with the wariness of someone expecting the delivery of bad news.

Marilyn appeared in the doorway to his office. The disapproving look from his assistant meant his outburst had been heard at her desk which meant it could also be heard out in the hall where officers and detectives might be milling about. The department was a notoriously gossipy bunch. A chief erupting the way he did, especially with Captain Tom Farrell sitting opposite him, would send tongues a-wagging.

As apologetically as Baumgartner could muster, he nodded once to his assistant. Marilyn reached for the handle of the door that separated his office from the lobby and slowly pulled it closed.

Farrell leaned forward. "You want to tell me—"

"DOJ lands in half an hour."

The captain's mouth slowly opened. "The Department of Justice is coming here? For what?"

Baumgartner shrugged. "We knew this could happen."

"But the info they requested, that was months ago. And it was routine stuff, right?"

"Nothing is routine with them," the chief said. "If they want something, it means they're watching."

"But I thought—"

"Stop thinking like a cop," Baumgartner snapped.

Farrell's jaw flexed as he set both feet on the ground. "I'm thinking like a captain."

"Of a police department."

"That's what I am." The captain's hands wrapped around the arms of the chair as if he was on a plane leaving the ground.

"You need—no, *we* need to think like bureaucrats who are part of a government agency. Arguably, the most powerful agency inside our country."

Farrell muttered, "I get it."

"Do you?" Baumgartner asked. "Justice effectively has oversight of all law enforcement agencies. If they don't like what we do or how we do it, they get to change it."

"I know that," Farrell said flatly.

Baumgartner lifted a hand. He'd upset his friend. He softened his voice when he said, "I know you do, Tom. Listen, I'm angry and I'm taking it out on you. Friendly fire.

I'll point it in a different direction."

"What do you think prompted this?"

"You're kidding." He might have been wrong for blasting Farrell, but the man seemed to be missing cues or purposefully ignoring the obvious. "Gary Stone," the chief said.

Farrell blinked several times before saying, "He was ambushed and… and we got his killer."

"You don't sound convinced."

The captain looked down at his hands as they rubbed together.

"What's wrong, Tom?"

"It's Stone," the captain said, his voice soft.

"You liked him."

Farrell nodded then shrugged.

"I get it. I liked him, too, but we can't let that blind us to the fact that we've had three dead officers—"

The captain looked up. "Three? One of those committed suicide—"

"Don't play semantics."

"I'm not. Suicide isn't even considered line of duty. How can DOJ use that to investigate us?"

"It's cumulative," Baumgartner explained impatiently. "They see three dead officers in a short time span, coupled with a series of officer-involved shootings."

Farrell's head jerked away but came right back. "A lot of departments have officer-involved—"

"Then I stepped in it when I tried to help the mayor with the Betty Rabe thing."

That gave the captain pause. "You think that has something to do with this?"

Baumgartner shrugged. "How would I know? It was all over the news. All I know for certain is they're here to see how we're doing."

"How we're doing?" Farrell parroted as he leaned forward. "What the hell does that mean—how we're doing? Is that what they said they want to find out? How we're doing?"

"Those are my words, Tom. Relax. They're coming out to poke around. If they find something, then they go back to D.C. and make a mountain out of it. If they find nothing, well, there's always another day."

Farrell shifted his position in his chair as he muttered, "Poke around."

"Come on, Tom. The hell is wrong with you? They want to see what's going on around here."

"Isn't this sort of…irregular?"

Baumgartner was surprised at how argumentative his captain was. "What's irregular is how many dead cops we've had."

"I get that, but—"

"What's irregular is how much we've been in the national news."

"I under—"

"What's irregular is how much crap I've had to eat lately, and it doesn't look like it's going to stop any time soon."

Farrell held his hands up in surrender. Baumgartner licked his lips and sucked for moisture in his suddenly dry mouth.

"Sorry, Tom. I can't seem to stop with the friendly fire."

"I get it. You just found out."

He nodded.

"Who told you, by the way?"

"A staff member in Justice. An old friend."

"Who?"

Baumgartner shrugged. "A buddy named Lou. We played football in high school before he ran off to become a lawyer. Anyway, he called me and gave me a heads-up. It's how the world works beyond the streets. Be nice to people and they'll be nice to you."

"Some friend. Half hour lead time isn't much."

"Half hour is better than nothing. I don't see any of your old friends calling to give you a warning about this."

Farrell smirked. "So what do we do now?"

"I call the mayor and you notify the captains and

lieutenants. Let the system take over from there."

"And what do we tell them?"

"What do you think we tell them? We tell them what's needed to protect the department."

Farrell swallowed as if he was fighting back the urge to vomit. "Are you suggesting…"

"Am I suggesting what?"

The captain's brow furrowed. "Are you suggesting we *lie* to them?"

"To who?"

"To DOJ."

"Seriously?"

"To protect the department. That's what you said."

Baumgartner stared at Captain Tom Farrell. For a moment, the man before him looked scared. It wasn't a look he'd ever seen before on his friend. It vanished almost as fast as he'd seen it and was replaced with a look he'd often associated with Farrell—concern for the department. Maybe Baumgartner had projected his own fears onto his captain. He rubbed his face and took a deep breath before speaking.

"No, Tom. I am not suggesting we lie to them. I would never suggest that. I'm also not suggesting we cover up anything. What I'm actually saying is this—less is more."

"Less is more?"

"That's right. Answer their questions. That's it. Don't offer up anything more. Tell your command staff to think before they speak. Advise them to pass that along to their officers as well."

"So act like we're on the stand and being cross-examined?"

"That's a good way of thinking about it. Maybe be a little friendlier than that, but you get the point."

Farrell leaned his head back and stared up at the ceiling.

"We're a good department made up of good people," Baumgartner said. "If we try to game this process, they'll sense it, and it'll only fuel their suspicion further. If we do that, we're screwed."

Farrell's head dropped back to eye level.

"Tell the captains and lieutenants what I just told you. Cooperate fully, but we don't need any eager beavers out there. Answer the questions that are asked. Truthfully. Then stop. And if that means one or two people take a beating over something, then so be it. It's better than the entire department falling under a consent decree."

The captain blanched. "Can that happen now?"

"No. They're kicking tires on this visit. That's all. If they find anything, then they'll be back to stick their foot up our collective ass. I'd rather avoid that."

Farrell's eyes dipped. "This isn't enough time to get ready."

"This isn't an inspection and we were fortunate to get a heads-up. Otherwise, they would have shown up in our backyard demanding an invitation to our barbeque."

"But—"

"I don't make the rules, Tom. I'm doing the best I can."

Baumgartner lifted the telephone receiver and his finger hovered over the number pad. The captain didn't take the hint and continued to stare ahead while he absently rubbed his hands together.

"Tom?"

Farrell's eyes focused. "Huh?"

"I've got to call the mayor. It's time to for you to let things roll downhill."

"Right," he muttered.

The captain stood and left without further word. Baumgartner considered the telephone in his hand, sighed heavily, then dialed the mayor's direct line.

Chapter 2

This is a waste of my time.

Spokane Police Detective Wardell Clint stood with his arms crossed in the bullpen of the County Sheriff's Investigation Division. This indication of frustration was the only tell he gave to Detective Cassidy Harris as she spoke about her investigation into the shooting death of SPD Officer Gary Stone. Crossed arms or not, she ought to be able to surmise what he thought of her case simply due to the weak-ass crap she was reciting. That was, if she were any kind of detective at all.

Despite his thoughts on her conclusions regarding this case, Clint supposed that Harris was decent enough at her job. She was a far cry better than the muscle-head with whom she was still partnered.

Shaun McNutt stood off to the side, his muscular arms crossed to mirror Clint's stance. To Clint, McNutt was more concerned about how he looked as a homicide detective than how he performed as one. He had little use for the man.

When Cassidy paused in her recitation, Clint spoke. "You've had this case for six weeks. This is the best you can do?"

Harris flushed slightly. She opened her mouth to reply, but McNutt hurriedly broke in. "Watch your mouth, Ward. Don't talk to her like that."

"My name is Wardell." Clint didn't bother looking at McNutt. It was clear the man didn't like him, but Clint didn't find that to be anything special. Lots of people didn't like him. "And I wasn't talking to you." He tilted his head forward slightly toward Harris. "I asked you a question, Detective."

Harris recovered quickly. "I don't answer to you, *Detective*. This is my case. This briefing is a courtesy."

"No, it's not," Clint said. "Per the Officer Involved Shooting Protocol Agreement, I am assigned as the shadow from the involved agency. I'm entitled to be with you every step of the way. But over the past four weeks, I've agreed to weekly briefings instead. *That* is a courtesy."

Harris clenched her jaw and sighed. "Why do you have to be so difficult?"

"I'm not difficult. I just expect people to do their jobs."

"Hey!" McNutt snapped. "I said, watch your mouth."

Clint ignored him. "Six weeks ago, a Spokane police officer was killed in the line of duty. More than that, he was probably executed in a clear ambush. And in those six weeks, you've discovered exactly what?"

"The case is solved, *pal*," McNutt growled. "We got the shooter. What more do you want?"

Clint let out a derisive snort. "The shooter was found dead at the scene, shot by one of our officers. So, forgive me if I'm not impressed by your investigative acumen. *You* didn't *get* anyone."

"Typical Honey Badger," McNutt muttered.

Clint focused on Harris. "Leon Strayer shot Officer Stone at 5606 North Havana. Officer Tyler Garrett returned fire, killing Strayer. Correct?"

"You know it is."

"We *all* knew it at the scene, six weeks ago. Tell me something I don't know."

Harris looked exasperated. "That's what I've been doing with this briefing."

"No. You've been detailing tasks."

"Tasks are important."

"They are," Clint agreed. "Tasks are crucial. But they are outputs. What's the outcome?"

"Look, I don't need you to lecture me on—"

"*Why* did Leon Strayer shoot Officer Gary Stone?" Clint asked.

"That's impossible to know. Strayer is dead."

Clint narrowed his eyes slightly. "So the only way to figure out a person's motive is if they confess it? You must be some detective."

McNutt dropped his arms and took a half step forward. Clint shot him a warning look. At the same time, Harris lifted a restraining hand toward McNutt. With a scowl, the male detective stepped back, crossing his arms again.

"Now you're just being a dick," Harris said to Clint. "Are you purposefully trying to insult me?"

"If that's what it takes to get you to think outside of the box."

"There is no box," Harris snapped. "That's a worn-out cliché. My job is to find and analyze evidence."

"Fine. My question stands. Why did Strayer shoot Officer Stone?"

"I have a theory," Harris said grudgingly.

Clint turned up his hand. "Let's hear it."

Harris hesitated, then said, "There was a third body at the scene."

"Richard Van Pelt."

"Right. He lived there. That's who Garrett and Stone were going to contact at the house that day. Apparently, they saw Van Pelt as a way to get to his half-brother, who was someone their Anti-Crime Team was targeting."

Clint nodded. The short-lived Anti-Crime Team had enjoyed significant success in its brief run.

"Van Pelt was killed with a shotgun, just like Gary Stone," Harris continued. "I believe that Strayer murdered Van Pelt. Officers Stone and Garrett arrived before he could flee the scene. He was trapped, so he decided to shoot it out."

"So your theory is that it was all a coincidence?"

Harris shrugged. "More like bad timing. Officer Stone didn't know what was waiting for him behind that door. He stumbled into an unplanned ambush." She peered more closely at Clint. "Why? Do you have a better theory?"

I do, Clint thought.

But not one I can share with you.

So instead, he shook his head and said, "No. I'm just the token black man on this detail."

Harris rolled her eyes. "You bust my balls with the race card? You don't have something better? Come on. Where's the legendary Wardell Clint conspiracy theories? The uncanny insight? Seriously, educate me."

Her sarcasm glanced off Clint without effect. "Even if your theory is correct, it doesn't explain why Strayer killed Van Pelt."

"I don't know why. Maybe something to do with his half-brother, William Schloss."

"But you interviewed Schloss," Clint said. "I saw the report."

"Then you know he didn't say squat," McNutt said. "Which means that Strayer probably killed Van Pelt over some junkie burglar BS vendetta. It doesn't matter. The case is sewn up. Why are you making this more difficult than it has to be?"

Clint didn't answer. Even if he could share all he knew, he wouldn't give McNutt the satisfaction. He realized this was the end of the investigation as far as McNutt and Harris were concerned. As a formality, they'd likely leave the case open until the remainder of the lab work came back, just in case any of those findings conflicted with their conclusions. But he expected they'd send over a preliminary findings report to the chief and the sheriff. The two chief executives would read about the tragedy of two aggressive police officers on a directed-enforcement team who stumbled upon a murder-in-progress, resulting in one officer killed and the other forced to take the life of a suspect.

Only Clint knew that wasn't what happened. The problem was proving it.

"Remember to copy me on all your reports," he said abruptly, then turned and strode away. McNutt muttered a curse after him.

Clint walked through the Sheriff's Office side of the

Public Safety Building, not making eye contact with anyone. His mind whirred through Harris's investigation one more time, looking for anything he'd learned that he didn't already know. There was nothing of consequence.

He should have expected that. He'd seen how Tyler Garrett had carefully orchestrated everything since that hot August night almost two years ago when he had been in the shooting that started this odyssey.

Todd Trotter was the unarmed suspect that Garrett shot to death on a traffic stop. Clint had been assigned to shadow Harris and McNutt for that investigation, too. While he had been sarcastic when he called himself the token black man on her case a few minutes before, that was exactly what he had been on the Trotter shooting. The chief himself had reportedly demanded he be assigned. Typical of the brass, the chief was more concerned about the *optics* of the situation than whether Clint was a good detective. A black officer had just shot a white suspect. It might have been the reverse of how the scenario played out to a bad end in some cities, but Clint could see how it would be a problem in Spokane. He still resented being assigned simply because of his race, though.

In the end, what he discovered stunned him, and he'd been dealing with it ever since. The enormity of Tyler Garrett's actions was only matched by the politics in play around them both. Clint developed enough circumstantial evidence to support an arrest, but it didn't matter. Politics trumped his facts. After initially backing away from Garrett after the shooting and an arrest for drugs found under his bathroom sink, the city abruptly changed direction and embraced him as a favorite son. The Trotter shooting was ruled clean, the drug charges inexplicably dropped, and Garrett was awarded a cash settlement to avoid a lawsuit. That effectively put Clint's investigation on ice.

Clint wondered now if he should have forced the issue right then, two years ago. If he had, would the chief have seen it the way he did? He wasn't sure. Baumgartner struck

Clint as old-school honest. The man believed in the truth but was pragmatic about it. Sometimes that meant swallowing a lie. And the mayor was a hard-headed, self-serving politician who wouldn't budge unless it benefited him. Once he decided that Garrett was more use to him as a hero than a sacrifice, it was a done deal, one that Baumgartner was forced to accept.

I hate politics.

A voice broke into his thoughts. "Wardell?"

He glanced toward the sound. It came from Jody Lauren, a crime scene technician. Her unit provided forensic services to both the Sheriff's Office and to the police. Clint had worked with her many times, and she was good at her job. He started his own career in the same unit, so if he had a soft spot for anyone at all, it was for the crime scene techs.

"How are you?" he asked, gesturing toward her swollen belly.

"Miserable." Jody grinned. "And I've got another eleven weeks to go."

Clint struggled for some kind of small talk. He quickly calculated her due date. "Tuesday is a good day to be born," he said.

Jody chuckled at that. "The way I feel, *any* day is a good day for this little parasite to come out."

Clint couldn't think of a response, so he forced a smile that felt more like a grimace.

Jody said, "Did you get the findings on the fingernail scrapings in the Meyer case?"

That piqued his interest. "Not yet. Did you?"

"No. But I checked with the lab early yesterday, and the supervisor there said they were working on them as we spoke. If they finished, the report might be in your box already."

Clint wondered briefly why the lab steadfastly refused to simply email reports, instead of using the antiquated interoffice mail system that was about as efficient as the pony express. "I'll check as soon as I get back."

"Sorry it's taken so long," Jody said.

"Not your fault. You did your part, getting the skin from under her nails in the first place. You can't control that they're backed up at the lab."

"I know. Anyway, I have to get to the bathroom." She patted her stomach. "I tell ya, this little girl must be Irish, the way she is stomping on my bladder."

Clint nodded his goodbye. He continued out of the county side of the building, and past the records division.

Like so many others, Jody was blissfully unaware that the murder of Sonya Meyer was also connected to Garrett. Clint hadn't suspected so when he was assigned the case as next up in the rotation. But when Garrett inserted himself into the investigation, Clint knew he was involved somehow. The officer claimed to be there at the behest of a councilman, who turned out to have been having an affair with Meyer. Even so, it wasn't the councilman's DNA Clint expected to find under Meyer's nails from where she'd scratched her assailant. He *hoped* to find Garrett's, but hope was not a plan. Besides that, Garrett had appeared uninjured at the time, so Clint was skeptical. Slam-dunk evidence like that had been nonexistent in his unsanctioned, off-book case against Garrett.

Most of his effort had involved following Garrett, who was notably careful, and finding little of value.

Things changed when Garrett was assigned to the Anti-Crime Team. His customary caution slipped. Clint's surveillance eventually caught Garrett meeting with a man named Earl Ellis. He'd been unable to get a good picture of the two together, but the lead still broke his investigation open.

Clint began following Ellis instead, and that soon revealed a network of drug dealers that the man met on an ongoing basis. One of them had a telltale fishhook scar on his cheek. It was only later, when Clint saw the dead man lying in a house on Havana Street, that he learned his name.

Leon Strayer.

The picture was immediately clear to Clint, even though he couldn't share it with Detective Harris. Garrett must have told Ellis to recruit a shooter. Ellis chose Strayer, whose task was to kill Richard Van Pelt in his home and lay in wait for officers Stone and Garrett. Garrett manufactured the reason for him and Stone to go to the house. When Stone came through the front door of 5606 North Havana Street, Strayer gunned him down. Then Tyler Garrett coldly dispatched Strayer.

Clint wasn't sure why Garrett chose to kill Stone. All he knew for certain was that Gary Stone was dead and Tyler Garrett was responsible.

He *knew* it.

He couldn't prove it.

Not yet.

In the aftermath of Stone's death, Clint watched with growing anger as the police department and the public further lionized Garrett. It galled him that a man could sully the badge the way Garrett so brazenly did and get away with it. And yet, what proof did Clint have? He had photographs of Ellis meeting with Strayer, but no physical evidence connecting Ellis and Garrett. To build a case even on circumstantial evidence, he needed to at least prove that connection. So far, he couldn't.

And now Ellis had disappeared, too.

Clint realized that he had to consider the very real possibility that Garrett had killed Ellis. As his only link to the rest of his criminal network, Ellis represented Garrett's greatest threat. But he was also Garrett's shield from the street-level dealers he employed. Since Ellis handled all those interactions, Garrett was insulated.

It was a quandary, and Clint wasn't sure how Garrett would resolve it. But the longer Ellis remained missing, the better the chances that Garrett had eliminated him. Which was a shame, because if he could have found a way to turn Ellis into a cooperating witness, Garrett's entire house of cards would come tumbling down.

Clint strode into the Major Crimes bullpen. Detective Marty Hill sat at his desk, hunched over and mumbling into a digital recorder. Later, a secretary would transcribe the report. The process was supposed to be faster and more efficient, but in Clint's experience, the timesaving was a push at best. He preferred to type his own reports. If the department really wanted to be more efficient, they'd mandate that detectives get some keyboarding skills.

At his own desk, Clint performed a quick yet surreptitious inspection to ensure that nothing had been disturbed. All his drawers and cabinets were still locked, though the locking mechanisms were chintzy. The nothing case file that Lieutenant Flowers had assigned him yesterday lay undisturbed on his desktop. He'd left the file, six inches away and perfectly aligned at a right angle with the edge of his landline telephone, as a ruse to see if anyone was snooping through his things. The still-locked drawers and cabinets suggested no one had, but he knew how easy the desk locks could be defeated. The file remained undisturbed, however, still perfectly square to the phone.

His diligence was mostly out of habit. He rarely kept his Garrett-related notes in his desk. Most of the time, he stored them in a locked box in his trunk and only reviewed them at home or in his car. On the rare occasion that he brought a file to his desk, he guarded it carefully.

Satisfied, Clint headed toward the mailboxes outside the lieutenant's office to see if Jody was correct about the lab report on the Meyer case. Halfway there, someone called his name.

"Wardell."

Clint recognized Captain Tom Farrell's voice before he turned. "Captain?"

"We need to talk."

Clint glanced around. They stood in the broad walkway that separated the detectives' bullpen and the secretary pool, and near the lieutenant's office. Clint couldn't imagine a worse place to discuss secrets.

"Not here," he said.

"Now!" Farrell snapped.

Before Clint could respond, the captain wheeled and strode away.

Clint considered ignoring him and continuing with his own business. But he knew Farrell would be back—they shared too many secrets for him not to return. Ever since the formation of the Anti-Crime Team, Farrell had seemingly become more and more unraveled. Clint didn't want to risk a slip of the tongue from the harried administrator, so he followed.

Farrell led him down the hall and out the west doors, an employee-only entrance. It was also a favorite place for smokers to congregate, in clear violation of the state law regarding proximity to a building entrance. There were no smokers now, however.

Ten yards away from the door, Farrell stopped and waited. Clint moved close enough to the captain to encourage a low tone of voice. Farrell got the point, as he spoke in a hushed whisper.

"DOJ is coming."

Clint pulled back in mild surprise. "Here?"

"Yes, here. Today."

"Why?"

"We don't know."

"So you're telling me things you have no idea about? Just to raise my blood pressure?"

"No," Farrell said. He waved his hand, irritated. "The chief figures it's because of everything. Stone, the business with the councilman, Garrett's shooting, all of it. It adds up to something, and they're interested."

"Good for them."

"Don't be flippant. This is serious."

Clint shook his head. "If the feds want to poke around, what do I care?"

Farrell's eyes widened. "Seriously?" He glanced around to make sure no one was nearby. "If they find out we've been running a secret investigation off the books on Garrett *for two years…*" He let the thought hang in the air.

Clint twirled his finger. "Then what?"

Farrell's expression was incredulous. "Have you suddenly forgotten how precarious our situation is here?"

"Precarious?" Clint shook his head at the word, finding it an overstatement. "DOJ coming doesn't matter. Do you really think that some half-assed fed is going to break open a case I've been trying to crack for two years?"

"That's not the point."

"It sounds like the point."

"Damn it, Wardell. The point is that when we bring this case in, it has to be done right. Otherwise, you and I will end up with our asses in a sling."

Clint shrugged. That much was true.

"Don't shrug like it doesn't matter," said Farrell. "I don't want any stink on this when we take him down."

Clint grunted. "Captain, you're aiming way too high. Everything about this case stinks. We can't avoid that now. There's only one thing we need to focus on."

"Which is?"

"Justice."

Farrell let out a long sigh of frustration. "Well, the Department of *Justice* is coming here on a fact-finding mission later today. And if they don't like what they see, they'll report back to Washington, D.C., and we'll have a full-fledged investigation on our hands. Once that happens, the most likely outcome is a consent decree."

Clint thought about that. He knew little about consent decrees, but he did know that if DOJ slapped one on the department, it was tantamount to a complete takeover. The ensuing demands would hamstring his efforts to bring down Garrett. Not only would everyone from the lieutenants on up be scrambling to create or modify policy or gather data, but that would all eventually roll downhill to the detectives and officers. Moreover, the increased, constant scrutiny might result in exactly what Farrell feared—the premature revelation of their two-year, clandestine investigation into Tyler Garrett before they had sufficient evidence to charge him.

Under the cloud of suspicion that came with a consent decree, he knew that it wouldn't necessarily be Garrett's wrongdoing that got the most attention. Clint and Farrell's methods would come under fire, and the DOJ investigators would almost certainly see that as proof of a corrupt department. Clint believed there was some minor crooked behavior going on at SPD and especially city hall, but outside of everything surrounding Garrett, things were a long way from corrupt.

"I see what you mean," he said.

"Good."

"We'll need to be careful."

"What?" Farrell shook his head. "Careful? No. We need to suspend the Garrett investigation while DOJ is still in the house. Stop everything. Once they leave, we can—"

"I'm not stopping anything."

Farrell's mouth hung open in mid-speech. He slammed it shut in anger and glared at Clint. Clint stared back, implacable. The battle of wills went on for thirty seconds, before Farrell spoke again. He enunciated his words clearly and emphatically.

"You *will* stand down, *Detective*. That's an order. Do you understand me?"

Clint nodded. "I understand. But like I told you once before, we're way past rank having anything to do with our situation anymore. Once we drop the hammer on Garrett, we'll both have our roles to play. You'll be the captain and I'll be the detective. Until then, I'm going to do what I need to do to finish this. I suggest you stop rubbing your hands together like a nervous old lady and get with the program."

Without waiting for a reply, Clint walked away, heading for the west doors. He was through them and several steps down the hallway when Farrell arrived at his side.

"Do not screw this up for us both," Farrell snarled, his

voice still barely above a whisper.

Clint didn't break stride. "I'd say you've already done that."

Farrell didn't have a reply. He walked next to Clint, seemingly in stunned surprise. Clint welcomed the silence. So far, all Farrell had brought to this investigation were demands and missteps. If the captain wanted to stand down while DOJ was present, that was fine with him. But Clint wasn't going to give Garrett any breathing room.

When they reached the entrance to the Investigative Division, Clint stopped. He gave Farrell a cold stare. "We're finishing this," he said simply.

Farrell stared back, his previous fury replaced with the look of a man lost.

Clint didn't care. He left him there and went back into Investigations. Before going back to his desk, he stopped by the mailboxes outside of Lieutenant Flowers's office. He shuffled through the small stack of papers in his slot but found nothing from the lab.

"That figures," he muttered, and headed to his desk to get to work.

Chapter 3

"You're on SWAT," the woman said. "Isn't that right?"

Irma Eddy smiled at Tyler Garrett with bright, watery eyes. Her hands shook slightly as she dabbed a bit of egg from her lower lip. She wore a black pantsuit with a red blouse.

"I was," Garrett said. "I left the team a while back."

When Irma leaned toward Garrett, her cloying perfume overwhelmed the smell of his own plate of eggs, bacon, and hash browns. She nodded as she said, "My husband was one of the founding members."

"Really?"

"He was really handsome in his uniform." She patted his arm. "Like you."

Gayla Stewart, a silver-haired woman seated next to Irma, bent toward her husband and loudly asked, "What's SWAT?"

Her husband, Bernard, rolled his eyes and whispered into her ear. He kept his gaze on Garrett as he spoke. Bernard was a pale, bald man with jowly cheeks that jumped and jiggled as he spoke. He wore a red Make Spokane Great Again pin on his gray suit jacket.

To Garrett, the Make Spokane Great Again folks were just a local spin on the national movement with a similar name. The intent was clear—return our town to the 1950s. In other words, make us white again.

When Bernard's explanation to his wife didn't get the desired result, he said a bit louder, "It's their group of tough guys."

"Oh!" she said and turned back to Garrett with wide eyes.

"High-risk entries," Garrett said. "Armed suspects. That type of thing."

Irma nodded knowingly to Gayla.

They were in the Greenwood Retirement Home's banquet room for its monthly civic meeting. About a decade ago, the retirees formed an ad hoc committee in response to the growing political divide in the country. They hosted speakers on a plethora of topics. Almost everyone accepted their invitation for two important facts—these people *voted,* and they spoke to their adult children about it.

This wasn't a city level event that required the monthly attendance of the mayor, a council member, the chief of police, or even a department command staff member. However, the civic activity group carried a certain amount of political weight, so the police department sent someone whenever the committee requested a guest speaker.

Along with Garrett, there were seven people seated at the table with him. Irma Eddy, Bernard and Gayla Stewart, and four other silver-haired women. Those four women were quiet, though, often tutting amongst themselves, but never engaging directly with Garrett. He'd randomly picked this table to sit at as he didn't know anyone staying at the home.

"And you're on patrol?" Irma asked. She rested an age-spotted hand on his bare arm. He was in his short-sleeved uniform.

Garrett nodded. "Day shift. Yes, ma'am."

"Good for you. Patrol is the backbone of the department. My husband spent his entire career on graveyard."

"That's where I wanted to be, but they moved me to days following my shooting."

"That's too bad," Irma said. "My husband wouldn't have stood for that. He was a tough man." She patted his arm once more then removed her hand to pick up her fork. "I'm sure things are different now."

He wasn't sure if she were referring to the times being different or the fortitude of the officers. Garrett chose to ignore either assertion for a variety of reasons, not the least of which was the environment. He lifted his head and looked about.

There were twenty tables. At each table were eight place settings and almost all the seats were filled. That meant a potential for one hundred sixty attendees. In all fairness, there were a few empty seats, so he estimated ten folks missing. In a room of nearly one hundred fifty people, there were only six people of color in the room—counting himself.

There were two elderly Asian women at different tables. They sat almost uncomfortably close to equally elderly white men. In the middle of the room was a Hispanic male who seemed especially animated while he talked with the patrons at his table.

Then there was the elderly black man who poured coffee to a table full of whites. None of them bothered to acknowledge his existence.

Nearby, a young ebony woman reached for what she thought was an empty plate. A frail elderly woman with a fake blond wig and a pinched face scolded her. The young woman smiled politely and hurried away.

Bernard Stewart asked something that Garrett didn't catch.

"Excuse me?"

When he spoke again, bits of food danced in Bernard's mouth. "I said, what's your topic?"

"I don't have one."

"You don't?"

Garrett shrugged. "I was asked to come and give a patrol officer's perspective on the city."

Bernard waved his fork in small circles as he spoke. Bits of hash browns fell off as he did so. "That's what we asked for, sure, but you've got to have a message. Otherwise, you'll just ramble for thirty minutes."

Garrett's eyes traveled around the table, meeting the eager eyes of those sitting with him. Captain Dana Hatcher tasked him with this assignment. She told him he was the highest-profile patrol officer she had and believed him more than suited for this task. Some ladder climber in the department would have seen it as an honor, but sitting here amongst these monied socialites, the duty irked him.

Garrett felt tired and the several cups of coffee he already consumed were not giving him the jolt he needed. Perhaps something else would. A mischievous smile spread across Garrett's lips. "How about this for a message? We're the best paid garbagemen in the city."

Bernard blinked several times and the women remained silent.

Garrett immediately regretted the remark. "I'm kidding."

"If you don't think this is serious," Bernard said, "if you don't think this meeting is serious, you don't have to be here." The elderly man waved his hand in a motion indicating the room. "We consider our meetings important and that is why we invited your department to participate."

The women at the table paid rapt attention to Bernard now. He was not the head of the civic committee nor was he responsible for the department's invitation, but it was clear he held some charm amongst the ladies. When he had surveyed the room earlier, Garrett noticed the distinct imbalance when it came to women. A man, even an insufferable boor like Bernard Stewart, would carry some sway in a place like this.

"It was a joke," Garrett said.

"I asked a question about your topic and you respond with a wisecrack? Is that how most officers treat the citizenry?"

Garrett didn't like the man's tone nor the manner he was being spoken to, yet he managed to say, "I apologize."

The elderly man with the coffee carafe now stood nearby, but it seemed only Garrett took notice. The man's eyes had been on Garrett during this exchange and they took on a sudden sadness, an almost disappointment.

"Then I ask again," Bernard said, "what's the general message of your presentation?"

Garrett looked away from the server and down to his plate. The eggs had grown cold and he hadn't touched the sausage. When he looked up, Bernard Stewart glowered back with a power the old man had no right to feel.

He chose his words carefully. "I guess my message would be..."

Garrett wanted to tell the table full of elderly whites that there was no point to it all. That law enforcement was simply an exercise in futility—an endless treadmill of arrests and re-arrests. If any of those arrestees ever were charged with an actual crime, most pleaded to a lesser offense to avoid any jail time. Or if they decided to go before a judge, they would get a jury of their peers, which meant mostly unemployed or underemployed citizens who weren't smart enough to figure a way out of their civic responsibility. The system was rigged against the cops and everyone was in on the scam—including the cops.

Instead, he said, "...that we've got a pretty good city here."

His tablemates seem to breathe a little easier at that. The server next to him clucked his tongue, though.

Irma absently held her coffee out for a refill and said, "But there's been so many shootings."

"All cities have shootings," Garrett said. He watched the server pour the black coffee into the white porcelain cup. The server shook his head and stole a glance at Garrett.

"I mean shootings with officers," Irma said. "And one of ours was killed."

"That was my partner."

"He was *your* partner?" Bernard said. His hand rested on the table now, a fist wrapped around his fork.

Garrett nodded.

"I'm sorry," Bernard said, and he appeared genuinely remorseful.

Many of the women muttered their condolences.

"It was over drugs, right?" Bernard asked. His eyes moved about the table. "That's what the newspaper said."

"We don't know why he was shot," Garrett said. "The detectives are still investigating."

The elderly server moved about the table now, offering refills of coffee. Several of the women dismissed him with irritated waves.

"But you have to suspect…" Bernard said.

Garrett knew the role he was supposed to play and after his earlier attempt at levity, he wasn't about to do that again. Bernard wanted him to say something to feed his agenda, so he gave it to him.

"I believe it was over drugs. The man who shot him was a junkie."

"A junkie," Gayla muttered.

"A person addicted to drugs," Bernard said.

"I know what a junkie is, Bernie."

He rolled his eyes and returned his attention to Garrett. "And you still think we have a good city?"

"I do."

"What do we need to do better?"

"More police officers," Garrett said.

The elderly server harrumphed and walked away from their table.

"We're severely understaffed for a city of our size," Garrett continued.

It was a tired argument, often trotted out by the department brass at budget times, but Garrett was looking for something safe that wouldn't offend these people. Besides, it was true enough.

"I've often said that." Irma patted his arm and glanced around the table. "We need more police, especially as Spokane has changed."

Not changed, he thought. *Darkened.*

"Anything else?" Irma asked.

"Directed policing."

Bernard licked his lips. "What does that mean?"

"Using analytics to go after the criminals before they have a chance to commit more crimes."

"Is that a real thing?" Irma asked.

"We had an Anti-Crime Team—"

"The officer who was shot was part of that," Bernard said.

Garrett nodded. "Just because there was a casualty doesn't

mean the war wasn't righteous."

The table fell silent and several utensils hovered in front of open mouths.

"That team," Garrett said, "was making a real difference. We were going after active criminals, the ones who were the real problem, in the worst neighborhoods. The chief shut it down after Officer Stone's death."

"And you think that was a mistake?" Bernard asked.

Garrett didn't really care, but he nodded, nonetheless.

"What can we do to help?" Bernard said.

"Yes," Gayla chimed in, "what can we do?"

"Talk to your city councilman." Garrett caught the eyes of several of the women at the table and corrected himself. "Council*person*." The ladies nodded appreciatively. "Make your voice heard. Tell them we need that team back on the street."

Bernard tapped the table then pointed to Garrett. "That's your message. You tell that message up there and our group will definitely be in the ear of the city council. That'll give us something to get excited about."

An elderly woman stepped to the podium at the front of the room. She tapped a finger against the microphone, the resulting booms quieted the chattering crowd.

"Good morning, everyone," she said before inviting up their special guest and that morning's speaker—Spokane Police Officer Tyler Garrett.

Chapter 4

The GMC Denali rocked then swayed as it moved into the furthest left lane of Interstate-90. Édelie Durand gripped the file spread across her lap and looked up.

Behind the wheel, Esteban Curado's eyes flicked to the rearview mirror. "Sorry about that."

"What happened?"

Curado thumbed toward the car on the right. "Guy jammed his brakes."

Durand lifted her eyebrows, grunted an affirmation, and returned her gaze to the file.

From the passenger seat, Danielle Watson said, "You should have let me drive, Esteban."

"Steve," he said flatly. "You know I prefer *Steve*."

They were silent for a couple moments before Curado asked, "And why should I have let you drive?"

"Because you're too busy sightseeing."

"And you wouldn't be?" he asked.

"I went to law school here," she said and waved toward the windshield. "I had enough of this podunk town by the time I finished. Couldn't wait to get away."

Durand glanced up from her file. Even though the city of Spokane neared, her thoughts were on the opposite side of the country and her two-story brick home in the Washington, D.C. neighborhood of Kingman Park. It's where her husband Roland was, as he dealt with—

"What's wrong, Edie?"

Her eyes slid over to meet Watson's who had now turned in her seat to look back at Durand. Danielle Watson was an attractive woman with tanned skin, short hair, natural eyebrows, and expensive eyelashes.

"Huh?"

"You look upset. Find something in the file we didn't cover?"

Durand ignored Watson's question and lowered her head. What had her face betrayed? No one in the division knew what she and her husband were going through and she had no intentions of sharing her personal life with her staff.

She did her best to remove any emotions from her face. "We're going straight to the department this morning. Get your bearings as soon as you can." When she looked up, Durand caught a brief exchange of glances between her subordinates. Pretending not to have noticed, she continued, "Three days is all we've got."

"We know," Watson said. "We went over this back at the—"

"So?" Durand snapped. "We're going over it again."

Watson stared at her and blinked repeatedly.

Curado's head turned slightly away. His eyes remained on the road ahead, but his peripheral vision would no longer be able to pick up what was occurring inside the vehicle.

Durand refused to look away from her subordinates, though. If she showed any weakness now, they would know something was wrong. She'd rather they just thought she was a bitch.

Watson finally said, "Yeah, okay."

Esteban Curado's head returned to its normal position and he studied the road straight ahead.

Durand inhaled a long, slow breath through her nose before calmly saying, "We're out of here Friday morning and back home. Our recommendations need to be ready by Monday morning."

With a gentle, almost apologetic tone, Watson asked, "We're working the weekend?"

"If we have to. Otherwise, we work on the flight. We work at the hotel. Everything is work for the next seventy-two hours. Is there a problem with that?"

Watson frowned, shook her head, then faced forward in

her seat.

Durand dropped her gaze back to the file.

There were plenty of attorneys on staff and she appreciated most of them. Curado and Watson weren't any more special than the next. They were expedient for this assignment and she wasn't about to coddle them. Nothing in this world was more important than the man back home and if she had a choice, she would have stayed there. However, a depleted savings account, a mortgage to pay, and ever-rising medical costs demanded she work. Her best course of action was to do her job quickly and effectively then get out of Spokane. The truth was, there had been too many Spokanes lately and she didn't know how many more she could take.

Without looking up, Durand said, "Let's review some things. Tell me about Gary Stone."

"Stone was a three-year police officer." Watson's voice was devoid of its usual enthusiasm. "A member of the department's Anti-Crime Team. He was—"

"Describe that," Durand interrupted.

"What?" Watson said, tilting her head back toward Durand but not bothering to turn around.

Curado didn't wait for the interpretation of Durand's demand. "The ACT was a six-man team made up of four officers, one detective, and a sergeant."

Watson flashed a look of irritation toward her fellow attorney.

"Its mission," Curado continued, "was directed enforcement against high-profile offenders using crime analytics."

Durand nodded. Esteban Curado was a lean man in his late thirties. He'd been with the department for nearly a decade now and had been on her team for the last two.

"Stone was a member of this team," Watson jumped back into the conversation. "He was gunned down during a search for one of these high-profile offenders. His partner—"

"Tyler Garrett," Curado interrupted.

Watson frowned at the man behind the wheel. "May I

continue?"

Curado ignored her question and checked the driver's side mirror before changing lanes.

"Garrett shot and killed Officer Stone's assailant," Watson said as she turned in her seat to face Durand. "No motivation has been tied to Stone's killing. The sister agency, Spokane County Sheriff's Office, is still investigating the case. Therefore, no ruling has been made whether Garrett's shooting was justifiable or not."

"Can't imagine it won't be," Curado said. "Stone was murdered, and Garrett returned fire almost immediately. Seems it would have been a slam-dunk review by the county."

"Everyone has to jump through hoops," Durand muttered. "Even us."

Curado eyed her with curiosity.

"All that is public information," Durand said, "so the first thing I want you to do is get your hands on the initial shooting report. Better yet, get the county's report."

"What if the county says no?" Curado asked. He didn't bother looking back when he spoke.

Durand inhaled deeply again and glanced out her window. "Ask nicely."

Curado said, "What if—" but Watson chopped off his question.

"We'll handle it," she said assertively.

Durand glanced down to her file for a moment then asked, "Tell me about Tyler Garrett."

"Former SWAT officer," Watson said. "Recipient of the Lifesaving Award."

"He's been involved in two shootings," Curado added. He flicked the indicator to signal a lane change just as he moved around a slow-moving pickup. "The first was two years ago, an ambush after he initiated a traffic stop and was targeted by shooters from a nearby house."

Watson said, "The victim in that shooting was a white male. A known criminal. No gun was found at the scene.

Even so, the shooting was ruled justified by the investigating agency. The county sheriff again."

Durand nodded with satisfaction. They had reviewed the files back in D.C., but she wanted to ensure her attorneys had the pertinent details committed to memory so they could think on their feet. She disapproved of those subordinates who had to constantly refer to a file while interviewing witnesses. It looked weak and ineffectual.

"What do we know about the ambushers?" she asked.

Curado looked in the rearview mirror. "Nothing."

"I've been—" She gripped the file as Curado hit the brakes, then accelerated to move around a semi. "I've been thinking about that."

"Sorry," he said into the mirror. "These Washington drivers…"

Durand smirked and reset the file on her lap.

Watson's brow furrowed. "I've been thinking about that, too."

Édelie Durand waited patiently for her subordinate to begin.

"My father was a cop," Watson said, "and I've got to say, if someone ever shot at him, I don't think the department would have rested until they had the shooter identified."

Curado's eyes met Durand's in the rearview.

Watson continued. "And this wasn't just a shooting, if there can be such a thing. It was an ambush—a planned and coordinated attack. And SPD leaves the question of who was responsible unanswered? They've never identified possible suspects? What the hell?"

Durand cocked her head. "They had other problems that might have pulled attention away from that."

"You mean the murdered detective?" Curado suggested.

"Butch Talbott," Durand said. "Killed in Liberty Lake."

"Where is that, by the way?" he asked.

"East of here," Watson said and pointed straight ahead. "And their police department never found *his* shooter, either."

"State patrol assisted in that investigation," Curado added.

"That makes it worse." Danielle Watson's head swiveled between Durand and Curado. "You see my point, don't you? Two cops. One dead. One ambushed. No arrests. Isn't that suspicious?"

"What are you suggesting?" Durand asked.

"Maybe it's a cover-up."

"A cover-up?" Durand asked.

"Why not?" Watson said. "It's happened before."

Durand waited for Curado to meet her eyes in the mirror, but his gaze remained firmly locked on the road. She turned her attention back to Watson. "I agree with your assertion that it looks suspicious but be careful to jump to a conclusion without knowing the facts."

Watson lifted her chin to the file in Durand's lap. "We've got the facts. We reviewed them back home. We even got the reports from Liberty Lake to give us a fuller picture."

"There's a lot of area still to shine some light on." Durand noticed a name in the file and her finger dropped to it. She tapped a chipped fingernail under it several times before saying, "I want to interview Tyler Garrett."

"Today?" Curado asked. "We'll get him set up—"

"No," Durand said. "*Last.* I want to interview him after we get an understanding of the department's culture. We'll conduct our reviews and interviews then I'll sit with him. Did you read the media coverage that I emailed you?"

"It wasn't very complimentary," Curado said. "Most of the local politicians don't think very highly of their own police department. Even the mayor, apparently its most vocal supporter, suspended the chief for an improper report filing on a rape investigation."

"The thing with the teenage girl, right?" Watson said. "If that isn't a cover-up, I don't know what is."

Durand rubbed the edge of the folder. There had been a recent incident that appeared as if the mayor and the chief colluded to hide a rape allegation against a councilman. The young woman who attempted to report the attack ended up taking her life. It didn't appear that anyone did much of an investigation into the handling of the case beyond the mayor's suspending of the chief for three days.

"If I read between the lines," Watson said, "it sure sounds like their chief is bulletproof."

Durand sniffed dismissively. "Nobody is bulletproof."

They drove in silence for a couple minutes. As the Denali exited the freeway and pulled to a stoplight, Curado asked Watson, "So this Garrett, you think what? He was infected by the culture somehow?"

"How could anyone not be?" Watson said as she dropped back into her seat. "Everywhere we've gone, it's the same thing—male-dominated groups, drunk on testosterone and the idea of us versus them, protecting citizens they look down upon. How do they not get infected by that?" She tapped her chest. "*I* would get infected by that."

Curado glanced once at Watson but didn't bother responding. He shook his head and remained silent.

"Don't let your personal biases affect how we do business," Durand reminded.

Watson looked back to her supervisor. She rolled her lips into her mouth and nodded once.

Durand caught a reflection of a smile hinting on Curado's lips. His eyes danced with delight at his fellow attorney's dismay.

"That goes for you, too, Steve."

Curado's smile faded.

Durand's chin tucked into her chest and her eyebrows raised. "Don't think I'm not aware of your biases as well. We all have them, and we need to watch for them constantly. The division is relying on us for an objective recommendation. Understand?"

The two attorneys glanced at each other before mumbling like scolded children, "Yes, ma'am."

Durand dropped her attention to the file again. She hadn't read a single word from it during the trip. Instead, the words seemed to blur together whenever she looked at it. The file had given her a convenient excuse to avoid conversation on the plane and allowed her time to be alone with her thoughts.

As far as she was concerned, she needed to get into this town, assess if there was a problem, and get out. It was as simple as that. She was not there to fix anything that was broken nor develop a long-term plan to do so.

All she had to do was slap the hornet's nest and see if anything flew out.

And if something did, she'd go home and call in the exterminators.

Chapter 5

Captain Tom Farrell washed his hands at the sink. His stomach gurgled and his bowels felt loose, but there was nothing he could do about that now. The captains and lieutenants were assembled in one of the conference rooms down the hall. It was up to him to break the news to them about the Department of Justice, answer their questions, and give them their marching orders. It was a task that required him to appear calm and confident.

He felt neither.

Farrell turned off the faucet and shook water from his hands. Then he reached for a paper towel. The nervous pain that wrenched in his gut was unlike any he'd felt before. For a moment, he wondered if he was having a heart attack.

No such luck, he told himself.

He dried his hands and tossed the used paper towel toward the garbage. The wet, limp brown paper caught the rim of the container and fluttered to the floor instead. Farrell stared at it for a moment, then muttered, "Screw it," and left the restroom.

This all went back to Tyler Garrett. Outside of that, he had nothing to fear, and this department had nothing to fear, from the Department of Justice. Sure, the Betty Rabe incident with the philandering councilman had been dicey, but Farrell blamed most of that on the mayor. Aside from Garrett, he believed that the Spokane Police Department was a good one, with cops who worked hard, and who cared.

But Garrett was a cancer, and like cancer polluting the cells around it, Garrett had polluted others around him.

Including Farrell.

Even if DOJ discovered the entire slate of Garrett's

crimes, that wouldn't be the story, he knew. The story would be how a crooked white captain conducted an off-book investigation of a black officer for two years.

He could see the headlines, and the narratives that people would fill in. He'd only be half-surprised if Garrett didn't somehow manage to come out of it a hero again, just like he did after the Trotter shooting and everything that followed.

He made it to the open conference door far too soon. Before entering, he took a deep breath and tried to steady himself. Then he walked in.

The murmur of conversation ceased as soon as the assembled group saw he'd arrived. He motioned for one of the lieutenants to close the door and began.

"Here's what's happening," he said. "We are going to have a visit today from the Department of Justice."

The room exploded. Questions flew at him in a torrent, most of them angry in tone. Farrell gave them a few moments, then raised his hands for quiet.

"I know you're wondering why. So are we."

"Who's we?" Captain Dana Hatcher asked. She stood along the wall, her arms crossed.

"The chief and I," Farrell answered

A low murmur went through the group, and Farrell realized he'd made a mistake. He may have been Baumgartner's closest confidante, but he was also the same rank as several other captains in the room. Baumgartner had abolished the assistant and deputy chief positions many years ago, immediately after being appointed as chief of police. He tended to rotate the traditional second-in-command duties amongst the various captains. But since the days of Garrett's first shooting, Baumgartner had kept Farrell closer than anyone else. Farrell knew this had not gone unnoticed.

"Was there a command staff meeting I missed?" Hatcher asked, barely containing her sarcasm.

"No," Farrell said. "It was an impromptu discussion. The chief only found out about it this morning."

"What are they doing here?" asked one of the lieutenants.

"He already told you," Hatcher said. "*They* don't know."

Farrell clenched his jaw. With the ongoing Garrett situation and now DOJ swooping in, the last thing he needed was a renewed skirmish in the cold war he'd found himself engaged in with Hatcher. Given how things turned out, he wished he'd never heard of the Anti-Crime Team. He should have let the idea die when Hatcher proposed it and the chief threw up a stop sign. Instead, he helped convince Baumgartner, who responded by putting him in charge of the unit. Not only did he fail to ensnare Garrett like he'd hoped, but he made a career-long enemy of Hatcher in the process.

He pressed on. "The chief believes their visit is exploratory. The media coverage we've gotten over the last couple of years has been highly critical, some of it inflammatory. DOJ sees smoke, so they're here to find out if there's any fire."

"Exploratory, Captain?" Lieutenant Keon asked doubtfully.

"It's nothing to worry about," Farrell said, hoping his words were convincing. "It should be painless."

"I had to have exploratory surgery of my colon last year," Keon said. "I'm here to tell you, it ain't painless."

Some nervous laughter rumbled through the group, but most of it sounded forced to Farrell's ear.

"The chief's directions are simple," he continued. "If one of the DOJ investigators asks you a question, answer it, and answer truthfully."

"Of course we'll be truthful," Hatcher said. "We're the police. We don't lie."

"I realize that," Farrell said. "That goes without saying."

"But you just said it."

"I was…affirming it."

"Oh." Hatcher muttered something out of the side of her mouth to the lieutenant next to her, who smirked.

Before the Garrett mess, Tom Farrell would have torn into Hatcher right then. Captain or not, he was senior to her and she was being both insubordinate and disrespectful. But right now, he didn't have the energy. Besides, he understood why she hated him. If he were in her place, he'd feel the same way.

"Answer all of their questions," Farrell repeated. "But don't offer anything. Just answer what is asked, and no more."

"Sounds like when we're on the witness stand," Keon said. "Are we on trial, Captain?"

"No. But we think…" Farrell winced, then corrected himself. "The chief believes they are fishing. They're looking for something to be wrong, and more information is just more of an opportunity for them to see ghosts in the bushes."

"You think they're here because of Stone? Or because Tyler Garrett's been in a couple shootings?" This came from Bo Sherman, a newly made sergeant. Farrell wasn't sure why a sergeant was in the room, but guessed Sherman was standing in for his lieutenant on days off or sick. "If a cop is always running toward danger, sooner or later he's going to end up in a critical incident. Or doesn't DOJ realize that?" Sherman said, then quickly added, "Sir."

Farrell shrugged. "I don't know if that's the reason."

"It's not about Garrett," Hatcher replied immediately. "It's about leadership, and how it has responded to officer-involved shootings, political scandals, and the murder of one of our own." She fixed her gaze on Farrell. "That kind of thing gets the attention of the feds."

Farrell noticed how Hatcher had used *it* instead of *we* when she referred to leadership, thereby excluding herself. The way she rattled off her statement made him pretty certain she'd picked it up from her friend, Councilwoman Margaret Patterson. That coalition was danger from another corner he wished he didn't have to worry about.

"If we're transparent with them," Farrell said, trying to salvage the meeting, "then it'll end up being about nothing, except to validate to them what *we* all already know—that this is a clean department made up of good people."

There were some muttered positive replies, but just as

many dubious looks. Farrell suspected it wasn't because the leaders in the room didn't agree with his sentiment about the agency. Rather, it was born of a deep suspicion of the feds and the prevalent concern that if they wanted to find something dirty, that's what they'd see.

"Let your sergeants know what's going on," Farrell said. "And make sure the troops don't worry about it and focus on getting the job done like always." Everyone kept staring at him, so he added, "That is all."

The assembled group shuffled out the door. He noticed Keon and several other lieutenants scowling. Hatcher studiously ignored him while Barry, the administrative captain, seemed unaffected by the news. He wished he could be so blissfully ignorant.

I've got to get through the DOJ visit, and then find a way to close out the Garrett case before they come back.

He toyed with the idea that they might not come back, but he knew that rarely happened. When the feds looked for corruption, they almost always found something good enough to slap that label onto it.

Farrell waited until the room was empty, then sank into a nearby chair. He was already drained, and the day had barely begun.

Chapter 6

Officer Ray Zielinski arrived at the Public Safety Building via a route he couldn't remember using for many years—the public entrance. To add insult to injury, he had to wait in the long line out front as it wended forward toward the metal detectors at the security checkpoint inside.

Zielinski kept his head down and shuffled forward with the line. The young man in front of him had the earnest, frantic look of a mental, something that he'd seen plenty on patrol, so he didn't want to make eye contact and invite conversation. The overpowering essence of cologne wafted from behind him, mixed with someone's pungent body odor. He wasn't sure if the smells came from the same person or not and didn't care to investigate. His mind didn't let him off that easily, though, and he guessed the sources were a lawyer and a junkie, respectively. He used an old patrol trick, breathing shallowly through his mouth, to endure it.

The experience was radically different than swiping his ID card at the west doors or pulling his patrol car into the basement sally port. But those methods of entry were reserved for cops, and since his suspension, he barely qualified as one.

He slowly made his way through the front door and into the lobby. The line crawled as each person removed items from pockets or placed a briefcase or bag on the conveyer belt to go through the X-ray machine. Or whatever kind of rays the machine used.

Zielinski had purposefully traveled light this morning. Just his keys and his wallet. He removed his driver's license to show the security guard when his turn came. He no longer carried his police identification. They'd taken it after he was placed on suspension.

Administrative leave, he reminded himself. That was the official term, and it was what Lieutenant Sutherland had called it when he collected Zielinski's gun, badge, and ID. He supposed it sounded better than *suspended*, but it amounted to the same thing. At least he was still getting his paycheck during this process.

How long will that last?

Zielinski pushed the thought away. Just a bump in the road, he told himself. Every officer with a long career had a few of them. The fact that his happened over some overzealous, off-duty police work didn't make any difference.

He hoped so, anyway.

Zielinski was fifth or six in line now, so this small torture was almost complete. Or that's what he thought until someone addressed him.

"Officer?"

Zielinski glanced up. One of the security guys in a pale blue uniform shirt was looking right at him.

Oh, please no.

"Officer?" the heavyset guard repeated. He beckoned to Zielinski. "You don't have to wait in line. Come on up here."

Everyone in line stared at him. Several scowled, though he caught a couple inquisitive expressions, and a young man with a military haircut grinned at him.

"Officer?"

Zielinski didn't want to move, but immediately realized that he would only prolong the situation if he didn't. It reminded him of someone wanting to give him a cup of coffee on the house while he was on duty. To refuse only called more attention to what was happening and ran the risk of offending the giver. Better to accept it and leave a tip worth two cups of coffee.

Without a word, Zielinski stepped out of line and joined the security guard, whose name tag read Amos. He held out his driver's license, but the guard waved it away. "I know who you are."

"You do?"

Amos nodded. "I live next door to Lyle Bunney. That dude that shot at you?"

Zielinski suppressed a wince. "I remember."

"I know he seems pretty crazy, but he's a decent guy. I appreciate what you did."

"I arrested him."

"But you didn't shoot him. And you coulda."

Zielinski peered closely at the man. "How do you know this?"

"Lyle told me."

"Huh." Zielinski grunted. "Well, thanks."

He started to go through the metal detector, but Amos held out a hand to stop him. "You don't need to do that. Here." He unclasped the security rope next to the metal detector and pulled it aside for Zielinski. "Have a good day, sir."

Zielinski thanked him and headed past, ignoring the angry stares he was sure were being fired at his back from the others in line.

"Why does he get to skip the line?" someone asked.

"He's a cop," Amos said, almost proudly.

Zielinski went directly to the front desk for the city police. The desk was staffed by a patrol officer and a senior volunteer. Citizens brought complaints, sought advice, and filed reports there, although Zielinski knew that online resources had diminished the importance of the front desk.

Even so, there was another line of people waiting. He didn't recognize the senior volunteer, who was busy listening to a very animated woman explain something. But the man in uniform was Sergeant Kelly Ragland. Zielinski figured the sergeant must be filling in for an absent officer.

Sergeant Ragland noticed him immediately. He held up his finger to stop the person talking mid-sentence and came around the desk to greet Zielinski. He didn't know what to expect from Ragland, so when the sergeant gave him a cool greeting of "Officer," he wasn't entirely surprised.

"Sergeant," he responded in kind.

"Follow me."

Ragland led Zielinski through the outer doors, swiping his card with a bit more flourish than Zielinski thought necessary. They went down a short, familiar hallway with a couple of small conference rooms and the Crime Analysis unit. He noticed the conference rooms were full and recognized some of the lieutenants busy arguing about something. Before he could process that, the two of them turned sharply left into the section of hallway widely known as Mahogany Row, where all the command brass was located. Another pair of lieutenants walked past, only one of which Zielinski recognized. Both studiously avoided making eye contact with him, though he noticed Lieutenant Larry Keon cast a furtive glance his way as they passed. The contempt in the fleeting look was apparent.

Zielinski tried to ignore them and kept walking. When they reached one of the open conference rooms a little further on, Ragland said, "In here."

The small room had a table with six chairs around it. A whiteboard hung on one wall. Zielinski looked back to Ragland. "Thanks," he said.

"I'm not supposed to leave you here unescorted," Ragland said. "But I have duties to attend to. Can I trust you to stay in this room until Dale Thomas arrives?"

Zielinski scowled at the sergeant's condescending tone. "What if I have to go to the bathroom?"

"You hold it. Or piss all over everything. That seems to be your thing."

Zielinski shook his head in disgust. He wanted to tell Ragland where to go, but if he ever got through all these troubles, he didn't want to find an insubordination charge waiting for him on the other side.

"I'll be fine," he said through gritted teeth.

Ragland turned and left.

Zielinski listened to the sergeant's descending footfalls on the tile floor until they faded.

So this is what it feels like to be on the outside.

He left the door halfway open but chose a seat out of sight of anyone walking past. No matter how confidential Internal Affairs matters supposedly were, he knew people talked. Facts were shared, and if facts were unavailable, speculation filled in until it became accepted *as* fact. Some people might hear about him searching for a wanted suspect on his day off and think he made a good arrest. Others might wonder what his motivation was and think he was dirty. Right now, he didn't want attention from either.

I'm not dirty. I've had some bad luck, and maybe even messed up a little, but I'm not a dirty cop. Not like Tyler Garrett.

Ever since Clint had filled him in on Garrett's actions, which Zielinski had already suspected, it amazed him how Garrett somehow managed to come out looking like a hero, while Zielinski was on paid administrative leave, his career in jeopardy.

He waited for almost ten minutes before Dale Thomas shuffled in the door. The union president looked flustered. Zielinski couldn't remember ever seeing him appear that way before. A lawyer by trade, Thomas usually exuded confidence.

"This will have to be quick," Thomas said without a greeting.

"Why? What's up?"

Thomas waved away his question and lowered himself in the seat opposite him. "No time." He placed his phone in front of him on the table. "Has anyone contacted you directly?"

"No. Dale, what—"

"If they do, you know not to talk to them, right? Everything goes through me, or my aides."

"No one has."

"And you're keeping out of trouble?"

"Seriously?" Zielinski said, shaking his head. "This is

starting to feel like I'm meeting with a probation officer."

"Don't be like that. This is the process."

"The process sucks," Zielinski snapped. He tapped the table with his first two fingers. "I need to get back to work."

"These things take time. But that's so we get it right. You want to get back to work, that's the cost."

Zielinski leaned forward. "I need the money, Dale."

Thomas gave him a confused look. "You're on paid admin leave. Are you not getting your regular check?"

"No, I am. But that doesn't cut it. I've had to take some construction work on the side, but it's only day work, so it isn't steady. Besides, swinging a hammer isn't going to put my kids through college."

Thomas's face took on a concerned expression. "Ray…" He stopped when his phone buzzed. Thomas quickly looked at the screen and swiped several times. He let out a small sigh. Then he looked back up at Zielinski. "Your finances are your own issue. I can't help you. You'll need to find a way to live within your means."

"Live within my means?" Zielinski repeated, shocked.

"It's something we all have to do." He glanced down at his phone when it buzzed again. His eyebrows knitted. "We need to move this along."

"I'm sorry I'm such an inconvenience to you," Zielinski snarled.

Anger flashed in the union president's eyes. "You're not my only member. There are three hundred others who need my services."

"But I'm the one sitting in front of you *now*."

Thomas pressed his lips together. He took one last look at his phone, read something for a moment, then swiped it away. He'd barely looked up at Zielinski before it buzzed once more. "This is routine follow-up, Ray. Nothing has changed in your case. Internal Affairs is investigating. When they're finished, the case will be reviewed by command. It's all standard."

"Sitting at home with an ulcer doesn't feel standard to

me."

"I understand that you're worried."

"Should I be?"

Thomas hesitated, and Zielinski's stomach fell.

"The Darold Barden arrest you made on your day off is questionable," Thomas said.

"The guy had a warrant."

"He did. But asking why you were there in the first place is a reasonable question. It's odd, Ray. And Internal Affairs feasts on odd."

"Funny. I thought they only ate cheese."

Thomas didn't smile.

"Because they're rats," Zielinski added.

Thomas waited a beat, then continued. "Barden's saying that you forced your way into Alejandra Sanita's apartment."

"That's bull. She invited me in."

"He says you spent the whole day hassling everyone who knows him, trying to run him down."

Zielinski didn't answer. That part was true.

"He's also telling IA that you went by his house a few days prior. That all of this is you doing a favor for a buddy because Barden is seeing your buddy's ex-girlfriend."

Also true.

"How bad is it?" he asked Thomas.

"I think you should prepare yourself for the very real possibility that when all is said and down, you'll take a significant hit."

"What does that mean? Suspended without pay? What?"

"It depends on which of the allegations are founded."

"What's the range I'm looking at?"

"I'm not a soothsayer."

"I'm not asking you to read the friggin' tea leaves, Dale!" Zielinski hollered. "I just want some idea what I'm facing."

"Don't yell at me."

"I'm not yelling!"

The phone on the table buzzed. Thomas reached for it. Zielinski slapped his hand over the lawyer's, trapping it on top of the phone. "Tell me," he said.

Thomas pulled his hand away, and the phone with it, but he didn't look down at the device. "I don't like to speculate, but if I were to do so, I'd say that a month's suspension without pay is the likely floor."

"The floor?" Zielinski licked his lips. "Then the ceiling is…?"

"Termination."

Zielinski leaned back, deflated. He'd known this was theoretically a possibility, but he'd spent the last few weeks convincing himself that it wouldn't happen. Thomas's words dashed those hopes.

"Fired," he mumbled. "They're really going to fire me." Absently, he rubbed his stomach while he spoke, as if to massage away the internal ache.

"That's always the worst case," Thomas said. He glanced at his phone, then spoke distractedly while he scrolled. "And only if the investigation sustains the complaints. If that happens, we'll do everything we can to mitigate the penalty."

Zielinski sat perfectly still, dumbfounded. He was going to lose his job. No, his *career*. He couldn't believe it.

When Thomas stood, he whipped his gaze back to the rotund lawyer. "Where are you going?"

"We're done here. And I've got even bigger problems to deal with."

"Bigger?" Zielinski balled a fist. He wondered if his situation would get any worse if he decked his own union representation.

"The Department of Justice just landed in Spokane," Thomas said. "They're on their way to jam a fist down our throat."

"DOJ?" Zielinski struggled to process the news. "What do *they* want?"

"I just told you." Thomas walked toward the door. "I have to go," he said, and disappeared from sight.

Zielinski listened to another set of footfalls fade away. Over the past few weeks, he had vacillated between anger and deep worry over his situation. Now, he only felt numb. He sat in the conference room for several minutes, waiting for one of those emotions to return. When neither did, he rose and showed himself out of the police department that he still thought of as his own.

Chapter 7

Clint rapped on the door of the green and yellow house. There was a new paint job on the door, a deep shade of red, and the yard was nicely tended. Clint figured a landscaping service took care of the lawn and the bushes, though in this neighborhood, it wouldn't surprise him if an enterprising young man handled it. But the door? He was nearly certain that Mrs. Aurelia Ellis had painted it herself, seventy-one years old or not.

As if on cue, the latch clicked, and Aurelia Ellis was before him. The elderly black woman wore a stylish dress of burnt orange that hung loosely from her tall, thin frame. She held the door open wide but stood squarely in the center of the entryway. From inside, Clint could smell baking bread.

Aurelia's expression was neutral, but the message was clear, as it had been on his previous visits. She would talk to him, be respectful of the law, but he wasn't going to be allowed into the house.

This was one of those times he wished he could have brought Marty Hill along with him. Clint was an able interviewer but did best when there was a direct line of questioning to pursue. Here, he knew that he couldn't ask her the only two true questions he had for her. Not yet. The situation required rapport building, not his strongest suit.

"Hello, Mrs. Ellis." He forced an awkward smile.

"Detective."

Clint glanced around at the sky and the clouds. "It's a nice day."

Aurelia Ellis nodded primly.

"Only a two percent chance of rain, I heard on the radio."

"You don't say."

Clint nodded. He took a deep breath and let it out. He glanced around the neighborhood before saying, "Barometric pressure's nice, too."

She frowned and crossed her arms. "Detective Clint."

"Yes, ma'am."

"May I ask you a question?"

"Yes."

"You aren't much good at small talk, are you?"

Clint shook his head. "No, ma'am. I have little use for it, if you want the truth."

"Well, that makes two of us. So while I do enjoy the sun on my face, I have a chair on the patio that is much nicer than here at my front door."

Clint took a stab. "Are you inviting me inside, Mrs. Ellis?" He glanced past her. All that was visible was a beige wall about ten feet inside, with a hallway opening to both the left and right. A free-standing coat rack was nudged up against the wall, holding a sparse two jackets. One was a pink raincoat, and the other a light blue windbreaker.

"No, Detective," Aurelia answered, her tone congenial but firm. "I am inviting you to ask your questions and leave."

Clint admired her directness. In a way, he appreciated her loyalty, too, even though it was hindering him now.

"I only have two," he said.

"That's all you ever have."

"Is Earl here?" Clint asked.

"No, sir, he is not. I haven't seen him in two months."

Clint wasn't sure if he believed her. She was believable, that was certain. And her denial sounded much the same as the ones she'd made on his previous visits to her door. But she could be lying to him. If so, she was good at it.

"Do you know where he might be?"

"He *might be* anywhere," Aurelia said. "But as to where he is at this moment, I have no earthly idea."

Clint cocked his head. "You wouldn't lie to me, would you, Mrs. Ellis?"

"No, Detective."

"You do know it is a crime to lie to the police officer engaged in an official investigation, right?"

"I am aware of that. Now, if you'll excuse me, that has been *four* questions, and I believe I've answered them all." She reached for the door and began to close it. "Good day, Detective."

"One more question, if you don't mind."

Aurelia stopped and gave him a look that somehow expressed patience and exasperation all at once. "What is it?"

"What did you do, before you retired?"

"How is that relevant?"

"It's not. I'm merely curious."

"I can assure you it was nothing illegal."

"I believe you. What did you do, though?"

She paused, as if gauging the value of answering him. Then she said, "I was a schoolteacher. I taught English, grades six, seven, and eight."

"Here in Spokane?"

She nodded. "Shaw Middle."

"Thank you. Have a nice day, Mrs. Ellis." Clint turned and walked away. Behind him, he heard a pause, and then the door close.

He'd thought perhaps she was an English teacher from her use of language, and when she corrected him, it cemented his suspicions. It was a fact that didn't really matter, but Clint still felt good about knowing it as he made his way back to his car. It may have felt like an interview inside his own head, but he was pretty sure it came out as small talk. Maybe he wasn't so bad at it, after all.

Good thing, too, because that was a skill he sensed he was going to need in the days ahead.

Chapter 8

Tyler Garrett's cell phone buzzed with another text message.

When he pulled to a stop at the intersection of Rowan and Alberta, he grabbed the phone. The message was from his friend, Bo Sherman. *You hear? DOJ on premises.*

He had heard, in fact. Bo's text was the seventh—

Garrett's phone buzzed again.

It was another text message. Eight now. This one came from another friend, Detective Marty Hill.

Dude! DOJ kickng tireS bcause of sTone? reeks of BullSht

For someone whose profession demanded attention to detail, Hill was all thumbs and spelling errors when he communicated via text. Normally, this made Garrett smile.

Today, though, he frowned.

He looked up at the rearview mirror and saw the impatient face of the driver behind him. Garrett checked left and right to see the cars at the other stop signs were patiently waiting for him to proceed. He accelerated through the intersection then let his thoughts return to the problem at hand.

The Department of Justice was on the SPD campus.

He slipped his phone into a pocket of the duty bag seatbelted onto the passenger seat.

Truth be told, he wasn't quite sure what to make of their visit. Oh, he knew DOJ was the big, bad boogeyman from a hill back east, but just what they could do to him and his department, he didn't know.

And was it anything he really needed to be concerned with?

There were plenty of things a patrolman had to worry about—those things usually had to do with guns and people with ill intentions—and there were things the brass had to worry about—those usually had to do with budgetary constraints and political ramifications. That's why he never had had any career inclinations to go higher than patrol.

Climbing the career ladder meant less time in a prowl car and more time in the hallowed halls of SPD where he'd be on his knees kissing someone's fat ass for his next opportunity. Out here, though, Garrett didn't have to pucker up for anyone. Out here, he created his luck and he took what he wanted.

He turned onto Decatur Avenue and drove slowly through the northside neighborhood. A block in he stopped in front of a boarded-up house with a yellow notice stapled to its door. He scanned the neighborhood. It was made up of blue-collar residents and most of them should be at work. *Should be.* There were still a lot of cars in driveways and along the curbs in front of neighboring houses.

This was the problem with his current day-shift assignment. If he wanted to do anything while in uniform, it had to be done in the light of day and in front of others. He never had that concern while he worked power shift—the assignment that overlapped both swing and graveyard shifts. He was slated to spend the rest of the year working days. Yet another unfortunate result of Captain Farrell's ill-fated Anti-Crime Team.

Garrett's lip curled slightly at the memory.

The four-officer Anti-Crime Team was created for two purposes. Its outward mission—the one Farrell sold to anyone listening—was to catch high-profile offenders. The actual mission, which Garrett learned later, was to entrap him.

In the end, the team flamed out after the gunning down of Officer Gary Stone. Garrett was there when it happened and was the only man who knew exactly what occurred. He was also the only person who knew *why* it happened, but he wasn't going to devote any more thought to a man he knew to be a rat.

Rookie Jun Yang, the academy princess, was also on the

team. After Stone's death, she quit the department entirely. Word around the department was she returned to the military. Probably so she could feel safe again, Garrett mused.

And rounding out the team was the old man, Ray Zielinski. After the team broke up, he just happened to step into a mess of his own doing and got suspended for it. Classic Zielinski. The scuttlebutt was Ray might even get terminated. Couldn't happen to a nicer guy.

Garrett's eyes returned to the boarded-up home—a so-called zombie house. They were becoming fewer as the Code Enforcement division worked with the city attorney to apply the nuisance ordinance. By doing so, the city could force the owners of record to clean up their properties. And if those owners failed to do so, the city would push the property to be sold.

These zombie houses had been a goldmine for Garrett.

He climbed out of his car. For the past several years, he'd hidden money and drugs around the city in houses just like this. At first, it was to secrete cash and dope he'd stolen from a dealer or a crime scene. Hiding stuff in a zombie home was a cheap and effective way to keep his then wife from finding anything suspicious. If he rented a storage unit, she might find that. Plus, it'd be in his name. If he kept a girlfriend, she could find her. But how the hell would his wife ever know about a zombie house?

The money or drugs never stayed in the abandoned homes for long. They were only temporary storage places, especially when he learned to play the game. Then the money and drugs were put into circulation. Round and round they went, building newer and bigger piles. Now, most of his cash and dope were no longer hidden but kept in plain sight. It was entrusted to a handler—Earl Ellis being the latest—and a network of dealers.

Using the houses didn't come without some risk, though, but even the stock market tanked occasionally, and banks were only insured to a certain limit.

Once, he lost some drugs when an enterprising bum broke

into a house and discovered what he had hidden. There was another house that burned. He'd hidden about five thousand dollars in that one. He chalked those losses up to the costs of doing business.

There was even a house in the Hillyard neighborhood where he killed a former associate and let him rot for a few days. He eventually controlled the outcome of that situation by reporting the body by way of a concerned, yet never verified, citizen.

In a neighborhood like this, however, Garrett only entered an abandoned home while in uniform. The silver shield on his chest was a ticket to places others couldn't go without arousing suspicions. If he walked into this boarded-up house in plainclothes, a neighbor would most assuredly be alarmed and immediately call 911.

Hello? Police? he imagined the caller saying. *There's a black man entering the vacant house next to me.* In the predominately white city of Spokane, a call like that was sure to get a response from the police department.

Instead, since he was in uniform, he would appear to be a cop performing a standard security check. Feel free to go about your business. There's nothing to worry about. The neighbors might actually be thankful a uniform was in the neighborhood, even if that officer was a man of color.

Garrett walked up to the front door and made a big show of checking its security. When he was done, he descended the stairs as he continued to scan the neighborhood. He casually strolled around the house, opened the low gate, and stepped into the backyard.

"They was just here."

It was a frail woman's voice. He turned and searched for its origin. She stood in the shade of an apple tree near the three-foot high chain-link fence. The handle to an oxygen tank was in her left hand. Tubes ran from it to her nose. Her silver and gray hair looked wiry and unwashed. Age spots covered her sallow skin. The purple housecoat she wore was caught up on the oxygen tank and revealed more leg than

Garrett cared to see.

"Excuse me?" he said.

"The maintenance peoples," the woman said. She pointed toward the rear of the house he was at. "They put some new wood up. Made a big racket about it, you ask me."

Garrett stepped to where there should have been a back door. Instead, a large piece of plywood had been hastily screwed into the frame. An unnecessarily large amount of screws were used to attach the board.

He slipped his hand into his pocket and grasped the thick wad of bills that he had planned to add to the secret cache that he had already hidden inside this house.

"Looks like they did a good job," the woman said.

"Looks like," Garrett muttered.

He didn't like holding onto this much cash—he now had a couple thousand in his pocket—and he didn't like keeping it at his apartment. Cash led people to ask questions. And cops with too much cash led people to watch them closely and suspect the worst.

Besides hiding his cash in zombie houses, he kept some with his girlfriend, Tiana. He didn't want her too involved with his business activities, though. If push came to shove, he didn't know how well she would stand up under pressure. She was already holding ten grand of his. Giving her more would be exposing too much.

When the oxygen tank hissed, Garrett glanced to the woman. She reached up for a yellowish-green apple and pulled it from the tree. As she pretended to examine the fruit, her eyes slid over to him.

He'd stood here for too long now. Garrett nodded toward the woman and she waved the apple at him.

While he walked back to his car, his fingers fiddled with the bills in his pocket.

Both the change to day shift and the disappearance of Earl Ellis were putting a crimp in his business dealings. A dip in earnings wasn't a big deal. Money was just a way to score the game. Some days you're up and others you're down. It happens.

And he knew he could he deal with the shift change. All he had to do was make it to the end of the year then he would rotate back to power shift.

But the loss of Earl? That was a bigger pain in the ass than anything. He needed to know what happened to the man, then he could take appropriate action. If Earl was hiding to avoid the police, Garrett could set up a safe method for them to keep in contact. Easy-peasy and life moves on. If the man bailed on the whole operation, Garrett could find a replacement. A bit of a pain, but he'd done it before. Again, life moves on. But if he turned against him…

No. Not Earl. He wouldn't rat. Garrett knew that much.

Which left him right back where he started. Not knowing anything. He felt like he was chasing his tail trying to find the man and that was irritating him.

Garrett dropped into his car and turned to his Mobile Data Computer to check the list of calls waiting for an officer response. There was a report of a garage burglary, a non-injury collision, a shoplifter, and something that read like a neighborhood dispute. All of them could wait. They could wait forever as far as he was concerned.

He tightly wrapped his fingers around the steering wheel as if he were choking the life out of a man. His lips pulled back from his teeth before he uttered, "So where the hell are you, Earl?"

Chapter 9

With his arms crossed, Chief Robert Baumgartner sat at the head of the conference table. To his immediate right sat Tom Farrell. To the chief's left, but a seat away, was Dana Hatcher.

The three of them were silent, each lost in their own thoughts, as they awaited the arrival of their guests.

Guests, Baumgartner thought sarcastically.

That's like saying a swarm of locusts was just an annoyance.

The Department of Justice team was in the lobby of the Public Safety Building working their way through the metal detectors. Maybe he should have sent someone up to greet them and escort them back. Perhaps show them some deferential treatment.

Screw that.

They should jump through the same hoops as anyone else, especially given what they were about to put him and his team through.

If he hadn't gotten a heads-up call from his friend Lou, this DOJ detachment would have caught everyone off guard. As it was, they were scrambling to notify the entire department, from commissioned officers to civilian employees. Fat lot of good it would do.

Who knew what these feds wanted to see or who they might want to interview. Or what phantom wrongdoing they would think they uncovered in the process.

A fluorescent tube flickered above him—an annoying warning that the bulb was about to die. His eyes went to it and he growled, "You're kidding me."

Both Farrell and Hatcher stared at him with the

ineffectiveness of people used to dealing with stubborn cops, not failing lights.

"Chief?" Marilyn said. His assistant was in the doorway to the conference room. Her wide eyes indicated that she had heard his expletive. "Justice is here."

Behind her were three people in expensive-looking suits.

Baumgartner stood and forced a smile. Farrell and Hatcher joined him in standing, but their faces remained impassive.

A dark-skinned woman in her late forties stepped forward. Her brown eyes seemed to be filled with not only wisdom, but a weariness reserved for someone many years her senior. Using her left hand, she flipped open a black leather wallet to reveal a Department of Justice seal and an identification card. A diamond wedding ring was on the appropriate finger.

"Édelie Durand," she said. "Deputy Chief. Special Litigation Section."

Baumgartner blinked. "Special Litigation?"

Durand motioned to the two people with her. "Steve Curado and Dani Watson."

When introduced, they both presented their wallet credentials. Their ID cards showed them with the same title—Attorney.

Great. Just what he needed—lawyers poking around his department.

The chief waggled his thumb between his subordinates. "Captains Tom Farrell and Dana Hatcher. Investigations and Patrol."

Everyone politely nodded at each other, but no one bothered to shake hands.

Baumgartner cleared his throat before asking, "So what's the deputy chief of the Special Litigation Section doing here?"

"As you may know, I work for—" Durand squinted and glanced up at the flickering fluorescent light. When she returned her gaze to the chief, she continued, "I work for an assistant attorney general who works for the attorney general.”

The chief nodded. He understood the organizational structure of the Justice Department.

“The attorney general,” Durand continued, “serves at the pleasure of the president who has taken a recent interest in local law enforcement agencies that have shown, shall we say, a propensity for violating the civil rights of the citizens they are sworn to protect.”

The chief’s face warmed. “And you think we’ve done that?”

Durand paused for several moments as if considering an appropriate response. She kept eye contact with Baumgartner during that time. Eventually, she shrugged. “I don’t know.”

Baumgartner glanced to Farrell then Hatcher before returning his attention back to Durand. “Then why are you—”

“Over the past couple of years,” Durand said, as if the chief hadn’t been speaking, “the Spokane Police Department has had several high-profile events—*negative* events. One of those even involved you, Chief.”

He kept his mouth shut now. She was referring to the reluctant assistance he gave the mayor in hiding a relationship between a councilman and a seventeen-year-old girl. If he could go back in time, he would punch the mayor in the mouth just for asking him to help. An arrest for assault would be easier to own up to than what he actually did.

Next to him, Dana Hatcher seemed to struggle with holding back a smile. Baumgartner’s eyes narrowed, but Durand continued.

“In this same time period, two officers have been killed in the line of duty.”

“That is an anomaly,” Baumgartner blurted.

“We realize that,” Durand said confidently. “Before these two officers, it was more than forty years since the last officer was killed on duty.”

“Which means—”

“Four decades,” Durand said and held up as many fingers.

Baumgartner ground his teeth together. She was

grandstanding. This woman from Washington, D.C. was letting him know that she had done her homework. Big deal. He didn't have to open his mouth any further and let her smack him around. This wasn't his first rodeo.

Édelie Durand looked to her female associate when she asked, "By the way, Chief, we watched with profound interest the events surrounding Officer Tyler Garrett."

Next to him, Farrell straightened.

"His shooting," Baumgartner said, "was reviewed by an outside agency and deemed justified and within all policies and procedures of our department. Officer Garrett did nothing wrong."

Farrell seemed to bristle further.

"It *was* deemed justifiable," Durand said, "yet the city still paid out three quarters of a million for an improper search of Officer Garrett's house that led to a questionable arrest on drug charges. Those charges were quickly dropped, weren't they?"

Baumgartner glanced at his captains but neither looked in his direction.

"Officer Garrett hasn't suffered any undue pressure from the command structure due to this situation, has he?"

"I can assure you, he has not. Officer Garrett is a stellar patrolman with an impeccable record. Our command staff stands fully behind him."

"That's good," Durand said. "Because we wouldn't want to stumble into a hostile work environment as part of our investigation."

Damn it.

He needed to say something now—*anything*. Otherwise, he'd just look petulant as she took pot shots at his department. Or worse, he'd look like he was actually hiding something.

Baumgartner pulled back his shoulders. "Law enforcement *is* a hostile work environment."

Captain Hatcher winced.

"We understand fully," Durand said and glanced between

her staffers. When she returned her attention to Baumgartner, she said, "We look forward to talking with your officers."

The chief looked to Farrell who stared straight ahead. The captain's face was ashen.

What the hell is wrong with him?

"You can talk with whoever you like," Baumgartner said.

"A number of questions concerning your department have been raised," Durand said. "And most of this came from reading news reports."

"You can't always believe the news," Baumgartner said.

Durand's smile softened into condescension. "Now, Chief, please don't use the fake news angle on us."

"The local media doesn't like us," he blurted. There was a surprising whine to his voice, and he was embarrassed to hear it.

"They don't like any of us," Durand said, "but we still do the work we swore to perform. We're all professionals, aren't we?"

Both attorneys behind her crossed their arms now. Baumgartner was sure it was a move meant to intimidate, and it irritated him. Especially since Farrell stood next to him looking like he had seen a ghost. To make matters worse, Hatcher seemed like she was enjoying watching him squirm. He swallowed but did so with some difficulty.

"Relax, Chief," Durand said with a dismissive wave. "This is only a fact-finding mission. It's not a takeover of any sort. We only want to look around and ask some questions."

"Then what will you do?"

She studied him for a moment.

This woman is actually *studying me.*

Finding something she liked, Durand nodded with satisfaction. "We'll go home and make a recommendation."

"As to what?"

Durand nodded. "As to whether or not a full-scale investigation is needed. If that's the case, there'll be a heck of a lot more attention than two attorneys and a deputy chief can give."

Baumgartner remained silent. What better course of action did he have right now?

Durand glanced down at her wedding ring. "I can assure you of two things, Chief Baumgartner. One is that our investigation will be thorough. The other is that it will be objective. There is no agenda here. We will follow the facts, nothing more."

Yeah, right.

"So I'm assuming your staff and officers are aware of our arrival."

That threw him for a moment. "How would we know you were coming?" he asked. Both captains turned to him, but he ignored them. "We were never notified of your visit."

Durand frowned. "You didn't receive a phone call this morning?"

Baumgartner's brow furrowed.

"I'm sorry," Durand said. "Maybe my information was bad. I thought Lou Nelson was a friend of yours."

"Lou?"

Durand's frown faded. "That's right. I asked him to call. Give you a heads-up when we landed."

The chief suddenly felt cornered. He opened his mouth to say something, but she beat him to it.

"Chief…" Durand glanced at both Farrell and Hatcher before continuing. "Did you really think a friend you send a sporadic Christmas card to would risk his career to tell you we were on the way?"

"But *why*?" His words were half his normal volume.

"Why the call? I figured it would ease the shock of us showing up. Maybe help you acclimate to the idea of us being here so we could avoid all the wailing and gnashing of teeth that usually slows things like this down."

That wasn't the reason, Baumgartner knew. Durand wanted to show she knew things about him that he would be surprised she knew. And to keep him off balance. Well, it worked, on both counts.

Farrell and Hatcher watched him with concern. They were

looking to him for leadership and, by God, it was time he delivered. He needed to take control of the meeting.

Chief Robert Baumgartner stood a little straighter, pulled his shoulders back, and thrust his chin out. "They'll be no wailing and gnashing. We'll provide whatever you need."

"I would expect nothing less," Durand said.

"We have nothing to hide," Baumgartner added.

Durand only stared at him in response.

Baumgartner let the silence sit for a few moments, then said, "Also, I've called the mayor and alerted him to your visit."

"I appreciate that."

"He said he would make himself available for you anytime, but I said we'd be over later in the afternoon. I figured you'd want to—"

Durand held up a hand. "I'll meet with him now."

"Oh."

"*Alone.*"

Baumgartner licked his lips.

"You understand the reason for that, don't you?"

"Yeah, sure," he mumbled.

If you're going to discipline a police department, you probably don't want to reveal you cards to the chief of police before you start the process.

His stomach roiled.

Durand looked to both her attorneys then back to Baumgartner. "I need someone to show around my staff."

"Dana and Tom," Baumgartner said, his voice almost a whisper now "They can escort them around."

"That'll be fine."

Baumgartner couldn't believe how embarrassing this initial meeting had gone. It should have been a simple introduction, but Édelie Durand had put him on notice that he was not the big dog in his own yard. No one had ever done that before. Not Mayor Sikes. Not a councilperson. No one.

Then this woman walks into his conference room and kicks him in the balls in front of two captains and her staff. It was humiliating. He needed a private meeting. Perhaps if he could have a few minutes of back and forth with her, he could understand how he mishandled this initial meeting.

Baumgartner turned to Farrell. "Why don't the four of you get started on the tour? Let me sit with Mrs. Durand so we—"

"Chief, I need to be clear about something." Durand spoke in a neutral voice, but Baumgartner could hear the steel in her words.

"By all means."

"This is a DOJ investigation. We will set the agenda, including who to interview and when."

"I get that, but—"

"That includes when we conduct our official interview with you."

Baumgartner inhaled deeply and forced a smile that Durand didn't bother to return. "Can I have some time," he said, "after your return from the mayor's office so we can sit and chat? Maybe get acquainted?"

"If there's an opportunity. Meanwhile, we're going to need this conference room for the next few days. For interviews, file audits, that sort of thing. You understand." Durand glanced up at the flickering light. "But if that blinks the entire time, we're probably going to get cranky. Get it fixed, will you?"

Durand didn't wait for Baumgartner to respond. Instead, she spun on her heel and walked between her subordinates. They, however, lingered behind and watched the chief and his captains with intense curiosity.

Baumgartner's face felt warm and he could feel wetness under his arms. He knew he was sweating. It had been a lot of years since someone had caused him to sweat like that. Despite Durand's neutral, if curt, demeanor, he felt the weight of the DOJ presence settling on his shoulders. His sense of control, always a strength, was shaken.

"If you'll excuse me," he said to Curado and Watson.

He didn't bother saying goodbye to his captains before slipping between the two DOJ staffers.

The chief walked as calmly as he could down the hallway, past Marilyn's desk, and into his office. Carefully and quietly, he closed the door. Robert Baumgartner shuffled to his desk before dropping heavily into his chair.

He bent forward and whispered, "Damn. This is going to be rough."

Chapter 10

Thick tension hung in the air. Captain Tom Farrell stared at the doorway following the chief's departure. He wished he could escape the conference room, too. His knees felt weak. His mind flitted distractedly through a quick succession of thoughts, barely exploring one before another pushed it aside.

I've never seen the chief get put on his heels like that before. Even when attacked by the mayor, a reporter, or a city councilmember, Baumgartner always handled the exchange deftly, like a boxer who could take a blow but keep to the fight plan. The cold, calculated way Durand knocked him around was stunning.

And Hatcher liked it. Even through his own shocked response, he'd been able to see that. Just under the professional veneer of impassivity, he saw a shadow of perverse satisfaction. What was the word for that? *Schadenfreude*, that was it.

None of that matters. They're going to find out everything.

The silence stretched out, and tension rose with it. Farrell knew he should be the one to break it, since he was the senior captain. But that last thought kept him stapled to where he stood, unspeaking, staring after his departed chief.

Captain Hatcher cleared her throat. "Well, why don't we each show one of you around, to give you the lay of the land?" She motioned toward Watson. "Counselor?"

"No," Watson said flatly. "We'll stick together."

Hatcher frowned. "All right. What would you like to see?"

"Let's start with Investigations."

Straight for the jugular. That brought him out of his temporary shutdown. "That's fine," he stammered, "but let's give you a quick once around first. That way you'll have a sense of where everything is."

"They said what they want to see, Tom," Hatcher said. She lowered her voice slightly when she said, "Let's just take them there."

"We will. I'm only suggesting we do a brief tour first."

"We're not real estate agents," Hatcher grumbled.

Farrell ground his teeth together, his worry and stress shifting toward anger. Why did Hatcher have to make things difficult? Despite their differences, they should be showing DOJ a united front. He opened his mouth to reply, but Watson interrupted.

"Officers," she said firmly. She glanced at her partner then back to Farrell and Hatcher. "If you don't mind—"

Farrell's frustration boiled over. "It's *captain*, actually," he said, interrupting her in turn.

"Excuse me?" Watson gave him a surprised look.

"I'm a captain," Farrell said. "It's a rank I earned. I haven't been an officer for many years."

"I misspoke. If we could—"

He motioned with his head toward Hatcher. "Same for her." He sensed Hatcher watching him but couldn't gauge her response in his peripheral vision.

"Fine." Watson bit off the word. "But is that really how you want to play this?"

"Dani," Curado began, but she shot him a look that silenced him.

Farrell felt all the steam go out of him as soon as it had risen. What was he doing poking the bear? But now he saw no graceful way to back away from the exchange.

I've screwed this up worse than Baumgartner did.

"I'm not playing at anything," he said evenly. "You're here for information, right? I am just making sure your information is accurate."

In his peripheral vision, he saw Hatcher roll her eyes.

Watson glared at Farrell for several seconds before she spoke. "Very well, *Captain*. Give us a brief walk around the police station for orientation purposes, and then take us to the

Investigative Division."

"Of course." He started for the door, brushing past the two DOJ attorneys. He didn't look to see if they followed.

Hatcher fell in beside him. Watson and Curado remained several paces back.

"What the *hell* are you doing?" Hatcher whispered. "Do you *want* them to slap a consent decree on us?"

Farrell didn't answer. He knew she was right. Getting into a pissing match with DOJ was foolish. His fear turned to anger and then he'd let both control his actions, responding without clear thought. The exchange with Watson accomplished nothing other than to alienate her, probably making her even more motivated to find something wrong or shady within his department.

She won't have far to look. He'd just painted a target on his own back.

When he didn't reply to Hatcher, she said, "Tone it down. Be a professional."

He didn't answer that, either. He just kept walking forward, hoping to get through what lay ahead of him.

That was all he could do now.

Chapter 11

"This is bullshit," Mayor Andrew Sikes said.

Seated in his office, Sikes was clearly doing his best to project an air of casual professionalism. He crossed one leg over the other and draped his left arm along the back of the leather couch. His right hand drummed absently on the ankle of which it rested.

However, his face was beet red and large beads of sweat formed on his forehead. His shirt collar was unbuttoned, and his blue tie appeared hastily tied and askew.

Édelie Durand sat quietly opposite him and watched.

The mayor had shown up to the meeting already purpled and perspiring. She had nothing to do with this physical reaction.

By showing up unannounced, Durand had interrupted his workout. For fifteen minutes, she waited patiently near his assistant's desk. During this time, Durand texted with her husband to check on his condition. Roland said he was having an *okay* day, which she knew was code for a difficult one. She texted supportive messages to him, never leaving for a drink of water or a bathroom break. Her constant presence caused the mayor's stolid assistant to grow increasingly anxious as evidenced through ever more furtive glances between her and the clock on the wall.

When the mayor finally trotted onto the seventh floor, tugging at his tie, his assistant intercepted him. They exchanged hushed yet hurried words. She tried to tamp his mussed hair in place, but Sikes pushed her away.

After quick introductions, the mayor demanded that his chief of staff be allowed to sit in on their meeting. Durand flatly said no and threatened to leave. Sikes eventually relented.

Then the mayor stammered his way into an insistence on his assistant taking notes of their meeting. Again, Durand said no. If he wanted notes, she said, he could take them himself.

She really didn't care if his chief of staff or assistant were in the meeting, she only wanted to see how the mayor would react. She wanted to see the man under some level of pressure.

Now, he was doing his best to display an air of casualness. His choice of words, however…

"Complete bullshit."

Durand lifted her eyebrows. "How so?"

"You waltz in here like you own the place."

"By *you*, I assume you're implying the federal government."

"You're damn right, I am."

Durand nodded.

Sikes wiped sweat from his forehead then rubbed the palm of his hand along the side of his blue suit pants. "Without warning, I might add."

"I warned the chief we were coming."

"Bullshit."

"I had his friend call him when we landed."

The mayor's Adam's apple bobbed up and down before he asked, "His friend?"

"His friend at Justice. I made sure the chief got a call."

Sikes wiped the side of his face followed by another palm swipe along his pant leg.

"We did our homework before arriving," Durand continued. "We know things about your police department, your city, and you."

"Me?" Sikes seemed genuinely surprised to be included.

"I came over as a courtesy to introduce myself and explain why we're here."

The mayor smirked. "That's a requirement. You can't operate in my city without me knowing about it. You gotta get my permission."

"Your permission?"

"That's right."

She stood and moved to the window. "*Your* city?"

"That's what I said. And if you want to operate here, Mrs. Durand—"

"It's Ms., actually," she corrected.

The mayor waved his hands dismissively. "Honest mistake. You're wearing a wedding ring."

Durand glanced down at the diamond solitaire. An image of Roland flashed through her mind, but she pushed it away. There was work to do if she wanted to get back to him, and that work was going to be a lot easier if the Honorable Andrew Sikes was on the sidelines.

"Ms. is the standard these days," she told him. "A woman shouldn't be defined by her marital status. Miss and Mrs. are patriarchal terms."

"Oh, please," Sikes said. "Next thing you're going to say is that you kept your maiden name."

Durand almost smiled. The mayor walked right into it. "Maiden name is an antiquated term. But yes, I kept my family name. I did it to honor my mother and father. And before you ask, my husband was very supportive."

"I'll bet he was," the mayor sneered.

Durand shifted gears. "May I ask you something?"

"That's what you're here for, isn't it?"

"How is it you were able to survive the cover-up of a rape allegation against a councilman?"

"I never—"

She turned back to look out the window. Nearby was a beautiful park and an arena. In the distance, a square monolith stood out like an ugly, sore thumb. The Spokane River ran by the base of city hall.

"There wasn't any cover-up," he said. The tone of the mayor's voice had softened slightly.

"What's the name of your river?" she asked.

"The Spokane. And that allegation was disproved."

Durand inhaled deeply before turning away from the window. "A councilman had a relationship with a seventeen-year-old."

"Yeah, but I didn't."

"When she reported the rape to your office, you asked Chief Baumgartner to handle it quietly."

Sikes swiped more sweat from his forehead before drying his hand along the side of his pants.

"Or am I misunderstanding the chain of events?"

"Baumgartner," Sikes said. "Baumgartner handled it that way. I never wanted it to be quiet."

Durand cocked her head. "You didn't?"

"Not me. No way. Baumgartner was looking for leverage. It was what he wanted. He's a political shark, that one." The mayor shook his finger at her. "He suggested we keep it quiet. It was his idea. He said we should find out if there was something there. And if there was, we could use it against the councilman."

"How would you use it?"

The mayor repeatedly blinked as he considered an answer.

"Should I repeat the question?"

Sikes shook his head. "I don't know how he would use it."

"So the chief presents a cockamamie idea like that and you went along with it?"

Another swipe and another wipe along the pant leg, but the mayor kept his mouth shut. His hand settled around his ankle and he angrily grasped it. She wondered if he imagined strangling her.

"And when it all blew up?" Durand asked.

"I disciplined him."

She nodded. So far, the mayor was confirming everything she had read in the newspaper's coverage of the events. "A three-day suspension," she said. "You sure showed him."

Sikes flexed his jaw. "I'm still the damn mayor and you need to show some respect."

She closed her eyes and nodded several times. When she opened her eyes she said, "Mr. Mayor." She paused to let it stand out from what she was about to say. "That girl killed herself."

New beads of sweat formed on the mayor's forehead. She was no longer sure these were from his workout. "We don't know if that had anything to do with—"

"A three-day suspension for the chief and the councilman walks away from his post."

Sikes pointed at her. "I kicked out that little sneak, too. The one that caused the whole thing."

"Who's that?"

"Gary Stone. Baumgartner's spy."

"The officer who investigated the girl's allegation."

"That's right. He's the one to blame."

"And you kicked him out of where exactly?"

"Here," Sikes said and pointed absently toward somewhere on the seventh floor. "He had an office just down the hall."

"So you removed him from city hall after the newspaper reported this incident?"

"I couldn't trust that little creep no more."

"You think he leaked the story?"

"He denied it. So did Baumgartner. But who else could it have been?"

Durand smiled. "So what you're telling me, Mr. Mayor…" Again, she paused when she used his official title. "Is that you punished a whistleblower?"

His eyes widened. "That's not what I did." Realizing his initial reaction was too small for the gravity of Durand's accusation, Sikes jumped to his feet and stared at her. "He never blew a whistle. He never gave me a chance to fix anything. That little bastard *talked* to the news."

"And you know that how?"

The mayor's fists balled. "I know because I know."

Durand nodded and turned back to the windows. "And the chief got three days off."

"That's right. Without pay."

"And you got nothing."

"I think you're over-simplifying—"

"You've had a string of bad luck under your administration."

"Bullshit," Sikes said. "That's bullshit. I've done great things while in office. Better than any administration before me. All you've got to do is look around to see what I've done. There's been more—"

Durand spun to him. The move surprised the mayor, and he took a reflexive step back.

"Two dead cops," she said and held up as many fingers. Then she pointed both those fingers at Sikes. "Those deaths happened on *your* watch."

"Baumgartner," he blurted. "It was his watch, too. Those cops are Baumgartner's responsibility."

"But he's *your* chief of police."

"*My*… so that's how it is, huh?" Sikes straightened and wiped his brow again. The two stood in an uneasy silence for several moments. Finally, Sikes spoke but his words were careful and slow. "What if he's gone? You know what I'm suggesting, don't you? If that happens, does that get rid of you?"

"Me?"

The mayor clucked his tongue. "The federal government. Don't play dense. If I agree to dump Baumgartner, can I make this whole thing go away?"

At that moment, Édelie Durand imagined Mayor Andrew Sikes to be Humpty Dumpty. He had fallen off his wall and been mightily cracked, but he was still in one piece and trying to reclaim his place atop his perch. She needed to push him off his ledge again.

"Why haven't you found the shooters who ambushed Tyler Garrett?"

Sikes lowered his head as he thought. As he did so, she realized she was going to have to thank Dani Watson for this line of questioning.

"Mr. Mayor?"

He looked up. Confusion was in his eyes.

"The shooters?" Durand repeated. "How come you—"

"I thought we *had* arrested them." His tone was no longer combative.

She shook her head. "As far as we can tell, no arrests. Not for that."

"Baumgartner," he muttered.

"But the city did pay Garrett three-quarters of a million as a settlement for false arrest." She held up a hand. "Please don't say Baumgartner. He wasn't the one who told you to settle."

His eyes bounced around for a moment before he said, "My former chief of staff. Heavy on the former."

"Your former—"

"That's right. My biggest mistake was trusting the advice of someone I shouldn't. He wanted to sabotage my administration. The little traitor ran against me in the next election. I think he was setting me up all along, from way back."

Durand inhaled deeply. She had heard enough.

"Thank you for your time, Mr. Mayor."

"Wait. Aren't we going to discuss the logistics for your visit? That type of thing?"

"This here," Durand pointed to the floor, "was for us to meet. It wasn't to set the grounds for anything. That will come later."

"Later?"

Durand nodded. "If we open a formal inquiry."

"You're not doing that now?"

She shook her head. "We're only here to get the lay of the land."

"Of course," Sikes said, forcing a smile that looked close to reptilian. "Of course."

He extended a sweaty hand.

Durand politely bowed and headed for the door. Before leaving, she said, "Mr. Mayor?"

He had remained standing near the couch.

"Huh?"

"In the incidents we discussed, there was never one name mentioned as having any culpability in these matters."

"Who's that?"

"You."

Sikes touched his blue tie. "Me?"

"Do you think you have any responsibility in what's occurred?"

His brow furrowed and he smirked. "What did *I* do?"

Durand shook her head. "We'll be in touch."

Chapter 12

Ray Zielinski nursed a beer at end of the bar of the Happy Time Tavern. The small, rectangular establishment was barely larger than a three-car garage, but it still afforded him some measure of privacy.

He'd been debating whether or not to order a shot for the past half hour while watching a courtroom reality show on the small TV mounted on the wall. The dispute involved damage to a borrowed car, which reminded him a little too much of his own situation. The entire mess he was in with Darold Barden started with a minor collision in his patrol car.

I should've just reported it. If I had done that…

If he'd done that, what? There would have been a founded collision investigation, resulting in some sort of sanction. His concern at the time was that he already had two open demeanor investigations in Internal Affairs. If either of those had come back founded, the collision would have served as a springboard to greater punishment.

Like suspension, you mean?

Zielinski shook his head ruefully. Suspension, even without pay, wasn't a big deal to him anymore. Not when he was looking at the possibility of termination. All because the guy he bumped into with his cruiser had called in a favor. Get the abusive guy who was dating his ex-girlfriend to leave her alone. It sounded simple, but it had grown into a mess. He wished he could ask for a do-over, take his preventable collision finding along with the reprimand or suspension that went with it. It was far better than the jackpot he was in now after paying back the other driver for not reporting the incident. In the end, Zielinski inserted himself into a stupid situation that he only made stupider, and now here he was.

In a bar, in the middle of the day.

Was it even noon yet?

He glanced at his watch. A little after one. Well, that was good, at least. He wasn't an alcoholic on top of everything else.

Above him, the TV plaintiff whined to the TV judge about the TV defendant. All three parties seemed more concerned about their performance than the actual outcome of the case. Zielinski wondered if the dispute was real, or if it had been contrived for the drama of the program. Reality television that was scripted. The thought made his head spin.

Maybe he did need that shot.

He hesitated, though. The Happy Time was, as the name would suggest, a friendly hole-in-the-wall place. Cops were welcome alongside every other walk of life. But it wasn't a cop bar, so he wasn't insulated. His words and actions were still on display and seen through the public lens. It wouldn't do for him to get sloppy drunk. Sitting here in the middle of a weekday was bad enough.

If he'd wanted to get hammered, the place for that was the Maxwell House, the last true cop bar in the city. There, he was just another guy getting his drink on. The non-police patrons were used to cops, having shed most of the preconceptions that much of the public had, so he didn't have to worry about upholding the dignity of his position.

Of course, like everything else in his life, the Maxwell House was fading away, at least as a cop bar. His generation still frequented the place, but the younger cops flitted from popular bar to trendy brewpub, and the tradition of the Maxwell House slowly died.

It didn't matter. He couldn't show his face there right now anyway. He was persona non grata at the department, and he was sure that extended beyond the walls of the Public Safety Building to include cop bars. So he sat at the Happy Time instead, where at least no one would find him. He sipped his beer, longed for a shot, and watched a contrived courtroom argument on a television that hung above the bar.

"Hello, Ray."

Zielinski turned to the stool next to him in time to see Detective Wardell Clint settle onto it. While he gaped in astonishment, Pamela, the daytime bartender, walked down.

"Seltzer water," Clint told her. "My day isn't over quite yet."

She nodded and moved away.

"Whuh-what are you doing here?" Zielinski sputtered.

"I came to speak with you."

"No, I mean, how did you know I was here?"

Clint frowned. "I talked to the subcontractor you've been working for. He said there weren't any jobs today."

"You talked to…?" Zielinski shook his head in surprise.

"You weren't at home, either. So I figured the most likely option was that you were having a liquid lunch somewhere."

Zielinski wished it weren't true. No work on a weekday? He should have called his kids. They were out of school for the summer. He could have taken them to the zoo or something. Then he remembered Spokane no longer had a zoo. Besides, his kids were too old for the zoo and they mostly avoided doing things with him unless they had to.

He couldn't get past the fact that Clint had found him. "How'd you know I was *here*, though?"

Clint gave him the same frown again. "Come on. You're not going to show your face at the Maxwell House. After that, there's only four police-friendly bars left in this town that you'd be likely to go to."

"Where else did you look?"

"This was the first place, but I got lucky." He shook his head. "Don't look so amazed. It isn't exactly rocket science."

Pamela plonked a club soda in front of Clint. Zielinski watched as the detective removed the lime and bit into it, then followed that with a swig of the soda water.

When Clint framed it that way, Zielinski supposed finding him wasn't such a tall order. He'd become predictable, a man of habit. Unfortunately, most of those habits were bad ones.

"What do you want?" he asked, suddenly irritated with

Clint having disturbed his solitude.

"DOJ has arrived in Spokane," Clint pronounced.

"I heard."

Clint raised a brow, as if impressed.

"Don't look so amazed. I had a meeting this morning with Dale Thomas, but I don't know any more than them being in town."

A faint hint of a smile touched Clint's lips. "This is only the beginning, an exploratory trip. They'll scare together a few facts that fit their opinion of Spokane as a corrupt police department in a corrupt city, and then they'll scuttle back to Washington, D.C. and make their report. That's when the big guns come out."

"You make it sound like a foregone conclusion."

"Son, please. This is the federal government we're talking about here. All of this is for show, so they can get what they want."

"You mean a consent decree."

Clint nodded. "Justice comes in, takes over the department, and remakes it in a kinder, gentler, more politically correct image. Uncle Sam saves the citizens from the evils of a corrupt local police." He shook his head. "It's a song they keep playing over and over."

Zielinski didn't answer. Wardell Clint's conspiracy-ridden view of the world was legendary, and he had no desire to see how deep the man thought the rabbit hole went.

"What do I care? That's for the brass to worry about."

Clint huffed. "You know better than that. Crap rolls downhill, not up. Under normal circumstances, that's what you should be worried about."

"Normal circumstances?"

"As in common. Everyday. Run-of-the-mill."

"No, I know what normal means, but what do *you* mean?" Zielinski wondered if Clint was referring to his current situation, and the looming danger of a long suspension or getting outright fired.

Clint glanced at Pamela, who had propped open the

service door. She held a lit cigarette past the threshold and leaned out to take a drag. Seemingly satisfied that she was out of earshot, Clint said, "When DOJ comes in and takes over, our chance to nail Tyler Garrett goes with it."

Zielinski's stomach fell. He'd heard enough about the golden child of the department to last a lifetime. Then a thought occurred to him. "Wait, wouldn't DOJ being here help catch Garrett? That's the kind of thing they're looking for, isn't it?"

"Don't be naïve."

"Maybe having outsiders—"

"DOJ isn't interesting in taking down individuals," Clint said brusquely. "Their interest is in taking over departments. I'm sure they'd delight in finding out all about Garrett, but only because they would use it to point to systemic corruption, to justify a consent decree."

Zielinski mulled it over. "Still, it might cast a little sunshine on things."

Clint snorted. "You want sunshine, go to San Diego. Trust me on this. If DOJ comes in, the odds of Garrett seeing justice go down considerably. And I wouldn't put it past the crafty son of a bitch to go running to them himself if he gets hemmed in. Cut a deal for immunity and tell them whatever they want to hear."

Zielinski let out a heavy breath and watched his beer ripple from it. He felt incredibly weary. "I don't care," he said. "I've got troubles of my own."

"And those aren't going away," Clint agreed. "But our window to bring in this case is closing fast."

Zielinski took in Clint's words. He recalled the hot August night, two years ago, when he'd been the first to arrive on the scene of the Todd Trotter shooting. His own words echoed back to him now.

Tell me this was a good shooting.

Garrett had assured him it was. And the city and the prosecutor had eventually agreed with him. But Zielinski had suspected differently, and that suspicion blossomed into outright certainty. His time on the Anti-Crime Team with Garrett only reinforced that belief. Then, in the aftermath of Gary Stone's death, Clint had confirmed it for him.

"It isn't my problem," he said, though his words rang hollow even to his own ears.

"Not your problem?" Clint cocked his head. "Is this the same man who came to my desk, hounding me about what a dirty fiend Tyler Garrett was? Huh? Begging me for information? The same man who—"

Pamela flicked away her cigarette and closed the back door. She went to the sink behind the bar and began to wash her hands.

Clint noticed and lowered his voice. "The same man who I took into my confidence after what happened to Stone?"

Zielinski took a slug of his beer. "That was then, this is now."

"That is a platitude, not a philosophy." Clint leaned forward into Zielinski's personal space. "Do you want to risk this man going free? After all that we know he's done?"

Zielinski avoided eye contact, glancing up at the TV. "What I'm supposed to do? I'm not a detective."

Clint scoffed. "Detective is a title. You know how to investigate."

"It doesn't matter." Zielinski turned and met Clint's gaze. "I'm on suspension."

"Which means you have free time."

"It also means I don't have any police authority. So don't ask me to do something I can't."

Clint stared at him, his expression strange. He reached for his seltzer and took a slow sip. When he finished, he put the glass down heavily. He inhaled as if to speak, then paused to think for a moment. Finally, he spoke, his words sounding as they were forced from his lips.

"Ray, I need your help."

Zielinski stopped. Wardell Clint, the Honey Badger, had just admitted to needing help. He couldn't be certain, but he was willing to bet those words had never come out of Clint's mouth before.

Clint seemed uncomfortable, but he pressed on. "There isn't enough time for me to do everything I need to do before the DOJ main event arrives. It's going to be tricky enough with their little scouts poking around the department over the next few days."

"You need my help," Zielinski repeated, still surprised.

Clint said nothing. He stared at him, waiting.

Zielinski pushed aside his surprise and thought about it. Then he shook his head. "I can't."

"Can't or won't?"

"Same difference."

"There's a big difference between can't and won't," Clint insisted.

Zielinski pressed his lips together in frustration. "Fine. I *can't* because I've got work some days, and besides, I'm suspended. I won't do anything to make my situation worse. I'm probably going to get fired as it is."

"Probably," Clint agreed.

"Oh, thanks, Ward." Zielinski rolled his eyes and slapped the bar. Pamela looked up in mild surprise, saw nothing of interest, and looked away. "That's what I need to hear right now."

"The truth, you mean?"

Zielinski didn't answer. He returned his gaze to the television, pointedly not acknowledging Clint.

"And my name is Wardell," Clint said. "You know this."

"Well, then, screw you, Ward."

Clint didn't seem surprised or put off by the reply. He sat quietly for a while, sipping his club soda and waiting. Zielinski knew it was an interrogation tactic. Silence was a powerful tool, something people often felt compelled to fill. He'd used it himself on occasion during interviews on patrol. He wasn't going to let it work on him now, though. He stared defiantly at the screen while the judge ruled in favor of the plaintiff and the defendant had an orchestrated meltdown.

Minutes went by. Clint finished his drink and pushed the

glass away from him but made no move to get up from the stool. In a low voice, he finally said, "Butch Talbott. Justin Pomeroy. Gary Stone. And those are just the cops whose deaths he's responsible for. There's at least another seven or eight civilians on the list, depending on how you want to count."

Zielinski didn't answer.

Clint rose from his seat. "But you enjoy your beer, Ray."

Zielinski snapped his head toward Clint and growled, "You don't think I want to help? I'm *suspended*, okay? I can't risk it."

"I don't need you to do anything risky."

Zielinski hesitated. "No?"

"No," Clint said.

"Then what, Ward?"

"Wardell," Clint corrected.

Zielinski stared at him, saying nothing, his jaw set.

Clint stared back for a moment, then relented. "I need you to watch a house."

Chapter 13

Édelie Durand lifted her glass of wine to examine the smudge of lipstick on the rim. Her thumb rubbed across it as she thought about her husband back in D.C.

When they were out somewhere, he would make a big act of sipping from her wine glass. He would always put his mouth directly over her lipstick mark. The first time he ever did it, she accused him of stealing a drink. He defended himself by claiming he was only stealing a left-behind kiss. After that moment, it became a game—a ritual, almost— whenever she left lipstick on the rim of a wine glass.

She missed him tonight.

Earlier, they had talked for a few minutes via Skype on her laptop. She'd ordered room service and planned to eat while they caught up on the day's events. Unfortunately, Roland was tired and needed to end the call early. After that, she found she'd lost her appetite and left her meal untouched before eventually joining her team downstairs at the bar.

Durand looked up as the waitress arrived with Danielle Watson's whiskey and Esteban Curado's beer. She quickly handed them off and disappeared deeper into the lounge. The three of them were in The Peacock Room of The Davenport Hotel. It was a fancier hotel then she had imagined they would have been booked. But she didn't handle the travel responsibilities for her department and, therefore, needn't worry about the rental rates of different hotels in different cities. It wasn't her bailiwick. No, hers was to find malfeasance and wrongdoing wherever she was pointed.

If it existed.

From speakers hidden somewhere, a song she'd never heard ended and another one started. It was something she recalled her father liking. She listened to it for a moment and struggled to name the song and its singer. The voice was familiar. Her head bounced along with the gentle beat. A small smile creased her lips when the chorus hit—"Nobody Wants You When You're Down and Out"—and she remembered Bobby Womack.

She was thankful for the brief musical interruption and the trip down memory lane.

But there was still work today. She rubbed her thumb once more across her lipstick mark and allowed herself a final thought of Roland. Then she turned away from her glass to face her team.

They were in the middle of some idle chatter. When they noticed her watching, they stopped their conversation.

She set her glass down on the table in front of her and asked, "How did the tours with the captains go?"

From her left, Watson snorted. "Priceless. Like two bickering children forced to play together by their parents."

Durand glanced to Curado. "You didn't walk them separately?"

He shook his head. "Dani thought it better to keep them together."

"They were at each other almost immediately," Watson added. "I wasn't sure we'd have a chance to see that again. I think it proved to be the right thing to do."

"You could have gotten a head start on building individual rapport," Durand said.

Watson shook her head. "You don't understand, Edie. There's something going on with those two—"

"Bad blood," Curado confirmed.

Dani pointed at her counterpart. "And you agree, right? It was worth seeing them together?"

Curado nodded. "There's definitely something between those two. Something deep."

"Any idea why that is?" Durand asked.

"Maybe they used to bang," Watson suggested.

Durand flinched at her subordinate's use of the vernacular.

"Whatever it is," Watson said, "Hatcher definitely has an ax to grind."

"And Farrell," Curado said, "he seemed frazzled. Almost—"

Watson leaned forward. "Don't you dare say he's henpecked, Esteban."

Curado's face flattened. "I wasn't going to say that. And it's Steve."

Ignoring the squabbling of her subordinates, Durand said, "While we were in the conference room, I saw the reactions of the captains. She seemed to be enjoying my conversation with the chief."

"Oh, and he *loved* you," Watson said with a chuckle. "When he left the room, he almost did it at a full run."

Curado fought an eye roll, stopping it at about halfway, but Durand still noticed it. He asked, "How was your meeting with the mayor?"

"Informative."

"How so?" he asked, scooching to the edge of his chair.

"The mayor doesn't take responsibility for anything," Durand said. "Everything is the fault of someone else."

"So we've got an absence of leadership?"

Durand shrugged. "Maybe in city hall. He wants to be a sunny day leader. Claim all sorts of wins, but when the chips are down, he shifts the blame to someone else."

"Baumgartner?" Watson asked.

"Mostly. But he pushed some to a former chief of staff. I'd like to find out who that was. He even tried to put some on Gary Stone."

"The dead officer?" Curado asked.

Durand nodded.

"He's the mayor," Watson said. "The buck should stop with him. Isn't that what they say?"

"Sikes wouldn't agree to that," Durand said. "He's the type of guy that if the chief was getting a medal, he'd be right there with his arm around his shoulders. He's also the type of guy that would shove the chief and his medal under a bus to save his own career."

"I wonder how much loyalty Baumgartner has for a guy like that," Curado said.

"Probably not much," Watson said, "which means the chief might be prone to make decisions outside department policy."

Durand studied Watson for a moment. When she turned to Curado, he only shrugged.

A blond woman in her mid-thirties approached the group. She wore slacks and a light-colored blouse. Over her left shoulder was a low-slung purse. "Excuse me."

The three of them turned to her, but only Durand responded. "Yes?"

"Are you with the Department of Justice?"

Durand's eyes slid to Watson then Curado. She slowly stood and her attorneys rose with her.

"What's this about?"

Durand tensed when the woman reached into her purse. She only relaxed once the woman pulled out a notebook and a pen. Paperclipped to the cover of the notebook was a business card.

"Kelly Davis." The woman handed the small card to Durand.

"You're a reporter?"

"Word is you're here to lay the groundwork for a consent decree."

"No comment," Durand said.

"But will you confirm that you're with the Department of Justice?"

Durand read the card once more then held it out for the reporter. "I'm not confirming anything."

"You're not denying it, though."

"Good day, Ms. Davis."

Kelly Davis studied Durand for a moment then closed her notebook. She dropped it in her purse. "Keep the card," she said. "You might want to give me a call."

"I highly doubt it."

Davis nodded to Curado and Watson then left the lounge. The three of them remained standing until they saw her exit the hotel lobby.

Watson chuckled as she retook her seat and picked up her drink. "That department definitely has a leak in its security."

Curado said, "Could have been city hall. Edie went there to meet the mayor. Maybe one of his staff did it."

"And maybe the mayor himself did," Watson said and lifted her drink in salute.

Durand tossed the card on the table. "Doesn't matter," she said as she picked up her wine glass. "Let's talk about the plan for tomorrow."

Both of her subordinates faced her.

"We've only got three days, so let's maximize our time. We'll make this a top-down process but allow for some freedom to deviate. Dani, I want you to interview the chief."

Watson's brow furrowed. "Me?"

"Yes, you." Durand again studied the lipstick mark. It was only a faint hint of a smudge now that she had rubbed it so many times. "He's all about respect. I'd imagine that goes for the chain of command, too. Let's see how he responds to you interviewing him."

"Might get his back up," Curado said.

"Maybe," Durand said, "but maybe it keeps him on his heels. At least at the start. Everything is about getting them off balance. If there's something they're hiding, that's when it'll come out. Understand?"

Danielle Watson glanced to Curado then back to her supervisor. "Yeah. Okay."

"In the conference room, I didn't ask about the status of Garrett's ambush investigation."

"I noticed that," Watson said.

"But I want you to bring it up. Be prepared, though. He might have gotten a warning from the mayor about the topic. I asked His Honor about it, and he looked like he'd seen a ghost, but he was quick to move on to a subject he liked better."

"Which was?"

"How to save his skin."

"Ugh."

Durand faced Curado. "And Steve, you'll interview Captain Farrell."

He nodded.

She sipped her wine. "You said he appeared frazzled."

"Having never met the man, I'm guessing, of course." Curado took a drink of his beer and wiped his lip. "But I can't see a guy behaving like that, giving off those kinds of signals, and rising to captain. Has to be something new. Something recent."

"Then I want you to be his friend," Durand said. "His best friend, if you have to. But I want you to find out what has gotten the man so upset that he's about to jump out of his skin. Maybe it's personal, but if it's not…"

"Got it," Curado said.

"That means you'll be talking to Hatcher?" Watson asked.

The Bobby Womack song was over, and she couldn't place the new one. She knew she'd heard it before. It was from the mid-seventies, she believed. Another sad song about missing love by moments. She hadn't missed love. She found it, held it, treasured it. But she was about to lose it forever and there was not a damn thing she could do about it. She looked to Watson who stared expectantly at her. "Hmm?"

"Hatcher," she said. "You'll talk with her?"

"You said the woman has an ax to grind."

"I did."

"Then I'll be her grindstone," Durand muttered.

Watson laughed and held up her drink. "To finding the dirt."

Curado lowered his drink. "Why would we toast that? We should be hoping we don't find anything."

"Are you kidding?" Watson snapped. "This is what we do."

"No," Curado said. "We're here to ensure the department is complying with the law. If they do that without us hammering them, that's a win for the city. It should be a win for us."

"The win for us is rooting out corruption."

"If it's there," Curado insisted.

Watson took a healthy sip of her whisky. "Don't be so offended, *Esteban*. Power corrupts. It's human nature. The fact that some cops get corrupted by power doesn't make them evil, it makes them human."

"Most cops don't get corrupted, *Danielle*. That's my point. Most of them do the job with honor. Like my brother does."

"And like my father did," Watson bristled, though Durand wondered how much of it was from the point Curado made or from him using her full name. "They're not the reason we exist. We exist because not everyone does the job that way. Police culture—"

"Is mostly positive," Curado interrupted. "Aside from a few big cities."

Watson laughed at that. "This is one instance where I can say size really *doesn't* matter. You don't think there's corruption in small town America? That's naïve."

"You say that because you see corruption everywhere."

"I see what is there. I don't wear blinders."

As her subordinates continued to argue, Édelie Durand tuned them out. Slowly, she leaned her head back to the edge of her chair and looked up toward the ceiling. She struggled to remember the name of the song. Durand closed her eyes and tried to hear the singer over the noise in the bar.

She really wished she could remember the name of the song.

Chapter 14

The white Audi was parked in the driveway again.

The driveway of *his* house.

Garrett dropped his gaze, anger brewing in his chest. Technically, per the court, it was her house now. But since he was the one making the mortgage payment on it, he believed he still had the right to consider it his.

He wasn't stupid, though. He knew how the law worked. Over the years, he had arrested enough idiots who thought they were smarter than some divorce judge. None of them were.

It didn't mean he had to like it.

He worked, fought, or bled for everything inside that house. That included her.

His eyes returned to the Audi. It was the third night in a row that the car was there. Parked on his side of the driveway, no less. Like it belonged there.

An unpleasant thought occurred to him.

It might have been there longer than three nights in a row. He only discovered the car three nights ago. He tried to recall the last time he was by the house in the evening. Weeks, maybe. A month?

He found the car when a bout of melancholy struck, and he decided to drive by the house late at night. A bit of nostalgia had hit him in the heart, and he wanted to check on her and the kids. He used to do it when they were together. Often swinging by late at night for a drive through the silent neighborhood with his patrol car. He never let her know. He only wanted to protect his family. It was a private way for him to show his love.

Back when they were still the Garretts.

Back when everything was still perfect.

When he first saw that car in his driveway, he didn't know what to make of it. Maybe she'd gotten a new ride and didn't tell him. That seemed plausible. She'd been secretive lately. Holding stuff back. Now, he knew why.

She didn't get a new car. She got a new lover.

A gray-haired white man named William Cardwell.

No. William Jefferson Cardwell.

A fag name if there ever was one. Except that fag was sticking it to his ex-wife. The mother of his children.

Fourteen years older than her.

Did she have daddy issues? He wondered about that. If so, he never noticed them before.

He let out a long slow sigh and relaxed the fists he had balled.

Cardwell was a real estate agent who lived in the wealthy South Hill neighborhood. Garrett knew a fair amount about him now. He'd done some homework after running the Audi's license plate through Department of Licensing.

He wasn't supposed to use the system for personal things like that. But how would anyone know, really? He ran license plates all the times in a search for stolen vehicles. Then he would run the names of the registered owners in a search for warrants. He had plausible deniability if anyone ever asked why he ran the name of William Jefferson Cardwell.

Garrett slipped out of his car then quietly closed the door. As he walked toward the house, *his* house, he pulled a knife from his pocket and flicked it open. The weight in his hand felt good.

At the rear of the Audi, he bent and stopped. He flipped the knife over, raised it for a strike into the side of the tire, and suddenly paused.

What the hell am I doing?

He froze like that for a minute as he considered what he was about to do. Then he straightened and closed the knife. He turned around and walked back toward his car.

Tyler Garrett wasn't the type of guy to slash a tire to get

an ounce of retribution. He wouldn't do that, especially if it meant alerting someone that they had made an enemy. No, it was better to let a sleeping dog lie.

For a while, at least.

He quietly got back into his car, started the engine, and drove away. His anger began to dissipate.

Soon enough, he'd come up with something special for William Jefferson Cardwell. That's when he'd get his pound of flesh.

A pound was better than an ounce.

That's the type of guy Tyler Garrett was.

TUESDAY

The truth is rarely pure and never simple.
—Oscar Wilde, playwright and poet

Chapter 15

Captain Dana Hatcher's hands wrapped around her cup of coffee. She stared into the black as if it contained some secret.

Édelie Durand watched the captain struggle with her thoughts.

They were seated at Indaba Coffee in Kendall Yards. The shop was walking distance from the department. They made small talk—the weather, mostly—until they arrived and ordered their drinks. An espresso for Durand. Plain drip coffee for the captain.

Durand wanted to talk away from the station. She thought a change of venue might loosen Hatcher's tongue, especially if she wasn't being constantly reminded of her duty as a captain.

The conversation started easy enough. When asked what she thought of the department and its officers, Hatcher defaulted to the expected position of support. Good men and women doing a hard job, the captain had said. She then built a house of platitudes around that central base.

When Durand asked what she thought about Chief Baumgartner's leadership, Hatcher mumbled, "It's fine," and clammed up to stare into her coffee.

That's how they'd been for the last several moments.

"It's okay, Dana," Durand said. "We're only talking."

"Talking," Hatcher muttered. She lifted her eyes. "You know who you should talk to?"

"Who's that?"

"Maggie Patterson."

"Maggie?"

"Margaret. She's a councilwoman. She'll give you an

earful about the chief. I have her number, if you want it."

"All right, but I want to hear what you have to say."

Hatcher turned to look out the window.

"Let's do it this way," Durand said. "We're really interested in a few key incidents. Namely, the murders of Officer Gary Stone and Detective Talbott." She had the captain's attention now. "We'd also like to discuss the shooting of Todd Trotter by Officer Tyler Garrett."

Hatcher slowly put her coffee down. She then crossed her arms.

Mirroring Hatcher's body position, Durand crossed her own arms. "There was also a shooting that Officer Ray Zielinski was involved in that—"

"Ray didn't shoot anyone," Hatcher interrupted.

It was an interesting reaction, Durand thought. Up until then, she had been aloof in the conversation, but the mention of Zielinski brought a quick response.

"Why do you think that was?" Durand asked.

The captain tightly pursed her lips. She probably realized she'd answered too quickly about Zielinski.

Durand wondered if there was some sort of relationship between them. Confidantes? Friends maybe? Perhaps lovers? None of that mattered unless it came to violating policies and laws to protect one another.

Finally, Captain Hatcher said, "Ray's a professional."

Durand accepted the answer for now. It wasn't worth digging any deeper on, but she made a mental note to look for any connections between Hatcher and Zielinski in the reports they were reviewing.

"Were you involved with the ambush of Officer Tyler Garrett?"

Hatcher cocked her head.

Durand smiled apologetically. "Poor phrasing. Were you involved with the investigation of the ambush that led to the shooting of Todd Trotter by Officer Garrett?"

"No."

"Do you have any thoughts on why the department has

still not found those involved with the ambush?"

Hatcher's brow furrowed.

"You didn't realize it was still an open question, did you?"

"I didn't."

"It seems a number of people have forgotten about it. You would think Chief Baumgartner would want an answer to that question."

Hatcher's furrow deepened. "He should. Yeah."

"And Captain Farrell. He's the head of Investigations. Shouldn't he want his team investigating who was responsible for the ambush?"

Hatcher began to slowly nod, and she relaxed her arms. Throwing Farrell into the mix seemed to make her happy. Casually, Durand mirrored her action.

"But why wouldn't you be upset about the unsolved mystery as to the shooters?"

"I didn't know."

"You didn't know?"

"I mean I wasn't involved in the initial investigation. I thought it was being looked after."

It seemed a reasonable answer, but Hatcher slowly lowered her eyes as she was lost in thought.

"What is it, Dana?"

"Garrett."

"What about him?"

"You'd think he would make some noise about this. I mean, I'd want to know who shot at me and why."

"Huh." That was something Durand *hadn't* considered. "Why do you think that is?"

The captain shrugged. "Probably some macho SWAT code."

"As in a typical testosterone reaction. Rub some dirt on it and everything will get better?"

Hatcher chuckled. "That sounds about right."

Durand's eyes flicked to the silver bars on Hatcher's collar. "How many female captains are on the department?"

"I'm the only one."

"And lieutenants? How many are female?"

Hatcher's eyes narrowed. She paused before answering. "None."

"What about sergeants?"

"Where is this going?"

"I'm just making conversation. I can get this data elsewhere if you don't want to—"

"Three. There are three sergeants."

"Three. So, four women in leadership positions in a department of three hundred plus officers."

Hatcher crossed her arms again. "What are you saying?"

Durand shook her head. "I'm not saying anything."

"Yeah, you are. You're saying something. You're just not being direct about it."

"A direct question, then. Do you like the way the department is run?"

"It's fine," she snapped. "I already said that."

"Okay. Let's talk about Gary Stone's murder."

"No," Hatcher said. Her face was reddening.

"Why not?"

"I don't want to."

"I can't compel you."

"That's why I said no."

"Dana, I'm sorry if I upset you. This was supposed to be a friendly conversation."

"A visit by Justice is *never* friendly."

Durand nodded in understanding. "Sort of like when the police show up. The law says you have a right to not be afraid. But when a cop has a badge, a gun, a nightstick, and some handcuffs, that's a lot of intimidating tools for you not to be concerned with."

The captain remained quiet.

"So what about Gary Stone upsets you?"

She looked out the window.

"Was it the actual murder?"

Hatcher slowly shook her head but continued watching

something outside. Her voice was soft when she eventually said, "It shouldn't have happened, but it happens."

"Then what is it?"

"It's stupid," the captain said. "Besides, it's nothing that matters for what you're doing."

"Why don't you let me decide that?"

Hatcher faced Durand. "I've used that on suspects before."

"I don't consider you a suspect."

"Then why are you here?"

"Because something stinks. We've smelled it all the way across the country. Spokane popped up on the radar a couple years ago with all the press the police department got. It's basically been on the radar that whole time. Maybe there's something. Maybe there's nothing. We could be all wrong. If that's what it is, then great. All we did was come out and have a few conversations. But maybe what we smelled was a piece of rotting fruit. And we need to get rid of it before it spoils the whole barrel."

"You don't think the whole barrel is already rotten?"

"Do you?" Durand asked.

"No."

"If that's the case, why don't you tell me what bothers you about Stone's murder?"

With a single finger, Hatcher tapped the edge of the table. "It's not the murder. It's how Stone got there."

"To the site of the murder?"

"No, to the team. ACT. The Anti-Crime Team." She sighed. "This is going to sound petty."

Durand shrugged. "I'm sure I've heard worse."

"The team idea?" Hatcher tapped her chest. "It was mine."

"Uh-huh."

"And Tom Farrell stole it."

"He stole it?"

"That's right. He totally stole it. With Baumgartner's blessing, I might add. Then he put people on it who had no business being there."

"Stone, you mean?"

"And Jun Yang. I mean, she was still on probation. Who thinks that's a smart idea?"

"Why would he do that? Put a rookie on a team?"

She blurted, "Because he's an idiot."

Durand raised her eyebrows.

"I didn't mean that. I'm sorry."

"Don't worry about it," Durand assured her. "It won't go into any report."

Hatcher rested both of her hands on the table and nodded. "I appreciate that. That was uncalled for. I shouldn't have said that."

"It's okay, Dana. Really. What was it about Stone, though? He wasn't a rookie, so what reason was there to keep him off the team?"

"He wasn't street ready. Ask Garrett or Zielinski. I'm sure they'll confirm it."

"And Yang? What will she say?"

"Who knows? She quit after Stone's death."

Durand sat back and inhaled deeply. "So what I'm hearing is this. Captain Farrell stole your idea for a directed enforcement unit and staffed it with a couple officers who had no business being on such a team. Basically, he endangered the lives of two officers."

Hatcher's eyes widened. "Damn. When you put it that way—"

"I didn't put it that way, Dana. You did."

Captain Dana Hatcher wrapped her hands around her cup of coffee and pulled it into her chest. She then stared into the remaining black liquid and searched for an answer.

Finally, she muttered, "Yeah, I guess I did put it that way, didn't I?"

Chapter 16

Wardell Clint paused at the front door of the small house, listening. Inside, the drone of a television provided the baseline of sound, almost overwhelming the two voices he heard. One was distinctly female. The other was less identifiable, but he believed he knew who it was.

Veryl Wooley.

Wooley was a street-level drug dealer. As a homicide detective, the only time Clint would normally be interested in someone like him was if he was a witness, victim, or suspect in a murder. But Wooley was different. During his surveillance of Earl Ellis before the man disappeared, Clint had observed the two men exchange what he believed were money and drugs on several occasions. Since he knew Earl Ellis was Garrett's second-in-command, his interest in Veryl Wooley spiked accordingly.

He'd never once spoken to Wooley, so he couldn't tell if the second voice belonged to the skinny white man or not. But despite not having personal contact yet, Clint knew a lot about the man. His multiple drug arrests for possession with intent to deliver told the simple story of his role within Garrett's little cartel.

So far, Wooley had managed to avoid prison, though Clint was convinced that it wasn't necessarily because of any criminal skill, but rather the purposeful ineptitude of the criminal justice system itself. Some of his arrests went uncharged. Others were dropped without explanation in the official record. He only had two convictions. The first was pleaded down to mere possession. Wooley was sentenced to seventeen days in jail, which was coincidentally the time he'd already served awaiting trial before the plea agreement.

The second charge was supposed to be vacated by drug court but remained open. Clint assumed that meant Wooley had agreed to treatment of some sort. Like so many instances he was aware of, it seemed likely that the arrangement had failed.

Failed for Wooley. Not for him, though. For Clint, it provided a nice lever, one he intended to use, even as a bluff.

He listened a little longer, trying to make out the words in the conversation, but the television muddied the sound. Clint raised his hand and rapped on the door.

The voices stopped. He heard some shuffling inside, then the female's voice. "Who is it?"

Clint knocked again. "Spokane Police Department!" he announced loudly. "Open the door."

There was another silence, but no sound of movement. Clint had been prepared to take the door if he needed to, but it appeared that his quarry was going to go the route of hiding rather than fleeing.

The lock rattled and the door swung upon. A woman with dishwater blonde hair stood in front of him. She wore a man's white sleeveless undershirt that was too tight, outlining her large breasts. "What's wrong? I didn't call the cops."

"What's your name?" Clint asked.

She hesitated.

Clint glanced down to the notebook in his left hand, though the action was more for show. He'd memorized his notes about her. "Are you Lori Moran?"

She folded her arms under her breasts and scowled at him. "If you already know, why are you asking?"

Clint slipped the notebook into his jacket pocket. He not only knew her name, but the name of the strip club where she worked. He wasn't sure if she waited tables or worked on stage, but given what he'd seen thus far, he leaned toward the latter. She was carrying more than a few extra pounds, but still had a decent enough figure.

"I need to talk to Veryl," he said.

"Veryl who?"

"Veryl Wooley," Clint said.

"I don't know anyone named Veryl."

Clint gave her a flat look. "Then I suggest you ask the man who went into this house five minutes ago and who you don't know is named Veryl Wooley to come to the door. Now."

Moran was unfazed. "Don't you need to show me your badge or something?"

Clint brushed his jacket aside, revealing the badge clipped to his belt.

"Fine," she said. "Then I want to see a warrant. And I'm calling my lawyer."

"I don't need a warrant. But you may need a lawyer if you're not careful."

"Are you *threatening* me?"

"You've already lied to me in order to protect Veryl and keep me from talking to him. If you continue to hinder and delay my investigation, I'll arrest you for obstruction. Then you'll need a lawyer."

Moran peered at him closely, as if trying to decipher his words. Clint didn't know why—he'd been very clear.

The conversation lost its relevance when Clint saw a flash of movement behind Moran, headed toward the back slider door.

"Stop! Police!"

Wooley didn't stop.

Clint shoved open the door and brushed past Moran in pursuit.

"Hey!" she yelled in surprise. "You can't do that!"

Clint ignored her. He ran through the small living room, hurdling over the coffee table. Ahead of him, Wooley threw open the glass sliding door and fled across the small deck and into the backyard. As Clint approached the slider, a tawny shape leapt from the yard onto the deck, snarling furiously.

It took a half second for the image to register. When the pit bull let out a throaty bark, Clint skidded to a stop. The dog barked again. Its muscular frame tensed to leap forward. Clint reached out and grasped the door handle. As the pit bull launched itself at him, Clint slammed the door shut. The dog's head struck the glass with a powerful thump. The blow didn't seem to have any effect, as the animal continued snarling and barking. Saliva flew at the glass and was smeared as the dog tried to bite at him through the obstacle.

Clint looked up to see Wooley going over the fence and into the alley. He flicked the lock on the slider door and turned around.

Moran was looking at him, a cruel expression on her face. "He likes dark meat," she said, her words dripping with contempt.

Clint ignored the barb. He hustled past her and out the front door. His mind whirred through possibilities and courses of action. He settled on returning to his car. Jumping in, he fired up the engine and sped up the block and around the corner.

No sign of Wooley.

Speeding up again, Clint drove to the next residential street, stopping in the middle of an uncontrolled intersection. He looked in all directions, scanning for movement. All he saw were a few regular citizens engaged in routine activity.

Cranking the wheel, he headed up the street directly behind Moran's house. Wooley couldn't have gotten far. Even a fast runner would still be within two blocks. And now Clint had the advantage, being in a car.

He rolled down the windows so he could hear the outside environment. Someone might shout in surprise at a strange man running through their backyard. Or he might hear the crashing sound of a less-than-sturdy fence giving way under Wooley's weight as he tried to clamber over it.

Nothing.

At the end of the block, Clint slowed to a stop again. He scanned all four directions. No sign of a running man.

He considered the possibility that Wooley had gone to ground. Like in any residential neighborhood, there was any number of viable hiding places within a block of Moran's house. Given time, Clint could search them all. A K-9 unit would be much quicker, but he didn't want to call for one. Given the time of day, it was unlikely one was on duty, so the response time would be considerable. More than that, Clint didn't want to call attention to this arrest.

Where did he go?

Clint started forward, intending to go to the next block away, when he suddenly had a realization. Instead of asking where Wooley might go, he should have been thinking about where Wooley expected a cop chasing him to look. Or more to the point, where a cop *wouldn't* look. The answer was someplace he'd already been.

He took a right and drove until he reached the alley that ran behind Moran's house. He turned into it, slowing down. His eyes searched every possible hiding place. Before he'd gone one lot in, a skinny white man in a black T-shirt rose from behind a garbage can and fled up the alley toward Moran's house.

Clint slammed the car into park and leapt out. He sprinted behind Wooley, closing ground rapidly.

Wooley looked over his shoulder, his expression strangely calm. "What do you want?" he yelled, still running.

"Stop!" Clint called in reply.

Instead, Wooley turned and lowered his head as he sprinted harder.

Clint pumped his arms, pushing himself. They were nearing the fence behind Moran's house. If he got there, Clint expected Wooley to climb over. That would complicate matters. He would have to decide whether to go around or follow the suspect. If he followed, the dog on the other side of the fence was sure to attack, which left Clint with only one option—to shoot the animal.

Reaching deep down inside himself, Clint put on another burst of speed. He caught Wooley just as the man was reaching for the top of the fence. All it took was a small shove in the small of the back to send him tumbling into the wooden slats, before collapsing to the ground.

Clint took a moment to catch his breath. Wooley surprised him by using that delay to spring to his feet. On the other side of the fence, Clint could hear the pit bull snarling and attacking the barrier. But Wooley didn't try to retreat. Instead, he raised his fists and beckoned at Clint.

"Come on, then, moolie! Let's do this!"

Clint shifted his stance slightly, and let his hands hang loosely at his side. He could have drawn his gun and ordered Wooley to the ground, but he didn't think the man would comply, and he wasn't willing to shoot him if he didn't.

He eyed Wooley placidly, waiting. The criminal didn't disappoint. He lunged toward Clint, throwing a looping right hand at Clint's head.

Clint stepped forward, short-circuiting the power of the attack. With his left hand, he deflected Wooley's punch. Using his right fist, he struck Wooley in the chest, pivoting his own hips as he did so. The force of the blow sent the skinny man staggering for two steps before he fell to the ground in a heap.

Clint waited.

Wooley rose again, though not as quickly as before. This time, he charged at Clint completely without technique. He screamed in rage as he ran, reaching for Clint as he drew near.

Clint side-stepped at the last moment. He caught one of Wooley's grasping hands at the wrist, twisting and turning. Once Wooley reached the end of his charge, Clint used the man's own momentum, redirecting it in a circular fashion and using his two-handed grip at Wooley's wrist to guide him downward.

Wooley crashed to the ground for a third time. He let out a grunt when he fell.

Clint adjusted his technique, maintaining the wrist lock and taking control of Wooley's elbow as well. He lowered a knee into the man's back, causing him to grunt again. Then he levered Wooley's arm against his other knee.

"Ow!" Wooley screamed. "I give!"

Clint said nothing. He used his free hand to remove his handcuffs and ratcheted one cuff onto Wooley's exposed wrist. On the other side of the fence, the pit bull's fury remained unabated as it growled and yelped, battering and clawing at the wooden barrier.

Once both of Wooley's wrists were secured, Clint assisted him to his knees, and then to his feet. Without a word, he led the man down the alley toward his police car.

The interrogation room was bare. Just a table, three chairs, and a short bar along the wall near the table. Clint knew that the cuff rail was a violation of the fire code, but so far no one had pushed the matter. He imagined DOJ would change that.

Wooley rubbed his wrist after Clint unlatched the cuff that had restrained him to the bar. He glowered at Clint but didn't voice any of the usual complaints. Instead, he just wiped both hands on his black concert T-shirt with the words *Der Stürmer*.

Clint had noticed the shirt in the alley on the way back to his car. While Wooley waited in the box, chained to the wall, he'd stepped out to grab a photograph from his file for the interview. He used the opportunity to do a quick bit of internet research. What he'd found hadn't surprised him.

"You're a music fan," Clint said, sitting down opposite Wooley.

"None of that jungle jump crap you probably listen to," Wooley sneered.

"I like Muzak," Clint deadpanned.

"Huh?"

"Elevator music. The kind they play at the mall."

"I don't go to malls," Wooley said. "Why did you arrest me?"

Clint considered pushing him on the T-shirt angle but decided to wait. He knew the friendly approach was out for this interrogation, though. That was fine with him. He did better when it was contentious, and when he could bring logic to bear on the suspect.

"Ten months ago, you had a charge suspended pending vacation in drug court. You violated the terms set in place by the judge, and that charge is now active again." Clint gave him a cold smile that was more of a grimace. "You've been violated."

"No way. I didn't get a notice. They can't violate you without a notice."

"You keep a consistent mailing address?"

Wooley shifted uncomfortably.

"Because," Clint continued, "you are not the easiest person to get in touch with."

Wooley scowled. "I like my privacy. The government doesn't need to know my business."

"I tend to agree."

Wooley's scowl took on a suspicious edge. "You're part of the government, you dumb ass."

"I'm a public servant. And the city is a far cry from the federal government."

"Government is government. None of you needs to know anything about me."

"Maybe, but it does make it difficult to give you court notices." Clint brought the conversation back on point. "And once the court has done its due diligence in attempting to make notice, the judge can proceed with a violation. Which, in your case, is exactly what he did."

"You're lying."

"I'm a cop. I'm not allowed to lie."

Wooley let out a snort. "That's a good one. No, you're a cop and you're a…well, that's reason enough right there for me to know you're lying."

"When I book you into jail, it won't feel like a lie, I can guarantee that."

"Then book me."

"I will. After we talk."

"I'm not saying jack. Get me a lawyer."

Clint didn't react. When he'd looked into Wooley's vacated charge, he couldn't find out if he'd failed to meet the terms or if the slow bureaucracy that was the criminal justice system simply hadn't caught up on its record-keeping. Normally, he would have waited until he knew for sure, rather than try to bluff an experienced criminal like Wooley. But DOJ's arrival forced his hand. He was running out of time.

"I said, get me a lawyer, *boy*." Wooley's lips twisted into a cruel smile. "And then get on back to the fields."

"Here's your situation," Clint said, keeping his tone even. "I book you on your violation and you sit in jail until you get sentenced for the charge, or you talk to me. If you tell me what I need to know, I won't book you. I'll let you contact the court and work things out."

"Lawyer," Wooley repeated.

Clint leaned back slightly. "You don't like me much, do you?"

"I don't know you. But I don't like your kind, no."

"Baptists?"

"What? No. Your *people*."

"Cops, you mean?"

"No! Well, yeah, cops, too. But we both know what I'm talking about here."

"Then why won't you say it?"

Wooley shook his head and motioned to the camera in the corner of the room, near the ceiling. "I ain't stupid. I'm not risking any sort of made up hate crime."

"That camera isn't activated."

"Sure it's not."

"I'm confused," Clint said. "I'm offering you a way out of your situation, but you won't take it. Now if you were keeping quiet on account of a white guy, I'd understand. Pale solidarity and all that. But the man you're defending is black."

"I don't know what you're talking about."

"Earl Ellis," Clint said.

"Who's that?"

Clint slid a photograph in front of him. It was one he'd taken of Ellis and Wooley meeting at a park. He'd chosen a shot that caught the pair in the middle of a hand-to-hand exchange.

Reluctantly, Wooley looked at the picture. Clint saw a flicker of a reaction, but then the criminal veneer descended again. Wooley looked up at him and shrugged. "Nice Photoshopping."

"It's real, I can assure you." He tapped the photo. "And that's you."

"So what? I don't know the dude's name."

"What's he giving you?"

"If you don't know, then I guess it doesn't matter."

"I want to know where he is," Clint said.

"Want in one hand and crap in the other," Wooley responded.

Clint gave him a hard look. "You can walk on all of this. Do you realize that? You give me Ellis, and you cooperate, and I can guarantee none of this comes down on you. That includes the drug court charge."

Wooley laughed. "You won't let that go, will you? Well, you messed up, boy. Because I did everything that I was supposed to. I went to the classes. I even got the stupid little certificate. It's at Lori's house. So there's no way the judge issued a warrant for me." He glared at Clint. "You're full of it."

Clint hid his disappointment and forged ahead. He tapped the photograph of Wooley and Ellis again. "I've got you. But who I want is Ellis. Trading up is my preference, but if you don't do it, someone else will."

"Maybe so. But not me."

"I still don't get it." Clint motioned toward his T-shirt. "That band is a white power band. You clearly have a problem with black folk. But here you are," he motioned toward the photo again, "doing business with a black man. Not just doing business but taking orders."

"I don't take orders from anyone, least of all one of you."

"It looks like it in this picture. Am I wrong? Are you the one giving him orders? Should I be charging you as the head of this operation?"

Wooley's eyes narrowed. "I'm not in charge of nothing. But I don't take orders neither."

"So why work with this black man?" Clint tapped the picture of Earl Ellis. "Why not give him up and go free yourself?"

"I'm not admitting diddly."

"Theoretically, then. Why would a white man who hates black people do business with one?"

Wooley seemed momentary conflicted. Then he said, "Theoretically?"

Clint turned up his palms.

"Because the most important color is green, that's all."

That's when Clint knew the interview was over.

He booked Wooley into jail for assaulting an officer. He knew it wasn't a charge that would hold water in the long run, but it took the man out of circulation for the next few days. After that, it wouldn't matter.

As he drove slowly through the East Central neighborhood, he felt the burn of having lost the interview. It was his own fault. He hadn't been armed with all the facts, and so his bluff had fallen apart. The DOJ visit had him pressed for time, but that was no excuse. He should have found a way to get the accurate information.

Ellis. Ellis was the key to everything. The man could give up the entire network and put Garrett at its head.

Once everything was out in the open, other evidence could be brought to bear on Garrett. For instance, if the bullet from the Ocampo quadruple homicide matched the one in Detective Butch Talbott's death, that would prove the same gun was used for both. The previously flimsy evidence that linked Garrett to each scene would get stronger when one considered that the two scenes themselves were linked. At some point, coincidence would become correlation.

That reminded him. He needed to check to see if the results had come back from the lab on the Ocampo bullet yet. The case was Marty Hill's, but he could manage a surreptitious look at the file. Once the finding was back, he'd need to think of a way to get Hill to compare it to the Liberty Lake shooting in which Detective Talbott was shot and killed.

Clint pressed his lips together in frustration. He hated even thinking of the dead man with the title of detective. Talbott was as dirty as Garrett and had sullied the badge just as badly. Clint despised them both for it.

As he approached his destination, he spotted Ray Zielinski's beat-up ride parked up the street. He slowed, and when Zielinski saw him, Clint gave him a nod as he passed. Then he drove to the front of the house and parked. He got out of his car, walked up to the red door, and knocked. A few moments later, Aurelia Ellis answered it. Her face bore the same placid expression of respectful noncompliance. Behind her, the pink raincoat and light blue windbreaker hung on the same coat rack as always. And just like the last time he'd been at her door, the pleasant smell of something baking wafted from inside the house.

Some things don't change.

"Hello, Mrs. Ellis," Clint said. "How are you today?"

Chapter 17

When Chief of Police Robert Baumgartner walked into the conference room, he paused. He suddenly understood how the family of bears felt when Goldilocks visited their home.

Danielle Watson sat at the head of the large table—a spot customarily reserved for him. She already had several folders opened and spread in front of her.

On the right side of her was a yellow pad that she'd been making notes on.

To her left was a small cup of Starbucks coffee with its lid removed. A mostly eaten croissant sat directly on the table. Its crumbs were scattered about.

She held a crumpled napkin in her hand as she read a document.

Baumgartner coughed to get her attention.

When she looked up, Watson blinked a couple of times before checking her watch. "Chief," she said and tossed the napkin to the table. She returned her attention to her notes and absently waved toward a chair along the side of the table. She muttered, "Thanks for making time this morning."

Goldilocks. That girl broke into that home. She committed a damned felony.

The chief pulled a chair out and sat. It had been at least a decade since he sat in the middle of the table. He didn't like the view from here.

Watson finished jotting down her thought and looked up. Her eyes appeared slightly red. Baumgartner wondered briefly if she was hung over. After taking a sip of coffee, she flipped over to a clean sheet on her notepad. "Tell me about the Anti-Crime Team."

Baumgartner glanced over his shoulder to the conference

room door. "Isn't Ms. Durand joining us?"

"It's just you and me," she said.

"Is she too busy?"

Watson raised her eyebrows. "For what?"

"To sit in on this interview. I would have thought—"

"She had other things to do."

Other things to do? He had other things to do yet he showed up like a schoolboy about to get scolded. "What does she have to do that's more important than this interview?"

"I don't know. Important things a deputy chief does."

Baumgartner's lip curled. "I'm a chief."

Watson shrugged. "Important things a deputy chief at The Department of Justice does. She assigned me your interview. I do as I'm told."

He frowned. He knew what this was.

"You would expect the same of your subordinates, I assume." Watson popped the last of the croissant into her mouth and spoke while she chewed. "Doing what they're told, I mean."

Having him interviewed by Danielle Watson was another one of Durand's power plays. Since that was the case, she would expect him to be upset that he was being interviewed by a subordinate—a younger woman no less. Well, Ms. Édelie Durand could kiss his ass. He knew when he was being played and he wasn't going to fall for it.

"So about the Anti-Crime Team," Watson prompted.

"What about it?"

"Do you think they stepped out of line?"

"How so?"

She shrugged. "I don't know. I'm asking you. We're requesting all their reports so that—"

Baumgartner leaned forward. "What do you think they did?"

"I didn't say they did anything. I was asking—"

"You can't go on a fishing expedition."

"A fishing expedition? An officer was killed, Chief. I'm asking if you or your department did a critical evaluation as to why—"

Anger flared in Baumgartner's stomach. "How dare you talk to me like that."

Watson straightened. "Like what?"

"Down to me." The back of Baumgartner's neck warmed, and he felt a tightening around his temples.

"I apologize if you think I was talking down to you. I wasn't. I'm seriously curious if you did an after-action review of the shooting—"

"Of course, we did."

"—before you disbanded the team."

Baumgartner remained silent.

"Is there an official report?"

"No."

The way she spoke to him was getting under his skin. He knew that's what she wanted, and it was working. It bothered him because of that, and he struggled to control his growing anger.

"Who made the decision to disband the team?" she asked.

"I did."

"Did you discuss it with anyone else?"

"I'm the final decision-maker. It doesn't matter who I discussed it with."

Watson softened her voice. "Chief, I'm not trying to be argumentative. The reason I ask is simple. Are you the type of man who seeks counsel, or do you make decisions on your own?"

Baumgartner inhaled and held the breath for a beat. Then he said, "I spoke with Captain Farrell before taking that course of action."

Watson made a note on her pad.

"But the ultimate decision was mine to make. Officer Stone's death is on me. It's my department. He was my officer."

Watson's pen hovered over the pad of paper as she studied him. "We're not looking to assign blame for Officer Stone's death."

"Your line of questioning suggests otherwise."

She gently laid her pen down. "With teams like that, like the ACT, there tends to be an opportunity for noble cause corruption. I'm not saying there was, nor even suggesting it. However, I'd like to know if you took that into consideration during the formation of the team."

Baumgartner smirked. "Of course, we did. It was an early concern and we assigned a sergeant to the team as a way—"

Watson interrupted, "That would be Sergeant Ragland, correct?"

He was surprised she didn't need to consult the files laid out in front of her. So far, she hadn't looked once toward them. He wondered if spreading the folders about was for appearances. He wouldn't put it past her. Many things about this DOJ team seemed to be done for the sake of appearance.

"Ragland was our replacement," the chief said. "The original sergeant had a family emergency. His wife died in childbirth."

"Did you approve of Ragland's leadership of the team?"

"Ragland did a fine job. He is an experienced sergeant who knows how to lead men."

Her eyes narrowed and she lifted her pen. It rolled through her fingers as she thought. An intimidation tactic, Baumgartner thought.

"Jun Yang," Watson said.

"What about her?"

"She was on the team."

"I know."

"She was a rookie."

Baumgartner nodded.

"Why would you put a rookie with little street experience on a directed enforcement team?"

"She had experience. She was military police before joining the department."

"Military police is the same as civilian law enforcement?"

"It's similar." Baumgartner's words rang hollow to his own ears. The way Watson cocked her head, he was sure she heard the emptiness in his statement, too.

"Who picked Jun for the team?"

"I did," Baumgartner said.

Watson shook her head. "I get you want to protect your department, Chief, but whose responsibility was staffing the Anti-Crime Team?"

He stared at Danielle Watson for several moments. Baumgartner then looked at the American and Washington State flags that stood at the head of the room. When he turned back, he said, "I did. I staffed the team."

She made a note on her pad.

"Following Officer Stone's shooting—"

"His murder," Baumgartner insisted.

"—Officer Yang quit the department."

"Your point?"

"Did she give any reason why?"

"She didn't have the stomach for the job," the chief said. "Lots of..." he shouldn't have paused, but he did it to spite her, "*people* don't have the stomach for the job. They go to places where it's safer. Where they can pretend what they're doing is law enforcement."

Baumgartner was disappointed when Watson deftly parried his verbal jab. "But you just said that military police is similar to civilian law enforcement."

He walked into that one. He went for a cheap shot and she jabbed him in the nose. He thought about saying, *Similar, but not the same*, but realized the futility of the argument. Instead, he remained silent.

Danielle Watson lifted her eyebrows then made another note on her pad.

As he watched her write, Baumgartner became mad at himself. He hadn't done anything wrong prior to his interactions with Édelie Durand and Danielle Watson, but both times he'd gone and stepped on himself. He'd told his own officers many times over, less is more in situations like this and here he was violating his advice. He had made his situation worse by talking too much. He should have been quiet, respectful, and just answered the woman's questions.

Why the hell did I have to take the cheap shot?

When she looked up, Watson asked, "Can I ask you about the ambush of Tyler Garrett?"

He exhaled a breath he hadn't realized he'd been holding.

At least now, they were into older, safer territory. This was something the county had investigated, Wardell Clint had shadowed, and the whole damn thing was put to bed. If he just kept his cool, he could avoid making any further mistakes.

Baumgartner nodded. "Ask away."

"How come the department has never found those responsible for the ambush?"

The chief again fell silent. Not because he wanted to, but because he was seriously struggling for an answer.

Had they really not found the shooters?

It took him a split-second to realize they hadn't. When that hit him, the next thought was, why the hell hadn't they? Had his department taken their eye off the ball? He definitely had. Why? How did this happen?

Questions continued to flood his thoughts.

What led his investigators to look away from this? This should have been a burning question. A top priority. They shouldn't have turned away until it was answered or until they exhausted every resource trying to get to the truth.

An officer was ambushed.

A decorated officer, no less, and this was how they treated him? What was that doing for Tyler Garrett's morale? What had it done to the department's morale knowing that those responsible for the ambush were still running around unaccounted for?

His eyes darted around the room as he continued to question just what the hell happened.

He would need answers from Tom Farrell. As the head of the Investigative Division, this should have been a priority. It should have been at the top of his list. Any leads might have grown cold after two years, but he didn't want something as important as this to be overlooked.

Who was investigating the ambush, he wondered? Wasn't it—

"Chief?"

"Huh?"

Danielle Watson watched him with inquisitive eyes. Her pen hovered over the yellow pad. "The ambush?"

"Yeah."

She leaned forward. Her eyes searched his when she asked, "Am I missing something or did your department drop the ball?"

Baumgartner's face warmed.

That damned Goldilocks. She should have been arrested for burglary.

Chapter 18

"Starbucks, huh?" Captain Dana Hatcher sat down at the small corner table.

Zielinski slid back his chair slightly to make room for her legs under the table. He doubted anyone who knew either of them would spot them having coffee, but it didn't matter. There were plenty of civilians who might interpret the tangle of long legs under the table as something romantic and, since Hatcher was in uniform, inappropriate. He and Hatcher had endured those false rumors in the past, and he had no desire to reignite them.

"You've got a problem with Starbucks?"

"The McDonald's of coffee houses?" Hatcher removed the lid from her cup and blew on her coffee. "Nope, no problem."

Zielinski liked Starbucks. He always knew what he was getting, and he always got what he wanted. There was some comfort in that. He realized that was probably the same reason people went to the golden arches, as well.

"It's better than your office," Zielinski offered. He left out the fact that while on suspension he couldn't meet her there without an official invitation anyway.

Hatcher glanced around the crowded Starbucks. "It is nice to get out amongst the people. Things are getting nasty inside the department."

"I've got news for you. It ain't so great *outside* the department, either."

Hatcher turned to him for the first time since she'd sat. Her eyes filled with concern. "I'm sorry, Ray. How are you doing?"

"Getting by," Zielinski said.

"That's your everybody answer. I need your Ray and Dana answer."

Zielinski hesitated. He had a long and trusted relationship with Hatcher, dating back to her time as his sergeant. She'd always been a good listener, coupled with giving sound advice. But as she climbed the ladder, it became more difficult for him to confide in her. In addition to that, lately she sometimes misunderstood him entirely. That had been the case when he tried to share his misgivings about Tyler Garrett. She'd been as blinded by Garrett's public image as everyone else.

Without thinking, he said, "That's not the easiest thing to do with you sitting here in full uniform, captain's bars staring me in the face."

Hatcher nodded slowly. "I know. Rank is scary, huh?" She looked intently at him, feigning meanness.

Zielinski cracked a smile.

She's still Dana. Sure, she may have changed, but so have I.

"A smile?" Hatcher said. "Careful, your face may get stuck that way."

Zielinski let the expression fade naturally as thoughts of his current situation filled his mind again. "I'm worried," he admitted. "I'm losing everything."

"Like what?"

"My kids, for starters. They skip out on almost every visit now."

"That's their age. They'll come back to you."

He shook his head. "That's just something people say. I don't think it's true."

Hatcher shrugged. "I all but froze out my own mother from the time I was seventeen until I was almost thirty."

Zielinski winced. "That's not helping, Dana."

"My point is, I came back." She thought about her mother for a moment. "For the most part. But my mother was horrible. What you've got going with your own kids is just teenage anger along with some divorce blame. They'll come back, as long as you keep making it clear you want them to."

"I hope so," Zielinski whispered, his chest tightening. "But the truth is, I'm going to run into problems supporting them if I lose my job."

"Who said you're losing your job?"

"Dale Thomas said it could happen."

"Dale Thomas is a tool."

Zielinski didn't argue, since he mostly agreed. It didn't matter, anyway. Thomas may have been a tool, but when it came to defenders, he was Zielinski's best chance.

"I'm surprised Mister President had time for you," Hatcher continued. "He's been flitting around ever since DOJ arrived, acting like they're here to investigate him or something."

"I know. He cut our interview short because of it."

Hatcher blew into her coffee and sipped it. She grimaced. "Say what you will about the feds. At least they have good taste in coffee."

Zielinski looked at her questioningly.

"I met with one of them," Hatcher explained. "At Indaba."

"Fancy," Zielinski commented. He didn't really care about DOJ. He'd been hoping to talk to Hatcher about his Internal Affairs case, but he could tell she was gearing up to share something. He tried to shift gears into listening mode.

"Fancy coffee for fancy words," Hatcher said. She took another drink, her eyes hardening. "You know, I used to think of DOJ the same way most cops think about Internal Affairs. Cops investigating cops, you know?"

"That's what they are."

"No, they're not. They're *lawyers* investigating cops. And I got a harsh lesson on that, I can tell you." Zielinski noticed her jaw flexing as she seemed to be reliving some moment from her meeting with DOJ. "They don't interview you, they interrogate. No, they *cross-examine*. And this Durand woman, she backed me right into a corner. Had me questioning Baumgartner's leadership on the record."

Zielinski was surprised. "I thought you liked the chief."

"That's not the point," she said. "I think he's been a good leader, in the past. But he's also screwed up a few things more recently."

"Just ask Margaret Patterson," Zielinski said.

Hatcher's eyes narrowed. "What do you have against Patterson?"

"Me, personally? Nothing. But over the past few months, she's up the chief's ass every chance she gets."

"That's her job."

"To mess with the chief over everything?" Zielinski gave her a knowing look. "I realize she's your friend, but…"

"But what?"

"Well, when she attacks the chief, she's attacking the entire department, isn't she?"

"Not necessarily. I'd say she's trying to make it better by holding its leader accountable."

"Okay." Zielinski didn't want to argue. He had only a rudimentary grasp on city politics anyway. Right now, his concerns were much closer to home. "Can we move on? I want to ask you something."

Hatcher took a drink of her coffee. "Sure." Her voice held the slightest tone of disappointment, but he couldn't worry about that now.

"I know some things are going to take a backseat while DOJ is here, but I was hoping you might know something about my case."

"Isn't that a question for Dale Thomas?"

Zielinski frowned. "I already told you how he handled our meeting. And you've seen it yourself. You said so."

"I did." Hatcher seemed to be thinking something over before she spoke. "Ray, what you're be asking me is a lot."

"I know."

"I'm not sure you do. It doesn't matter, though, because I would have done it for you. I wouldn't have broken any policies, but I would have found out enough to at least reduce your stress level while you waited this whole thing out."

Zielinski nodded along as he listened. He believed her.

Hatcher had always focused on taking care of her people at least as much as she did on completing the mission at hand. In his opinion, that's what made her such a great leader.

"But things are different right now," she continued. "DOJ being here complicates everything. I can't risk doing anything that looks the slightest bit out of line. Especially not with Internal Affairs. That's one of their favorite places to fish."

Zielinski stopped nodding and looked down at his hands. "I get it."

"Don't pout, Ray."

He glanced up at her, his gaze narrowing. "I'm not pouting!" Several patrons turned their way. Zielinski lowered his voice and continued, "I'm thinking, okay? My life is unraveling here, so give me a break."

Hatcher's eyes flashed with anger. "You want to know the truth about that? It's unraveling because of bad decisions *you* made."

Zielinski stared at her, shocked.

"Yes, Ray," Hatcher continued. "Those wounds are self-inflicted. For example, why in the hell did you go all Lone Wolf McQuade on that guy Barden?"

"I…" Zielinski stopped. He couldn't answer her without revealing another bad decision he'd made. More than one.

Damn, she's right.

Just as quickly as it flared up, Hatcher's ire seemed to fade. "Look," she said, "you can't change the past. I hope this works out for you, but there is nothing I can do to help you right now. Maybe after DOJ has gone, or when the process gets to the review phase, but for now, you've just got to hold on and hope for the best."

"Okay," Zielinski whispered.

"And for heaven's sake," she added, "stay out of any more trouble. That's crucial. You can't afford any more springboards for Internal Affairs. Progressive discipline is a real thing."

"Okay," Zielinski repeated.

Hatcher gave him a long look, then went back to her coffee. They sat in silence for a long while, and when the conversation renewed, they skirted anything important. Instead, they skimmed along the surface of mundane matters, filling the time with empty words until their coffee cups were empty, too. Then Hatcher made her excuse that she needed to get back to work, and Zielinski thanked her for meeting him.

"Anytime, Ray," she said, before she left.

But Zielinski knew better.

I'm losing her, too.

He got into his car and headed east. He drove mechanically, his body remembering every turn that he needed to make without him having to think about it. He was a career patrol officer and knew the city like the back of his hand.

He recognized Clint's Impala half a block away from Aurelia Ellis's home, parked under a tree that provided some shade and a small measure of camouflage. He pulled in behind, flipped open his cell phone, and dialed Clint's number.

The detective answered on the first ring. "You're late."

"I had something to do, Ward."

"*I* have things to do. And my name is Wardell. Would you like it if I called you Raymond?"

Zielinski wouldn't, but he wasn't going to tell Clint that. "I don't care. It's my name."

"My condolences on that."

That was a good one, Zielinski had to admit. For a guy who didn't have much in the way of a sense of humor, Clint surprised him sometimes.

"Anything?" Zielinski asked.

"No. But you can see a little bit of the alley entrance from here, so keep an eye on that."

Zielinski clenched his jaw. He didn't need to be told how to watch a damn house.

"I got it, Ward. Take off."

Clint severed the connection. A small, grim smile creased

Zielinski's mouth. He half-expected Clint to flip him the bird as he drove away, but instead Clint only made a U-turn and left the neighborhood, already focused on his next task.

Zielinski nudged his own car forward until he was tucked under the tree branches. He glanced toward the alley entrance to make sure it was visible. It was.

He leaned back in his car seat and watched.

Chapter 19

When Ray Zielinski pulled into the neighborhood, Tyler Garrett froze.

He thought for sure the man would have made him.

But Zielinski must have had other things on his mind since his eyes were locked straight ahead. The man rolled right past Garrett and pulled slowly behind a Chevy Impala parked underneath a shade tree.

Garrett had been standing at a bus stop with a baseball cap pulled low and his hands shoved in his pockets. It would have been difficult for the driver of the Impala to make him out from his position, but Zielinski should have had him cold.

If he hadn't been distracted, that is.

Sometimes it's better to be lucky than good.

He quickly abandoned the bus stop and moved around the corner to take up a position next to an overgrown arborvitae tree. It provided him better concealment, but still allowed him to see his targets.

So, two things were official now.

Wardell Clint was hunting Earl Ellis.

And Zielinski was in league with Clint.

Alone, Zielinski was of no concern to Garrett. But if Clint figured out a way to direct the man's anger, that might mean something.

For the last hour, Garrett had slowly moved his position about this neighborhood, watching the Chevy Impala parked in front of the house owned by Earl Ellis's grandmother.

During this time, he had the time to make two calls.

The calls really weren't important. Rather, they were something personal he wanted to set in motion. Now, he wondered if he should let these plans go until a later time.

Ray Zielinski missed seeing him when he pulled into the neighborhood because he was distracted. Garrett didn't want to miss something important because *he* was distracted.

He spat on the ground.

"What are you watching?"

Garrett hadn't heard her approaching. She was a smaller woman with curly white hair cut close to her head. He thought she was in her late seventies, but her ashy gray skin made it hard to guess.

She clutched a fluffy white dog to her chest. A thin leash dangled uselessly from her hand to its neck.

"Is it a drug deal?" the woman asked.

Garrett glanced around the corner to Clint and Zielinski. "No. Just a couple guys." Then he added, "White guys," to hopefully stoke the woman's fear.

"What are they doing?" the woman asked.

He shrugged. "They're parked."

"You think they're doing…*it*? Inside the car?"

Garrett turned back to her. "No," he said with a smile. It was a funny image, Clint and Zielinski going at it. "They're watching a house."

The woman eyed him then as if considering if he belonged in the neighborhood. Deciding he did, she turned her attention up the street. "They're probably cops."

"Probably."

The Impala's engine started, its brake lights momentarily flashed red, and the car drove away.

She shook her head. "Used to be a nice neighborhood," she muttered.

The woman crossed the street behind Zielinski's car and continued on her way. The dog never once touched the sidewalk.

Garrett took a moment to assess the situation. Earl Ellis was missing, and he wasn't taking Garrett's calls or responding to his texts. Even the man's own people didn't know where Ellis was. Garrett didn't know what had spooked

Ellis so bad to go missing.

Perhaps it was the killing of Leon Strayer, but Ellis had been part of that plan. He'd known it was coming. Garrett needed to get rid of the rat, Gary Stone, and they needed to sacrifice a man to do it. Earl was the one who offered Strayer up. Getting spooked over his death didn't make any sense.

But this—Clint and Zielinski? That could spook a man.

If Ellis ran because Clint had found him, why wouldn't he reach out? Maybe Clint had planted a fear in him, and Ellis was considering a play. If that were true, it would be a play the man wouldn't have contemplated if he was near Garrett.

His lip curled. The bastard was going to talk.

But his face quickly relaxed.

No. If he was going to turn, he would have done it by now and there would have been no reason to run. Ellis was hiding because he *didn't* want to talk.

So why hadn't he reached out to tell Garrett this?

Because he knew he was being watched. His eyes returned to Zielinski's car.

Yeah, Garrett decided that was why.

Earl may be a lot of things, but a rat wasn't one of them.

Chapter 20

"Thanks for taking the time to meet with me, Captain."

Curado stuck out his right hand over the top of Farrell's desk. Farrell grasped it. The lawyer's grip was firm but not overbearing, which he thought described the man himself.

"No problem, Mr. Curado."

"Call me Steve." Curado raised a brow questioningly and motioned to one of the chairs in front of Farrell's desk.

"Yes, of course," Farrell said. "Please have a seat."

As Curado settled into his chair, Farrell did the same. Having this interview in his office, on his own turf, had seemed like the best possible option when Curado had called earlier that morning. But now, instead of the familiarity of his surroundings bringing him comfort, the lawyer's presence here made him feel vulnerable.

"As I mentioned on the phone," Curado was saying, "this entire visit is only exploratory in nature. It's official, but unofficial, if that makes sense."

"It seemed pretty official when your boss was hammering away at mine yesterday morning."

Curado grinned, a little sheepishly. "Yes, well, Ms. Durand is a bit of a force. She's used to dealing with people in Washington, D.C. that require a…shall we say a strong front? I realize it doesn't translate so well away from the capital."

Farrell made a noncommittal sound.

"So," Curado said, "the chief said you oversaw Investigations?"

"That's right."

"And you're the senior-most captain?"

"Yes, by a couple of years."

"We noticed that your department has had an open assistant chief position for over a decade now. Do you know the reason for that?"

"Chief Baumgartner was our last assistant chief," Farrell replied. "When he was promoted, he didn't fill the position, so isn't that question better asked of him?"

Curado seemed to consider the point. "Perhaps," he concluded. "And hopefully my colleague will remember to ask about it. But do you know the reason behind the decision?"

Farrell thought about the question, searching it for any kind of danger lurking unseen in the shadows. He saw nothing, so he answered. "I'd say there were two primary reasons. One was budgetary, the other had to do with leadership development."

"The budgetary consideration being…?"

"The savings from the unfilled position funded another police officer on the street, plus a little extra. That little extra gave us some wiggle room if a training opportunity came along that we hadn't budgeted for, or if we had an equipment shortfall."

"Smart," Curado said. "And the leadership aspect?"

"The chief stated he wanted to spread the duties of a number two among the four captains and allow all of us the chance for professional development. If he'd made an assistant chief, those opportunities wouldn't be available."

"But doesn't that create more work for all of you?"

"Some. But it's good for our careers, too."

"I see."

Something in Curado's voice sounded off to Farrell. "What is it?"

"What? Oh, nothing."

"It sounded like something."

"It's just that…" Curado appeared a little uncomfortable. "We've heard that the chief seems to have relied on you a little bit more than your peers."

Farrell thought about it briefly, then shrugged. If this was going to be the nature of the DOJ inquiry, he'd be fine. "Maybe he does. It's not something I solicit."

"I'm not implying that at all. In fact, it would seem to me that it makes sense, you being the most senior captain."

"Then why ask about it?"

Curado smiled. "Captain Farrell…actually, is it all right if I call you Tom? Or do you go by Thomas?"

"It's Tom."

"Okay. Well, I can't stress this enough, Tom…these are just information gathering questions. I want to understand the dynamics of your agency, the culture of it, all of this. Those things help apply context to whatever facts we may discover about the incidents in question."

A flash of ice cut through Farrell's lower gut. "What incidents?"

Curado waved his hand. "We'll get to that, but I'm really not overly concerned. I mean, it seems like the local media is fairly anti-police."

"They hate us," Farrell agreed.

"See? So while some high-profile incidents and the ensuing media coverage is what got our attention at Justice, I'm confident that'll turn out to be all smoke and no fire. Or as my father used to say, all hat and no cattle."

"Your father was a rancher?"

"Yes, sir," Curado said. "He's got a nice spread in Texas."

Farrell saw an opportunity to direct the conversation away from topics he didn't want to discuss, if only temporarily. "You didn't follow in the family business?"

"No, sir. Neither did my brother."

"Was your father disappointed?"

"On the contrary. He pushed us in other directions. Said that ranch would always be there for us if we needed something to come home to, but that he wanted more for us than branding steers and stringing barbed wire. We took him at his word, too. I attended law school, and my brother went into law enforcement."

Farrell looked at him sharply. "Your brother is on the

job?"

"San Antonio Police Department. He's a sergeant."

Farrell wondered how Curado could do the job he did, having a brother who was a cop, but he didn't dare voice the thought. But he'd run out of idle chit-chat, too, so he fell silent.

Curado smiled again. "I know what you're thinking. My brother's a police officer, and here I am, investigating police officers. That's some cognitive dissonance there, right?"

Farrell nodded cautiously. "Seems like it."

"I experienced some when I first got the job offer from Justice. But like I told my brother, I know that the overwhelming majority of police officers in this country are like him. They're honest, they're dedicated, and they work hard at a crucial job. A job that keeps getting more and more complex and difficult, with fewer people qualified or willing to do it." Curado paused a moment, as if waiting for his words to sink in. Then he said, "If I investigate police agencies, that's what I'm going to find most of the time. Only instead of my opinion, there'll be empirical evidence of it."

Farrell watched him, unconvinced. The words Curado spoke were welcome to his ears, but he wondered if they were propaganda, or if the man truly believed them.

"Even when we find something wrong," Curado continued, "most of the time it is an issue of awareness or training. Occasionally equipment. We help those agencies out with training or material, and all's well that ends well."

Farrell thought about some of the DOJ grants Spokane had applied for and received over the years. They came from a different division of DOJ than the one investigating them now, but Curado had a point all the same.

"As for that small percentage we come across who are truly dirty?" Curado shrugged. "Doesn't everyone want police officers like that caught?"

"Yes," Farrell whispered.

He wished he could tell Curado about Garrett, but he

resisted the temptation. All he and Clint had at the moment was circumstantial evidence and speculation about Garrett, but their off-book investigation was a fact. He was sure DOJ wouldn't be worried about *context* when they found it out, either.

"Anyway, now you know where I'm coming from with these questions," Curado said. "Do you mind if I ask a few more?"

Farrell cleared his throat. "Sure, go ahead."

"Tell me about the Anti-Crime Team."

Farrell's stomach pinged. This was one of several places he did *not* want them poking around. But Curado was looking at him expectantly, his expression open, so he knew he had to answer. "It was a directed enforcement team created to target high-profile offenders."

"Who created it?"

"Who?" The question caught Farrell off guard. What did it matter? "Uh…it was originally proposed by Captain Hatcher. We modified the plan in command staff, and the chief assigned it to me."

Curado made a slight grimace. "Is that the reason for the rift between you and Captain Hatcher?"

How the hell do they know that?

"Me and…" Farrell shook his head. "No, we…there's no problem between us."

"I'm sorry, then. I thought I sensed some tension between the two of you yesterday."

They noticed that? Farrell cleared his throat again. He wondered what else they knew or had noticed, and his palms started to sweat. "I think we're all on edge with your visit," he said.

"But you haven't done anything wrong," Curado said. "Have you?"

"No. But DOJ has a reputation of finding the one fleck of pepper in the trainload of salt, even if it isn't there."

Curado nodded sympathetically. "I know. It's not true, though. Really, it isn't. Those kinds of statements are made by agencies who unfortunately have systemic issues that require our full involvement to fix. Once we're involved, we try to be thorough and get each and every aspect corrected. We definitely get into every little detail in those cases. I think that's why that rumor is out there."

"Maybe. But it still makes people nervous."

"So all is good with you and Captain Hatcher?"

Farrell forced a smile. "Yes."

"Good to hear. So, the Anti-Crime Team?"

"It was successful, for the brief time we fielded it. But then we lost an officer, and the chief suspended the team."

"That would be Officer Gary Stone, right?"

"That's right."

"Tom, who selected the team members?"

Farrell thought for a moment before answering. He knew he could default to the chief as the decision-maker. Ultimately, everything was his say. But the idea of saying that galled him. "I did," he said. "I chose all six members."

"I thought there were four officers."

"Plus a sergeant, and a detective assigned for investigative support."

"What criteria did you use for selection?"

Farrell swallowed hard. The truth was that he picked Garrett to trap him and the other three to be part of that trap. But he couldn't tell Curado that, so he started with the sergeant, who seemed the safest one to discuss. "I chose Sergeant McGinn because he had tactical expertise and I knew he'd run a tight ship."

"Were you concerned?"

"No," Farrell said. "But I'd seen how these kinds of teams can get out of control in other cities. Even good people can start bending the rules to put bad guys in jail."

"Noble cause corruption."

You mean like running a secret investigation of a murderous police officer for two years?

"Exactly. I didn't want to risk that happening, so I put a strong leader in place."

"Sounds wise to me."

"I thought so. But he had a family tragedy early on and had to be replaced. His replacement was less engaged, but adequate."

Curado raised an eyebrow. "That sounds like he did a poor job."

"No," Farrell said. "He just had some additional duties."

"All right. What about the detective?"

"Marty Hill is one of our best. He vetted the targets, did arrest paperwork, and worked up the search warrants for the team."

"How about the team members?"

Now we get to it. Farrell could feel his stomach gurgling nervously and hoped it wasn't audible to Curado. "Who do you want to know about?"

Curado shrugged. "Let's start with why you picked them."

"I'd just sent Stone to a surveillance school in Seattle," Farrell explained. "Yang had military experience. Zielinski is a veteran officer. And Garrett…"

Garrett was supposed to step into the trap, but instead he walked through it like a ghost.

"Garrett has significant tactical experience," Farrell finished.

"Makes sense." Curado glanced down at his notes for the first time since the interview had begun. Then he looked up and said, "Things didn't work out well for this team, though."

"No," Farrell agreed. He forced himself to keep his jaw from clenching.

"Stone was killed in the line of duty." Curado looked back down at his notes. "Officer Yang resigned from the department. Officer Zielinski is currently suspended. And Officer Garrett shot and killed a second suspect in as many years."

Farrell tried to go on the offensive. "What are you getting at?" Even to his own ear, his words lacked the verve of the self-righteous.

Curado looked up, meeting his gaze. "Just stating facts, Tom. But I'd like to get the context."

Farrell tilted his head left and right, stretching the tension from his neck. He was suddenly glad that Yang had resigned. She wasn't here, so she couldn't tell Curado or his posse about how he had used her as his eyes within the team. That, at least, was a blessing.

Curado waited, his expression still friendly and open.

"The context is that some career criminal shot a good officer," Farrell snapped. "And after that, I suppose Yang decided she didn't like being a cop. One of her partners got murdered. Who can blame her?"

"Not me," Curado agreed.

"Zielinski's a good cop who is accused of making one bad decision, and we're looking into that. But anyone who thinks ill of him should investigate the shooting incident he was involved in earlier this year. That'll tell you who he is. He had every justification to shoot but didn't. And Garrett..." Farrell trailed off.

Curado nodded, encouraging him. "And Garrett...what?"

Farrell wanted to scream that Garrett was a disgrace to the profession. That Curado's brother would be as ashamed of him as Farrell was. But he knew he couldn't. Bringing down Garrett had to happen in the right way, or the slippery bastard would wriggle free. And on top of that, there would be repercussions for Farrell because of his own secret methods.

"Garrett responded the way he was trained," he said. "I know it's getting popular these days to criticize a cop for actually winning a gun fight, but that's how we prefer it here."

Curado laughed lightly. "I think we all do, Tom."

Don't call me Tom, you fakey son of a bitch.

"An officer died," he said instead. "It had an impact, as it should."

"I'm sorry for that," Curado said. "I know it must have been hard."

Farrell accepted his condolences with a brief nod.

"And I'm sorry to dredge up these memories. I know the wounds must still be fresh. But it's my job to ask."

"I get it."

"What can you tell me about this incident with Bethany Rabe and a councilman?" Curado asked.

Farrell almost groaned.

Chapter 21

Clint found her at the park located less than a mile from her house on Five Mile Prairie.

Garrett's house.

Not anymore. She'd given him the boot, and since then there didn't appear to be much in the way of love lost. He'd seen plenty of interaction between Angela Garrett and her ex-husband since she'd kicked him out of their home. She kept it civil when the children were present, and never seemed to go beyond a quiet, biting remark even when they were alone. Those spiked when Garrett took up with a young woman named Tiana Kennedy and dipped again when Angela started dating a real estate broker named William Cardwell.

Clint imagined that last part stung Garrett the most. An older white man with money was shacking up with his wife. Clint didn't necessarily doubt that Cardwell had some issues of his own, but he was glad to see that Garrett had lost at something. Considering the man had been winning against all odds since he pulled the trigger and launched the bullet that killed Todd Trotter, Clint took a small but grim satisfaction in this one defeat.

Tyler Garrett lost his wife.

Cardwell wasn't with her now. Clint remained in his car, watching long enough to confirm this. He waited a little bit longer while the kids became fully engaged in their play. The boy, Jake, found a trio of other boys near his age and the group threw a small blue and green plastic football around. His little sister, Molly, made a friend on the climbing gear. For her part, Angela Garrett sat at the nearby bench, reading from a tablet and glancing up frequently to check on both of her children. She must have brought them here directly after her shift, as she still wore her nurse's uniform.

Clint got out of his car. He angled his approach so that she wouldn't see him until he was at the bench where she sat. Once he was there, he conspicuously stepped into her peripheral vision.

She looked up almost immediately. As soon as she recognized Clint, she scowled. "What do you want?"

Clint sat on the bench but left a respectful space between them. "To talk."

"I've got nothing to say."

He looked at her, his expression impassive. "I think you do." He noticed her name tag, which read *Angela Berg*. "Berg? That's your maiden name, isn't it?"

"What's it to you?"

Clint thought about it. "It supports a theory I have."

Angela flipped the cover over her tablet screen. "I can get a restraining order, you know?"

"Like the one you have against your ex-husband?"

"I dropped that."

Clint shrugged. "It's inconvenient to exchange the kids that way, isn't it? With a third party. Only you never really adhered to it, so I guess it doesn't matter."

"This is harassment. If I call your sergeant—"

"I don't have one. But I have a lieutenant. Would you like to call him?"

Angela looked at him uncertainly. "Maybe I will."

"I'll give you the number. Do you know what will happen if you call?"

"As long as you stop hassling me, I don't care."

Clint ignored her answer. "What will happen is my lieutenant will want to know why I made contact with you. When I tell him I'm investigating Tyler Garrett, he'll want to know why. When he hears why, he will promptly squirt out kittens and then call the chief. And after that, the world will change radically for all of us."

Angela stared at him. Her lips parted but no sound came out.

"Don't worry too much," Clint assured her. "That day is coming sooner rather than later, anyway. The only real question is this: when it does, what side of things do you want to find yourself on?"

Angela closed her mouth but said nothing.

Clint pressed on. "You're not part of his dirty, Angela. I know this is true."

"I don't know what you're talking about," she whispered.

"If you were part of it, you wouldn't have kicked him out." Clint leaned forward. "I don't need you to break this case open for me. I just need you to step up after it does."

Angela watched him, her lips pressed in a thin line.

Clint pushed forward. "Don't go down with him. Help take him down."

Something flickered in her expression, but he couldn't read it precisely.

"Do it for your kids," he finished.

Angela Berg didn't speak. She looked at Clint with an inscrutable expression for a long while. Clint waited patiently. He didn't know for sure how much she knew, but he sensed it was more than enough to help build his case. And while he didn't like to think in terms of trial strategy while he was still in the investigative phase, some things were worth considering in advance. Stripping Garrett of the last semblance of being a family man would be one more way to tear down the public image he'd built up for himself.

"Let me be perfectly clear," Angela said. Her tone was firm and unwavering. "I may be divorced from my ex-husband, but he is the father of my children. For their sake, I keep a cordial relationship with him."

"I realize that. That's not what I'm asking you about."

"I wasn't finished," she said curtly. She let a moment of silence stand as emphasis, then continued. "I don't know what you are talking about, and I want you to leave me and my children alone. If you bother me again, I will file an IA complaint. Are we clear?"

"We are." Clint stood. "But remember this—you're Angela Berg again for a reason, and we both know it."

He walked back to his car and drove away.

Chapter 22

"This is your fault." Mayor Andrew Sikes leaned forward in his chair and rested his elbows on the edge of his desk.

Robert Baumgartner tilted his head slightly.

"You heard me right," Sikes said. "*Your* fault."

Typical politician, Robert Baumgartner thought. Instead of voicing that, though, he said, "How's it my fault?"

"What? You think it's mine?"

"You're the mayor."

Sikes pounded the desk then pointed at the chief. "Don't you try that."

"Try what?"

"Passing the turd to me." The mayor shook his head. "This pile of garbage stays on your desk. Where it belongs."

"We're not in this together?"

Sikes laughed once. It was a mean bark that could have passed for a holler. "Together? It's your people they're investigating. Not mine. They're not down here investigating the utilities department."

"So SPD is my sole responsibility?"

The mayor's eyes narrowed. "I see what you're doing, you sneaky bastard. Let me clarify. When there's trouble, it's yours. You earned it."

That's what Baumgartner figured. He decided to change the course of the conversation. "I heard the head of their team interviewed you."

"A peach, that one."

"How'd it go?"

"Once I put her in her place, it went fine."

Baumgartner fought a smile. "Her place?"

"She thought she could tell me they were going to poke

around my city. Not on my watch, I said."

"They're still poking around."

The mayor clucked his tongue. "That's because I agreed to it, not because she told me she was doing it. What the hell is wrong with you?"

Baumgartner shrugged.

Sikes was quiet for a moment as he thought. His eyes dropped and he rubbed a finger under his nose. He stole a quick glance at the chief then lowered his gaze again. Finally, he looked up to say, "She made it sound like corruption is running rampant in your department. Quite frankly, it got me worried."

"No, it didn't."

"Don't tell me what I thought, Bob. She made some pretty scary observations. That's why I gave her free rein."

This time Baumgartner didn't fight his growing smile. "You gave her free rein, huh?"

"Like she can just walk in and take it? She needs my permission." Sikes frowned. "I did what I did because she made a good case."

"And if she finds something because of her free rein?"

"Then I'll clean up the department."

"That's not how it works."

"Don't tell me how it works. I'm not an idiot. You and your cronies like to think so. Don't shake your head. I know. Trust me, I know how you think."

Baumgartner wondered if he should point out that the mayor had just corrected *him* for suggesting that he knew what the mayor thought, and now the mayor was doing exactly the same thing to him. In the end, he figured it would be bad form.

"Anyway," Sikes continued, "Justice will give some recommendations. I'll follow the ones I like, then I'll—"

"You follow them all."

The mayor's eyes narrowed. "I'll follow the ones I want."

"If you don't do what they say, they'll slap us with a consent decree."

"You say it like it's the arrival of the boogeyman or something. Even the staff around here is afraid to say it aloud." He lifted his hands and wriggled his fingers. "Oh, consent decree. Does that scare the dickens out of you?"

"Should scare you, too."

Sikes smirked.

"A consent decree is a binding agreement between a police department and the federal government," Baumgartner said.

"I know what it is."

"If one is put in place, an outside entity that Justice designates will monitor us. We don't get a say in it. That monitor reviews everything. Every traffic stop. Every citizen contact. Every use of force. *Everything.*"

"I *get* it." Sikes crossed his arms and set his jaw.

Baumgartner continued. "They'll second guess everything we do. It's like having a juiced-up Internal Affairs on our backs, and it only goes away when Justice believes we've cleaned up our act in perfect accordance with their imposed guidelines. It's nonnegotiable."

The mayor's smirk returned. "Whatever. Won't happen."

"You can't say that."

"Let me fill you in on something. It takes two parties to have an agreement. Two. And I won't agree to it. Boom. Done. Problem solved. No decree."

Baumgartner stared at Sikes. He wanted to ask him why he always had to be so dense, but there were times the mayor acted this way just to knock people off-kilter. Perhaps that's what he was doing now. The chief couldn't be sure. "If you refuse, they will withhold their direct grants and block all other federal dollars going to our department. It's a lot of money. Nineteen percent of our personnel budget, for starters."

"We'll make cuts."

Baumgartner rode right over his comment. "To say nothing of the public relations disaster it would be. Every news jockey would be asking why we refused to cooperate.

So would our citizens. Trust in the department would drop like a hot rock."

"Maybe," Sikes muttered as his eyes drifted down to his fingers as they tapped along the edge of his desk. "Maybe."

"Maybe what?"

Sikes smiled maliciously then, and Baumgartner realized he'd bitten onto a hook that the mayor had dangled.

"Maybe I should go ahead and ask Justice to put that decree on the department now."

"Why would you do that?"

"It would allow me to get rid of you. Nice and easy." The mayor clapped his hands together a couple times as if cleaning dust away.

Baumgartner wasn't surprised. He and the mayor's relationship had been contentious for some time. Sikes had previously intimated that he wanted to get rid of Baumgartner, but the department's success and the chief's popularity made it difficult.

Sikes smirked self-righteously. "No one could say a thing about it then, could they?"

"No, they couldn't," Baumgartner said. "If Justice slaps us with a consent decree, there'll be calls for reform and one of the loudest would likely be for a change at the top."

Sikes leaned back in his chair and put his hands behind his head. "So you see my dilemma. Should I sit back and fight the inevitable? Or do I lean in and ask them for it now? Get ahead of the curve."

"When I said a change at the top, I was talking about you."

With a thud, Sikes dropped his chair forward. "Me?"

"Yeah, you."

"But the decree is for the police department."

"Which is part of the city."

The mayor's eyes jumped left and right. It seemed clear to Baumgartner that Sikes was looking for some path to victory. He decided to help him find it.

"Consent decrees aren't the death of a department and

they don't have to be the death of a police chief's career. They don't have to be the end of a mayor's career, either."

Sykes eyed him cautiously. "What are you saying?"

"To survive something like this, we need to do it as a united force."

"United?"

"We can't be split in leadership. We need to point in the same direction. Work as one, so to speak."

"But it's your department." Sykes barely hid the whine in his voice. "You're the chief."

"And you're the mayor," Baumgartner said. "You're ultimately responsible. And for a guy that wants to change the term limits around his office, I would think you would want the best story possible around you now."

"But a consent decree…"

"Like you said, it's nothing to be afraid of."

"You don't believe that."

"I believe this: we stay together, and we survive."

Sikes rubbed his mouth as he thought. "Bullshit," he muttered. "You're just trying to save your job."

"I'm trying to save yours, too."

"No," Sikes said. "You're screwing with me. I see what you're doing."

Baumgartner stood. He'd had enough. "Do what you want. Ask for the decree and get rid of me. I'll even throw this in the mix. If the consent decree comes down, I'll quit if you ask me."

"Huh?"

"You'll be doing me a favor." It was Baumgartner's turn to point a finger. "Because then I can talk openly about you."

Sikes threw his hands in the air. "What did I do?"

"Seriously?"

"Seriously. What did I do?"

"For starters, you meddled in the Bethany Rabe affair and caused a seventeen-year-old girl to kill herself."

"But I—"

The chief thrust his finger at the mayor. "And in a rush to

get a headline, you demanded we arrest Tyler Garrett, which ultimately cost the city three-quarters of a million dollars."

"That's not how—"

Now, Baumgartner tapped the side of his temple. "And I haven't forgotten all the dirty political dealings I've watched you do over the past. Or the lousy things you've said about the council. Without the badge holding me back, I'm just another private citizen. I'll be able to tell anyone I want about anything I want. Maybe I'll even write a book."

Sikes stood and put his palms on his desk. "That's blackmail!"

"No, Mister Mayor, that's the first amendment. It's not even slander, since it's all true. And when you're impeached, or recalled, or whatever the hell it is they do to a mayor, you know who the first person the next mayor is going to call?"

"They're not calling you! Don't be delusional, buddy."

Baumgartner chuckled. "No, the first person the *new* mayor is going to call is the *new* chief of police. They'll want to make sure my allegations about you are thoroughly investigated. Especially if the consent decree is still in place, they'll need to make a name for themselves. Show themselves to be a law and order type of mayor. Hasn't Maggie Patterson been pushing that idea around most of this year?"

The two men seethed quietly at each other for several moments. Outside, a siren from a fire engine wailed in the distance.

Finally, the mayor said, "So we're in agreement then?"

"Of what?" Baumgartner snapped.

"That a consent decree would be a disaster for the department."

The chief slowly nodded. "I'd say we're in agreement."

Mayor Andrew Sikes turned his palms up in frustration. "Then what the hell are you standing here for? Get back to your department and make sure they don't hammer us." Then his face transformed into a magnanimous smile. "I know I can trust you to do the job, Bob. You've always come through before."

Baumgartner left without further word.

Chapter 23

"Jake and Molly!" she hollered. "Your dad's here."

Angie Garrett stood in the open doorway of her house. She tried her best to keep her face passive, but there was a hint of malice behind her eyes. Her right hand clutched the door's handle. An unconscious signal that she would slam it closed at any moment.

Then he remembered she wasn't Angie Garrett anymore. She was Angela Berg again. She'd abandoned his name.

"They're not ready?" Garrett asked.

"We just got home from the park. Finally had some time to change my clothes."

His eyes traveled up and down her length. She wore a tight pair of tan shorts and a form-fitting T-shirt. Her feet were bare and her toenails unpainted. "You look good."

"Don't start."

"Why don't you grab some sandals and come with us?"

"What about your girlfriend?"

Garrett ignored her question. "It'll be the four of us. Like old times."

Angie looked past him toward his car. Tiana wasn't with him so there was nothing for her to see. He was supposed to pick his girlfriend up after getting the kids, but if Angie said yes, he would call and break their date. But more than likely...

She shook her head. "Wouldn't be a good idea."

"Why not? You got something better to do? Hot date maybe?"

Her eyes hardened.

"You seeing someone?" Garrett asked.

Angie crossed her arms. "Does it matter?"

"Do the kids know?"

She paused, as if considering a lie, probably knowing damn well that Garrett would ask questions once they pulled away from the curb. It was a violation of the parenting plan to talk about the other parent, but that was all just so much legal talk. He knew she did it because he was doing it.

"I just started seeing him," Angie said.

A lie. "What's his name?"

"You wouldn't know him."

You would be surprised. "How do you know? I know I lot of people."

"I know your friends," she said. "He doesn't run in those circles."

"What circles are those?"

She opened her mouth to say something then slowly closed it. Finally, she muttered, "Cops. He's not a cop."

Jake and Molly showed up then, one on each side of Angie. Their grins were in stark contrast to their mother's glare.

Garrett forced a smile. He reached out and put a hand on each child's head then pulled them toward him.

"Good for you, Ang," he said. Even though he didn't mean a damn word of it, his voice was soft.

"Thank you."

Garrett looked to his kids. "C'mon, guys. Let's go have some fun."

"I want to be a fireman," Molly said.

Tiana Kennedy smiled. Her face was at the same level as Molly's. "A fireman? Not a firewoman?"

Molly cocked her head. "Huh?"

The four of them were seated in a booth at the Carl's Jr. on Northwest Boulevard.

Tyler Garrett chuckled. "Why do you want to be a fireman, kiddo?"

"Because they put out fires," Molly said. She dipped a

french fry in ketchup and lifted it into the air. "And they save people."

"Dad saves people," Jake said.

Molly frowned. "Is that true?"

Garrett nodded. "Sometimes."

Tiana touched Molly's nose with a finger. "Your dad even has a lifesaving medal because of it."

His daughter scrunched her nose. "I thought the police arrested people."

"We do that, too."

Even though she hadn't taken a bite out of it, Molly dipped the french fry deeper into the ketchup. "That's what I thought."

Tiana was still bent over with her face near Molly's. "You don't want to arrest people?"

The little girl shook her head. "I want people to like me. People don't like the police."

Jake looked to his father. "Mom doesn't want me to be a policeman when I grow up."

Garrett put his hand on his son's head. "You can be anything you want, but I would like it if you did something else."

"Like what?" Jake asked.

"Something safe and inside an office."

"That sounds boring."

Tiana raised an eyebrow. "He sounds like you."

Garrett winked then checked his watch. "Hey, babe, I need to run for a couple minutes."

She straightened. Concern registered in her eyes. "What's going on?"

"A thing I gotta do." He glanced to the kids. "Ten minutes at the most, but I'll be right back. Can you watch them?"

Concern washed over Tiana's face, but she muttered, "Sure. Okay."

He stood, kissed her on the cheek, then said to the kids, "Be right back. Eat your burgers."

Outside, he opened his phone—the burner he kept for use

with his side business—and saw a text message from Royal Harjo.

Ready.

The house was only a few blocks away from the restaurant. It was a small rancher with an attached garage. A large picture frame window took up most of the east half of the house.

The exterior looked recently painted. Pictures online showed its interior was completely modernized—almost too nice for the neighborhood. Garrett had pulled the transaction history on the web and found that it sold earlier in the year. It was simple to understand what it was—a flip. Therefore, no one was living in it.

A For Sale sign proudly stood in the front yard. On it was William Cardwell's name and phone number.

Earlier that morning, while he'd been watching Clint outside Earl Ellis's grandmother's house, Garrett made two calls. The first was to Cardwell to set a showing on this house. His assistant took the call and gladly scheduled the tour. The next call was to Royal Harjo—a big man with a knack for physical violence.

Garrett drove slowly through the neighborhood, looping back by the small rancher several times. When he finally saw Cardwell's Audi, he pulled to the side of the road.

The Audi bounced into the driveway of the For-Sale house. Cardwell exited the car and trotted toward the front door. He was a tall, thin man in black slacks and a bright blue golf shirt. His gray hair looked expertly trimmed. Even from this distance, Garrett could see that Cardwell was filled with confidence bordering on arrogance.

The man held his cell phone next to an electronic lock attached to the front door. When it popped open, he removed a key and let himself in.

Garrett dropped his car into gear and crept down the street. When he was parallel with the picture window, he saw Cardwell fall inside the house. As he fell, the broker's hand slapped the window. It didn't break, but light shimmered off the vibrating glass.

It was hard to tell, but it appeared there was a masked figure standing near the window. Garrett glanced around and didn't notice anyone moving about the neighborhood.

Satisfied that no one else had seen the movement inside the For-Sale house, Garrett accelerated away.

When he returned to the Carl's Jr. parking lot, he checked his burner phone. He'd received one new text message.

Done.

He typed *Good. Will call again from new number.*

Then he snapped the phone in half.

He tossed the pieces into the trash can outside the entrance.

Inside, Tiana and the kids had finished eating. Jake was playing with his phone and Molly and Tiana were whispering to each other. Molly giggled as she did so.

Garrett slid into the booth next to his son and put his arm around him.

"Everything good?" Tiana asked.

"Definitely," he said. "What do you say we go shoot some mini-golf?"

"Yeah!" Jake said with a fist pump.

Molly's eyes lit up. "Can we get the cotton candy?"

Garrett smiled at his daughter. "Of course, kiddo. It's a great day. We should celebrate."

Chapter 24

Union President Dale Thomas leaned over and whispered into Sergeant Kelly Ragland's ear.

Édelie Durand waited patiently as this process repeated itself for the umpteenth time.

As Thomas continued to quietly advise his client, Ragland nodded but kept his gaze firmly affixed on Durand.

The men across the conference room table were a study in opposites.

Ragland wore a meticulously cared for police uniform. It was pressed to high creases, and there wasn't a speck of lint or dust anywhere on the dark blue polyester. His badge glistened so much under the conference room lights, she wondered if he polished it. However, the tidiness of the uniform couldn't hide the frumpy nature of the man himself. Ragland was overweight and his face was jowly. His eyebrows needed trimming and a couple long hairs peeked out from inside his nose.

On the other hand, Dale Thomas wore a tan suit that appeared straight off a rack at Men's Wearhouse. His white shirt looked as if he might have pressed it a couple days ago, and his tie was knotted haphazardly. That's where the low budget ended with this man. His hair was cut in a businessman's style, and his cheeks glistened as if they were recently shaved. His fingernails were clean and cut short.

Durand glanced down at her notes, not because she needed to be reminded of anything, but to stop herself from rolling her eyes at the union president's continued whispering.

Ragland had sought counsel's advice almost a dozen times already and Thomas had butted in a few when it wasn't even necessary.

When the sergeant finally spoke, he said, "I was assigned the position."

Durand sighed. "So you didn't want it?"

Thomas leaned toward Ragland again, but Durand lifted her hand to stop him. "Enough."

The union president straightened. "Excuse me?"

"Can we let the man answer a simple question?"

Dale Thomas pursed his lips before saying, "He has the right to counsel."

Durand smiled. "Of course, he does. I'm not implying he doesn't, but if he can't answer a simple question, it makes me wonder a couple things."

"Like what?" Thomas asked as he steepled his fingers.

Durand turned her full attention to Ragland. "Like is he putting you between us because he's done something wrong?"

The union president snorted. "The advice of counsel doesn't imply wrongdoing. Give me a break."

She faced Thomas now and shrugged. "Or maybe he's too simple to understand my questions."

Thomas's mouth dropped. "You can't say that."

"I'm not simple," Ragland protested.

"She can't say that," Thomas said to Ragland.

"If that's the case," Durand said, ignoring their protests, "then it's an obvious failure of this administration to properly vet their leadership candidates. If you both will agree that Sergeant Ragland is too simple to understand my questions—"

"I'm not simple," Ragland repeated.

Thomas laid a hand over his arm. "Kelly…"

"Then I'll make an entry to that agreement. We can end this interview right now and I'll have my proof that this department has been derelict in its duty."

Ragland yanked his arm free of the union president's hand. "I'm not simple," he said.

Durand raised her eyebrows. "But you've needed help on every question I've asked."

"He advised me not to talk—"

"Kelly!"

Durand glanced at the union president.

Thomas turned to his man and whispered, "That's not what I said."

Ragland muttered, "She called me simple."

"She's trying to get your goat."

"And you told me not to talk."

Durand waited patiently for the two men to decide a course of action. Ragland chose it for them.

He faced her and asked, "What was your question again? Did I want to lead the Anti-Crime Team? No, I did not want to lead that unit."

"Why not?"

"Because I was already the administrative sergeant. I didn't want additional duties."

Durand nodded. Now, she was getting somewhere. "So, the desire to not be on the team had nothing to do with the unit personnel?"

"The ones who were already assigned? I didn't care about them one way or another. I have a good job. Day shift hours. I didn't want to give it up. That's what I cared about."

"But you took the assignment after Sergeant McGinn's emergency leave?"

"I'm a team player," Ragland said. "I stepped up even though I didn't want to."

"And you weren't worried about the lack of experience from a couple of the team members?"

"You mean Yang?"

"And Officer Stone."

Ragland smirked. "I've never gotten to pick my people for any team. You work with what you're assigned. I figured this was more of the same."

"Did you make it known that you didn't want the assignment to ACT?"

Dale Thomas leaned forward then. "We registered a formal complaint with the department."

"And what happened?"

"Gary Stone was killed," Ragland said.

"The team was disbanded after that," Thomas added. "Our formal complaint no longer served a purpose. Sergeant Ragland was returned to his original assignment."

Durand made a note on her pad before asking, "How did you feel the team operated prior to Gary Stone's death?"

Ragland glanced to the union president who shrugged in frustration.

"Sort of dysfunctional," the sergeant said.

Thomas groaned.

Durand asked, "Can you explain?"

"Garrett and Stone were running around like they were Tango and Cash, taking doors—"

She interrupted, "I'm sorry, I don't get that reference."

"Taking doors?"

"Tango and Cash."

He glanced to Thomas who refused to look at him now. "It was a movie. Sylvester Stallone and Kurt Russell. Late eighties, I think. Doesn't ring a bell?"

"What did they do? This Tango and Cash."

Ragland sucked his lips in while he thought. Then he said, "They were a couple detectives. Sort of loose cannons."

Thomas moaned at that.

Ragland didn't seem to notice. "But they got the job done, you know? Great action. Funny wisecracks. Lots of explosions if I remember correctly."

"And that's how you saw Garrett and Stone?"

"Mostly."

Thomas rubbed his temples.

"And this made the team dysfunctional?"

"When they were getting all sorts of pats on the backs, yeah. Zielinski and Yang were all butt hurt over it."

"Butt hurt?"

"Upset. Jealous."

"Jealous of what?"

"Since they weren't the flavor of the month. And let's be

honest, Ray Zielinski is never going to be anyone's flavor. He's sort of a jerk."

"Kelly!" Dale Thomas yelled.

"What? He is. Even you've said so."

"Not in public," the union president protested. "And not on the record."

"What about Yang?" Durand asked.

"She was sort of a push around."

"A push around?"

"Someone who doesn't stand up for themselves. Truth be told, I was thinking maybe they were hooking up. I mean, she's a decent looker—"

"Damn it, Kelly!" Thomas shouted.

"But I couldn't get past the fact that it was Ray Zielinski. Have you met him yet?"

Durand shook her head.

"This guy could find a pile of crap in a mound of diamonds. There was no way he was getting with a young thing like Yang."

Dale Thomas turned in his seat to put his back toward Ragland.

"Was the team paired up like that on purpose?" Durand asked. "Garrett and Stone? Zielinski and Yang?"

Ragland shrugged. "They were that way when I took over."

"Which adds to your dysfunctional comment."

"Definitely."

Durand tapped her notes while she thought. "Officer Yang resigned from the department shortly after the death of Officer Stone."

"I know. I out-processed her."

"Do you know why?"

"It's part of my job as administrative sergeant."

"No," Durand said. "Do you know why she resigned?"

"Oh." Ragland considered, then shrugged. "Some types just aren't a good fit for police work."

"Which types?"

"The type that quits after something bad happens. The type that can't hack it."

"I see. Anything else?"

Ragland thought about it for a moment. "I thought the small team dynamic could lead to all sorts of noble cause corruption."

Durand straightened suddenly and Dale Thomas spun around in his chair to face Ragland. "Kelly! What is wrong with you?"

"What? What did I say?"

"By noble cause corruption," Durand clarified, "I assume you are referring to the slippery slope of officers believing that the ends justify the means when it comes to putting criminals in jail?"

"Yeah, that. I mean, that's how it starts—cops bending the rules or lying a little to make sure the case on some piece of crap dirtball is solid. Then pretty soon they're stealing money from drug dealers and shoving pokers up people's asses or whatever."

Thomas whispered, "For the love of God" to Ragland but the sergeant waved him off.

Durand asked, "You saw behavior on the Anti-Crime Team that you believe was corrupt?"

Ragland's face pinched. "I never said that."

"But you mentioned noble cause corruption."

The sergeant wagged a finger. "I said I could see the team formation leading to it. The potential was there. I even talked to Captain Farrell about it."

"You talked to Captain Farrell about noble cause corruption?"

"I brought my concerns to him, yes."

"What did he say?"

"He agreed. He said that's why they wanted a sergeant on the team. To make sure corruption didn't happen."

Durand made several notes before moving on to her next question. "Did you see one side of the team leaning more toward corruption than the other?"

Ragland chuckled. "You must be referring to Zielinski's troubles."

Thomas slapped the table. "Will you stop?"

"Which troubles would those be?" Durand asked.

Thomas grasped Ragland's arm and glared at him.

The sergeant glanced down to the trembling grip and sighed. When he looked back to Durand, he said, "You should probably ask Ray Zielinski about that."

The union president exhaled audibly then patted Ragland's arm. He left his hand in place, however.

Durand studied Sergeant Ragland for a moment then referred to her notes. After a time, she asked, "As the administrative sergeant, do you think you had the apparent authority to lead a team like ACT? Especially with a couple operators you just described as Tango and Cash and an officer like Ray Zielinski who you described as having a propensity for getting himself into trouble?"

Dale Thomas's hand tightened again around Kelly Ragland's arm, but the sergeant tugged himself free.

"Apparent authority? Who needs that when I have *actual* authority?" Kelly Ragland smiled and tapped three fingers repeatedly next to the stripes on his sleeve. "I'm a sergeant. They did what I told them."

Dale Thomas put his head in his hands and groaned.

Édelie Durand stood and said, "Thank you for your time, Sergeant Ragland. You've been very helpful."

Chapter 25

Detective Wardell Clint heard Lieutenant Dan Flowers say his goodbyes to Detective Marty Hill on his way out of the Major Crimes bullpen. That reminded him that he needed to check his mail. He headed toward the bank of mailboxes located near the lieutenant's now unoccupied office.

Along the way, he passed Marty Hill, who was leaning back in his chair with an open file on his lap. When Hill noticed Clint, he gave him a nod. "How's it going, Wardell?"

"Fine," Clint said, because he knew that was what people wanted to hear when they asked that question. It seemed like a waste of time and energy to him, but so did most social niceties. He kept walking, then he remembered what else was expected of him. "How about you?"

Hill lifted his foot off the ground and flexed his knee. Despite the audible crack on the first flex, he didn't seem to have any difficulty with the movement.

"Healing up," Hill said. "Finally almost human again."

"Let me know how that feels," Clint said, and continued around the corner. Behind, he heard a sound from Hill, but couldn't decide if it was a chuckle or a sigh.

His mailbox contained a stack of papers of various sizes, including a couple of interoffice envelopes. He leafed through the notes, discarding several unimportant ones in the nearby trash can. When he saw that one of the envelopes was from the lab, he opened it Inside, he found what Jody had told him to expect soon—the results from the Sonya Meyer case.

Reading as he walked, Clint reviewed the findings. Most were what he had expected. Meyer's blood work was clean except for a trace of THC. That didn't surprise him, given that marijuana was now legal in Washington State. The fact Meyer was not of legal age to imbibe was also not a surprise. The dissonance of eighteen being the legal age to be an adult but not to indulge in adult beverages or cannabis was something Clint had long ago accepted.

He reached his desk and sat down, flipping through the paperwork until he reached the one piece of evidence that he had hoped would bear results. Meyer had been brutally—and clumsily, Clint noticed—murdered in her home. In the struggle, she had managed to scratch her attacker, as indicated by the skin that Jody discovered beneath Meyer's fingernails when she did the scrapings on scene. Clint had requested DNA analysis, knowing that if he got a match, this was powerful evidence against the suspect.

He also knew it was unlikely to be a match for Tyler Garrett, though Garrett was the man he believed was possibly behind Sonya Meyer's murder. Garrett had even come to the crime scene, supposedly at the behest of the councilman who'd been involved with the young woman. Garrett's presence contaminated the scene and would negate the value of most physical evidence that placed him there. Skin beneath the victim's nails would be difficult to explain, however.

Clint read the lab results.

DNA Extraction from sample 13B, 13C, and 13D: Successful.
DNA Analysis: Complete
CODIS Database Search: Match Successful
Subject Identified: Ezekiel Hetzel

"Ezekiel Hetzel," Clint murmured. The name sounded familiar, but at the moment he couldn't place it. It didn't matter, though. The lab report included his basic information, so Clint entered his criminal identification number into the local computer system. His disappointment that the match hadn't miraculously been to Tyler Garrett was tempered by the fact that there *was* a match. While it didn't give him a silver bullet for his case against Garrett, the match was a huge development for the Meyer case itself.

He found Hetzel in the computer system. The man's alias of "Skunk" was listed along with his birthdate, last known address, and physical descriptors. His most recent arrests also appeared on the first page of the record. But Clint was drawn to the field he habitually checked first: status. Often, he discovered people he was interested in were currently incarcerated or wanted on outstanding warrants. When he saw the status of Ezekiel Hetzel, he frowned.

Status: Deceased

Hetzel was dead.

Clint noted the date of the entry and saw that it was only a couple of weeks after the Meyer homicide. The timing seemed suspicious to him, but he knew that criminals led dangerous lives. With a click, he accessed the official report of Hetzel's death. The attending detective was Leanne Hollander. Clint skimmed through her description of the scene. Hetzel had been found in the basement of an abandoned home at the bottom of a short flight of stairs. The body was estimated to be at least ten days old at the time of discovery. Cause of death was difficult to determine at the scene, but the autopsy later revealed a broken neck with some indications of strangling as well.

Someone choked him and threw him down the stairs. Clint flipped through the remainder of the pages until he reached the original patrol report. The responding officer's name blared at him from the screen.

Tyler Garrett.

A small thrill went through him. He quickly read Garrett's account. While on his way to conduct follow up on a hit-and-run, he claimed to have been flagged down by a citizen. The citizen complained of a suspicious smell coming from a nearby abandoned house. Garrett investigated and discovered the deceased.

Clint sat back, thinking. The chain of events cascaded

through his mind.

Ezekiel Hetzel murders Sonya Meyer.

Tyler Garrett shows up and uses a pretense to intrude onto the homicide scene.

Ezekiel Hetzel is murdered within days.

Tyler Garrett discovers Hetzel's body weeks later.

The events had to be connected. There was just too much coincidence at play for it to be otherwise. Even the location Hetzel was discovered convinced Clint of this. He'd followed Garrett to several different abandoned houses throughout Spokane. Commonly called zombie houses, these empty homes once belonged to people who were foolish enough to use easy credit to punch above their financial weight class. When the real estate crisis hit, and they found themselves upside down in their dream home, foreclosure was the result. The bank had owned hundreds of these properties throughout Spokane in the immediate aftermath of the crisis, and Clint reckoned there were still dozens of them scattered throughout the city. These zombie houses afforded many criminals a safe place away from prying eyes where they could do their dirty deeds. Garrett was no different.

Clint believed Garrett met his cohorts inside these houses and wouldn't be surprised at all if he hid drugs or money there, too. And though he didn't recognize the address where Hetzel was found, he was certain it was one of Garrett's haunts. When he needed to dispose of Hetzel, he'd chosen that location to do it.

But can you prove it?

That was the question, the challenge he had been unable to overcome for two years. Were these facts suspicious? Certainly. Did they prove anything? Not by themselves. But in Garrett's case, seeming coincidence after coincidence had occurred. At what point was there enough circumstantial evidence for even a skeptical mind to accept his culpability?

Who was Hetzel to Garrett? Clint suspected the man was just another lackey, perhaps a precursor to Ellis. But why would Garrett have sent Hetzel to murder Sonya Meyer? As a favor to Councilman Hahn?

The trail of breadcrumbs certainly seemed to lead there. The connection between Meyer, the victim, and Hetzel, her attacker, was now concrete. A defense attorney might argue that skin from Hetzel under Meyer's fingernails only proved that she scratched him, not that he murdered her. But Clint thought the evidence was damning. The connection to Garrett, however, was a tenuous one. Garrett had discovered Hetzel's body in the course of his duties as a police officer, that was all.

Clint searched through the report for the name of the concerned citizen who had alerted Garrett to the body. There was no listing in the section for persons involved. Then he found Garrett's convenient explanation in the officer's own narrative:

Upon ascertaining that the victim inside the abandoned residence was deceased, I notified dispatch of the situation and the need for investigative follow-up. I then returned to my vehicle to further interview the yet-unidentified complainant who had alerted me to the suspicious smell at the house. However, she was no longer in the area, and my attempts to locate her were not successful.

Clint shook his head. He doubted very much that this anonymous citizen actually existed. He found it far more likely that Garrett himself had killed Hetzel in the aftermath of the Meyer murder, and left the body in the abandoned house to be discovered at a later date. But once more, what he believed was still a far cry from what he could prove. And if he was unable to link Garrett to the murder, then Garrett's connection to the councilman was unimportant.

He rose from his chair and began pacing the short stretch of floor behind his desk. This latest development was one more in a case full of them. He wondered if he had lost perspective, due to being so close to the facts for so long. Perhaps there was probable cause, and he wasn't seeing it. Or maybe he didn't have anything but steam, and he wasn't seeing *that*.

Walk through it, he told himself.

Make the case.

Clint stopped pacing and sat. He flipped to a new page of his legal pad and started to make notes. He didn't bother writing in code, preferring to use all his energy to consider the case. He could shred the notes afterward, anyway.

He imagined standing, file in hand, before a skeptical prosecutor with no foreknowledge of the case. What would it take to convince *her* to charge Garrett? What gave him not just probable cause, but enough for a jury to convict Garrett beyond a reasonable doubt?

Clint sorted his case into bullet points, occasionally drawing an arrow to move one point higher or lower in the list. He noted the source of each piece of evidence, and what its impact was. He scribbled furiously for twenty nonstop minutes, before leaning back and looking at what he had.

The case was sprawling, a fact he knew would work against them when things eventually went before a jury. As he examined his bullet points, he realized that it could be divided into three separate prongs.

The Ocampo drug conspiracy.

The Sonya Meyer homicide.

The ambush and murder of Officer Gary Stone.

One, two, three.

In the Meyer homicide, he'd received evidence that seemingly solved the crime, or at least the question of a perpetrator. Hetzel's connection to Garrett suggested the motive behind the murder, as well. Clint wasn't sure how much more he could accomplish on this case as it stood alone but knew it would eventually fold into his larger investigation.

Clint shook his head. It was a lot for someone to take in if that person hadn't been part of the situation from the very beginning. The Tyler Garrett saga had been long and twisting, but with two consistent outcomes. Garrett left chaos in his wake, and yet Garrett seemed to get away at each turn.

The thought burned darkly in Clint's gut. If there was one

thing he was certain of in this world, it was that it was an unfair place in need of justice. And Tyler Garrett was in need of more justice than most.

Clint wanted to bring it to him.

He turned his eye toward the evidence pertaining to the Ocampo prong. He knew that Garrett had been in league with Ernesto Ocampo, a drug dealer. Along with Detectives Talbott and Pomeroy, they'd ran a small drug operation. When Garrett decided to cut out his partners and deal directly with Ocampo, the pair of detectives responded by luring him into an ambush. The trap failed, and the bait, Todd Trotter, was killed. That is what started the entire messed up journey two years ago.

Talbott upped the stakes when he planted drugs in Garrett's house. It was clear to Clint that Talbott was betting the drugs were enough to either get Garrett out of the way or bully him back into line.

He lost that bet. When Talbott confronted Garrett outside of a Liberty Lake apartment, Garrett returned fire and killed him. All the witnesses said a black man shot in self-defense, but none of them were able to identify Garrett. This included Derek Tillman, Garrett's high school friend, outside whose apartment this deadly encounter just *happened* to occur.

Can you prove it? Any of it?

"No," Clint grunted. Pomeroy had confessed everything to him shortly before his supposed suicide, making the confession useless to him now. Talbott was dead, too. Tillman refused to talk at the scene, and Clint doubted his position had softened over time. That left Ocampo, but Garrett had made short work of him, too.

Along with three others, Ocampo was murdered in his north Spokane home. Clint knew it had been Garrett, but what evidence did he truly have?

He scanned the pages he'd written, searching for the answer. Nona Henry? She was an eyewitness to Garrett going into and then leaving Ocampo's residence at the time of the quadruple homicide. On the surface, this seemed compelling.

But there were problems with it. Henry was elderly and her eyesight was less than stellar. She had seen Garrett at a distance. Garrett was black and she was white, and defense attorneys had been very successful in pointing out how inaccurate witnesses were when making an identification of someone outside the witness's own race. Besides that, due to the media coverage of the Trotter shooting and subsequent events, Garrett's image had been plastered all over television for several days. His face would be familiar to her because of that. All these facts stacked up against Henry's positive identification. It wasn't enough to completely negate it, at least in Clint's mind, but it was enough that her identification couldn't be the centerpiece of his case.

What else did he have to link together this little cabal, then? If the drugs found at the Pomeroy scene were ever tested and shown to match the drugs at the Ocampo scene, that would link Pomeroy and Ocampo, but not Garrett. He had to link Garrett to Ocampo, and Nona Henry's fragile identification wasn't enough.

Clint had long suspected that Garrett had used the same gun when defending himself against Talbott and when he killed Ocampo. The lab should have made that connection by now, but he hadn't heard anything about it. Perhaps Marty got the results and kept them to himself, but such a connection would be big news, so he doubted it.

Of course, even if bullets from both scenes were conclusively proven to come from the same gun, what was there to say that Garrett fired that gun?

Nothing.

That was the problem. Much of his evidence was his own testimony, which he knew would make any prosecutor hesitate. Relying on a detective to make a case sometimes worked but if a jury failed to connect with the detective or if just one juror didn't like or believe that detective, the case was shot. That's why forensic evidence and witness testimony were paramount.

He shook his head. He didn't have much in the way of

forensic evidence or witness testimonial evidence. But circumstantial? There was plenty of that. Talbott was shot by a black male outside Derek Tillman's apartment. Derek Tillman was a friend of Garrett's. Then Ocampo was killed, and Nona Henry identified Garrett entering and exiting the house. Taken individually, perhaps those facts remain unconvincing. But at a certain point, they begged the question: how likely was it that this exact confluence of events occurred, all centering around one man, and yet remained mere coincidence? The sheer volume of the coincidences added up to correlation.

As Clint saw it now, he had two strong cards to play. If the Ocampo bullet matched the Talbott bullet, all the weight of all the circumstantial evidence reached a breaking point, at least for everything that happened in the aftermath of the Trotter shooting two years ago. And if he could find Earl Ellis and convince the man to become a cooperating witness, Ellis would provide sufficient evidence for much that had happened more recently.

More recently? That seemed like a weak way to describe the murder of Gary Stone.

He glanced up at the sound of motion nearby. One of the evening janitors was reaching for a trash can and dumping its contents into the larger container on her cart. Clint recognized the woman, who most of the detectives mistakenly thought was Russian. Clint knew better. She was from the Ukraine.

Clint glanced at his own trash can, which was empty. Unlike some of his colleagues, he only used it for true garbage. Any scrap of paper from his official investigations went into the shred bin. Any Garrett paperwork he no longer needed, he burned himself.

The janitor gave him a perfunctory smile as she drew near. "All empty still?" she asked, her accent thick but her words easily understood.

He nodded.

"Always. You are very clean man." Her smile ticked up a

notch and her eyes joined in.

She has a nice smile.

Stay on task. He gave her a professional nod and turned back to his file.

Build the case.

Get the Ocampo bullet match to the Talbott bullet, and that links Garrett. Test the drugs from Pomeroy's suicide, which strengthens the case, along with Nona Henry's identification and all the circumstantial evidence.

That's one.

Ezekiel Hetzel murdered Sonya Meyer. Garrett found Hetzel's dead body.

That's two.

And three?

Three was pretty straightforward, too, the more Clint looked at it. Leon Strayer had ambushed and killed Officer Gary Stone. Garrett had shot and killed Strayer immediately after that. To everyone who had investigated, including the hapless county homicide detectives, it looked like a clear-cut case of an officer returning fire after his partner was shot. To Clint, it looked like Garrett was following the first rule of assassinations.

Kill the assassin.

Because dead men don't talk.

So far, it had worked, like everything else Garrett had gotten away with. But Clint had seen Garrett meeting with Ellis, though he wasn't able to get a photograph. He *did* get photographs of Ellis meeting with Strayer. Several of them on more than one occasion.

All of it painted a clear picture to him, one very different from the public view of the situation. Of course, he had the advantage of knowing that Captain Farrell had foolishly taken Stone into his confidence regarding Garrett and his plan to trap the dirty officer.

Farrell's trap fared no better than Talbott and Pomeroy's did. Clint didn't know for sure how Garrett figured out that Stone was a mole inside the Anti-Crime Team. He suspected

Stone simply told him, as the younger officer had come more and more under the sway of Garrett's larger-than-life persona. Either way, Garrett made his decision, told Earl Ellis, and Ellis gave the task to Leon Strayer.

But can you prove it?

Clint stared down at his work. Strayer was dead. Stone was dead. Only Ellis remained. Ellis could detail this murder-for-hire plot and put Garrett at the head of their new operation. He was the linchpin.

Ellis.

That's three.

Clint pushed the notepad away and rubbed his tired eyes. So many moving parts. So many places for a defense attorney to trip up the case.

His stomach rumbled. He glanced at the clock and was surprised to see it was almost seven. He'd been at this for hours and had come to the same conclusion he always did. He needed just a little more, so that when he slapped the cuffs on Garrett, they stayed on. Anything less, and he risked not only a failed case, but increased scrutiny on him and Farrell for their off-book investigation. DOJ would feast on that.

Clint rose and walked through the bullpen. Most of the desk lights were off and all the desks were empty. He listened and heard no movement or signs of anyone present. That decided it for him. He made his way to Marty Hill's desk.

When he reached it, he hesitated. He'd never broken into another detective's desk before. The truth was, he'd never even slid open an unlocked drawer to borrow a pen. He respected private space since he expected others to do the same for him.

Clint worked his jaw, considering for a moment. Then he realized there was no decision to make here. He'd come too far.

There were a few files in a plastic file rack on the desktop, but he quickly determined that none were the Ocampo file.

He tried the file drawer and discovered it was locked. He went back to his desk and returned a short time later with a thin tool that he inserted into the lock, making short work of the crude mechanism.

Once inside, he flipped through the files. Hill appeared to sort his older files by report number, which also meant they were in reverse chronological order. It didn't take long to find the Ocampo file. He pulled it out and set it on Hill's desk, opening it. He leafed through the organized contents until he reached the lab reports. Turning to ballistics, he found the report he was looking for.

He didn't even have to read the official report. Hill had a small yellow sticky note in his own handwriting on it.

Examined and entered—no match.

Clint blinked at that. No match? He wanted to say that was impossible, but of course that wasn't true. So what *was* possible? Logically, either he was wrong in his belief that Garrett had used the same gun, or…what?

Or Liberty Lake hadn't submitted their bullet for testing yet.

Clint frowned. That hardly seemed likely. Maybe Garrett had used two different guns. Going even further away from his working theory, maybe someone other than Garrett had been responsible for one of the shootings.

He shook his head. There was too much circumstantial evidence in support of Garrett's involvement.

That left Liberty Lake. Clint resolved to go to the neighboring department tomorrow to find out. It wasn't his place, but he couldn't let that stop him. He was the only one trying to bring about any semblance of justice here. If he had to violate a few points of protocol, so be it.

Clint returned Hill's file to its place and locked the drawer. Then he packed up his own notes, locked his desk, and went home for the night. But on the way, he drove past Aurelia Ellis's house, just in case.

Zielinski was watching the home, and there was no sign of Ellis.

Clint drove home, weary to the bone.

Chapter 26

This damn DOJ visit. They're going to blow everything.

Tom Farrell sat at the dinner table, poking absently at his potato. The sound of Steve Curado's patronizing voice still rang in his ears. Even worse, so did his own weak replies to the lawyer's questions.

He had to give them credit. They zeroed in on exactly what he had been most worried about. He knew the department was overwhelmingly clean, and if DOJ looked just about anywhere else, that's what the investigation would show. But like a pack of bloodhounds, they smelled what was rotten. And even though the rot emanated from Tyler Garrett, Tom Farrell knew it had infected him now.

This is going to get ugly before it's over.

"Tom? Did you hear me?"

Farrell shook his head slightly and looked at his wife. "I'm sorry, what?"

Karen Farrell frowned. "You haven't heard anything I've said."

"Sure I did."

"Really? Then what's your answer. Red or blue?"

"Blue," Farrell replied, picking what seemed like the safer color.

Her frown deepened. "That's interesting, because I asked if you thought we should replace the washer and dryer."

The sinking feeling in Farrell's stomach got another ping. "I'm sorry. I'm a little distracted."

"No kidding." Karen took a deep breath and let it out. Then she reached out and touched Farrell's forearm. "What is it?"

He put down his fork. For the thousandth time, he wished

he could just tell her everything, but the time for that had passed, and now wouldn't come again until everything was finished. "It's DOJ," he said, not entirely untruthfully.

Karen stared at him for a few moments, then stood suddenly. She picked up her plate, then grabbed his, and marched into the kitchen.

"Hey!" Farrell said. "I wasn't done."

"Well, I am," she snapped back at him. He heard the dishes clatter into the sink. A moment later, Karen reemerged from the kitchen. "Do you think I'm a fool, Tom?"

"Of course not."

"Then why do you talk to me like one?"

Farrell looked at her, confused. "I…"

"You've been distracted for months. You've been acting strangely for months. And you've clearly been stressed out to the max *for months*. So don't try to tell me that all of this is because of DOJ's arrival. They just got here." She crossed her arms. "Tell me the truth, Tom."

Farrell didn't answer. He closed his eyes, then rubbed his palms into them.

"What is it?" Karen asked.

"I can't…"

"You *better*," she snapped. "This has gone past all of the supposed rules of confidential information. If something is having this big of an impact on you, I need to know."

"It's not that easy," he said.

"You think living with you like this is easy? Seeing whatever it is eat away at you?"

"Karen…"

"Tell me, Tom. Is it work?"

"I told you. It's DOJ."

She shook her head, her jaw set. "They may be adding to it, but you've been this way for too long. It's something else."

"I told you what it was."

She hesitated. Then she said, "Maybe it isn't work. A while ago I joked about you having a mistress, back when you were running the Anti-Crime Team. Do you remember?"

"I remember."

"I'm starting to worry that I shouldn't have made that joke. The way you're not talking to me makes me wonder if that's what it really is. An affair."

Farrell laughed, but it came out as a derisive bark. "That's *not* it."

"Then tell me what it is. Maybe I can help."

If Wardell Clint can't help with this, I don't think you can.

"Honey, I am telling you the truth. Yes, I have been stressed out. A lot has happened, and there is a lot of pressure on me. DOJ being here only amplifies that, but I've been dealing with all of the things that brought them here for a while now."

"Like what?"

"I can't tell you."

Karen stood in front of him, her arms crossed. She glared at him in sullen silence. Farrell felt like he should say something, but no words came. So he just returned her gaze, waiting.

Finally, she spoke in a low voice. "In all the years we've been married, you've never told me that you can't share something with me. Never. You tell me it's confidential so that I know never to disclose it to anyone. And then you tell me, Tom. That's what you've always done."

"This is different," he said.

She stared at him a little longer. Then she said, "That's what worries me."

She left him there, at the dining room table. He heard her head upstairs and knew he wouldn't see her for a while. Not that he blamed her.

He was suddenly thirsty. He reached for his glass of water, but it was empty.

Chapter 27

The waitress arrived with their drinks. A Pendleton whiskey for Watson and a pale ale for Curado.

"And your cabernet," the waitress said. She placed a tall glass in front of Édelie Durand.

The three of them nodded to the waitress and she moved off.

They were again seated in the Peacock Room, although tonight they'd gotten a round table near a window. People of all types meandered by outside on the sidewalk. There were young couples holding hands, businessmen and women leaving their offices late, and the wandering homeless who always seemed to be mumbling to themselves.

Durand's thoughts were on her husband, Roland. She hadn't been able to Skype with him before getting together with her team. He had texted to say that he was going to bed early. Unfortunately, Roland spent most of his life in bed now. What that text really meant was that he was going to sleep. She wouldn't get to talk with him until tomorrow morning. That put her in a sour mood.

"As I was saying," Dani Watson said, "when I asked Baumgartner about Tyler Garrett's ambush, he shit a brick."

Durand grimaced behind her wine glass.

"How so?" Curado asked.

"Want my honest opinion?"

"No, I want you to lie to me," Curado said. "Probably like you do to your boyfriend."

"Ouch," Watson said, "but well played. Anyway, I think Baumgartner forgot about it."

"About an officer getting ambushed?" Curado leaned back in his seat. "I don't buy it."

She waved off his disbelief. "He didn't forget that Garrett was shot at. He's not stupid. I'm saying he forgot that the shooters hadn't been found. My question surprised him."

"Doesn't he have someone investigating it?"

Watson smiled. "After he phased out for a moment, he said it was still an open investigation."

"Two years later?" Curado glanced at Durand. "You would have thought they closed it by now."

"Exactly," Watson said. "That's my point, exactly."

Durand lifted her wine glass. She wasn't wearing lipstick tonight so the only smudge on the rim was oil from her skin. There weren't any left-behind kisses. Her mood soured further, and she shifted her gaze to Curado. "Anything about the Farrell interview surprise you?"

He sipped his beer and thought for a moment. "He seemed sort of evasive."

She glanced at Watson before asking, "Sort of?"

Curado smiled. "It was hard to tell if he was being so on purpose. He flipped the interview on me, you know? Started asking about me, my brother the cop, how I could do this job. That kind of stuff."

Watson nodded. "Classic avoidance."

Durand cupped her wine glass in both hands. "Go on."

"Avoidance," Curado muttered as if reconsidering his thoughts on Farrell. "Right. Anyway, I gave him some rope and answered his questions. When I brought it back around, I asked about his relationship with Captain Hatcher. I thought it would be a simple question for us to ease back into the interview with, a softball, if you will, but then he stumbled all over himself. Stammered quite a bit just to assure me there was no problem between the two of them."

Durand set her wine glass on the table. "That's not what Hatcher said."

"Yeah?" Watson said. "What did she say?"

"She said she came up with the idea for the Anti-Crime Team."

Watson chuckled. "Like she invented directed

enforcement teams. The woman sounds delusional."

"She claims she brought the idea to the table," Durand said, "and then Farrell stole it."

Dani Watson's face flattened. "Farrell stole it?"

Durand nodded. "That's what she said."

"The bastard," Watson blurted.

Durand didn't bother to hide her displeasure of her subordinate's cursing.

"Farrell gave her credit," Curado insisted. "He told me the chief assigned it to him, but he gave her full credit. No stammering with that part of his statement."

"Could they both be telling the truth?" Durand asked.

Her subordinates glanced to the other then back to her. "Maybe," Watson allowed, and Curado nodded his agreement.

Durand lifted her glass for a sip then paused. Over the noise of the bar, she heard a song she recognized. It was an old one that always brought a feeling of melancholy to her. As Eric Clapton sang "Tears in Heaven," she fought back the sudden desire to go to her room, crawl into bed, and pull the sheets over her head. She faced the windows and did her best to ignore the music. Passersby did little to distract her from Clapton's heartbreaking tune. When Dani Watson said something that caught her attention, she reengaged with the conversation.

"What was that? What did you ask?"

Watson was surprised at Durand's forceful tone. She carefully repeated her question. "I asked if he thought maybe Farrell felt guilty for stealing Hatcher's idea."

"But he didn't steal it," Curado said.

Dani Watson frowned. "C'mon, you know what I mean. Does he feel guilty for it getting assigned to him?"

Curado shrugged. "I don't know. It's possible. Does it matter?"

Watson sipped her drink then pointed with the glass still in her hand. "It does if he got a man killed with an ill-gotten team. Can't sit well."

"Do you think he lied?" Durand asked.

The question stopped both of her subordinates and they watched her.

"About what?"

"About how he and Hatcher got along?"

"No," Curado said. "And if he did, it was a small one. Maybe to protect their positions. I think he was forthright with everything else. We talked about how he staffed the team, about each—"

"Baumgartner," Watson interrupted, "he told me *he* selected the team personnel. Both can't be telling the truth."

Durand inhaled deeply as the music continued to bother her. "Baumgartner is the chief. Everything his people do are his ultimate responsibility. Perhaps he was taking the position that he would run interference for them. That's not a lie."

"It's not truthful," she said.

"It's leadership," Durand muttered.

"You'd do that for us?" Watson asked.

Édelie Durand glanced between her two subordinates then sipped her wine. The song was thankfully almost over.

Watson watched her with concern. "You okay, Edie?"

"I'm fine," she said. "What about the people? Did Baumgartner or Farrell say anything about the people on the Anti-Crime Team?"

Curado nodded. "I asked why Farrell picked Gary Stone and he said he had just sent him to a surveillance school."

"Did he send him to the school for the team?" Durand asked. "Or was he sent before Farrell knew he was going to be on the team?"

Curado blinked several times but didn't answer.

"That's an important distinction. It would have been an important question, Esteban."

Watson remained silent as Durand leaned slightly toward Curado who bristled at his supervisor's use of his given name.

She continued. "Hatcher told me that Stone didn't have

the experience to be on a team like that. So why was he there?"

"The surveillance school," Curado offered.

"Which brings it right back to my question. Did Farrell send him to the school so he could justify his existence on the team? Or did he realize later that the skill was worth having on the team?"

Esteban Curado shook his head. "I didn't ask."

"So Stone wasn't street worthy," Watson said softly.

Durand nodded as she leaned back into her chair. She breathed a little easier now that the song was over, and the music had moved to something she had never heard before. "Hatcher said the same thing about Jun Yang. That she was inexperienced. Did Baumgartner or Farrell say anything about her?"

"When I asked about her," Watson said, "I thought the chief was going to tell me women can't do police work."

"I don't think he would say that," Durand said.

"Me neither," Curado chimed in.

"I was there," Watson said, tapping her chest. "That's what he was intimating."

"Were you giving him the Dani Watson special?" Curado asked.

"What's that mean?"

"You know what I mean. He might say that if you were kicking the man in his—"

Durand coughed. "Kelly Ragland didn't think she belonged on the team either."

They turned to her.

"The sergeant said that?" Curado asked.

"Why would he say that?"

"He called her a push around," Durand said. "He thought she might have been in a relationship with Gary Stone. The man dished on Garrett and Stone, too. He called them Tango and Cash."

Curado's brow furrowed. "Tango and Cash?"

Watson laughed. "C'mon, Steve. Where's your man card?

Sylvester Stallone. Jeff Bridges."

"Never seen it," Curado said.

"Or was it Kurt Russell?" Watson muttered.

Curado mimed pulling something from his breast pocket and tossing it on the table. "My man card."

Watson raised her glass to him. "They're not a good thing to be compared to," Watson said. "Tango and Cash were hot shots."

Durand pointed at Watson. "Loose cannons. That's how Ragland described them."

"That works," she said.

Curado frowned. "So Stone was inexperienced, but his sergeant compared him to a loose cannon?"

Durand nodded. "Yeah."

"Interesting," Watson said. "Any feedback on Zielinski?"

"Farrell called him experienced," Curado said.

Durand lifted her glass. "Hatcher suggested the same, but Ragland thought him susceptible to noble cause corruption, especially in light of some recent troubles."

"What kind of troubles?" Curado asked.

"The kind Dani will find out about when she stops by Internal Affairs tomorrow," Durand replied.

Curado smiled slightly at her words.

"Noble cause," Watson said thoughtfully. Then she asked, "Did the sergeant use those exact words?"

Durand nodded. "The union president cut him off after that. Watch out for that one if he shows up to an interview, by the way. I got lucky with Ragland since he was a talker, but anyone else might listen to that man's advice. He's suggesting they not talk with us."

The three of them sat quietly for a few minutes. Each lost in their own thoughts. Finally, Watson asked, "So the plan tomorrow? We interview Zielinski and Garrett?"

"Zielinski, yes. Garrett is still last."

"Why last?"

"A gut feeling. A guy gets screwed by the system like he did, he's either going to carry a lot of wisdom or a ton of anger. I don't want our investigation tainted if it's the latter."

Durand said, "Make sure you interview Detective Wardell Clint, though. He shadowed the investigation into Garrett's shooting incident with Todd Trotter. He might have some interesting insights we won't get from the official paperwork."

Curado nodded. "And you, boss?"

"I'm going to talk with a councilwoman Captain Hatcher recommended I speak with." Durand took another sip of wine, thinking. "Keep getting files, too. I want to get as much as we can to take home with us. After this visit, I'm not sure how compliant SPD is going to be without a mandate."

Chapter 28

"It was nice spending time with the kids today." Tiana Kennedy smiled. "Molly makes me laugh."

"She likes you," Tyler Garrett said.

"I like her."

They were seated on the suspended bridge of Twigs Bistro and Martini Bar. The bridge hovered above the lobby of River Park Square. They had a view of not only downtown's Post Street through the large front windows, but the entire mall below. The din of activity added to the ambiance. They had ordered their meals and were each sipping a cocktail.

"Jake really wants to move in with you," she said.

Garrett nodded. "Someday."

"When he's old enough to decide for himself?"

"He's old enough now," Garrett said, "but the courts discourage it until they're sixteen. After that, they can drive themselves around. Then what can you do? There's no stopping them after then."

Tiana frowned. "He's having a tough time with her. I'm not sure he can wait until he's sixteen."

"He say something to you?"

"When you went out, he did. He's not happy. He misses you. He also talked about her new boyfriend."

"He hasn't told me much about him."

Tiana widened her eyes and frowned at the same time. "He's afraid to."

He pulled slightly back. "Why?"

"He thinks you'll do something."

Garrett smirked. "Like what?"

She shrugged. "Hurt him maybe."

"I wouldn't hurt the guy."

"And that's what I told him, but Jake is still worried. He knows how tough you are, and he says this guy isn't so much."

Garrett sipped his drink and glanced down to the crowds milling below the suspended bridge. After getting seated, Garrett had excused himself and gone into the restroom. Standing in front of the sink was a large Native American man in a Chicago Blackhawks jersey, baggy jeans, and Timberland boots. His hands were in the sink, but nowhere near the running water.

Garrett checked underneath the stalls to make sure no one was seated there.

"We're alone," Royal Harjo said.

"This is for you," Garrett said, and held out a wad of bills.

Harjo's hand enveloped the cash and quickly slipped it into his pocket. "Anything else?"

"We're good for now. Unless you've heard from Earl."

"It's quiet out there," Harjo said. "Like the man vanished or something."

"Stay safe," Garrett said and patted him on the shoulder as he left the restroom.

Now, back in the restaurant, he watched customers ascend the three levels of escalators.

Tiana lifted her drink to study it. "I'll also say this. Jake doesn't like that his mom is messing with a white man."

"He's white?" Garrett asked. He pretended a little surprise, but not too much to upset Tiana.

"Yeah and he doesn't like it."

"All right. I'll talk with him."

"What are you going to say?"

"What can I say? His mom can see who she wants to see."

Tiana put her hand over his. "He's a sensitive kid. If you want me to—"

"I'll talk with him," Garrett repeated. "It'll be okay."

She patted his hand. "I'll be here if you need me."

His cell phone rang, and he pulled it from his pocket. "It's Angie," he said and showed her the screen.

Tiana's face hardened. "Perfect timing."

"I'll call her back."

"Better take it now," she said. "Otherwise, she'll keep calling. You know how she is."

Garrett swiped across the screen to answer. "Hey."

"Ty?" Angie said. Her voice was soft, which made it hard to hear above the noise of the mall. "Can you talk?"

"Sure," he said.

Tiana crossed her arms.

"My…the guy I'm seeing…"

"Yeah?"

"Where are you? It's really noisy."

"I'm out. What's going on?"

"The guy I told you about? He was assaulted today."

"Okay."

Garrett looked to Tiana and rolled his eyes, but she didn't smile.

"It happened in one of the homes he has for sale," Angie said. "Can you believe that? It doesn't make sense. Someone jumped him for no reason."

"A lot of attacks don't make sense. Did he call the police?"

Tiana's brow furrowed and she leaned forward. Garrett was sure she was trying to hear his ex-wife on the other end of the call.

"He did report it," Angie said. "Fat lot that's going to do. There's no witnesses. He had to go to the hospital."

"What happened?"

"Fractured occipital bone. Broken nose. A couple teeth were…He's a mess, Ty."

"Is he still there?"

"At the hospital? No. I just brought him home. To my house, I mean."

Tiana mouthed the words, *What's happening?*

Garrett held up a finger as a signal for her to wait.

"I don't mean to sound rude, Ang, but what do you want me to do about it?"

"I was hoping…" Her voice trailed off. "I mean, maybe you could…I don't know, look into it. Maybe?"

Garrett inhaled deeply before answering. "Yeah. Okay. Text me his name."

"Really?"

"And do you have the report number? For the assault?"

"I'll text that to you, too," Angie said.

"Then I'll look into it," Garrett said. "I can't promise anything, but I'll see what I can do."

They said their goodbyes and ended the call.

Tiana's lip curled when she asked. "What was that about?"

"You wouldn't believe it if I told you."

"Try me."

"Her new boyfriend got beat up."

Tiana's eyes narrowed. "Did you have anything to do with it?"

"You kidding?" Garrett said with a laugh. "Why in the hell would I do something like that?"

She relaxed then and their food arrived. As Tiana picked up her knife and fork, she said, "I'll tell you one thing."

"What's that?" Garrett said.

Tiana pointed her knife at him and scowled. "I'm not exactly thrilled that the first thing she does when there is a problem is to call you."

Garrett smiled. For some weird reason, the whole thing made him happy.

WEDNESDAY

Don't compromise yourself—you're all you have.
—John Grisham, *The Rainmaker*

Chapter 29

Ray Zielinski slept fitfully in the front seat of his car throughout the night. Each time he awoke, sometimes only after dozing for a few minutes, he rubbed his eyes and tried to force himself to remain alert for as long as he could. Periodically, he drank the coffee he'd brought in a thermos, mixed with a healthy infusion of Baileys Irish Cream liqueur. The booze made him sleepy, but the caffeine kept him awake, and he told himself the two canceled each other out.

The sky remained black, pierced only by the needle points of stars and a half-shrouded moon. He looked at his watch. The glowing hands told him it was shortly after three. He considered calling it a night. A few hours of real sleep in his bed would freshen him up, and he could be back by midmorning. It wasn't like he was punching a clock here. Clint had no concrete ideas about when Earl Ellis might return anyway.

Zielinski shook his thermos. It was nearly empty. He poured the remains into the thermos cap that doubled as a cup. The last of the spiked coffee filled it about a third of the way.

Drink this. Then go home.

It seemed like a fair bargain.

He sipped the coffee, which was barely warm at this point. That alone should tell him he was over-achieving in his duties as Clint's lackey. But what else did he really have to do? Wait around for Internal Affairs to finish its investigation? For his career to end?

Zielinski scanned the street for the thousandth time that night. Nothing moved. Barely anything had, unless you counted a few people coming home late, or the pair of raccoons he spotted working on a trash can just three houses down. That had at least entertained him for a while, watching the furry bandits try to figure out how to get the swinging lid to stay up. They seemed to be making progress when one of the returning cars frightened them off. It turned out to be the homeowner of the garbage can in question. Zielinski wondered if they knew how narrowly they'd avoided having their garbage can burglarized.

So much had to do with chance, he mused. If he hadn't been sent on a certain call, or if he'd been paying attention while on the way, things would have happened quite differently. Unfortunately for him, fate didn't intercede, and now he was where he was.

Which was screwed.

I'm going to lose my job.

And then what? Go back to the construction work he'd dabbled in? Compete for work with men half his age, for less money and no benefits?

His kids would love that. They already hated him, but at least they couldn't say that he didn't provide. That was about to change.

Or maybe not. He held out some hope that the Internal Affairs investigation would have a few holes, and that Dale Thomas would then punch bigger holes in it. During the review process, he had a friend in Dana Hatcher, who would see things through that lens.

Or would she?

He frowned. Most leaders he'd known in his career drank the company line Kool-Aid at some point. They changed, and usually not for the better. Hatcher always seemed different, but since being promoted to captain, he'd seen signs that she was falling prey to this same path. She was drinking the Kool-Aid, too.

Bottoms up and welcome to the dark side.

The inevitable loss of another good one to the brass made him sad, but he'd seen it so many times that it was hard not to be cynical about it.

If things didn't go his way on the IA front, there was really only one other possible route to salvation. It was that slim chance that had him sitting in his car at three o'clock in the morning, watching a house at the behest of Wardell Clint. Clint had been clear that Ellis was the golden ticket. He could put Garrett at the head of a drug operations ring, and more importantly, as part of the conspiracy to murder Gary Stone.

Zielinski hadn't particularly liked Stone. The officer had been pampered in his short career and hadn't earned it. In the time they spent on the Anti-Crime Team together, all Zielinski saw was Stone emulating his hero, Tyler Garrett.

Some hero.

Zielinski had long held his own suspicions about Garrett. Even so, when Clint had finally revealed all he knew about the man, he was shocked. Shocked at what Garrett had done, and that he'd managed to get away with it so far.

I might have messed up, but at least I'm not dirty.

Garrett was. He needed to be stopped. And if being part of that somehow saved Zielinski's own career, so be it. He deserved a break.

Zielinski raised his cup to his lips, then stopped. A small flash of light caught his eye. It came from the street almost directly in front of Ellis's house. A moment later it disappeared.

He put down his coffee and leaned forward, peering into the darkness. The sliver of light appeared again, lasting for several seconds before it was dampened. A slight reddish glow remained.

Zielinski immediately recognized the tactic. He'd used it himself on patrol at night. Cup the end of the flashlight before turning it on. Spread a finger to allow a little light through, directing it in the desired direction. It was light discipline, straight out of Patrol Procedures 101.

That thought sent a jolt through him. Could it be Tyler Garrett? Clint had theorized that Garrett could be looking for Ellis, too.

He hesitated, watching carefully. The silhouette was

difficult to make out, and race was impossible for him to determine. But the man had the same basic build as Garrett. Or Ellis, he realized. It could be either one.

The light played peek-a-boo again while Zielinski considered his options. Exit the car and try to sneak up on the man? Wait and see if he went inside the Ellis residence? Call Clint?

"To hell with that," Zielinski muttered.

He flicked the ignition key, and his sedan rumbled to life. At the sound of the engine, the man froze for a split-second, then turned away.

Zielinski turned on his headlights and flipped on the high beams. At the same time, he dropped his car into gear and leapt forward.

The man was already running.

Damn!

Zielinski accelerated the half block to where the man had been standing, keeping his eyes fixed on the fleeing silhouette. He lurched to a stop, flung open his door, and gave chase. The first few steps were painful, as the long hours of sitting had stiffened his muscles. But after a half dozen strides or so, he hit his rhythm, pumping his arms and breathing deeply.

The shadowy man ahead of him had made it to the alley that ran behind the Ellis home, sprinting through an unfenced yard to get there. He surprised Zielinski by turning left, away from Ellis's house. If it was Ellis, why didn't he instinctively run to where he felt safest?

Because it's Garrett.

A shot of adrenaline zinged through Zielinski. He cut around the front of the same house, taking advantage of the unfenced backyard to close some distance on the suspect. When he turned into the alley himself, he was only about twenty yards behind the man.

That was all. Twenty yards between him and a saved career.

Zielinski put on a burst of speed. The coffee and Baileys

sloshed in his belly, but he ignored it. He drove forward, pumping his legs like aged pistons.

Fifteen yards now.

"Stop!" He tried to shout the word, but his voice was raspy and breathless. "Police!"

The man kept running.

Zielinski pressed on, finding the energy for another burst. Before he knew it, he was almost within grabbing distance of the man.

"Stop!" he ordered again. His own hoarse voice sounded foreign to him.

In the dim ambient light, he saw the man turn his head and look over his shoulder. He couldn't make out features or the man's expression. The action slowed the suspect's pace slightly, and Zielinski seized the opportunity. He powered forward and tackled him to the ground.

Zielinski's knees scuffed along the hard dirt of the alley. They immediately stung with pain. He grunted but refused to let go as the two of them toppled to the earth with a thud.

The man cursed and wriggled to get free. Zielinski reached up to clasp a meaty hand onto the man's belt. As the man struggled and pulled away, Zielinski kept a strong grasp. He flailed around with his other hand, trying to find purchase on some other part of the man's body.

Suddenly, the tugging against his hand that held the belt seemed to stop. The man's pants had slipped off his waist and down his legs. The jeans pooled around the man's ankles, and he'd risen to a seated position, kicking and thrashing to get his feet free.

"Enough of this," Zielinski growled. He rose up on one knee and lunged forward with his free hand. He'd intended to strike with an open palm but on the way, his hand instinctively curled into a fist. That fist thundered into the man's chest with all the force Zielinski could muster from a crouched position.

The sound of the blow was somewhere between a slap and a thud. The force of it knocked the man flat on his back, where he lay still for a moment. Then he groaned and curled his legs in slightly.

Zielinski let go of the man's belt. He spotted the flashlight where it had fallen from the man's grip and grabbed it. Then he snapped the light on him.

A white man with stringy black hair and a patchy, wispy beard stared up at him, squinting and blinking against the harsh light.

Zielinski almost groaned in dismay. Just his luck.

Not Ellis.

Not Garrett.

"Don't move," he ordered out of habit.

The man put his hands to his chest, rocking slightly. "The hell, man?"

"Police," Zielinski repeated. "What's your name?"

The man moaned, not answering.

"I didn't hit you that hard," Zielinski said. "Now, what's your name?"

"Paul."

"Paul what?"

"Brown."

"Paul Brown?" Zielinski repeated.

"What the hell? Yes, Paul Brown. Why'd you hit me?"

"Why'd you run?"

"I didn't know who you were."

"I told you who I was."

"Not until the end there."

Zielinski replayed the foot pursuit in his head. He couldn't remember when he'd first identified himself as the police, so maybe Brown was telling the truth. Then another thought struck him. He shouldn't have said he was the police. He was on suspension.

"Why'd you hit me?" Brown repeated.

Zielinski didn't answer. He squatted on his haunches, keeping the light shining in Brown's face. "What were you doing?" he asked.

"Running."

"Before that."

Brown hesitated. Then he said, "I locked my keys in my car."

It all became clear to Zielinski in that moment. To be certain, he ordered Brown to place his hands on his head while he did a quick check of the man's pockets. The jeans were still tangled around his ankles. Zielinski found what he expected. A screwdriver and a several pieces of porcelain from spark plugs.

Brown was a vehicle prowler. The porcelain bits were used to shatter car windows, and the screwdriver was for prying. Crude tools, but effective ones.

"What are these?" Zielinski asked, holding the porcelain chunks in his open hand and extending them into the halo of light.

"What are what? I can't see anything."

Zielinski dipped the light slightly. "These," he said, giving his hand a shake.

Brown glanced at the porcelain and shrugged. "I never saw those before."

"I just took them out of your pocket."

"Tried to plant them in my pocket, more like."

Zielinski let out a long, frustrated breath. This was a mistake, all of it. He could only hope that no one on Ellis's block had seen him react, and that his cover remained intact. If Clint heard about this, he'd shit enough bricks to build a wall.

"Where's your backup?" Brown asked.

Zielinski broke out of his reverie. "Huh?"

"It's just you. Where's your backup?"

"Don't worry about it." Zielinski stood up and tossed aside the porcelain pieces. "Pull up your pants."

Brown didn't move right away. Instead, he kept looking up at Zielinski suspiciously.

Zielinski tilted the light so that it glared directly into Brown's eyes again. "Your pants," he said. "Now."

Brown averted his eyes. He pulled his pants most of the

way up, then unclasped the belt, stood and completed the job. As he fastened the belt buckle, he said, "Show me your badge."

"Shut up."

Brown shook his head. "You ain't no cop."

"Yeah, I am."

"Then show me your badge."

Zielinski was almost glad he didn't have a badge to flash, because he knew he would have done so.

Stay out of trouble. That's what Hatcher had told him. She even said it was crucial.

Yet here he stood.

"You ain't got no badge, do you? And I can smell the booze on your breath." Brown sounded more confident every time he spoke. Zielinski knew he needed to do something about that.

"Here's the situation," Zielinski told him. "I can take you to jail for attempted vehicle prowling, possession of burglary tools, and resisting arrest. Or—"

"That's fake," Brown spat, "and so are you."

"This is for real," Zielinski said.

"Then show me your badge, you old drunk."

Zielinski wanted to grab the man by the front of his shirt and blast him with a punch right into his smug face. Instead, he said, "I have bigger concerns than you." He shifted and hurled the screwdriver up the alley into the darkness.

"Hey!"

"I'm keeping this," Zielinski said, bobbing the flashlight.

"You can't do that," Brown objected.

"Go," Zielinski ordered. "Before I change my mind."

Brown scowled, shaking his head. "You dirty piece of crap," he muttered. Then he turned and headed up the alley in the direction he'd been running.

Zielinski followed his progress with the flashlight. He watched as Brown stooped and retrieved the screwdriver he'd thrown, then continued on. Once the man reached the far end of the alley, Zielinski snapped off the light and retraced his own steps.

His car was still where he'd left it, the engine running and the door standing open. He took a moment to be grateful it hadn't been stolen. He got in, dropped the lights from high beam to low, and executed a three-point turn. Then he drove out of the neighborhood. Brown's words burned in his ears.

You dirty piece of crap.

He was done for the night.

Chapter 30

"I'm sorry," Jean Carter said. "I thought she would have been here by now."

Édelie Durand frowned, gave a half shrug, then turned her attention back to her notepad. She'd brought along a couple files and was taking the opportunity to review them.

Durand had shown up at city hall without an appointment and asked to speak to Councilwoman Margaret Patterson. Her assistant, the woman who now stood at the door anxiously watching Durand, had phoned Patterson to let her know she was in the offices of the city council members. Patterson stated she would be there in ten minutes and to find a conference room for them to meet.

That was twenty-two minutes ago.

"I'm really sorry."

Durand glanced up at the woman. Jean wore a muted red dress and her dark hair was cut short. Her hands remained loosely clasped in front of her, yet her eyes couldn't hide her worry.

"It's fine," Durand said. "I showed up unannounced."

"You sure I can't get you something?"

Durand's hand hovered over her file. "I've got everything I need."

Jean turned to leave then stopped. "Excuse me, ma'am. May I ask you something?" Her voice was soft, and her words respectfully chosen.

"You can ask whatever you like," Durand said. "Whether I can answer is a different question."

Jean glanced at her hands then asked, "Is this about Gary?"

Durand put down her pen. "Gary Stone?"

She nodded.

"He was your…?"

"Friend. He was my friend."

Durand leaned back in her chair. "His death is partially why we're here. I can tell you that much."

Jean gnawed on her lip then nodded. "That's good."

"Why is that?"

"Because I don't want him forgotten."

"He won't be," Durand said. Thoughts of her husband flashed through her mind. She'd been able to talk with him for a few minutes that morning. "Especially if you keep remembering him."

Her eyes suddenly glistened. "That's my worry, you know? I mean, someday, not right away or anything, I'm going to wake up and not think about him. Maybe I'll even go the whole day through. I don't want that to happen."

Sadness washed over Durand and she turned back to her notepad. Images of her husband alone in his bed played in her head. The cancer slowly eating him while she helped save another city that didn't want to be saved. She lifted a trembling hand to cover her mouth.

"Sorry to keep you waiting." A woman brushed past Jean as she hurried into the room. She wore a green pantsuit with a black blouse. "I'm Margaret Patterson." She thrust her right hand out as the left tossed a leather briefcase onto the conference room table. "My friends call me Maggie."

Durand remained seated while she shook Patterson's hand. She tried to ignore the waver in her voice as she introduced herself.

Patterson smiled broadly then jerked her head toward her assistant. "Did Jean talk your ear off?" The councilwoman scanned the table. "Jean, are you kidding me? Why haven't you gotten Mrs. Durand a coffee or water?"

"She didn't want—"

"You want a coffee or something?" Maggie asked Durand.

Durand thought briefly about correcting the councilwoman's inappropriate use of her gender title.

Instead, she shook her head and muttered, "I'm fine."

Patterson dropped into a chair. When she looked up, she said, "Close the door, Jean. And bring me an espresso. Oh, and something to eat."

Jean appeared slightly embarrassed and smiled awkwardly toward Durand. When she faced the councilwoman, she asked, "What do—"

Patterson lifted her palms and made a face of mockery. "Make a decision."

The assistant lowered her head and backed out, closing the door as she went.

"A nice woman," Patterson said, "but she's taking longer to acclimate to her role than I would have expected. Anyway, thank you for meeting with me. Dana said to expect your call. I figured we would have set an appointment or something."

"I don't have much time," Durand said. "My schedule has to be flexible."

Patterson tapped the table. "Totally understand. Totally do. So what can I tell you to help make your case?"

Durand picked up her pen. "My case?"

"You're here to build a case for a consent decree, right?"

"We're determining if one is needed. We hope that it's not."

"What do you mean?"

"It's in everyone's best interests that a police department conducts their business appropriately without our intervention."

Patterson smirked. "But this department *needs* a consent decree."

Durand crossed her arms. "Why do you say that?"

"Because the chief is out of control."

"Baumgartner? What has he done that's—"

The councilwoman laughed. "Did you hear about the Bethany Rabe thing? About how he and the mayor covered up a rape accusation? I should have Jean bring down my file on that. You should see it. I've got all the newspaper clippings from it. When Jean returns with my coffee, I'll send her back up for it."

"No need. We have a file on that incident."

"There you go," Patterson said with a clap of her hands. "There's your decree, right there."

Durand shook her head. "That's not enough. We need to show a repeated pattern of behavior concerning civil right violations."

"Civil rights?"

"That's correct."

"But Baumgartner acts with impunity."

"Impunity?" It was Durand's turn to smirk. "How so?"

"The mayor is afraid of him. He doesn't hold him accountable."

"Afraid of the chief of police?"

"Yes," Patterson said.

"I've met the mayor. He doesn't seem afraid of much. And according to news reports, he suspended the chief for three days after what happened—"

"He had to do *something*," Patterson said. The exasperation was clear in her voice. "Otherwise, he would look weak. He had to show he had a grasp on Baumgartner's leash. But it was all for show."

Durand didn't appreciate her analogy. "If you're worried about him so much, can't the council remove Baumgartner?"

"No," she said. "He serves at the pleasure of the mayor."

Durand shrugged. "That's not worthy of a consent decree."

"What about him not promoting women?"

"Explain."

"That's a civil rights issue, right?" Patterson tapped the table repeatedly. "There's a distinct lack of women being promoted over there."

"The imbalance—"

"Exactly," Patterson interrupted. "That's exactly what I'm talking about—the imbalance."

Durand was about to explain that she'd already spoken

with Captain Hatcher about this very issue, but the councilwoman's enthusiastic interruption revealed her bias. Therefore, Durand decided to push on the other side of the issue and see how Patterson would respond.

"The imbalance is an issue for civil service to address. The Justice Department will step in if clear discrimination is apparent."

"Your job is to find problems like this and fix them."

"Just because there's a disparity in women supervisors doesn't mean there's an inequality in opportunity. We'd have to look at a multitude of factors. Such as, how many women applied for promotion? How did they score on their tests? What are the—"

"Maybe," the councilwoman interrupted again, "the tests are biased toward men. Ever think about that?"

Durand took a deep breath. "Of course, we have."

Patterson shook her head, sighed, then threw up her hands. "If you're not here to help put this department in line, then what are you here for?"

"I'm here for the truth," Durand said and closed her folder.

"What are you doing?"

"Thank you for your time," she said and stood.

"That's it?"

"That's it."

"We've barely spoken for five minutes."

"I've gotten what I've needed."

"Listen, lady—"

Durand scooped up her files and notepad.

"I didn't bust my balls—"

She stepped toward the conference room door as Patterson's voice rose.

"—to get down here just so you could—"

When the door swung open, Jean Carter stood there with a cup of coffee and a muffin in her hand.

"—walk out on me in the middle—"

"It's over?" Jean whispered.

"For me," Durand said and stepped past her.

"You kidding me?" Patterson yelled from the conference room.

Jean's mouth slowly opened.

Durand muttered, "Good luck."

"Waste of my damned time!" the councilwoman shouted.

The deputy chief didn't bother to turn around as she headed toward the elevators.

Chapter 31

William Jefferson Cardwell stuck out his hand and Tyler Garrett shook it.

"Wish this could have been under better circumstances," Cardwell said with a slight lisp.

Garrett glanced back as Angie slid the glass door closed to leave the two men alone on the deck. Her smile was kind before she turned to deal with the kids.

"Yeah," Garrett said, turning toward the white man who patiently waited to sit at the picnic table.

Cardwell's face was messed up. The left side was badly swollen, and his eyes were darkened like a raccoon's. Several bandage strips were taped across the bridge of his purpled nose. His lips were cut in several places and when he spoke, two of his upper teeth on the left side were missing.

It looked like he had been in a car collision while not wearing a seat belt.

Royal really did a number on him. Might have to give him a bonus.

When Cardwell started to sit, Garrett moved toward the deck railing. This caused the man to pause mid-squat with his eyes firmly on Garrett. Even though he was physically uncomfortable, Cardwell had remained standing out of politeness.

Garrett stared into the backyard where he used to play with Jake and Molly, where he had invited his department buddies over for beers, and where he once made love to Angie under the stars. Now, it looked different somehow. Almost like a stranger's yard.

He fought back a smile as Cardwell straightened. The man had decided to wait on sitting.

"Angie and I appreciate you looking into this."

The lisp sounded ridiculous. It was probably only temporary from the cut lips and broken teeth, but Garrett hoped it was permanent. He couldn't see Angie dating an older white guy with a lisp.

Tyler Garrett nodded at Cardwell's comment, but continued looking into his former yard.

Why was she with this jerk off? Was it because he had money?

Garrett had money when he was with her. She didn't know about it because he wanted to keep her safe from his other life. If he told her about the money, would she still be with him?

"Guy did a real number on me," Cardwell said. He sat now, politeness be damned.

That irked Garrett, truth be told.

Just for that, he should turn to the man and tell him about banging Angie in the middle of this same backyard. He could explain how he clamped a hand over her mouth to muffle her catlike moans because he feared the neighbors might hear. He could share how they giggled like teenagers afterwards as if they had just gotten away with something naughty. Then Garrett wondered if it would bother Cardwell to know that about his new girlfriend—*his* ex-wife.

The way Cardwell looked expectantly up to him, he doubted it.

Garrett moved his neck to the side and popped it. The man would probably be one of those understanding types. The kind of guy who would say the woman had a life before him and none of it mattered now. Weak mother—

"Is there anything you need…?"

"Need?" Garrett asked. "From you?"

Cardwell seemed taken aback. "Like the phone number of the guy who set the meeting?"

"You already reported it."

Besides, Garrett had broken that burner phone and thrown it into the trash. That number was about as worthless as

Cardwell had been in his fight.

"Right," the white man said. "So you read the report?"

"I did. As I told Angie, I'm not sure what I can do, but I'll ask around."

"Who will you ask?"

Garrett leaned an elbow on the deck railing. "Excuse me?"

"I didn't mean any offense. I was only—"

"I'll ask lowlifes and mopes. Who do you think I'll ask? I doubt they're people you know."

Cardwell looked chastised and he turned away. Garrett glanced toward the sliding glass window and realized Cardwell was examining their reflections.

"Listen," Garrett said, "this is weird."

"Weird?"

"You're seeing my wife."

"Oh, hell. I thought you two were divorced."

Garrett sniffed. "We are. Force of habit. Still weird seeing someone new in my house. Thinking about you in my bed."

Cardwell's complexion, the parts that weren't bruised or broken, blanched. Garrett thought the man might vomit. "I didn't think of it that way," he said.

"It's fine," Garrett muttered, even though he didn't mean it. He pushed off the railing and moved toward the door. "I'll ask around."

"Angie said," Cardwell blurted, but he never finished his thought.

"Said what?"

"She said I should get a gun."

Garrett shook his head. "Don't get a gun," he said as if talking to a small child.

"But you have one, right?"

"Sure."

"You carry it with you?"

"All the time." He reached behind his back to touch the gun tucked into the back of his pants. He didn't pull it out, though. Cardwell seemed scared enough just by the motion.

"But I…I shouldn't get one?" he asked.

Garrett asked, "Can you fight?" but he knew the answer.

Cardwell pointed up to his face. "This is why I want the gun."

"So, someone comes up to you, threatens you, and you pull out the gun. They'll take it away from you unless you can fight. Then you get killed with your own gun."

Cardwell looked away.

"I'm not trying to make light of what you went through. I'm trying to help you survive."

The white man rubbed his hands together.

"Be smart. Don't do things that will get your ass beat."

Cardwell turned back to Garrett. "What did I do to deserve this?"

"I don't know, man. Maybe do some soul searching. Figure out who you might have ticked off."

"But I didn't tick off anybody."

"I don't know," Garrett said with a wave of his hand. "Maybe it was karma."

"Karma?"

He shrugged. "Maybe you're paying the price for something you did in a previous life."

"Oh, man," Cardwell said. He bowed his head and stared at the deck floorboards. "I hope not."

Garrett frowned. Seriously? What the hell did Angie see in this guy?

He left him then and stepped into the house. He slid the glass door closed, not bothering to see if Cardwell followed him.

Garrett hugged his kids and kissed them goodbye. Jake mumbled something he didn't understand. He was too distracted to find out what he wanted.

Angie's eyes were on the white man sitting alone on the deck and not him.

That pissed Garrett off.

Jake pulled at his dad's hand.

I should have messed Cardwell up worse. We should have had this conversation up at the damn hospital.

Jake mumbled something again.

"See you around," Garrett muttered to his ex-wife, but she didn't turn to look at him. He headed toward the door as his son stood silently watching.

Angie absently hollered "thank you" as he stepped through the front door, but she didn't bother to follow him outside and ask what was wrong.

That bothered him.

The whole thing bothered him.

And *that* pissed him off.

Chapter 32

The first two things that Wardell Clint noticed about the Liberty Lake Police Department headquarters was that it was much smaller than Spokane's, and much nicer. He supposed that held true as a metaphor for the department itself.

The building was new and modern, but decorated to evoke the quiet, small town charm that had long been the brand of the bedroom community. Many of its citizens commuted to Spokane daily, causing a miniature rush hour that turned the ten-minute drive on Interstate 90 into a thirty-minute trek.

Clint had interacted with Liberty Lake PD on several occasions but had never been to its headquarters. As he walked in, he noticed that there was no security station. He realized that was because the police station stood alone, away from the rest of the criminal justice campus, which included municipal courtrooms and a small detention center. Any felony arrests were booked into the county jail and the cases were adjudicated in Spokane Superior Court.

At the front desk, he was greeted by a familiar face. Officer Jerry Anderson was a former SPD officer who had lateraled to Liberty Lake. Clint had always liked the heavyset officer, considering him a good cop. He reminded Clint of Marty Hill, both in friendliness and competence. Sometimes cops lateraled away from a bigger city because they couldn't handle it, but in Anderson's case, it seemed that the man's laid-back nature was a perfect fit for the style of policing a community like Liberty Lake expected.

Anderson looked surprised to see him. His surprise melted into a smile, but that expression shortened into a slight scowl. Clint knew why there was a run of emotions.

"Hello, Jerry," he said.

"How're you doing, Wardell?" Anderson's tone wasn't warm but remained polite.

"I'm still at it," Clint replied. "They've got you working the front desk now?"

Anderson lifted his left arm. He wore a brace encompassing his hand and forearm. "Light duty, until this heals."

"What happened?"

Anderson smiled slightly. "I punched a guy."

Clint raised his eyebrows. "Why? Did he cut in front of you in the buffet line?"

Anderson chuckled. "Nice one." He patted his belly. "I was down fifteen pounds before this happened. Sitting here on my ass all day, I packed it right back on."

Clint didn't respond, waiting for the story he knew was coming. Every cop he knew loved to tell tall tales. He expected Anderson wouldn't brag, though. He didn't need to. Despite his appearance, Anderson was as strong as a bear. Clint had seen him in action on two occasions and had been impressed.

Anderson surprised him, neglecting the opportunity to jump into a war story. "I hit him in the forehead," was all he said. "Broke my hand. Good thing it wasn't my gun hand, or I'd be sitting at home on medical leave."

"The pay's the same."

"I'd go crazy sitting around doing nothing. Anyway, why are you here, Wardell?" The slight suspicion had returned to his eyes.

"I need to see Detective Rogers."

Anderson looked at him. "I don't know if that's such a good idea."

"Why not?"

"He doesn't like you."

"No one likes me." Clint spread his hands. "Otherwise they wouldn't call me names behind my back, right?"

Anderson looked conflicted. Then he said, "I think he's still mad at the way you stepped on his homicide scene."

"That was two years ago."

"He holds a grudge." Anderson was quiet for a moment. Then he added, "I was a little mad at you, too, if you want the truth."

"I'm sorry," he said, and he meant it. Jerry Anderson was a good guy and a solid cop, and Clint's actions that day had taken advantage of both of those traits.

"I believe you," Anderson said. "I thought a lot about it after you lied to me. Eventually, I decided you were just upset. It was one of your friends who was shot, right?"

Clint blinked. Butch Talbott was the furthest thing from a friend of his, even *before* he discovered the detective was dirty.

"Anyway," Anderson finished, "I tried not to take it personally."

Clint nodded. "I'm sorry," he repeated.

"I know," Anderson said. He stood up, affixing a *Be Right Back* magnet to the front of the desk. "Come on. I'll take you back to him. I think he's in-house."

Clint followed. He doubted Detective Alan Rogers left the comfy confines of his desk chair for much besides lunch or a manicure, but he kept his opinion to himself.

Anderson used his ID card to lead him through two sets of doors and into a typical office area. The furniture and computer equipment looked newer than Clint was used to, but everything else seemed familiar.

"His desk is in the small office there, next to the sergeant's." Anderson pointed.

"Thank you," Clint said.

"You want me to hang out for a few minutes?"

"Why?"

Anderson shrugged. "I dunno. Just in case. Or to walk you back."

Clint shook his head. "It'll be fine."

He walked toward the small office. The door stood open, so Clint didn't bother knocking. Rogers spotted him as he entered and hurriedly shut down the window he was looking at on his computer screen. The glimpse Clint caught looked to him like YouTube.

"What do you want?" Rogers asked, masking his surprise with a sneer.

"I want to talk about the Butch Talbott homicide."

"Why? You didn't finish stomping all over my case last time you were here?"

Clint clenched his jaw. With an effort, he said, "That was unfortunate. It shouldn't have happened."

Rogers sat back in mock astonishment. "Well, will you look at that? The mythical Honey Badger is apologizing to little old me? Who'da thunk it?"

Clint ignored the jibe. "Your case is still open, correct?"

"Homicides always remain open until solved. You know that."

"And you haven't solved it?"

Rogers narrowed his eyes. "What's that supposed to mean?"

"Nothing. It's a question."

Rogers continued to stare at him, as if looking for additional meaning. Then he said, "No, I haven't solved it yet. I can't even say for sure it's a murder. It could be justifiable homicide."

"Because the shooter acted in self-defense."

"May have," Rogers corrected. "If you believe all the witnesses."

"Why would they lie?"

"Why does anyone?" Rogers leaned forward. "I won't know for sure until I can identify the mysterious black male everyone saw but nobody knew."

"No movement on that front?"

"Not yet. I have a theory. You wouldn't like it, though."

"What's your theory?"

"No." Rogers shook his head. "First, you tell me why you're here."

Clint let it go and moved on to his request. "I'm interested in the bullets from your scene."

"Which ones?"

"The ones fired by your mystery man."

"Why?"

"I'm wondering if they might match up to a different case. One of ours."

Rogers leaned forward further, his interest piqued. "Which case?"

"Doesn't matter," Clint said. "Unless the bullets match."

"Typical SPD," Rogers groused. "Wanting info but not willing to share."

"I've got no problem sharing if we get a match."

"You've got the gun in your case? Because I don't."

"I know. Neither do we."

Rogers sat back, disappointed. "No gun to match the bullet to? Then why bother?"

Clint stared at him in disbelief. "You're kidding, right?"

"No." Rogers looked slightly unsure of himself. "Matching a bullet to a gun is the point of examining both, right? If you only have one—"

"You stupid amateur," growled Clint.

"What did you call me?"

"Unbelievable. You didn't submit the bullet to the lab, did you?"

Rogers's face turned red in anger. "You can't talk to me like that. This is *my* office."

"Just answer the question—did you send it in?" Clint asked.

"No," Rogers admitted. "Why would I?"

"They can match bullets, too," Clint told him. "Bullet to bullet."

"What?" Rogers suddenly looked confused, his anger faltering.

"A bullet is like a fingerprint. They can match one bullet to another just like they can match one fingerprint to another. You don't need the gun for a bullet to match another bullet any more than you need the person for two fingerprints to match." He shook his head in disgust. "How do you not know this?"

"I…I do," Rogers stammered. Clint couldn't be sure if he was telling the truth or not. "I just didn't see the benefit."

"You didn't see the benefit of finding out if the same gun was used in another crime somewhere else? You didn't imagine how that match might lead you to the shooter in your own case?" Clint narrowed his eyes, peering closely at Rogers. "How many homicides have you worked, Alan?"

"This was my second," Rogers whispered.

"A police officer is killed, and you get the case? Your *second*? Where the hell was the state patrol investigator on this one?"

Rogers cleared his throat. "The state was deferring to the local jurisdiction on their assist cases. Their new chief didn't want them taking over."

"They should have taken this one."

Rogers seemed to recover from his shock. "All right, you made your point. I'll submit the bullet to the lab."

"Give it me," Clint said. "I'll walk it over for you right now."

"It's my case. I'll do it."

"Today," Clint said forcefully.

Rogers scowled. "Yes, today."

Clint pointed a finger. "You better call in whatever favors you've got stacked up over there to get it moved up to the front of the line, too. A police officer was killed, and he deserves better than some damn strip mall detective working on his behalf."

"That's enough!" Rogers stood up. "I don't know who you think you are, coming into *my* police department, and yelling at me in *my* office, but—"

"I'm a working detective," Clint snapped, cutting him off. "Something you wouldn't know anything about."

"Get out!" Rogers pointed at the door. "I've had enough of your holier-than-thou crap. Leave!"

Clint weighed the value in staying longer and decided it wasn't worth it. He'd made Rogers angry enough to want him to leave, and that was enough. If he pushed him any further, he might drag his feet on submitting the bullet.

He turned sharply without another word and walked out of the office. Officer Jerry Anderson was still standing where he'd seen him last, rooted to the spot with a look of disbelief and disappointment plastered on his face.

"I'm ready to go," he said.

Anderson hesitated a moment, then got his bearings. "Okay," he said, and led Clint out of the secure area. When they were past the last door, Anderson turned to Clint. "Why do you always have to make things so difficult, Wardell?"

"I don't make things difficult," Clint said. "They manage to be difficult all on their own."

"No," Anderson said quietly. "They don't."

Clint stuck out his hand. "Thank you, Jerry."

Anderson looked at the proffered hand for a long moment. Then he took it and shook glumly. "Good luck, Wardell."

Clint left the building and headed to his car. Despite Anderson's misgivings, his visit had been a success. He'd convinced Rogers to submit the bullet and managed to aggravate him just enough to avoid having to share any details about his own case. This was an instance in which his reputation had worked to his advantage.

He wondered if he needed to worry about the state patrol getting involved but doubted it. Rogers was right about the new chief's policy of a kinder, gentler approach to assisting agencies. Plus, hadn't he read in the news that the WSP was embroiled in some sort of a jurisdictional struggle with the Seattle-area municipalities? He doubted the agency had the time or inclination to ride herd over a small town like Liberty Lake. They probably saw Eastern Washington as the beginning of flyover country, anyway.

As he got into his car, his phone buzzed. He glanced at the text. It was from Lieutenant Flowers.

DOJ Investigator Curado wants to interview you. Contact him.

Flowers had included Curado's cell phone number.

Clint put the phone down and headed toward Interstate 90. He didn't have time to talk to those crooked jokers just yet. He had more important things to do. With his actions today, he had started a timer. When the bullet analysis was completed, the results would ping both Detective Alan Rogers and Detective Marty Hill that their cases were related. From there, it would be a short road to Tyler Garrett.

He didn't have much time left.

Chapter 33

Captain Tom Farrell changed hurriedly back into his uniform. He was still damp from his shower, and his black dress socks stuck to his skin as he pulled them on. He managed to get fully dressed and run a comb through his short hair.

He'd tried to bleed off some of the nervous energy he'd been feeling by hitting the treadmill during his lunchtime. Midway through his workout, the chief had texted him, asking him to come to his office. Baumgartner didn't like to be kept waiting, and Farrell didn't need one more thing hanging over his head right now, so he cut his exercise short, showered quickly, and got dressed.

As he walked out of the locker room and down the stairs to the main floor, he wondered what the chief wanted. How could things get worse? He'd bungled his interview with Curado, he knew. Maybe that was what the chief wanted to talk to him about. Or had DOJ discovered the off-book investigation he and Clint had been orchestrating for the past two years? This could be his moment of truth.

A terrible thought struck him. What if DOJ interviewed Clint and *he* told them everything?

Farrell had never considered Clint to be untrustworthy, and the man had no love for authority in general and the federal government in particular. But if the detective were faced with a *him or me* situation, how would he respond?

A second thought came to him. Clint might not even require an ultimatum. His single-minded goal of bringing down Garrett was what informed his every decision. If he became convinced that DOJ could help him accomplish that objective, he might be willing to tell them everything, repercussions be damned.

Farrell's stomach gurgled. He knew that would follow shortly with a need for him to go to the bathroom. In the past, he had jokingly used the term "crapping water" to describe someone who was terminally nervous about a situation. He never thought he'd experience it himself.

The worst part so far had been Karen, though. He could deal with the stomachache or the embarrassing trips to the restroom. He could even deal with the fallout of a ruined career, if it came to that. Bringing down Garrett was worth all that. But he didn't want to lose her, too.

When he reached the chief's outer office, Marilyn saw him and waved him through. "He's waiting for you."

Great.

He tapped once on the door and walked in. Chief Robert Baumgartner was seated at his large wooden desk, staring at his monitor. He looked over at Farrell when the captain entered.

"Where have you been? I texted you twenty minutes ago."

"I was upstairs on the treadmill," Farrell explained.

Baumgartner grunted. Then he pointed to the screen. "Have you seen this?"

All Farrell could see was the back of a computer monitor. "Seen what?"

Baumgartner frowned and spun the monitor sideways so that they could both see it. A video player filled most of the screen. Baumgartner adjusted the time slider at the bottom and hit play.

The program was a popular local talk show that fancied itself as Spokane's answer to *Meet the Press*. Baumgartner had appeared multiple times, and even Farrell had gone on once to discuss the realignment of the Investigative Division a few years ago. The host was a local institution who was well respected by most people in the city, though Farrell always thought he was a little on the pompous side.

"DOJ is in the house," the host intoned gravely. "The Department of Justice is here in Spokane, investigating the police department. This is something that many have clamored for in the face of the questionable shooting of Todd Trotter, the mystifying arrest and then exoneration of Officer Tyler Garrett, the police handling of the city hall scandal earlier this year, and most recently, the shooting death of Officer Gary Stone. At the same time, there are others who claim this inquiry is entirely unnecessary and represents nothing more than continued federal meddling." The host paused a moment to let his monologue resonate with the listener, then continued. "I have with me today guests from all sides of this question. First up, retired police sergeant Sam Gallico. Good afternoon, Sam. Nice to have you on again."

Gallico was a lanky man who wore a light blue button-down shirt and a bolo tie. "Thank you. Nice to be here."

"Great," Farrell muttered. "What does Sergeant Judas have to say?"

"Just watch," Baumgartner said. "He's not even the worst of it."

On the video, the host continue to address Gallico. "You've long been a vocal critic of the police department, Sam. Why is that?"

Gallico smiled bitterly. "I spent twenty years in the belly of the beast. That gives a man some perspective."

"To be fair, your perspective has often skewed toward the negative."

"And to be fair," Gallico responded, "so have the actions of the Spokane Police Department. I mean, just look at the events of the past two years. The Todd Trotter shooting is still a mystery, as far as I'm concerned. An unarmed civilian was shot in the back, but somehow that's ruled as a justified shooting? Then you've got the arrest of Tyler Garrett for drug possession, a charge that conveniently went away when the city decided the man was a hero for some reason. After that—"

"Can I jump in here for a moment?" The camera shifted to an elderly white male seated on the other side of the host. A graphic quickly appeared under the man, giving his name as

Bernard Stewart.

"Please do," said the host. Then, for the benefit of the viewers, he added, "Mr. Stewart represents a civic group based out of the Greenwood Retirement Home."

"Community," Stewart corrected. "Greenwood Retirement Community."

The host smiled indulgently. "My mistake. You wanted to comment, sir?"

Stewart nodded his head. He fixed Gallico with a hard stare. "I know you once worked for the police department, Sergeant, and I respect that. But have you ever met Officer Tyler Garrett?"

"No," Gallico admitted. "But I've seen what—"

"I have met him," Stewart interrupted. "I've broken bread with the man, and I've looked into his eyes. And I can tell you that what I saw was a good man doing a hard job for us. A job you don't do anymore, I might add."

"I'm retired," Gallico said. "As I assume you are. I did my time, believe me. But I'm not the point of this discussion, the department is. And for years now, the chief has repeatedly shown a lack of leadership. In addition to the debacles I already mentioned, he was suspended over the city hall scandal earlier this year. And worst of all, another police officer died on his watch—Officer Gary Stone."

"Did you know that the police department is severely understaffed for a department its size?" Stewart asked. "Maybe some of these problems are the result of too few cops on the street."

Gallico shook his head. "They've been beating that tired drum for years now. Too few cops might be a legitimate challenge, but it doesn't cause corruption, and corruption is why DOJ is here. As they should be."

The host turned away from Gallico and addressed his third guest. "Police department staffing is a budgetary matter, and the city council is responsible for the city budget. Joining us is Councilwoman Margaret Patterson. Thanks for coming on the show, Councilor."

Margaret Patterson wore a cream-colored business blouse with a long, thin gold chain. She smiled at the host. "Always a pleasure."

"What do you say to Mr. Stewart's point that the police department is understaffed?"

"I'd point out that the police department is the largest budgetary item for the city after public works. It takes up a significant chunk of our revenue, eclipsing the fire department, parks and recreation, and all of our social programs."

"I heard that Spokane has something like one-point-two officers per thousand citizens," Stewart said. "Portland is over two per thousand, and Seattle closer to two and a half."

"I'd like to see the source for those numbers," Patterson replied.

"They're public record."

"All right." Patterson smiled. "I'm not saying that we couldn't use more police, but there are other concerns that also affect our citizens. We don't have the luxury of staffing at the same levels that Seattle or Portland does. Not if we want to maintain our infrastructure."

Bernard Stewart waggled a finger at the councilwoman. "Based on the potholes I had to deal with on my way down here, I'd say you're not doing that anyway. It's like driving through Iraq or something."

Patterson's smile remained. "Our road crews are working hard to patch those up, Mr. Stewart. But that's my point—we need some balance in the budget. It can't all be police. Frankly, with the size of the police department budget, it falls to leadership to be a good steward of the people's money."

"You don't believe Chief Baumgartner has done so?" the host asked.

Sam Gallico snorted.

Patterson smirked slightly. "My criticism of the chief is as publicly known as Mr. Gallico's. In addition to his colossal failures in leadership on these large incidents, there is the question of how wisely he has spent the funds allotted to him by city council."

"Then find a way to give him more," Stewart asserted.

Patterson and Gallico both shook their heads.

"When someone mismanages resources," Patterson said, "you don't solve the problem by giving him more resources to mismanage."

"Exactly," Gallico agreed. "And let's not lose sight of the reason we're here today. It isn't because Robert Baumgartner might have trouble balancing a checkbook. DOJ doesn't care about that. They're here because of concerns about corruption. And I think their concerns are valid."

"Councilwoman Patterson, do you agree?"

Patterson kept her expression neutral. "I also have concerns. If the Department of Justice is the right vehicle to resolve those concerns, then I am in support of that."

The host nodded sagely. "That brings us to our final guest, Councilman Cody Lofton. Welcome, Councilor."

Lofton looked ten years younger than he actually was. He was impeccably dressed in a stylish suit and appeared relaxed when he smiled slightly at the host. "Thanks for having me."

"Your stance on this, sir?"

"Simple," Lofton said. "I think we should withhold judgment until we see what DOJ finds during their inquiry." He opened his hands and held them up. "Unless you have an agenda, what other stance is there at this point in the process?"

The host seemed to sense conflict brewing and stirred the pot. "We've heard three other stances from my other guests. Are you saying that they all have an agenda?"

"No," Lofton said smoothly. "All I am saying is that the most reasonable thing we can do is allow this inquiry to run its course. If DOJ determines there is a need for further investigation, our stance should be to cooperate—no, to *facilitate* that investigation. If, on the other hand, they determine that there is nothing to be concerned about, then that is a nice reassurance to have about one's own police department, isn't it?"

The host seemed mildly disappointed at Lofton's answer. He tried a different tactic. "Do you agree with Mr. Stewart that SPD is understaffed?"

"Yes," Lofton said without hesitation. "But I also agree with my colleague that our budgetary considerations can't be single-minded. We have to balance the varied needs of our citizens. I'd love to put another dozen cops on the street tomorrow, but not if it means shutting down city-subsidized daycare for single moms who need that service to be able to work. It's a difficult balancing act. When you come right down to it, I think the real answer is fostering economic growth that increases our city revenues so that everyone benefits."

"So you want to raise taxes?" Stewart accused.

"Not necessarily, but—"

Baumgartner hit the pause button. "It goes off the rails for a while after that, with a bunch of tax and spend versus free market blather. They eventually get back on track, but then it's mostly Gallico and Patterson taking potshots at me." He spun his monitor back into place. "That woman hates my guts."

"Dana's friendly with her. Maybe she could talk Patterson into easing off a little."

Baumgartner considered. "Maybe. It's possible that it's not personal with Patterson, only political."

"Speaking of politics," Farrell said, shaking his head, "Lofton was chief of staff to Mayor Sikes during the Garrett shooting. How does he get away with not answering questions about that? From what you've told me, he was behind all of the flip-flopping the mayor did."

"He claims Sikes has executive privilege and won't discuss any specifics concerning his time as chief of staff."

"Is that true?"

"It is."

"Then the mayor should make a public statement releasing him from it. Then Lofton would have to answer a few hard questions of his own."

Baumgartner stared at him in disbelief. "Tom, what are you thinking?"

"What do you mean?"

"The mayor can't relinquish executive privilege piecemeal. It's an all or nothing thing, like pleading the Fifth Amendment."

"Oh." Farrell hadn't realized that.

"There's no way Sikes wants to give Lofton free rein to spill all his dirty little secrets. Especially not while he's trying to get term limits rescinded." Baumgartner looked more closely at Farrell. "Did that not occur to you?"

"I guess not."

Baumgartner watched him for a moment longer. Then he asked, "How'd your interview with DOJ go?"

"Fine," Farrell said immediately, his stomach tightening.

"Who interviewed you?"

"The Hispanic guy. Curado."

"I got the snippety blonde," Baumgartner said. "What did they dig away at?"

"Garrett's shooting," Farrell answered. "And the Anti-Crime Team, of course."

Baumgartner scratched his chin. "That's pretty much what they came at me with, too."

"It makes sense that they would focus on that," Farrell said with a confidence he didn't feel. "A cop was killed."

Baumgartner made a vague sound of agreement. Then he gave Farrell an odd look. Farrell couldn't be sure, but he thought there was a hint of suspicion in the chief's gaze. "They hit on something else that had to do with Garrett, too."

"What's that?"

"His other shooting. Trotter."

Farrell felt sweat prickling under his arms and beneath his hair. "Why? The county investigators did that investigation, and the DA ruled it justified."

"I know that. We were both at the meeting in the mayor's office, remember?"

Farrell did. That had been his only true chance to come

forward with what he believed about Garrett at the time, but it was swept away almost immediately as the mayor orchestrated the outcome he desired most. Butch Talbott became a fallen officer instead of a crooked cop, and Tyler Garrett was enshrined as the hero of an apologetic city.

"It's not the justification of the shooting they were curious about," Baumgartner continued. "They asked me about the ambush."

Farrell swallowed. Sweat ran down his sides. "What about it?"

"That smartass little millennial investigator asked me a question I didn't know the answer to, and that's never a position you want to be in as chief." He kept his eyes on Farrell. "She asked about the status of our investigation into who the shooters were in that ambush."

"It was the county's case," Farrell said weakly.

"So it's still open? They're still looking for the shooters?"

"I don't believe so. They ran down every investigative avenue on that angle, but the results were inconclusive."

"Inconclusive? Yet they closed the case?"

"They were focused on the shooting and the death of Trotter, and whether there was any criminality in that. Who tried to kill Garrett was secondary, and in the end, there just wasn't an answer."

"Which means that those shooters are still out there." Baumgartner tapped the desktop with a thick finger for emphasis. "They tried to assassinate a police officer and they are still out there."

No they're not. Because Garrett shot Talbott in Liberty Lake and according to Clint's theory, he also forced Justin Pomeroy to kill himself in his own kitchen.

"Tom?"

Farrell cleared his throat. "I suppose you're right."

"And you're okay with that?"

"No," he answered firmly. "I'm not."

"If the county gave up on that angle, why didn't we pick it up? Once the question of Garrett's shooting was deemed as justified, there shouldn't have been a conflict of interest anymore."

Farrell considered the question. The real answer was that he and Clint had done exactly that, but all of it off-book. Once the mayor dictated the official history of events in that meeting, the threshold to prove a different truth rose significantly.

Baumgartner was looking at him with a slightly confused expression. Flummoxed, Farrell struggled for an answer. His hesitation seemed to irritate the chief.

"Are you telling me that we have no one looking into who those shooters were? No one looking at the attempted assassination of one of our own?"

Farrell swallowed. Sweat had beaded on his brow, and now streamed down his temple. "No, sir."

"I have to say, Tom...I think you dropped the ball."

Farrell didn't reply. Couldn't. The cognitive dissonance of being reprimanded for not doing what he secretly *was* doing made his head hurt. That he may still have bobbled the ball in that effort wasn't lost on him, either.

"Though I suppose I did, too," Baumgartner said, his tone conciliatory. "We'll need to regroup and get on this, as soon as DOJ is out of our house."

"Yes, sir."

The chief leaned back in his chair, steepling his fingers. "I don't know, Tom. What do you think?"

Farrell cleared his throat again. "I'm afraid you're going to have to be more specific, Chief. Which part?"

Baumgartner scowled, then sighed. "I'll make it simple. Do you think we have a corruption problem in this department?"

"No." Farrell's answer came easy. He didn't see systemic corruption. He saw three bad actors—Garrett, Talbott, and Pomeroy. Their corruption was extreme, but isolated. It had certainly touched others and affected them, but it wasn't an agency-wide problem.

"Neither do I," Baumgartner agreed. "But do you think

DOJ will see a corruption problem?"

Farrell considered the question for so long that the chief finally cocked his head expectantly. With some reluctance, Farrell answered. "I think they will. They are already looking through a lens of expectation that it exists. Enough bad things have happened for them to decide that the dots connect, whether they do or not."

Baumgartner nodded slowly. "I think so, too." He sat forward and looked at Farrell. "That makes it our job to do what is best for the department."

"What's that?"

"We ask for help."

Farrell blinked in surprise. "You're...you're going to *ask* for a consent decree?"

"No," Baumgartner said. "But there's another option. I can ask for their help in the form of a technical assistance letter. It's a formal, nonbinding letter, offering us suggestions in a variety of areas. Policy, procedure, and so forth. If we adopt most of those changes, it might be enough to keep them at bay, and avoid a consent decree."

"It sounds like a risk."

"Life is a risk," Baumgartner said. "But a TAL is far better than a consent decree. We can cherry pick the best recommendations from their list, the ones that really will be beneficial, and implement them. It'll be a lot of work for command staff, but it keeps us from being wholly taken over by DOJ. And we might even be able to find a way to get some federal grants in the process."

Farrell digested the information, not speaking.

Finally, Baumgartner said, "What do you think?"

Farrell cleared his throat again. "It sounds like a great idea, Chief."

"Good," Baumgartner said. "It's going to be a delicate process, but I think we can pull it off. We just need everything to go smoothly until the investigators here finish their visit. Once they get back to Washington, I'll hit DOJ with my request. It should work."

Farrell thought about the Garrett case that he and Clint were trying to bring in. He wondered how DOJ would react to that level of corruption, regardless of how singular it was. He had a feeling their reaction wouldn't be to send a letter with some suggestions.

"Tom? I want your honest thoughts on this."

Farrell smiled weakly. "Sounds good," he managed.

Chapter 34

Ray Zielinski took another nip of Baileys and coffee, watching the Ellis home. As a veteran patrol officer, he had spent plenty of time in the car, but most of that involved driving. This stakeout routine was painful to him. He decided that if this was how detectives worked, he was glad he stayed a patrolman.

Then he realized Clint hadn't been on surveillance at all for the past couple of days. So it seemed that what detectives really did was get a patrol schlub to do their surveillance work for them.

Not that it mattered There'd been no sign of Ellis. He was starting to wonder if there ever would be. Maybe the man had another place to hide out. Or fled the state. But Zielinski was becoming increasingly suspicious that Garrett killed Ellis and buried him in a deep hole somewhere.

He started to think about getting some food. It was well after lunch. These days, he chose his lunch destinations by which one had one-dollar specials. He tried to remember where those were today, and then realized he wasn't sure what day *today* was.

"Good Lord," he murmured, taking another sip of his spiked coffee. "My life is so screwed."

His phone buzzed. He debated not looking at the text, since it was most likely from one of his ex-wives with something snippety to say to him. But this was also the way that Dale Thomas kept in touch, and if there had been an update in his case, he wanted to know.

He flipped open the phone and read the text.

This is D. Watson from Dept. of Justice. Chief's office provided your number. I need to interview you ASAP.

Acknowledge receipt so we can set a time.

"Oh, great," he said, tossing the phone onto the seat next to him. "Just what I need." He knew DOJ wanted to talk about the Anti-Crime Team. What the hell was he supposed to tell them, now that he knew all that he knew? Was he supposed to lie? Spill his guts?

Damn feds.

He wasn't going to "acknowledge receipt," at least not until he'd had a chance to think it over. And get some food. He took a long slug of the cool liquid in his thermos cup and debated his destination again. Before he could decide between a taco and a hamburger, Clint's Impala slid up beside him.

There goes lunch.

The passenger window slid down, so Zielinski turned his own key and rolled down his window.

"Anything?" Clint asked.

"Did I call you, Ward?"

Clint's eyes narrowed. "Is that a no?"

"That's a no."

"My name is Wardell."

Zielinski didn't reply but gave him a sour look.

Clint stared back at him for a few moments with a flat expression. Then he said, "Let's try the door."

"You want me with you?"

Clint nodded. "I'm going to need you to do some knocking over the next couple of days. It'll go better if she already knows you."

"I don't need an introduction from you to talk to some dirtbag's mother," Zielinski said.

"This mother is a grandmother. And she's a nice woman, so we're going to show her some respect." Clint's tone made it clear that he would brook no argument. "Plus, if I vouch for you, then you don't have to show her a badge or ID, which you don't currently have. Now, come on."

Clint raised his window as soon as he finished speaking, pulling forward just past Zielinski's car.

Zielinski sighed. The man was abrupt, but he had a point. Zielinski got out of his car and trudged to Clint's. He opened the door and clambered into the front seat. He noticed that Clint's car was meticulously clean. The interior smelled slightly of Armor All and whatever utilitarian brand of aftershave Clint wore.

Probably Old Spice, Zielinski thought disdainfully. He was an Aqua Velva man, himself.

Clint drove the short distance to the home and parked at the curb. They both exited the vehicle and walked to the door. Clint stood directly in front of the door, something that Zielinski smirked at. Clint saw his expression and gave his head a short shake. "A seventy-year-old woman is not going to blast me through the door with a shotgun," he said.

"No, but her criminal grandson might."

Clint considered Zielinski's words. After a moment, he shuffled slightly to the side.

The door opened and Zielinski got his first look at Aurelia Ellis up close. The expression etched on her regal face was friendly but firm. She wore a loose-fitting tan smock and small gold hoop earrings.

"Hello, Mrs. Ellis," Clint said, in a stilted but friendly voice that Zielinski couldn't ever remember hearing from him before. It was polite…and *kind*.

"Detective," Aurelia Ellis replied, her tone neutral.

Zielinski could smell some sort of spicy dish cooking inside. He tried to peer into the interior of the house, but the entryway dead-ended at a wall, with openings going left and right. All he could see was a coat rack with a pink raincoat, a light blue windbreaker, and a heavy gray overcoat.

His stomach rumbled. As soon as this little dance was over, he was going for some lunch. He decided it would be tacos.

"Your dinner smells delicious," Clint said.

Zielinski tried to keep a straight face. Had Clint just *complimented* her?

"Thank you. It's my mother's recipe. Shall we discuss the

weather next, Detective?"

"That won't be necessary," Clint said. "You know why I am here, ma'am."

"Same reason as always. And like I've told you before—"

"Where is he hiding, Mrs. Ellis?" Clint asked it abruptly, and with unwavering confidence.

Aurelia Ellis stopped for a second, clearly rattled by the question. Zielinski was surprised, too, but even more than that, he was intrigued by her reaction. He'd seen it often enough to know what it meant.

"Detective," she said, her tone wavering slightly, "I don't know what you think, but he is not—"

Clint held up his hand. "Mrs. Ellis, don't. Listen to me. I know he is hiding in the house. Now, you can tell me where and let me in to take him down to the station so we can talk, or you'll force my hand."

Aurelia pressed her lips together. "I don't know what you mean."

"I mean that if it doesn't happen the way I described, then I will be forced to arrest you for lying to me. Then I'll have to call for SWAT to surround the house. When they've done that, a K-9 officer will send in his dog to find Earl. He will find him, Mrs. Ellis. Those dogs rarely fail on outdoor tracks and never in an enclosed space. The thing is, when the dog finds him, he will bite him."

"That's barbaric!"

"It's what the dog is trained to do. I can't say I love the idea, given the way some of these dogs have been used in the past on people like you and me, but I don't get a say in the matter. If the K-9 goes in, he bites. But you *do* have a say in it, ma'am. Earl is leaving in handcuffs with me today. That is a fact. But he doesn't have to get bit by a dog, and your neighbors don't need to get a peep show with the SWAT team surrounding your house."

Zielinski was impressed with Clint's finesse. He wasn't sure how much of what the detective said was true, since he didn't have probable cause to charge Ellis yet. But he was betting that Aurelia Ellis didn't know that.

"You can keep him safe, Mrs. Ellis," Clint said. Zielinski detected a trace of sympathy in his voice. "It's all you can do in this situation, really."

Aurelia Ellis stood in her doorway, her eyes fixed on Clint. Clint stood impassively, waiting for her response. Zielinski readied himself in case she tried to slam the door.

Finally, Aurelia spoke in a quiet voice. "He's in the spare bedroom."

He's here? A surge of adrenaline zipped through Zielinski's chest, sending his heart racing. *How'd he get past me?*

Zielinski shot a sideways glance at Clint.

The detective didn't notice. "Where is that?" he asked Aurelia Ellis.

"Take a right at the coat rack and it's down the hall on the left."

"Is he armed?"

"Of course not."

"Thank you, Mrs. Ellis. Please wait here."

"On the porch?"

"Yes, ma'am. It'll be safest."

"You said you wouldn't hurt him."

"And I have no intention to. But I don't know what his intentions are, ma'am, and I want to make sure you're safe."

Aurelia paused a moment, then stepped out onto the porch. "He's a gentleman, my grandson. He won't fight with you. Whatever else he is, he's a gentleman."

"I hope that's true," Clint said.

He stepped through the doorway. Zielinski followed. He noticed Clint didn't draw his gun, which puzzled him. If this had been a patrol call, they would have drawn their pistols and called out to the suspect.

And how did he get past me, damn it?

Clint took a hard right at the coat rack and started down the hall. As soon as he was out of the sight line from the front door, he pulled his gun from his holster. Zielinski reached down to his ankle holster and did the same, fumbling to remove his small .38 and still keep up with Clint. He cursed under his breath as he almost tripped and fell before clutching the pistol in his hand.

At the bedroom door, each of them took up a position to the side. Clint nodded to Zielinski, who turned the knob and pushed open the door.

"Police," Clint said loudly.

Earl Ellis sat on the edge of the made bed, his hands on his knees. He wore suit pants and a white business shirt, open at the collar. A maroon tie lay atop a suit jacket on the bed next to him.

"Hello, shitbird," Clint said, his voice much lower. He removed a pair of handcuffs from a case on his belt and handed them to Zielinski.

"Stand up," Zielinski ordered sharply.

Slowly, Ellis stood, keeping his hands open and at shoulder height.

"Turn around," Zielinski said. "Now!"

Ellis turned almost leisurely until his back was to Zielinski.

"Down on your knees," Zielinski told him.

"No."

No?

"I said, down on your knees," Zielinski repeated, more firmly this time.

"And I said no." Ellis spoke in flat tone, without rancor. "Do what you have to do, but I don't get on my knees for anyone."

Zielinski didn't hesitate. He gave the man a power nudge behind a knee. Ellis buckled but didn't fall, catching himself by bracing his hands against the bed.

"Hands *up*," Zielinski growled.

Then he felt Clint's restraining hand drop onto his shoulder.

"Just cuff him," the detective said.

Zielinski frowned, but did as he was asked. "Put your

hands on your head," he directed Ellis. When the man complied, he slipped his .38 into his jeans pocket and reached out to take Ellis by the wrist. Ellis didn't resist, and Zielinski cuffed that wrist and then the other behind the back. He performed a meticulous pat down, finding only a wallet. When he'd finished, he gave Clint an embarrassed nod.

"Let's go," Clint said.

They walked Ellis down the hall and out the door, past Aurelia Ellis. The elderly woman didn't speak as her grandson walked past, but Ellis did.

"Don't you worry, Grams," he said. "Everything will be fine."

Zielinski expected Clint to call for a patrol car, but the detective surprised him by stuffing Ellis into the back seat of his Impala. When he closed the door, he gave Zielinski a satisfied nod. "I guess you're done for the day," he said. "I'll call you when I need something else."

Now he was being dismissed. "That's perfect," he said sarcastically.

"What's the matter?"

"I didn't miss him," Zielinski asserted.

"So you say." Clint started around the back of the car toward the driver's side.

"I didn't."

"Maybe not," Clint said. "Our coverage hasn't been perfect. He could have slipped in while we didn't have eyes on the place."

Zielinski thought about the small gaps of time when he hadn't been on surveillance duty. It was possible, he decided. It was a better thought than the idea that Ellis made it into the house right under his nose.

Clint opened his car door.

"Wait," Zielinski said. "How'd you know he was in the house? You sounded so sure."

"I was."

"Why?"

"What did you see on the coat rack behind her?"

Zielinski thought about it. "A pink raincoat, a blue jacket, and a dark gray overcoat."

Clint nodded. "I've knocked on her door a dozen times since Ellis went missing. Every time, that rack held a pink raincoat and a blue windbreaker, and nothing else. Until today."

Zielinski grunted in appreciation. "So now what?"

"Now Mr. Ellis and I are going to have a conversation," Clint said.

Zielinski watched Clint get into his car and pull away. Then he got into his own car and started it up. He glanced toward the house to see Aurelia Ellis still staring after Clint's taillights. Her face was pinched with a mixture of anger and embarrassment, but most of all, disappointment.

He put the car in gear and drove home. He wasn't hungry anymore, but he needed a drink.

Chapter 35

Tyler Garrett sat in the corner of the Starbucks at Buckeye Avenue and Division Street. He sipped his black coffee and kept his eyes on the door. The music in this store always seemed abnormally loud especially combined with the hissing of the espresso machines and the banging of whatever the baristas hammered against the counters.

But Garrett liked the noise for the anonymity it provided him when striving to have private conversations in public places.

When Dale Thomas walked in, Garrett raised a hand.

The union president headed over. He wore a red Nike shirt, gray Adidas shorts, and white New Balance tennis shoes. The shirt was too tight and revealed his soft belly. The shorts drooped past his knees. To make matters worse, the man wore calf-high tube socks.

"Nice get-up," Garrett said.

Thomas checked out his choice of clothing. "What? I'm heading to the gym when I get done here."

"Want a coffee?"

The union president shook his head and sat across from Garrett. "What can I do for you?"

"I'm hoping to get the scoop."

"About DOJ?"

Garrett nodded.

"They're here to conduct an inquiry into—"

"I've heard that line already."

Thomas's eyes narrowed. "That's the official position."

"What I want to know," Garrett said, "is what are they really looking for?"

"In other words, do you have anything to be worried

about?"

"We're all looking out for number one, right?"

"What do you have to be worried about?"

Garrett laughed. "I've been in a couple shootings, man. One's been cleared and I'm still waiting for a ruling on the other. With DOJ poking around, it makes me nervous. Who knows if those feds are going to say I violated the rights of some mope?"

Thomas waved his hands in front of him. "You're overthinking this. Just relax. You're going to be fine. Your first shooting was good to go."

Garrett leaned forward. "And this last one? Do I have something to worry about that?"

It was Thomas's turn to laugh. "For taking out a cop killer? Are you kidding me? They're probably going to give you a medal. And the county detectives aren't going to come out against you even if they thought you might have done it dirty. They wouldn't have the balls. Which means the district attorney is going to rubber stamp it as justifiable."

He frowned. "How the hell would I know? No one talks to me about it."

"Listen. I'll reach out tomorrow and see what's what but believe me when I tell you to relax. That's probably the most righteous shoot any of us are ever going to see."

"You must have heard some of the questions they're asking, right?"

"I sat in with Ragland. So yeah, I heard some."

Garrett's face flattened. The Justice Department might have wanted to interview an administrative sergeant, but it was more likely they wanted to interview him because of—

"It's the Anti-Crime Team," Thomas said. "They're focused on that."

Garrett scratched his neck. "They think we did something wrong?"

"If so, they haven't said anything specific. It seems like they're pushing at the edges of something, though. Maybe they're going after directed enforcement teams around the country.”

“Maybe,” Garrett muttered. Almost as an afterthought, he asked, “How did Ragland do?”

“Talk about a mope.”

“What did he do?”

“He referred to you and Stone as Tango and Cash.”

“The hell is that?”

“From an old movie.”

“Why’s that bad?”

“Because the movie is about a couple of reckless cops who run and gun and get in trouble for it.”

“Huh,” Garrett said. “Ragland really said that?”

“That’s my point. Let me give you a piece of advice. Never compare a cop to some movie character because it makes my job harder. Got it?”

He nodded.

“I’ll tell you this, though. The damage he did to you was minimal compared to what he did to Zielinski. Unbelievable.”

Garrett contained his smile when he asked, “Yeah? What did he do?”

“The dumbass basically pointed toward the IA office and said, if you want to find corruption, go ask about my man, Ray Zielinski.”

Garrett leaned back. Maybe this wasn’t so bad for him after all. If the Department of Justice could find corruption in the form of Ray Zielinski, maybe they would pack up and go home, satisfied in the knowledge that the Spokane Police Department was already on top of it.

“Well,” Garrett said, “Ray did sort of earn the trouble he’s got.”

Dale Thomas shook his head. “There are some people who see a pile of crap heading toward the proverbial fan and get out of the way. Ray Zielinski is the only guy I know who stands in front of it, hoping the breeze will get better.”

On his way home, Garrett drove surreptitiously through Earl Ellis's neighborhood. He wanted to see if either Clint or Zielinski was watching Ellis's grandmother's house. Neither man was there, though.

This gave him pause as it had been days now that either man had been sitting on the house. What had changed?

Had an emergency pulled one of them away?

Or maybe DOJ required them to come by for an interview?

Or perhaps they found Ellis and no longer needed to sit off the house?

He immediately pulled to the side of the road and called Ellis's cell phone. Once again—he lost track of how many times now—the call went straight to voice mail. He hung up.

Then he called Aurelia Ellis's number. It rang repeatedly until the answering machine finally picked up. He listened to her recorded voice until it said to leave a message.

He considered doing so but didn't. A voice message from him would be a physical connection to Ellis. So far, the only thing that truly connected the two men were calls and texts from burner phone to burner phone.

Oh, Ellis knew about the setup of Leon Strayer killing Gary Stone, but there wasn't anything in writing. If the man ever decided to talk, it was his word against Garrett's.

And who was going to take the word of a drug dealer over that of a decorated officer?

Garrett pulled back into traffic and headed home.

Chapter 36

Earl Ellis didn't speak on the way to the police station, which was fine with Clint. He parked near the west doors in a lieutenants-only slot and walked Ellis into the building. Even though interview room one was open, he stuck Ellis in number four. Another detective looking for a place to park a suspect or a witness was less likely to look there. Then Clint returned to his desk for his file. He didn't need it for reference purposes, as he'd memorized the pertinent details. But a thick file was an intimidating image for a suspect to see, and it sent a powerful message.

As he started back toward the interview room, a man in an expensive suit approached. He was Hispanic and although he didn't quite look like a cop, his manner was similar. It wasn't difficult for Clint to guess who he was.

"Steve Curado," the man said, sticking out his hand toward Clint. "From Justice."

Clint stared at the proffered hand but made no move to shake it.

Curado held it there for another awkward moment, then dropped it. "We're conducting a small inquiry regarding a few incidents here in Spokane. I'd hoped to interview you today."

"I can't. I have a suspect in the box."

"Oh." Curado nodded understandingly. "Will it be a long interview? I can wait."

"It's an interrogation," Clint corrected him. "And it's going to take a while."

"How about tomorrow, then?"

"I can't say for sure. I'm busy. I have an overload of cases."

Curado took out his card and handed it to him. "Detective, I am on a short timeline here, and I do need to talk to you. If you can't do it today, it'll have to be tomorrow."

"So the world revolves around your calendar?" Clint snapped. "I just told you I have cases to work."

Curado didn't react. He simply nodded his head and said, "I'll see you tomorrow, then, Detective. Either here, or down in the chief's office."

Clint shook his head in disgust and walked away. Whether he could avoid an interview with the feds was secondary to him right now. He had Ellis, and if he could bring the man in, that would give him Tyler Garrett on a platter.

Ellis sat erect in his chair, waiting patiently for him. Clint unlatched the cuff attached to the man's arm, then removed the other cuff from the rail on the wall. Ellis rubbed his wrist while Clint folded the cuffs together and put them back in the case on his belt.

"What's the charge, Detective?"

Clint sat down. "We'll get to that. I want to talk to you about something first."

"No. Either charge me or release me. Better yet, call my lawyer."

"You're not a lawyer?" Clint asked. "I thought you might be, with all the fancy suits I always see you in."

"A man can't represent?" Ellis asked. "People might take you more seriously if you wore something besides those khakis and a collared shirt from Walmart."

"I bought this at Kohl's."

Ellis smirked.

"It's interesting to me," Clint said, "why a man with no record of employment dresses like he works at a firm downtown."

Ellis gave him a patronizing smile. "Believe me, Detective, if we keep going at it over fashion choices, that's one you're going to lose."

"I'm just asking questions."

"And I'm asking for a lawyer."

Clint shook his head. "No lawyer."

Ellis's smile turned mischievous. "Are you denying me my Sixth Amendment rights, Detective?"

"Fifth, too, you want to get technical about it." Clint leaned forward. "I'm doing you a solid right here. My advice—don't mess it up for yourself."

Ellis paused. His smile remained but Clint could see the gears turning behind his eyes. "I want it on the record," he finally said, "that I asked for a lawyer and you denied me access to one."

Clint pointed up to the camera in the corner near the ceiling. "You see a little red light?"

Ellis's eyes flicked to the camera and back again. "No."

"That's right. This is off the record. No video, no audio. And no lawyer, neither."

"I'm not agreeing to that."

Clint leaned back and crossed his arms. He grunted. "Maybe you're not as smart as I thought you were. I had you pegged as the brains, but maybe you're just an errand boy after all."

Ellis chuckled. "Appeals to my vanity won't work. If I ever end up in front of a judge, I'd rather be an errand boy than a kingpin."

"How would you like to not end up in front of a judge at all?"

"That's my goal."

"I can make that happen."

"So can I."

"Not indefinitely. But I can."

Ellis eyed him curiously. "How?"

Clint flipped open his thick folder. He shuffled through some of the paperwork, though he knew right where the photos he wanted were located. He wanted to emphasize the enormity of his case to Ellis.

When he found the envelope containing the photographs, he tapped them out into his hand. Then, one by one, he put them in front of Ellis, like a dealer dealing blackjack.

Snap. Ellis with Veryl Wooley, handing him a package.

Snap. Ellis with a yet unidentified heavyset black male, receiving an envelope.

Snap. Ellis with Kendra Cattage, receiving an envelope.

Snap. Ellis with a yet unidentified Native American male, delivering a package.

He watched Ellis as he laid each in front of him. The man kept a straight face, but Clint spotted micro expressions of surprise and then worry. That was good.

He held one photo in reserve.

Ellis looked at all four photographs for a long while, then looked up at Clint without a saying a word.

"Nice suits in every shot," Clint said. "I could send these to *GQ*." He tapped Veryl Wooley in one photo. "If it weren't for these underdressed raggedy asses here."

Ellis shrugged. "So you have some pictures of me. That doesn't prove anything."

"It does, actually. It proves association. And it demonstrates your position with the organization. Besides, these aren't the only photographs I have. There are many more."

Ellis managed to seem unimpressed, but Clint caught his tongue start to snake out to lick his dry lips before the man brought it under control.

He's cool. But I'm getting to him.

"What other photographs?"

"I might show you some of them," Clint said. "Or you might have to wait until your lawyer gets them in discovery before your trial. Since you're operating a drug ring, I'm sure the prosecutor will come at you with all kinds of charges. You'll be wearing threads from DOC instead of Hermes."

Ellis shifted slightly in his chair. "If you had a case, you would have charged me already. We wouldn't be sitting here."

"That's where you're wrong," Clint said. "We're here because I want someone else worse than I want you. And I'm willing to give you a walk to get him."

"Who are you talking about?"

Clint frowned. "Come on, Earl. Don't play dumb."

Ellis shook his head. "I don't know who you mean."

"Yes, you do. We both do. And you're in the unique position of being able to trade yourself right out of a prison sentence, if you're not too blind to see it."

Ellis swallowed slightly. "I want my lawyer."

"I already told you—"

"I want a lawyer!"

"NO!" Clint slammed the palm of his hand on the table between them. Ellis jumped slightly. "No lawyers," Clint snarled. "This is just you and me, and we are going to come to an understanding. This run of yours is over. It can end in prison, or it can end with you going your own way. But for that, you've got to give up Tyler Garrett."

"I don't know who that is."

Clint held up a hand and broke eye contact. "Don't say that to me. We both know it isn't true."

"I have no idea who—"

"Everyone in this city knows who Tyler Garrett is," Clint said. "So stop with the denials."

Ellis pressed his lips together but didn't reply.

"You know him better than most, though," Clint said. "The way I figure it, you're his right-hand man. His number two."

"No, I'm not."

"Yes, you are. You run his drug operation. You insulate him. And when he has a problem that needs to go away, you take care of that for him, too."

"I don't—"

Clint slapped the final photograph on the table in front of Ellis. He stared intensely at the man until Ellis lowered his eyes to look at it. Clint saw more micro expressions flutter across his face. Surprise, fear, perhaps even panic.

"That's Leon Strayer," Clint said. "The man with the fishhook scar on his face. And you."

Ellis glanced up at Clint and back to the photo.

"A few days after I took this photo, Leon Strayer gunned down Officer Gary Stone. He was then shot and killed by Tyler Garrett." He tapped the picture of Strayer. "First rule of assassinations. Kill the assassin."

Ellis swallowed. "I…"

"You are party to a conspiracy to commit murder," Clint said. "That's what you are. And that means you get charged just one degree below an actual murder. Some heavy weight there."

Ellis shook his head. "You can't prove that. All you have is a photograph."

"Maybe," Clint agreed. "But that's a long stretch of prison time to wager, isn't it? Even more than the drug conspiracy charges. Though if we roll them all into one, I think we can get to racketeering pretty easily. That brings in the feds and all their resources. Hurts your chances even more."

Ellis swallowed hard. Clint saw sweat starting to bead up at his temples.

Clint wagged his finger at him. "All of this, this massive weight, we can bargain it away, because Garrett is the bigger fish. He's a cop who has dirtied the badge, and that's worth more to me than any three of you."

"I can't," Ellis whispered. "So just book me into jail."

"You're afraid of him?"

Ellis looked away. Then he glanced up at the lifeless camera on the wall. Finally, he looked back at Clint. "There are some people in this world that just don't care about anything but themselves. The value of everything and everyone else is measured only by what that thing or that person offers them. Friends, family, lovers, they only matter as long as they have something to offer or fill some need."

"You're talking about a sociopath. You're saying Garrett's one?"

"I'm saying," Ellis said through gritted teeth, "that people like that won't hesitate when they are threatened. They will kill without a second thought. Without remorse."

Clint leaned forward. "If you know about other murders

Garrett has committed, that can strengthen your position here, Earl. Give you complete immunity."

Ellis shook his head. "You're not listening. You seem like a smart man, so consider this—how terrifying is a smart man who has no moral compunctions?"

Clint thought about it. "We can protect you," he said.

"Oh," Ellis waved his hand at him and sat back. "You really don't get it. We're done here. Get me a lawyer or take me to jail."

Clint was quiet for a few seconds, his mind ticking through his options. He had sufficient probable cause to book Ellis. He might even be able to compile enough evidence by the time the case went to trial for the prosecutor to secure a conviction. But that didn't matter. Garrett was what mattered. And he was running out of time.

Booking Ellis would only strengthen the man's resolve. The trappings of jail were nothing new to him, and they'd only serve to remind him of Garrett's long arm. Clint needed to put Ellis in a situation that would push him the other way.

He had to release him.

But not without painting a picture for him first.

"Earl," he began.

"Lawyer or jail," Ellis said, his voice firm.

Clint glared at him. "You're going to listen to me, or we will take a third option and that's the hospital." He pointed up to the nonoperational camera. "Whatever I *say* happened in here is what happened. You get me?"

Ellis shook his head. "Cops," he muttered. "The same everywhere."

"You've never been anywhere but Spokane," Clint said. "So don't act like you're all worldly. You've got roots here. You've got your false front neighborhood image. You've got family."

Ellis narrowed his eyes at him.

"Yeah," Clint said. "You better start thinking about that. Because once you're back out on the street, I will become your absolute worst nightmare. I will shadow you everywhere you go. I will arrest you for every little violation. You'll have a new arrest warrant every week. Not only that, I'll bring a horde of cops to your Gram's house with a search warrant and tear the place apart every three days. I'll wait until the two of you are in church, sitting in the front row worshipping, and I'll slap the cuffs on you for one of those chippy warrants right in the middle of a hymn."

"That's harassment," Ellis said, but his voice lacked conviction. Clint could tell he was envisioning what Clint had described.

"That's going to be daily operating procedure for me and you. And it's just the beginning." He motioned toward the photographs in front of him. "How solid do you think that crew is? When I snatch every one of them off the street, how many will roll up on you? Half? All of them? Because all I need is one, Earl." He held up a finger for emphasis. "All I need is one."

"You're crazy," Ellis said. "My lawyer will sue."

Clint scoffed. "Sue me? Get in line." He shook his head slowly. "Earl, this is the endgame. And you have to decide whether you want to talk or be talked about. I can bury you. It won't even be difficult. But you've been blessed with the opportunity to save yourself and your Grams all of that trouble. And here's the truly ironic part. All you have to do is tell the truth."

Ellis was quiet again. When he opened his mouth to speak, Clint read the denial in his face. He held up his hand to stop him.

"We've talked enough," Clint said. He removed his business card and reached across the table to tuck it into Ellis's shirt pocket. "I've been nothing but polite to Mrs. Ellis in all my visits to her home, and I've been nothing but honest with you here today. I'm going to do one more thing for you, Earl. One last thing. I'm going to let you go home."

Ellis gazed back at him, a mixture of suspicion and confusion on his face.

"You heard me right," Clint said. "I'm letting you go. I'll

even give you a ride home. You can let your Grams know you're all right. Eat some of that delicious smelling dinner. Her mother's recipe, right?" He leaned forward, lowering his voice and putting an edge in it. "But the clock is ticking, Earl. My offer is good until six o'clock tomorrow night. After that, it's open season."

Ellis sniffed slightly. "And if I call?"

"Then I guarantee you walk."

Ellis looked around the empty room. "Where's the DA saying that? You don't have the juice to make that happen. You're just a detective."

"I've already cleared it with her," Clint lied. The lie didn't matter. Any prosecutor with half a clue would jump at the deal. "She's the one who insisted on the deadline."

Ellis considered his words but said nothing.

"You want to talk now?" Clint asked. "Because I'm ready."

"No." Ellis shook his head. "No, I want to see my Grams."

"All right," Clint said. He'd made his play, and now he had to see it through.

He stood and Ellis did the same. Ellis held out his wrists for the handcuffs, but Clint shook his head. "No need for that."

Ellis dropped his hands to his side.

"We'll be talking again real soon, one way or another," Clint said, reaching for the door. "Whether or not I need my cuffs is up to you."

Ellis didn't respond. He remained silent during the drive back to Aurelia Ellis's home. When Clint pulled up in front of the house, Ellis got out. Clint let him go without a word. He knew he had just pushed a lion's share of his chips to the center of the table. It was a bold move, but he believed it was the right one. He'd know soon enough.

Clint drove away. He turned on the radio and lost himself in the sweet tenor of Coleman Hawkins's saxophone. It almost made the world go away.

Chapter 37

Édelie Durand stood at the edge of the bar and scanned the tables. It didn't take long to find them, as it was hard to miss Danielle Watson's wild gesticulations as she spoke. Esteban Curado sat opposite her, leaning back easily with a beer clutched in his hand. They sat at a high table on the north side of the lounge near another bank of windows.

They'd started drinking without her which was fine. She had planned to be down to the lounge thirty minutes ago, but Roland Skyped her and she wasn't about to let that moment get cut short.

"How's it going?" he'd asked after yet another wet cough that sounded painful.

"It's fine," she said, "but I want to know how you're doing?"

"Fine," he said. "Just fine."

Though separated by thousands of miles, they stared at each other with the aid of technology. "Fine" had been a code word throughout their relationship. Whenever either said it, they both knew it to mean the speaker was in fact, the opposite of fine, but did not want to talk about what was truly bothering them. This would allow them to sweep the problem under the proverbial rug and move on with life.

The few times they actually argued past the initial utterance of *fine* turned out, well…fine.

Durand chuckled. This simple act felt good as it had been some time since she'd laughed with Roland. Her chortle soon became full throated. Roland's face brightened and he joined her in laughter.

Unfortunately, his face quickly pinched, and he hacked. His features purpled as the cough worsened. This continued for several moments.

Durand's fists balled helplessly as she watched her husband struggle.

When he finally quieted, Roland whispered, "I guess I'm less than fine."

She didn't laugh anymore after that.

Danielle Watson noticed her at the edge of the bar and waved. Curado lifted his beer.

As she walked through the lounge, Durand noticed the song playing on the radio was Chicago's "You're the Inspiration." It was a sappy song and she'd always hated it due to that nature, but tonight it hit her. A lump formed in her throat as she walked over to the table where her team sat.

She didn't break stride and swallowed down her emotions. This wasn't a time to let herself wallow. When she arrived at the table, Durand didn't sit. She stood behind an empty chair with her hands on its back.

"We were wondering when you—" Watson said, but Durand interrupted her.

"Did you interview Wardell Clint today?"

"I tried," Curado said. "But he blew me off."

"How so?"

Curado put his beer down. "He said he had a suspect to interview."

"All day? What about Zielinski?"

Watson leaned forward. "I texted him and—"

"Texted?" Durand interrupted.

"*And* left a voicemail. But he never responded."

Durand sighed and lowered her head.

That stupid song, Durand thought, as the whiney Chicago tune continued to play.

"I'm sorry, Edie," Watson said. "We were able to get most of the files we wanted." She slid a file in front of Durand. "That's the Zielinski one from Internal Affairs. It took some negotiating to get it."

"Negotiating?"

"I was joking," Watson said. "They gave it up pretty easy.

I don't think they have a lot of love for this guy."

"We spent some time reviewing that file and the others we requested," Curado said.

"You can review those any time," Durand said. Her finger tapped the Zielinski file. "We're here now. Interviews are the most important thing."

"Can I ask—" Watson said.

"Who I talked to?" Durand snapped.

Watson glanced to Curado who lifted his beer to his lips.

"I talked with Lieutenant Flowers about his recollection of the Garrett ambush. I talked with Marty Hill about the Anti-Crime Team. And I talked with Councilwoman Margaret Patterson."

Both of her team looked down. She realized she'd been too hard on them. She was letting her personal life affect her work life.

And that stupid song was still playing.

She took a deep breath. "I apologize for snapping at you, Dani. You too, Esteban."

"Is everything okay?" Curado asked.

"Everything is…" Durand wanted to say fine, but instead she let the answer and its question fade. "Lieutenant Flowers didn't give me anything and Marty Hill is a company man."

"What's that mean?" Watson said.

"I think he has problems with the way things work, but he wasn't going to tell me what they were. Maybe he would share more during a formal investigation, but since this was informal, we just talked in circles. Smart man."

"And Patterson?" Curado asked.

"I finally understand the hostile environment that the chief operates within."

Watson turned in her seat. "What does that mean?"

"If the man doesn't have a friend in higher places, he might be likely to play the game a different way." Durand shrugged. "I don't know. I'll have to think on that some."

"Aren't you going to sit, Edie?" Watson asked.

"Not tonight. I'm going back to my room after this."

Watson and Curado glanced guiltily toward their drinks.

"Here's the plan for tomorrow," Durand said. "Dani, I don't care what you have to do, but you track down Ray Zielinski. If you've got to interview the man in his bathtub, you do it. Tomorrow's our last day, so we've got to wrap this up."

Watson nodded.

"And you," Durand pointed to Curado, "Get Wardell Clint. Same story as Dani. Sit on his desk, if you have to, but get an interview."

He nodded and pushed his beer to the side.

"As for me, I'm going to Seattle first thing."

"Seattle?" Watson said.

"I've got the first flight out. Five o'clock. I've scheduled an interview with Jun Yang at Fort Lewis."

"Is that necessary, boss?" Curado asked.

"Yeah," Watson added. "You're going to waste half a day traveling back and forth. For what? A rookie?"

"A rookie that several people seemed upset that we asked about. Don't you want to know what she has to say?"

Danielle Watson twisted her lips and raised her eyebrows.

"I'll take that as a yes," Durand said. "And both of you work together on Tyler Garrett. I want him ready for an interview in the afternoon. Start without me, if need be, but get him there by midafternoon. Understand?"

Both mumbled some form of acknowledgement.

Durand tapped the back of the chair. "In that case, I'll leave you to it. See you tomorrow."

"Edie," Watson said.

"Yes?"

"You sure everything's okay?"

She looked at the open and worried faces of her team.

Durand wanted to tell them about her dying husband and how she hated herself for leaving him to battle his illness alone. She also wished she could tell them how much she hated the job for sending her to places like Spokane. But that would mean lying to herself rather than admitting the terrible truth: she was also thankful for being sent to places like this so she could avoid watching the man she loved waste away.

Could they understand that contradiction? Or the guilt that came with it? If she started sharing, where would it end? With the help of a glass of wine, she'd almost surely detail how her family had long ago disowned her for leaving New Orleans to pursue a career in Washington, D.C. And if she did that, honesty dictated that she tell them how she spitefully ignored their repeated requests to reconnect.

She ached to share with them, with anyone, that she would be alone if…no, *when*, Roland passes. Doing so would mean finally admitting the selfish nature of her feelings.

Above all, she wanted to tell her team how afraid she was.

Instead, she said, "I'm fine," and headed for her room.

Chapter 38

When Tyler Garrett quietly slipped out of bed, Tiana Kennedy did not stir. He stood naked and watched her for a moment in the ambient light of her condo. He then turned and walked toward the windows that overlooked the street. There wasn't much activity down below. Not many people moving. An occasional car drove by.

Regardless of what his eyes told him, he knew that something was occurring out there. It involved him. He was sure of it now.

His gut told him that Earl Ellis was back in town. He wasn't positive, but it felt like it. And if he was right, the man had not contacted him yet. That was troubling.

Garrett would have expected the man to reach out immediately.

Had Clint and Zielinski gotten to him? And how would he know if they had? Clint wouldn't be stupid enough to have someone transport the man anywhere. Doing so would require a CAD notification, thereby putting Ellis's name in the system for everyone to see.

Maybe Clint would do that just to spook Garrett, to mess with his head. He would have to check call histories tomorrow to see if anyone had contact with Ellis.

But if Ellis *was* back in town and Clint *hadn't* gotten to him yet, why wasn't the man reaching out to Garrett? What was he up to?

Was he preparing to turn rat?

No, it still didn't seem like Ellis. The man was harder than that.

But what seemed more likely for Ellis to do would be to make a play for Garrett's network, the fledgling empire he had built of runners and dealers around town. Everything funneled through Ellis anyway. This was done to protect Garrett's name. It would also make him an easy target for Ellis.

The man could easily cut him out, but that would mean making a play to kill him.

Ellis wouldn't come at him straight. He was too smart. He'd come at him from the side or the back. Come at an angle that Garrett wouldn't see or wouldn't expect.

Garrett leaned against the window and watched a couple of women walking arm in arm on the sidewalk. He was disappointed they couldn't look up and see him standing naked high above them. The thought made him smile.

His grin faded, though, as he realized how Earl Ellis would attack him. He would come from the one angle he would never expect. The one he had repeatedly said wasn't possible from the man.

Earl Ellis *would* turn rat.

Doing so would get Garrett off the street and leave his network largely intact. If Ellis skated by the cops, he could walk in and keep doing business with Garrett's network. The suppliers and buyers would never miss a beat.

But what could he do about it? There wasn't much to do until he could find the man. He was going to have to make it a full priority now.

Which caused problems with not only the ever-watchful eyes of Wardell Clint and Ray Zielinski, but the lurking presence of the Department of Justice.

Garrett had misunderstood why they were here. Talking with Dale Thomas had helped him see some of it, even if the union president hadn't.

Everything Justice asked about led back to him in some way.

The Talbott shooting. It was him who killed the detective in Liberty Lake.

The Bethany Rabe incident. He was the one who leaked the story to the press.

And Gary Stone's death. Garrett had orchestrated that.

It all led back to him.

Well, maybe not the thing with the dead seventeen-year-old, but if they dug long enough, they would find he was involved beyond the leak of the story. Sonya Meyer was murdered because of her relationship with a councilman. He had orchestrated that then killed the man responsible for her death. No one would care about him, though. Cops don't care about homeless drunk addicts named Skunk.

So what should he do now?

Was it time to consolidate the money he had hidden around town? Should he pool those resources together and run?

Garrett's hand rubbed his bare chest. Running away with his tail between his legs was a distasteful proposition. Maybe if it was the only way out.

There were other ways out—nobler ways that wouldn't make him look like such a pussy.

But it all hinged on Earl Ellis.

If the man was actually in town.

He was going in circles now.

Garrett heard her then. She padded across the room until she was behind him. Her hand snaked around his belly and he felt her skin against his back.

"What are you doing out here?" Tiana asked.

"Thinking."

"About?"

"Stuff."

"Anything important?"

"Everything's important."

She slowly turned him around and pressed her naked body against his. "Is it anything that can wait?"

He felt himself reacting to her warmth. A smile crossed his lips. "It can wait," he whispered.

THURSDAY

If you think this has a happy ending,
you haven't been paying attention.
—Ramsay Bolton, *Game of Thrones*

Chapter 39

"I appreciate the driver you sent," Édelie Durand said.

"Perks of rank," Staff Sergeant Jun Yang said. She wore a camouflaged uniform that appeared to have been pressed. Her short dark hair was tucked behind her ears. "Besides, my guy was happy to get off base that early in the morning. Not a lot for us to do at that hour except maybe some traffic enforcement."

They were seated in a conference room of the 504th Military Police Battalion. Framed photographs of the unit in action lined the walls. At the far end of the room stood an American flag, an Army flag, and a flag for the brigade.

"Has anyone contacted you from SPD?"

Yang frowned. "Why would they do that, ma'am?"

"To alert you to our questions."

The younger woman slipped Durand's business card off the table and stuffed it into a pocket of her uniform. "I don't speak with anyone from SPD. Or about them, except for when you called and told me what our conversation was going to cover. I'm just glad I finally get to talk with somebody about it."

She was in her late twenties—twenty-seven to be exact—and wore no makeup. Durand decided she didn't need it. Her brown eyes had only the smallest hint of crinkles at their edges while the rest of her face was blemish free. Jun Yang appeared to be an attractive, confident woman.

"Is there something specific you would like to talk about?"

Yang shrugged. "Not really, no. The whole thing was so fu—messed up."

Durand smiled. Even though she hated cursing, she said,

"You can swear. It won't offend me."

"I appreciate that, ma'am, but it wouldn't be appropriate. I'll answer any questions you have and provide as much detail as possible."

"Let's start with this: why were you, a rookie, on the Anti-Crime Team? It would seem a group like that would need to be made up of experienced officers."

"I agree. I even asked that same thing. But Captain Farrell wanted an informant. Experience was secondary."

Durand was taken aback by how straightforward Yang made that assertion. "How do you know that?"

"He told me."

"Just like that?"

"Yes, ma'am. Just like that."

"And he thought you would assume that role because…"

"Of the incident at the academy. Are you aware of—"

Durand nodded. "I've read your file."

During the academy, Jun Yang had exposed several students who were cheating on their exams. This led to their immediate expulsion from the academy. Durand could only imagine the level of blowback this caused the woman. Yang did not seem to be in any hurry to rehash that incident, so Durand decided to remain with the current line of questioning.

"Why would Captain Farrell need an informant?"

Yang inhaled deeply before saying, "He wanted me to watch the other guys on the team."

"Zielinski, Garrett, and Stone?"

"No, ma'am, not Stone. I think Farrell had him pegged as an informant, too."

Durand tapped her upper lip with a fingernail. *Stone was an informant, too? What was the captain worried about?*

Yang's smile appeared apologetic. "I know this sounds crazy, but I've given it a lot of thought."

"I believe you," Durand said slowly. "Did the captain say what he suspected Zielinski and Garrett of?"

"He was very secretive about that."

"Secretive?"

"Yes, ma'am. He skirted the issue, but he wanted me to keep an eye out for anything that looked inappropriate."

"Inappropriate?"

"You know, wrong. Illegal."

"To see if they, Zielinski or Garrett, were somehow corrupt?"

"Or leaning that way. Yes, ma'am."

Durand fell silent for a moment while she considered what Yang had said. If it was true, then Captain Farrell suspected Ray Zielinski and Tyler Garrett of corruption or, at least, being susceptible to corruption.

But Yang's assertion didn't make sense. Zielinski had a history of questionable decision-making. Why put a man like that on directed-enforcement team if there was further worry that he was capable of corruption? In reality, he proved those worries right by getting further into trouble.

Which left only Tyler Garrett, whose record was exemplary going into the team and remained so coming out. The only blemishes, if they could be called such, were the officer-involved shootings he'd been a part of.

And if Farrell had suspected either man of corruption, why wasn't there a file on it? Why wasn't Internal Affairs looking into it? Maybe they were and had kept it hidden from them? But they had been so agreeable to giving Danielle Watson the file on Zielinski. Was that Internal Affairs throwing up chaff?

Durand refocused on Yang. "What's your opinion of Ray Zielinski?"

"He was…all right, I guess."

"Would it surprise you if I told you he was suspended?"

Yang looked up to the ceiling and pushed her lips from side to side as she thought. When she refocused on Durand, she said, "I guess that would depend on what he did."

"I can't tell you that because it's still an open investigation."

"Then I would say yes. It does surprise me that he was

suspended."

"But you said it would depend…"

"Ray was a confusing person to be around. He's a burned-out jerk who thinks the world revolves around him. He's also a caring person about the people he likes. If he got suspended for something related to his ego or a person he cares for, well then, I can see it. One hundred percent. But corruption? I don't see that."

"What about Tyler Garrett?"

Her lip curled. "He was a different type of jerk."

"How so?"

"Our first sergeant made us switch up partners. When we rode together, he sort of ignored me. When he drove, he didn't talk. When I drove, he played on his phone. I figured he was more interested in cultivating what some of the guys called the CDI factor."

"CDI?"

"The chicks dig it factor."

Durand smirked.

"Garrett looked sharp, talked smooth, always hyped up his game. Do you know what I'm talking about?"

She did.

"Anyway, that's what I saw at first."

"Then later?"

"He messed with Ray. A lot. Sort of twisted the guy up. I think Ray hated him because of it. And Garrett didn't really follow the directions the replacement sergeant laid out. He more did his own thing. Gary loved him, though. When those two were together, it seemed like Garrett really played with Gary like a puppet master does his toys."

"That's not a flattering portrayal of someone who's supposed to be a good cop."

Yang shrugged. "No, ma'am, but it's what I saw."

"Do you see him as being susceptible to corruption?"

She paused before answering. Finally, she said, "I don't know. I mean, I've seen guys get in trouble here—on the base. A lot of time people have no idea that they had it in them. Everyone kept telling me how great of a guy Tyler Garrett was, but he kept showing me a different person than I was led to expect."

"If you had to guess," Durand said, "who were you supposed to be watching?"

"As the team's designated rat?"

Durand nodded.

"Again, I've given this a lot of thought. I think Farrell was worried about Garrett for something."

Durand leaned forward. "How so?"

"I don't know, but at the shooting, Gary Stone's I mean, I caught Farrell watching Garrett. I didn't think much of it then. I just figured it was partly because Garrett had shot Gary's killer. But then I watched Ray talk with that detective—"

"Marty Hill?"

Yang shook her head. "The other one. The black detective."

"Wardell Clint?"

"Yes, ma'am, him. They were huddled up watching Garrett, too. It looked like a couple thieves planning to rob a man."

"Could have been like you thought. Everyone was watching him because the man had just shot a cop killer."

"And it might have been had I not seen the same thing at the funeral. The entire department was there. You can't imagine the turnout. Really big. Everybody was watching Stone's casket. Except those three—Farrell, Zielinski, and…what's his name?"

"Clint."

"Farrell, Zielinski, and Clint. Those three kept a close watch on Garrett the whole time."

"And you don't know why?"

"No, ma'am, and I didn't care to know why. After Gary's death, I realized I made a mistake."

"How so?"

Jun Yang shook her head. "I didn't want to end up dead

like Gary, or a burnout like Ray, or whatever Garrett is. I told Farrell the same thing when I out-processed."

"Whatever Garrett is? What's that mean?"

Her laugh was short and full of regret. "It means there's something wrong with him. What that is, I don't know. I didn't want to stick around long enough to get any of it on me. I'm not saying he's done anything bad. But he's not a person I want to hang around with."

"And that's why you left?"

"Partly. They also stole my confidence. Here, in this uniform, I matter. Back there, on that team, in that department, I didn't."

Durand studied her.

"I could have stayed there and fought maybe to regain my self-worth. Struggled to find some significance. Or I could have returned to the thing that made me happy." Yang smiled slightly. "It was an easy decision."

Chapter 40

Farrell retrieved a cup of coffee from the Major Crimes bullpen. It was his fourth of the day, and it wasn't even noon yet. He'd slept poorly and needed the caffeine, though he certainly didn't need the jitters that came with it. On balance, though, the trade-off was worth it to stay sharp.

Usually, he took advantage of the stroll through the workspace of his division to chat with a few detectives. The small talk kept him grounded, or so he believed. But today, his mind was whirring. The conversation with Baumgartner yesterday kept him spinning in circles and had burned in his thoughts all night. Even Karen had mentioned how he'd tossed and turned, using the comment to offer him another chance to come clean with whatever was bothering him. Instead, he made the general excuse of DOJ's presence and left it at that. She grudgingly accepted the lie, and Farrell could see the hurt in her eyes. He knew that things would come to a head with her soon.

Walking down the hallway, he passed a pair of detectives in nearly identical khakis and polo shirts. Each carried a single manila file folder under an arm. He wondered if there was anything in the files, or if they simply served as props to make the detectives look busy.

Now I sound like DOJ.

At Dana Hatcher's doorway, he slowed and glanced inside, hoping to catch her eye so he could give her a friendly nod. Their relationship had suffered ever since the Anti-Crime Team debacle, and he hoped to someday repair it. But Hatcher's light was off and her desk empty.

Probably having coffee with Margaret Patterson, sharpening their knives.

He momentarily chastised himself for his poor attitude. Sure, Hatcher and Patterson were friends, but that didn't mean anything.

He frowned.

He should go around the corner to Crime Analysis and get his thinking checked if he really thought *that* was true. Patterson was pure politics, maybe even more so than the mayor, if that were possible. Anyone associating with her, Hatcher included, was sure to have some of that rub off.

Farrell took a sip while walking but tipped the cup too far. Hot coffee spilled over his lip and dribbled down onto his shirt. He stopped short, cursing under his breath.

"You all right, Captain?"

Farrell glanced up to see Steve Curado stepping out of the Internal Affairs offices with several files tucked under his arm. He wondered immediately what the investigator wanted from those files. He doubted that he had them for show.

He realized Curado was looking at him, awaiting a response. Farrell swiped at the liquid on his shirt, but it had already soaked in. "I'm fine," he said. "Coffee's hot, though."

"Only way to drink it." Curado flashed an engaging grin, but Farrell thought he could see something devious in it. "Myself, I can't chew gum and walk at the same time, so I'd never even attempt drinking coffee on the run."

Farrell managed a half-hearted smile. "What are you up to? Or am I allowed to ask?"

"Sure, sure. No secrets here." Curado's smile never left his face. "I'm off to interview Detective Clint."

Tendrils of near panic shot through Farrell's gut.

Clint? What would he say? If it was the wrong thing, the entire house of cards he'd constructed could come crashing down around him.

Farrell shifted from one leg to the other. "Uh, do you want me present?"

Curado's expression melted into mild confusion. "What for?"

Farrell cleared his throat. He realized he'd been doing that a lot lately, a byproduct of his nervousness. "Detective Clint can be…a little difficult. Maybe having someone in authority there will help."

Curado's pleasant mien reappeared. "Thanks, but I think I have all the authority I need. Besides, it's best if we interview everyone individually."

"Sure," Farrell said. "Of course."

Curado signaled the end of the conversation with a nod and took a step to leave.

"Wait." The words were out of his mouth before Farrell had time to think about them. He wondered if they sounded as frantic as he felt.

Curado paused with an expectant look.

Farrell cleared his throat again. "Uh, I was just wondering…this is the final day of your trip, right?"

"It is."

"Besides Detective Clint, do you need any help arranging interviews?"

Curado seemed to consider the question. "I don't think so. Dani had a little trouble getting Ray Zielinski scheduled, but I'm pretty sure he came down for her."

"He's here?" Another wash of cold panic flooded over Farrell. Zielinski knew far less than Clint, unless the notoriously untrusting detective had shared more with him than Farrell was aware of. Even so, he still knew enough to open a crack for DOJ to insert a crowbar into and start prying.

"Is that a problem?" Curado eyed him curiously.

"No, no," Farrell said hurriedly. "I'm just a little surprised, is all. He's on paid administrative leave."

"We know. But since this qualifies as official police business, it made sense to have him come to the station, don't you agree?"

"Definitely," Farrell said. "It's no problem." He took a sip of his coffee. "What's your boss up to today? A final discussion with the mayor or the chief?"

"No," Curado said. "She actually flew over to Seattle this morning."

"Seattle's in trouble again?"

An appeasing smile crossed Curado's face. "No, she went over there to talk to a former employee. Jun Yang?"

Damn. Farrell's stomach fell. Outside of Clint, Jun Yang knew more about his true intentions in staffing the Anti-Crime Team than anyone else. She might not be entirely aware of the significance of her knowledge, but the very fact she had known she was the designated spy on the team, *his* spy, was enough to open another enormous crack for the DOJ investigators.

"Captain? You okay?"

Farrell stared back at Curado. Then he bobbed his head. "Yeah, yeah." He put his hand on his belly. "Just fighting a bit of a bug. Don't stand too close, it might be catching."

"Well, get healthy," Curado said. He gave Farrell a final nod and headed down the hall to the Investigative Division.

Farrell watched him go, his head spinning. When he realized what he was doing, standing in the middle of the hallway staring after the DOJ investigator, he gathered himself together and strode toward his office.

Jun Yang, he thought as he walked. His plant on the Anti-Crime Team to spy on Garrett. Later, he'd tried to bring Stone on board, but that had failed miserably. Zielinski was there for his potential as a spy, too, but no information came from that source until after Stone's murder, when Clint huddled together with the veteran officer. Yang was the only one to serve as Farrell's primary means of keeping track of the team.

Yang figured out her intended role, and she hadn't liked it. She called herself a rat, and rejected the job, rejected him, and when it came down to it, rejected the entire department.

He put his coffee cup on his desk but didn't walk around to his chair. Instead, he worked his way through the scenario.

Did Yang know who she was there to watch? He didn't think so, not initially. But what about at the end? When all was said and done, had she figured it out?

Her last words to him before she quit the job rang in his ears.

I don't want to end up like the other three, Yang had said. She didn't want to become a burnout like Zielinski or end up dead like Stone. And Garrett?

What had she said to him about Garrett?

I sure as hell don't want to end up as whatever the hell Garrett is.

"Whatever the hell Garrett is," Farrell whispered.

She *had* to suspect. Not just that something was off about Garrett, but that he knew it, too. After all, he'd put her in place to spy on the man, hadn't he? Jun Yang may have been a police rookie, but she wasn't a kid. She had some life experience, she was military police, and she was a smart woman. If she'd given any thought at all to this situation after she left, her opinion would only become more conclusive over time.

And she was sharing all that with the Department of Justice.

"It's tumbling down," Farrell murmured to the empty office. Two years of an off-book investigation that had yielded no definitive evidence. He wondered if DOJ would delve more deeply into Garrett, or if they would accept the mayor's version of events and focus on his own actions instead. He saw the narrative the way they might—a corrupt, white police captain trying to frame a black police officer. No, a *hero* black police officer.

He had to get ahead of this.

He had to go to the chief.

Farrell left his coffee on the desk and hurried from his office.

Chapter 41

Clint looked away from his Garrett file to glance at the small digital clock next to his desk phone. Ellis still had about six hours left. Clint didn't think it was worth being nervous about until the deadline was within a half hour or so, but that intellectual knowledge didn't entirely quell his concern. He'd gambled when he released the man. He still believed it was his best course of action. Not necessarily in the case against Ellis but to achieve his ultimate goal—bringing down Garrett.

He'd meant what he said. If Earl Ellis and every single one of his network of street dealers had to go free in order to nail Garrett, that was a trade he was willing to make. It was distasteful, and it went against the grain for him, but as a necessary evil, he knew he could stomach it. What he couldn't allow was for Garrett to escape justice.

"Detective?"

Clint turned toward the voice. The DOJ investigator, Curado, stood a few feet away. He scowled. "What do you want?"

"To interview you," Curado said congenially. "Unless you're still in the middle of that interrogation."

"No, but I am busy. Like I told you before, I have case work."

"I appreciate that," Curado said. "But I have a job to do as well, and today that includes interviewing you."

"Later," Clint said.

"I go back to Washington this afternoon. There is no later."

Clint grunted. *This* was Washington but leave it to a fed to use shorthand for the nation's capital. Of course, Curado would think the world revolved around that seat of power. He was a cog in that machine, after all.

"Detective, I don't mean to be difficult, but this is happening now. We can talk together like professionals, or I can go down the hall and get your chief involved, but—"

"Oh, by all means, don't bring my daddy into the situation," Clint snarled. "He might decide to ground me."

Curado looked at him. Clint could see the frustration clearly tearing at the edges of the fed's calm demeanor. "Detective…"

"Fine," Clint snapped. He rose from his chair, closing his case file. He slid open the desk drawer and put it inside, taking care to lock the drawer. Curado looked on with mild fascination. "Come with me."

He led Curado through the bullpen and to the row of interview rooms. He chose number four again and held the door open for Curado. The lawyer stepped inside, and Clint followed. The two of them sat across from each other at the small table. Clint waited, saying nothing.

"Do you want a union representative?" Curado asked.

Clint snorted. "Why? They're in bed with the brass and have been for years."

"You have the right."

"I don't need one."

"How about Captain Farrell, then?"

Clint's eyes narrowed. Did Curado know something? "Why would I want the brass in here if I don't even want a union rep?"

Curado shrugged. "He offered, so I thought I'd ask."

He *offered*? Clint forced himself to maintain a constant expression, but the revelation disturbed him. Once again, Farrell thought he was being crafty when all he was really doing was endangering the entire operation.

You can't trust the brass. Either they were out to get you, or they were incompetent. Either way, it represented a danger for him.

"So no rep, and no Farrell?" Curado asked.

Clint gave him a short shake of his head.

"That's fine," Curado said. "I prefer it this way. No white shirts, no lawyers, just be the two of us."

"Aren't you a lawyer?" Clint asked snidely.

Curado held up his hand in surrender. "Technically, yes. But most of my work is very similar to yours, Detective."

Clint didn't reply, but a thought sprang to mind.

You are nothing like me.

"So it's my hope," Curado continued, "that in an informal situation like this, no bosses around, you and I can have a meaningful conversation."

"I've got nothing to say to you."

"I think you do."

"All that confirms is that you think in the same head-up-ass way as every other fed I've encountered in my career."

"Every single one?" Curado countered. "Not a single good cop in the bunch?"

Clint hesitated. He'd actually come across more than one federal officer who was a good investigator, both from the FBI and DEA. He'd even had an agent from BATFE who had been the best of the bunch. She'd been the reason Clint's own aspect of that particular case broke open. But he wasn't going to tell Curado that. The man wasn't a real fed any more than the rats in Internal Affairs were real cops.

"I respect the work you do here at the local level," Curado went on. "I'd appreciate it if you respected the work my colleagues and I do at the federal level. Let's keep it real."

"Real?" Clint scoffed. "That's rich."

"I'm being sincere."

"That's what you want me to think."

"It's the truth."

Clint pointed at Curado's identification badge where it was clipped to the lawyer's jacket lapel. "There's the truth," he said.

Curado followed Clint's gesture to the badge. "All right," he said. "Yes, I work for the Department of Justice. I realize that can lead to a contentious relationship at times, but—"

"That's because you go looking for corruption and don't stop until you find some, even if you have to twist the facts to get it."

"You don't think police corruption exists?"

"I know it does. But not to the degree your agency thinks it does. And certainly not to the degree that the federal government itself is corrupt. But you don't care about that, do you?"

Curado frowned slightly. "All due respect, Detective, you don't know anything about me."

"True enough," Clint conceded. "But all due respect, I know your kind."

Curado's brows went up. "My *kind*? You mean brown people?"

Clint let out a snort. "Son, please. Don't try to play the color card with me. Besides, your identification card says Esteban, doesn't it? But you call yourself Steve. Doesn't sound to me like you're too concerned about being in touch with your roots."

Curado's jaw set. "I'm like anyone else of color in this country. I do what I can to make my way. It isn't always easy."

He shook his head at Curado. "Try being a black man in a city that's ninety percent white. Then have a go at policing that ninety percent for nineteen years. You do that and then maybe I'll listen to your race concerns. Until then, stow it."

He and Curado stared at each other from across the table. Clint could see a quiet fury brewing in the lawyer's eyes now. All trace of friendliness was gone. That suited Clint fine.

Finally, in a tight voice, Curado said, "What can I do to convince you to answer a few questions for me, Detective?"

"Get a court order."

Curado exhaled in frustration. "You're not doing your department any favors."

"That's between me and my department. Are we done here?"

Curado stared at him for a few moments longer. Then he said, "Yes. We're finished." He stood up.

Clint remained seated.

"Goodbye, Detective." Curado didn't offer his hand.

Clint said nothing.

After a moment, Curado left the interview room. Clint listened to him go but didn't follow him with his gaze. He waited about a minute, then rose and headed back to his desk. It wouldn't surprise him if Curado was already complaining in Lieutenant Flowers's office, but he didn't worry about it. He knew the feds couldn't compel him to talk without a court order, and he didn't care if that upset Curado and his pals. By the time they brought any revenge to bear on the department, the Garrett situation would be resolved.

As Clint approached his desk, he saw Detective Marty Hill standing in front of it, staring down at some paperwork spread below him on the desktop.

For the first time in a very long while, a cold trickle of dread found its way into Clint's chest.

Hill either heard or sensed his approach. He wheeled around, a single piece of paper in his hand. His usually friendly face was twisted in uncustomary rage and his eyes bore into Clint's.

"I heard you made a trip to Liberty Lake PD," Hill snarled.

"You broke into my desk?" Clint said weakly.

Hill ignored his complaint. "They fast-tracked the bullet Rogers brought them, since it was used in a cop's death. Straight to the front of the line. But you knew they'd do that, didn't you?"

"I can explain."

"Explain what? That the bullet someone shot Butch Talbott with somehow came from the same gun as the bullet we took out of Ernesto Ocampo's brain?" Hill's voice shook with anger. "I've been sitting at my desk since I got these results, trying to make sense out of it. I remember that day at the Ocampo scene. You were assigned to help me and

Hollander, but you were acting weird. You ran off to do who knows what and then you lied to me about it. I thought that was just you being you."

"Marty…"

"Shut up, Ward." Hill glared at him. "I called over to Liberty Lake and talked to that detective. He told me it was *you* who told him to request the bullet analysis on the Talbott bullet. That was the last straw. I knew you were hiding something. I just didn't know what it was, at least until I pried open your desk drawer."

He held up the piece of paper in his fingers.

"Now I know!" he barked.

Clint could see the single sheet of paper from where he stood. It was the photomontage he'd created for Nona Henry to look at, to see if she could identify who she saw going into and out of Ernesto Ocampo's home around the time of the shootings. She'd been certain of her identification, circling the picture of Tyler Garrett with her wavering hand.

"Is this for real?" Hill demanded. "Your witness ID'd Garrett?"

Clint nodded slowly. "Yes."

Hill let his arm drop to his side. "Unbelievable."

"Marty, now that you know, I can explain it all to you. You can help—"

"Help?" Hill shook his head. "You don't get it. I've got an unsolved quadruple homicide. A damn *quad*! And all along, you've had the answer. You've just been sitting on it. Why?"

Clint paused, suddenly aware that it was likely other detectives could hear this exchange. Finally, he said, "At the time, it was the only decision I could make."

Hill rolled his eyes. "So you just decided to tank my case?"

"I know it's hard to understand, but it was the right decision."

"Says who? You?" Hill shook his head savagely. "I am sick to death of your always-gotta-be-right, honey badger, on-the-spectrum act!"

Clint absorbed the insult, hoping that Marty's rage would expend itself and that they could talk rationally. Once Hill knew everything, Clint was sure he'd help close out the case. His, and Clint's. "We can make this work," Clint said evenly. "First, we—"

"*We?* There is no *we* in this situation. You made that decision already." Hill stabbed a finger at Clint. "I'll tell you what *I'm* going to do." He glanced around, then lowered his voice. "I'm going to the prosecutor and getting a warrant for Tyler Garrett. Then I'm going to the chief. After that, I'll stop by Internal Affairs, and let them deal with your lying ass."

Hill turned around, scooping up Clint's file from the desk.

"That's mine," Clint said.

"It's mine now," Hill snapped. "All of it should have been mine two years ago."

"Marty, I need that file."

"Screw you, Ward."

Marty turned and stomped away.

Clint remained standing a few feet away from his desk. The empty desk drawer stood open. He remembered how easily he'd managed to get into Marty's desk just a couple of days ago. He never should have left his paperwork so vulnerable.

That didn't matter now. What mattered was that the red button had been pushed. The missiles were launched. He only had a short time left before impact.

Clint stepped to his desk and picked up his phone.

Chapter 42

Ray Zielinski sat in the same small conference room where he'd met Dale Thomas earlier in the week. He'd briefly considered having the union president with him for this but rejected the idea. Thomas didn't seem too interested in helping him these days. Either way, he hoped this upcoming meeting went better than that one had, but he doubted it.

Through the open door, he saw Captain Farrell walk by in the hallway with a cup of coffee. The man's head was lowered and he shuffled with the same weariness that Zielinski felt. He had an idea what was weighing on the captain's mind. He wondered if it were possible that, when everything came out, he might fare better than Farrell did. He doubted that, too.

Farrell passed out of his field of vision. Zielinski listened to his footsteps until they stopped suddenly.

"Damn it," Farrell cursed.

Zielinski pursed his lips. What was that about? Then he heard someone else ask if Farrell was all right. The captain's answer sounded forced, as if his voice were stretched thin.

What is going on with that guy?

Zielinski listened in fascination to the conversation, straining to hear each word. He figured out quickly enough that the other man was one of the DOJ investigators. The way Farrell spoke to him made the captain seem guilty as hell. He wasn't even casual in the way he asked what the investigators were doing. Instead, he sounded worried. His excuses were feeble and his explanations lame.

When he heard his own name mentioned, Zielinski perked up further, but nothing of consequence was said. He found it interesting to hear that they were interviewing Jun Yang, though. He wondered what insight she might have. He'd learned from Clint that Farrell had put her on the team to spy on Garrett. He'd also tried to use Officer Gary Stone in that role.

Zielinski remembered Stone's crumpled body in the entryway of a shack of a house up in Hillyard. He was glad that he never got close enough to see the damage the shotgun did to the officer's face. That was the result of Farrell's plan. He'd messed that up, and now he was up the hall, making more mistakes. Zielinski felt a strange urge to run out of the conference room to stop the captain from talking.

You're only making it worse!

He didn't have to, though. The conversation finished, and a few moments later, he saw a Hispanic man stride past the conference room toward the Investigative Division.

Good luck, Ward.

Another minute passed before he heard more footsteps and a woman came through the door. She was tan, with short blonde hair and long eyelashes. Zielinski could see in her eyes that she meant business.

Game on.

"I'm Danielle Watson," the woman said, extending her hand. "Department of Justice."

Zielinski took her hand. Her grip was surprisingly firm. "Ray Zielinski."

"Thanks for making the time for me," Watson said, sliding into the seat next to him. Zielinski caught a waft of her perfume. It was expensive and heady. She set her file on the table in front of her but didn't open it. "I'll try to make this quick and painless."

"Like dental work," Zielinski joked darkly.

Watson gave him a parade float smile. "Let's get something straight right away, shall we?"

"What's that?"

"I've been to Internal Affairs. I know your situation. I have the reports here." Watson tapped her folder.

"Okay," Zielinski said, drawing out the final syllable.

"How'd you get that?"

Watson smirked. "We're Justice. Now, Officer Zielinski, I'm not saying you might be inclined to be less than cooperative with our inquiry, but I *will* say that cooperation would probably go a long way toward helping you out with your IA situation."

Zielinski digested her words, but they didn't make sense to him. How would helping DOJ do anything for him in Internal Affairs? He doubted Chief Baumgartner cared what the feds thought about disciplining his own officers. If anything, cooperating might *hurt* his standing with the chief.

Watson was staring at him, so he said, "I understand."

"Good." Watson flipped open her file halfway, shielding his view of the contents. "You were the first officer on scene when Officer Garrett shot Todd Trotter?"

"I was."

"Did you notice anything concerning?"

"Like what?"

"That's what I'm asking."

Zielinski hesitated. He *had* noticed something, almost right away. It was the first troubling piece of evidence that eventually led him to where he was sitting now. But he didn't know if he should share that with her. Then he realized it was already part of the official report, so he forged ahead.

"His dash camera hadn't been activated."

"That concerned you."

He shrugged. "I thought it was odd."

"Was it purposeful?"

"I have no way of knowing that."

"What else about that case concerned you?"

"I had nothing else to do with that case."

"No official duties whatsoever?"

"Not that I recall."

"How about from afar? What concerns did you develop while watching things play out?"

Zielinski rubbed his mouth. "I suppose I just hoped everything worked out for the best."

"For who?"

"Everybody."

Watson gave him a knowing look. "You're not that naïve, are you, Officer?"

Zielinski didn't know how to answer that, so he didn't.

After a few moments, Watson glanced back down at her file. "All right, moving on then. You arrested City Councilman Dennis Hahn for attempted suicide?"

"No."

She cocked her head at him. "That's not what the record says."

"Then the record is wrong."

"You didn't take Mr. Hahn into custody and transport him to the hospital?"

"I did," Zielinski said. "But it wasn't an arrest. Attempted suicide isn't against the law."

Watson pursed her lips. "Are you being purposefully difficult?"

"No. I'm just trying to be accurate. I didn't arrest him for attempted suicide. I contacted him and took him to the hospital for evaluation."

"I see. So once you 'contacted' him," Watson made air quotes at the word, "was there any chance he wasn't leaving the house in your custody?"

Zielinski sighed. "No, I guess not."

"So it's something of a difference without a distinction, isn't it, Officer?"

"He went voluntarily," Zielinski persisted. He knew it didn't matter, but it irritated him that someone who held others to task didn't seem to care much about being accurate herself.

"As you already stated, he was essentially already in custody from the moment you arrived. If he believed his committal was voluntary, then I'm sure that helped you with the process, and perhaps the paperwork, too."

"My paperwork was good."

"I'm certain it was. Here's the entire reason I'm asking

you about this: what else do you know about the councilman's involvement with Bethany Rabe?"

"Nothing."

She raised an eyebrow. "At all?"

"No."

"How about Sonya Meyer?"

"Who's that?"

Watson's eyebrows fell and she frowned. "She was murdered around the same time as you arrested Mr. Hahn. He was rumored to have been involved with her as well. Detective Clint is the primary detective on the case."

Zielinski shrugged. "Outside of my area of concern."

"Really. All right, let's turn to something closer to home. You were assigned to the Anti-Crime Team."

"I was."

"Why?"

Zielinski turned up his hands. "You'd have to ask the brass."

"Who, exactly?"

"Sergeant McGinn, I guess. Or Captain Farrell. I don't know who made the team selection."

"What was your role on the team?"

"Same as everyone else's. Catch bad guys."

Watson turned up the corners of her mouth. "Cute. What dimension did you bring to the team?"

"Experience?"

"So you were the team leader?"

"No."

"Who was?"

He remembered how Garrett had driven the team's actions once McGinn went out on compassionate leave and the ineffective Ragland took over. Was that what she was searching for? Dirt on Garrett? She'd started there, with his shooting. He knew from Clint that Garrett had injected himself into the Rabe situation, and even shown up at the Meyer homicide. Now she was focusing on the Anti-Crime Team. If DOJ was looking into Garrett, maybe he should help them. They had more resources than Clint did, and from what he'd heard, federal time was worse than state time.

Then Clint's words from their meeting at the Happy Time Tavern rang out in his ears, as clear as Watson's had been moments ago. How if DOJ came in, the odds of Garrett seeing justice went down considerably. And how Garrett might use the opportunity to cut a deal for immunity. Tell the feds whatever they wanted to hear.

No way. No way does Garrett get away with this.

"Sergeant Ragland was in charge," he said.

"What was your relationship to the other team members?" Watson pressed.

"We got along fine."

"Friendly?"

"We were professional."

"Things didn't go so well for your team, did they?"

Zielinski hesitated. "We put some bad people behind bars," he said carefully. "But, in the end, you're right. It ended badly."

"Officer Stone dead, Officer Yang off the department, and you suspended. Seems like Officer Garrett was the only one who survived that disaster."

Zielinski met her gaze. He felt the weight of all that he knew pressing outward from his throat, but his gut told him he couldn't trust this woman. Clint would say it was because she was a fed, but it was more than that. He knew anything he said would be taken in the most unfavorable light possible.

"I guess he's lucky," Zielinski said.

Watson closed her file. "I get the sense that you're not being one hundred percent honest with me, Officer."

"I get the sense that you always feel that way."

Watson stared hard at him. "Hazards of the job, I suppose."

Zielinski shrugged, feigning nonchalance.

"So I'll just make a note that you weren't cooperative," Watson said, "and perhaps we'll continue this discussion another time."

"I've answered your questions," Zielinski said.

"Not honestly."

"You get to decide that?" Zielinski asked. "I tell you what I know, all facts, and you decide I'm lying? What kind of bull is that?"

Watson stood, file in hand. "Stating facts we already know and withholding the complete truth isn't cooperation, Officer Zielinski. It's what we call malicious compliance. Trust me, I see it frequently. It never ends well for the person trying it."

Zielinski watched her turn and go. He wished for a moment that he had some sort of snappy comeback to hurl at her as she walked out the door, but nothing came to him, short of the tried and true *screw you!* He knew that would do more harm than good, so he kept his mouth closed.

Once he was sure Watson was gone, he leaned back and let out a long sigh. For a fed, that woman had been tough. Not the kind of person he wanted on his ass, which is exactly where she seemed to enjoy being.

Pain and worry brewed in his stomach. This was coming to a head. He could feel it. Everything. His IA cases, the Garrett situation, all of it.

Zielinski frowned. Resentment joined the emotional mixture in his gut. None of it was fair. Not the way things had turned out for him, and definitely not the way Garrett seemed to be skating out of danger every single time. The man lived a charmed life.

What goes around, comes around.

He used to believe that, after a fashion. What did they call it? Karma? Maybe it didn't act in a strict mathematical fashion, but he always thought that whatever a person put out into the world with his acts and deeds and intentions was usually what came back to him. He'd seen too many people do bad things and then end up with bad things happening to them not to believe it wasn't at least a little true.

On the wall, the thin red second hand twirled around the

face of the clock. He wondered how long it would be before they finally swapped it out with a digital one. After he was gone, most likely. Which looked more and more like it would be sooner rather than later, whether he deserved it or not.

Zielinski sat in the chair for several minutes, stewing on that thought. Finally, he decided that there was another truth he believed in. Yeah, what goes around, comes around. But it doesn't happen in a vacuum. Sometimes, you gotta be the one to bring it around.

That's what he intended to do.

He had to let Farrell know that DOJ was closing in. Then, together, they needed to corral Clint and form a plan. Otherwise, everything really might come crashing down, and Garrett really might win.

Zielinski stood and left the conference room, hurrying down the hallway toward mahogany row.

Chapter 43

Chief Robert Baumgartner stared across his desk at Farrell, not believing what he'd just heard.

"Two *years*, Tom? Are you *kidding* me?"

"Chief, I—"

Baumgartner held up his hand, his mind rushing, trying to catch up to this new revelation. He felt like he'd been watching a play in which the hero was all of the sudden revealed to be a villain. Every wrinkle and nuance of everything he knew about Garrett, about Clint, about Farrell, was now changed.

Oh, man. This is going to kill this department.

He glared at Farrell.

What have you done?

"Two years," Baumgartner mumbled again. "You sat on a murdering cop for *two years*."

"The mayor—"

"The mayor didn't know," the chief interrupted. He jerked a thumb toward his own chest. "*I* didn't know."

Farrell dropped his gaze. "I thought it was best that way. Until we had enough to guarantee a conviction."

"Do you know what you've done here?" Baumgartner asked him, still astounded. He shook his head unbelievingly. "Seriously. You should have told me two years ago, Tom, or not at all."

Farrell raised his eyes. "I thought…" He trailed off.

"It doesn't matter what you thought. What matters now is that I have to clean up this massive mess you just dropped on my desk. I don't know if I'm going to survive this, and worse than that, I don't know if this police department will."

Farrell's lip quivered. "I was trying to—"

"Shut up." Baumgartner leaned forward. "I need you to tell me everything. Don't leave anything out. I have to know every last detail if I'm going to stand a chance on this one."

Farrell opened his mouth but was interrupted by voices outside the office door.

"I need to see him *now!*" snapped a woman's voice. "I don't care what he's doing."

Baumgartner frowned. Rude interruptions like this were extremely rare, and even then, Marilyn usually handled them deftly. He didn't know who was being so insistent, but he knew for certain that whatever she wanted to talk to him about wasn't more important than what he needed to hear from Farrell right now.

The door to his office burst open, and Édelie Durand stepped in. His eyes narrowed in surprise and then anger. He stood to protest, but Durand beat him to the punch.

"I need to talk with you," she said in a tone full of resolve.

"I'm busy at the moment," Baumgartner said. "Give me thirty minutes and—"

"Not you," Durand said. She pointed at Farrell. "*You.*"

Farrell seemed to shrink in his seat. "Me?"

"Now," Durand added. "There's a conference room across the hall. Let's go."

"Wait a minute," Baumgartner said, his legendary anger flaring up. He wasn't sure what had gotten under Durand's skin, but he wasn't going to let her barge into his office and dictate terms like they were already under a consent decree.

A moment later, the weight of that thought settled on him, and some of the fire went out of his chest.

Durand fixed him with a cool gaze. "Or if you want to give us the room, Chief, I'm happy to have my conversation with Captain Farrell right here."

Baumgartner boomeranged right back into being angry again. "Across the hall is fine," he growled.

"Good." Durand beckoned Farrell with a crook of her finger.

Farrell stood slowly. He glanced from Baumgartner to

Durand, then back again. He looked beaten, even worse than when he confessed all that he'd done. Baumgartner gave him a hard look and tried to bore a single thought into the captain's head.

Don't make this any worse.

Durand turned around and left the room. Farrell followed her. Baumgartner stepped around his desk and scrambled out his doorway to catch up. He spotted Durand already standing across the hallway, holding the door open. Farrell was still in the waiting area, skulking reluctantly toward Durand. Baumgartner also registered Ray Zielinski, standing in the hallway in civilian clothes, gawking at the scene in front of him. His longtime secretary, Marilyn, watched on in surprise.

"Tom!" Baumgartner said in a low, urgent voice.

Farrell turned. He had the look of a condemned man.

"We're not finished," Baumgartner said. "As soon as you're done talking to her, you come find me. Are we clear?"

Farrell nodded dutifully.

"Immediately after," Baumgartner stressed.

"I will," Farrell said. He waited for any further direction from the chief, and when Baumgartner didn't add to what he'd already said, Farrell turned and trudged the rest of the way to the conference room. For his part, Zielinski disappeared down the hallway, probably eager to get out of the line of fire. Only Marilyn didn't turn away from the train wreck.

Baumgartner ignored it all. He looked at Durand. Their eyes met, and then she closed the door. The latch clicked in place, but Chief Baumgartner kept staring at the blond wood of the door, wishing for answers that weren't there.

Chapter 44

Tyler Garrett strode confidently through the parking lot of the public safety building. Earlier in the morning, he'd been called by a DOJ investigator to schedule an appointment. He tried to play the day-off card, but she wasn't having any of it. He didn't want her in his home, so he agreed to meet at the department.

He thought about inviting Dale Thomas along, but the man hadn't impressed him after his two shootings. Therefore, he was taking the "less is more" approach with the union president.

The phone buzzed in his left pocket. He pulled it out and flipped it open. It was a text message from Royal Harjo. *All's quiet on the home front.*

The moment Earl Ellis went missing, he should have put a man on the grandmother's house. He hesitated to do it while Clint and Zielinski were watching it, but he should have risked it for the intel alone. Now, he was hoping it wasn't too late. For a bit, he mentally chastised himself, but he couldn't do that anymore.

Now was time for business.

The phone in his right pocket buzzed. He tucked the burner away and pulled out his normal phone. It was a text message from Tiana. *Good luck, baby. I love you.*

His quickly responded with a *Luv U* and put the phone away.

When he got done with this interview, Garrett planned to task Harjo to go back through Ellis's network to see if anyone had heard anything from the man. Maybe Ellis had reached out to someone. It was unlikely, but Garrett should at least check. And he'd already exposed himself to Veryl

Wooley. He didn't need to expose himself to anyone further. Let Harjo do the dirty work. The man was built for it.

Garrett was also going to do some additional homework on Angie's boyfriend, William Cardwell. Garrett wasn't finished with him. He thought Harjo's beating of the man would have settled things, but it hadn't.

Sitting face-to-face with Cardwell had irked Garrett. Then seeing how Angie looked at him only served to anger Garrett. He didn't like the mental space it put him in. It made him feel weak.

A quick press of a fob against the west door and he was in the building. He walked down the short hall and took a right, past the Investigative Division and into the section of hallway known as mahogany row, a nickname Garrett was sure the brass gave themselves—the arrogant pricks. The hallway made another right turn at the chief's office, leading past Crime Analysis and a few other rooms before the door to the public foyer. That was where he found a blonde woman and a Hispanic man huddled close together with a woman in her early fifties. All of them wore suits and the constipated looks of federal employees.

Justice, my ass.

He started toward the group.

It was obvious that the younger suits deferred to the older woman because they nodded while she spoke. Her hands tapped together as she spoke, emphasizing her words. Her dark skin shone slightly under the hallway lights. When she was done speaking, the older woman abruptly turned and walked past him without acknowledgment.

As he neared, the blonde woman faced him. Recognition flashed in her eyes as if she'd seen him somewhere before. "Tyler Garrett?"

He nodded.

"Danielle Watson, Department of Justice." She pointed to her male counterpart. "Esteban Curado."

"Steve," the Hispanic man said and offered his hand.

Garrett reluctantly shook it.

Behind them, Marty Hill came through the door from the public foyer. His face was pinched with concern. When they made eye contact, Garrett smiled and lifted his chin in acknowledgement.

Hill's reaction was decidedly less friendly, though. His lip curled and he glared back.

Garrett lifted his palms in a *what's up?* gesture.

"We've got the training room reserved," Watson said.

Marty Hill didn't move. He stood there with his eyes firmly locked onto Garrett's.

"Officer?" Watson said. Her arm was held out, directing him toward a nearby room.

He glanced toward her and slowly followed Curado toward the doorway. Garrett glanced back at Marty Hill. The detective was gone.

What the hell was that about?

Inside the training room, several thick files were arranged on a table inside. A presentation made to intimidate, Garrett was sure he had nothing to fear, though. Everything he'd done while in uniform was already checked and given a department stamp of approval.

Curado pulled the door with the small window closed behind them.

Garrett sat so his back was to the far wall. The feds sat across from him. They both put their business cards on the table and slid them toward him. The embossed seal of the Department of Justice was in the right-hand corner. Under each of their names was a simple title—*Attorney.*

"This is an informal interview," Danielle Watson began.

"Informal?" Garrett said. "Way you made it sound on the phone, I had no choice."

"We want to talk with you—"

"But I can get up now and leave and you won't have anything to say about it?"

Watson sarcastically said, "Until we come back under the umbrella of a consent decree and compel you to speak with us."

Garrett's eyes flicked to Curado's. The man raised his eyebrows but didn't speak.

"Listen," Watson said. "We're trying to do this in a friendly manner."

"Right," Garrett said. "There's never anything friendly about a couple suits in an interview room with a cop."

The two feds eyed each other. It was an unspoken signal to transfer the lead.

Curado leaned forward. "Officer Garrett, do you mind if I call you Tyler?"

"Call me whatever you want but ask your questions so I can get on with my day."

"Tyler," Curado said. "I'd like to take you back to the night of the shooting with Todd Trotter."

"Why?"

"Because that's where my questions start."

Garrett tapped the table with a finger. "No. The county investigated that shooting, and the prosecuting attorney ruled it justified. I've been cleared."

"I'm not arguing that," Curado said.

"Then what are you saying I did wrong?"

Curado lifted his hands in defense. "Relax, Tyler. I'm not saying you did anything wrong. I simply want to ask some questions."

He wasn't sure what Curado's angle was, but there had to be one. The man's voice dripped honey.

"Were you happy," the lawyer asked, "with the way the city and the department handled your situation?"

"My situation?"

Curado didn't answer. He watched Garrett waiting for him to respond. It was an investigative technique. Ask a question and let it sit. Allow the interviewee to determine their own reasoning and start talking. The interviewer can dictate the course of the interview after that.

But he wasn't going to do that. He knew what they were doing so he remained silent. Let Curado answer his question or they could sit here silently.

Watson's chair squeaked as she shifted positions. "There was quite a stir-up following your shooting."

Garrett shrugged. "Worked out okay."

"You mean the settlement?" she asked.

"What else would I be talking about?"

"Can you tell us about your arrest for drug possession," Curado said.

"I was cleared," Garrett said. "There's nothing to tell."

Watson sniffed. "That case was dismissed. That's different than being cleared."

The small window in the door darkened then as Chief Baumgartner's face blocked out the light. His eyes filled with fury when they locked onto Garrett.

Steve Curado rambled for a moment, but Garrett couldn't hear his words. Instead, his heart raced, and the blood pounded in his ears. It had been a long time since an adrenaline dump bothered him, but at this exact moment, Garrett's hands began to tremble.

Baumgartner lingered for a moment, glanced both directions, then headed west—the direction toward the detective's office.

Toward Marty Hill.

Why were two men—both of whom who had always been easily approachable, one of which Garrett considered a friend—suddenly angry with him?

It didn't take long for his imagination to turn to Wardell Clint. *That mother—*

"Tyler? Officer Garrett?"

He shook himself from his thoughts and refocused on Curado.

"I'm sorry," Garrett said. "Can you repeat the question?"

"Would you mind explaining the drugs? We tried finding a reasonable explanation for them being in your house—"

"Under your bathroom sink," Watson added.

"—but we didn't find anything. You were arrested, booked, and the drugs were put on property. Then the charges were dropped. We'd like to know why."

Garrett slowly pulled his hands from the table and put them in his lap. It was a move that both DOJ interviewers noted as he saw them glance to each other. He didn't care. His hands were shaking.

If Wardell Clint had started talking, it would make sense for Baumgartner and Hill to be angry. However, if Clint had talked, why was he still sitting here with these Department of Justice flunkies and not in handcuffs?

Garrett's heart slowed slightly. Because the department hadn't told DOJ. They wouldn't want the feds knowing their dirt. They would wait until the suits were gone before they jumped him. That's how he saw it.

Which meant he still had a play.

He looked up and glanced from one DOJ lawyer to the next. Finally, he said, "I know where the drugs came from."

"Where?" Curado asked.

"It's a story that involves dirty cops."

"Who?" Watson asked, leaning forward.

"The department has known about this and kept it covered up for the past two years. If I tell you what I know, I want immunity and protection."

Both Watson and Curado straightened before glancing to the other. Curado picked up his pen and hovered it over his notepad.

"Immunity?" Watson said.

"I might say some stuff that ends up implicating myself."

"How do we know this is real?" Curado asked.

The cell phone in Garrett's left pocket buzzed. He put his hand over it, but it didn't buzz a second time.

He had to give them something fast. They would need to get approval for the immunity deal and that would take time—time he no longer had.

"Butch Talbott and Justin Pomeroy," Garrett said. "They were detectives here."

"We know," Watson said. "Talbott was killed in Liberty Lake."

"His shooter was never found," Curado added.

"And Pomeroy committed suicide," Garrett said. The two feds stared at him. "You knew that?"

"We did," they said unison.

"Did you review the report of that crime scene?" Garrett asked.

Both shook their heads. "No need. It was a suicide."

"You should have," Garrett said. "Packages of heroin were found with Pomeroy. The drugs found there will match the heroin that Talbott *planted* in my house."

"Planted?" Curado asked.

Watson rested both of her hands on the table. "How do you know the drugs will match?"

"Those two were dirty," Garrett said. "Like I said, the department knew it and they covered it up. They paid me seven hundred fifty thousand to keep me quiet."

Both federal agents leaned back in their chairs.

Garrett's heartbeat was almost normal again. His worries hadn't gone away. They were still there, but he felt a new game being played. A game he could win.

Watson leaned forward. "Why do you need immunity?"

"You mean aside from the fact that I just admitted taking money to stay quiet about a cover up?"

Watson waved dismissively. "So maybe you felt remorse and came forward as a whistleblower. Why ask for immunity?"

"Because when I finish that story, I'll need a lawyer."

"Give us something that we can go to our boss with."

Garrett wetted his lips as he thought. He was about to own up to something the department had hunted for two years. But if he could wrap himself in an immunity deal, then Wardell Clint and Captain Tom Farrell could never get at him.

"Detective Talbott," Garrett said. "His shooter has never been found."

Both feds stared at him.

"Do I need to draw a roadmap?" Garrett asked.

"You?" Curado said.

"You killed Detective Talbott?" Watson said.

"In self-defense. Yeah. He tried to kill me once before. Him and Pomeroy. They were the ones who ambushed me on patrol. When I stopped Todd Trotter."

Watson glanced at Curado then turned back to Garrett. "They ambushed you?"

Garrett nodded.

"That's why no one has ever been arrested," Watson muttered.

"Because the shooters were already dead," Curado said, his voice tinged with revelation.

"And the department knew," Garrett added with emphasis.

Watson lowered her chin. "You can prove this?"

He nodded even though he didn't have any proof.

"That still doesn't explain why the immunity request." Watson pressed.

"I've kept quiet for a reason," Garrett said. "I talk and I jam myself up. I know this. If you want to hear what I have to say, get me an immunity agreement. If not, I'll leave, and we'll pretend this never happened."

"You just admitted it to us," Curado said.

Garrett chuckled. "You never read me my rights. We aren't being taped or recorded. As far as the law is concerned, none of this is admissible. You should know that."

"We do know that," Watson said.

"Tyler—" Curado began but was interrupted.

"Get me an agreement. Then I'll sing to the heavens. You can record the hell out of it."

The phone in his left pocket buzzed again.

The lawyers looked at each other briefly before standing.

"Wait here," Curado said. "We'll go find our boss and discuss this with her."

The two lawyers slipped out of the room and pulled the door almost closed.

Garrett pulled the burner phone from his left pocket and flipped it open. Two new texts from Royal Harjo.

The first text was bad enough. *Think I saw him.*

But it was the second that made him realize his time in the training room was up. *EE Def here!*

If Clint or Zielinski grabbed Earl Ellis and brought him in, then his immunity deal wouldn't be worth the paper it was written on. The feds would protect him from killing a dirty detective in self-defense, but there was no way they would give a deal that would absolve him for the murder of Gary Stone.

He wasn't worried about Ellis talking about his drug dealing. Garrett could paint a picture to DOJ that he was working a case. That it was some sort of hangover investigation from his days with ACT. Of course, if he went down that road, he'd need to create a bunch of paperwork to cover his ass. That was something he'd like to avoid.

It wasn't a gun that brought down Al Capone. It was some paper.

Earl Ellis was the only person on this earth who could definitively link him to Stone's death. So Ellis had to go, and it had to be done quickly before Clint and Zielinski returned to his house.

Garrett snapped the phone shut, pushed his chair back, and ran from the training room.

Chapter 45

"Who were you investigating with the Anti-Crime Team?" Édelie Durand demanded.

Captain Tom Farrell started to answer, but she cut him off.

"Before you answer, let me share some things I've learned with you. Is that okay?"

Farrell swallowed.

"Dana Hatcher doesn't like you."

"I wouldn't say—"

Durand held up her hand. "Let me finish."

Farrell fell silent again and watched her like a child waiting patiently for a parent to finish a scolding. Normally, Durand would have been more tactful in the way she spoke about Hatcher, but she was out of time. Her flight back to D.C. was in a few hours, and they needed to wrap this up. The time for niceties was a couple days ago. Now was for cutting to the chase.

"It was obvious in the way she spoke about Chief Baumgartner and you. I took that into account when considering what she said."

"I appreciate that."

"She feels slighted that you got to run the Anti-Crime Team."

"It was her idea," Farrell said. "The chief decided it fit best under my division. I argued against that, but it's his decision where things like this fall."

"She's not likely to get over it very soon."

"That doesn't seem to be a Justice problem."

"It's not. She had concerns about the team, though, that went beyond it being under your division."

"She never voiced these concerns to me."

"Then I'll voice them for her."

Captain Farrell flexed his jaw.

"To confirm, there were four officers on the team. Tyler Garrett, Ray Zielinski, Gary Stone, and Jun Yang."

Farrell nodded. "That's correct. There was also a sergeant and detective, too."

"But four officers formed the core team."

"That's correct."

"Garrett and Zielinski are listed as senior patrol officers. That's a designation for officers with over five years on the department. Am I right?"

"That's right."

"And Stone had a couple years on."

"Roughly. Yes."

"With no street experience."

"That's not true." Farrell wagged a finger. "He had street experience in the FTO car. That's the field training officer program."

"I know."

"Then he spent the rest of his probationary period in a patrol car on the street. After that, he was assigned to city hall."

"Is that typical? For someone that inexperienced to be assigned that quickly to a specialty position?"

Farrell paused as if considering his answer. Finally, he said, "It happens sometimes."

Durand made a note on her pad. When she looked up, she said, "And Jun Yang? She had less than a year on, correct?"

"Correct."

"In fact, she phased out of the FTO program and went straight into the ACT. Isn't that right?"

"Well, yeah, but there were—"

"Is *that* normal? For a rookie with no experience to make it onto a specialty team?"

"She had military police experience—"

"Captain, please. She had no city police experience. So I ask, is that normal?"

The captain paused again. His answer was the same as before. "It happens sometimes."

"If I asked you to pull the records of other recruits, let's use the last ten years, who were assigned to a specialty detail before they were off probation, how many do you think we would see?"

"I don't know."

"Take a guess."

Farrell's face reddened. "I don't know."

Durand shook her head as she made another note. When she looked up, she asked, "Who selected the members of the Anti-Crime Team?"

Farrell wiped his face then said, "I did." A moment passed before he weakly added, "With the input of the chief."

Durand leaned forward. "So the chief had input on the team members?"

Farrell considered his answer before speaking. "I recommended the team. He approved them."

"Oh. How many detectives are under you control?"

"By division?"

"No. You're the head of the Investigations Division. I'm wondering how many detectives you have at your disposal?"

"Fifty-four, but they're spread across property crimes, special investigations—"

"Fifty-four," Durand interrupted. "So you have fifty-four investigators at your disposal."

Farrell crossed his arms. "They're not at my disposal. They have responsibilities."

"How many are working the ambush of Tyler Garrett?"

The captain blanched. "That case has been closed."

"I didn't realize you found those responsible for the ambush?"

Farrell blinked.

"Or have you?"

The captain remained silent.

"You have an officer who survived an ambush, fought back, and killed one suspect. Yet the additional shooter or shooters was never identified. Even the chief was surprised that they hadn't been found yet."

"It was a county case," Farrell said. "They were the lead on it."

"What about the dead officer in Liberty Lake? His shooter has never been identified either."

"Liberty Lake," Farrell said, "they were the lead on that case."

"Two dead officers and no arrests. You're defending the inability to find attackers of your officers with territorial justification?"

Farrell's eyes dropped.

"I flew to Seattle this morning."

The captain nodded but didn't bother to look up.

"So you heard that I was over there?"

He nodded again.

"Did you know that I went to speak with Jun Yang?"

Farrell looked up then.

"She had a lot to say."

The captain gnawed on his lip.

"She said she was brought on for a specific reason. It was a surprising one, actually. One I would never have imagined hearing from a young officer."

Farrell rubbed his mouth where he'd bitten it but didn't speak.

"She said she was brought on to be a rat. Your rat, to be exact."

The captain's shoulders slumped slightly. He still did not speak.

"So, back to my original question."

Farrell raised his eyebrows. He looked like a man about to vomit.

Édelie Durand put down her pen and leaned forward. She looked deeply into his eyes. "Just exactly *who* were you investigating with the Anti-Crime Team?

Chapter 46

Clint tapped at the keyboard, then reached for the mouse. The payroll program was a clunky application, and his clearance level as *user* kept him locked out of several functions. If he was a sergeant, he'd have supervisor clearance, and finding out Tyler Garrett's current work schedule would be easier. He'd already checked the CAD system to see if Garrett was logged on. Since Garrett was assigned to day shift, he should be listed. He wasn't, so that meant he was off today. If it wasn't his scheduled day off, Clint wanted to know the reason he wasn't on duty, and if it was a single day or more than one. With all his focus on the network surrounding Garrett recently, he hadn't followed the officer's movements as closely as in the past. His schedule might have changed. For all he knew, the man had left on a Mexican vacation.

I should have been on top of this.

If Garrett slipped the noose because of his own clumsiness…

"Ward!"

Clint turned to the sound of his misused name with a scowl. He doubted Marty Hill was back for a second round but was surprised to see Zielinski staggering up to his desk. The veteran officer was breathing heavily, and his face was painted with panic.

"What is it?" Clint snapped.

"It's Farrell," Zielinski said. "DOJ is going after him."

"What?"

"They're taking him down," Zielinski said. "He's in a room with one of them right now."

"You saw this?" Clint asked, his eyes narrowing.

"Yes." Zielinski took in a lungful of air and let it out. His breathing evened. "It happened right in front of me, down by the chief's office. I just finished my interview with DOJ and—"

"What did you tell them?"

"Nothing."

"You must have said something. Otherwise, why did they go after Farrell?"

"I don't know," Zielinski said. "But it was something else. I had the blonde lady with the short hair. The fed with Farrell is a black woman."

"How'd he look?" Clint asked.

"Farrell?" Zielinski shook his head. "Like a man walking to the gallows."

Clint frowned. Coupled with Hill's discovery of his case file, this latest development made it clear. Time was up.

"I'm going after Garrett," Clint said. "If Farrell spills to DOJ, that's it. They shut us down, and we don't get him." He didn't bother to tell Zielinski about Hill. It wouldn't change anything.

Zielinski looked around to see if anyone was listening. Then he leaned closer. "You've got enough to arrest him," he said. "But enough to charge? Enough to convict?"

"It doesn't matter. It has to be now. We get him in cuffs and hope the rest falls into place."

Ellis. Maybe Angela, too. Get Marty Hill on board, and bridge all the cases together, including the incomplete forensics. It could work.

"I'm in," Zielinski said. "I might be screwed, but at least I can do this."

Clint understood. He motioned toward the computer. "He's not on duty. I was trying to get his schedule from the payroll program, but the software's clunky." Clint rose from his chair. "We'll have to do this the old-fashioned way."

"Let's go," Zielinski said.

Before either of them could take a step, Chief Baumgartner strode angrily into the bullpen. When he saw Clint, he made a beeline for him.

"Uh-oh," Clint muttered under his breath.

When Baumgartner was an arm's length from Clint, he stopped. "Do you have enough to arrest Tyler Garrett?" he growled at him.

Clint stared at him, momentarily shocked. Next to him, Zielinski let out a small gasp.

Their reaction seemed to irritate the chief. "I know everything, damn it," he snapped. "Do you think I'm stupid? Now answer my question—do you have enough to arrest Tyler Garrett?"

"Yes, sir," Clint said.

Baumgartner pointed a thick finger at him. "Then go do it."

"Yes, sir," Clint repeated. He turned to Zielinski. "We'll try his girlfriend's condo first."

"What?" Baumgartner said. "No. He's in the training room up the hall with DOJ."

That surprised Clint, too, but it was a lucky break.

"Come on," ordered the chief.

He turned and headed out of the bullpen. Clint took three swift strides to reach his side. Zielinski trailed behind them.

As they left the Investigative Division, Baumgartner turned toward Clint with a glare. "As soon as he's in cuffs, get him in the box. I want a confession."

"I understand."

Baumgartner turned his eyes straight ahead again. Then he asked, "Was it your idea or Farrell's?"

"What part, Chief?"

"All of it," Baumgartner said. Then he added, "Keeping me out of the loop."

Clint didn't reply.

"That's what I thought," the chief said.

When they reached their destination, all Clint saw was an empty room with stacks of papers on the table.

We're too late He should have known it wouldn't be that easy.

Baumgartner's face pinched into a scowl. "He read me.

Damn it." Baumgartner slammed his fist down on the table, causing it to rattle from the force.

"What do you mean?" Clint asked him.

Baumgartner gave him a look of frustrated embarrassment. He pointed to the window in the door. "He saw me looking in on him during the DOJ interview. He must have read my expression and knew something was up. That's why he left early."

Clint knew that the chief was right. Garrett was like a wild animal that sensed danger and fled. The question was, where to?

Baumgartner's voice was low and dark. "You go get him, Wardell."

"I will." Clint thought for a moment. "Should we put it out to patrol? That would give us more eyes, and a wider net."

Baumgartner considered briefly but shook his head. "After what happened two years ago, how many of our own people will believe it? We already cried wolf once. He'll get tipped off."

Clint nodded. Someone sympathetic would tell him what was happening, and then he really would run for it. Right now, he was spooked but not certain. He might still go to a familiar place, making it easier to find him.

Baumgartner leaned forward. "Besides, I want to keep this off DOJ's radar until they're gone. *We* bring him in, not the feds. We fix our own mess."

"All right," Clint said. That was fine with him. Only there was no *we* about it. He was going to take down Tyler Garrett. No one else.

Baumgartner pointed at Zielinski. "And *you* stay the hell away from this."

Zielinski swallowed but didn't answer.

Baumgartner returned his gaze to Clint. "Do it," he said, and walked away, headed toward mahogany row. Both Clint and Zielinski watched him go.

"What the hell just happened?" Zielinski whispered.

"I've been blessed by the man," said Clint. He turned to Zielinski. "You should go home."

Zielinski shook his head. "I'm not staying away from this."

"You heard the chief."

"I don't care. I'm not going."

"This needs to be as clean as possible," Clint argued. Before the chief's directive, he'd been fine with Zielinski's help. But that changed when Baumgartner gave a clear order.

Zielinski snorted. "Clean? Are you kidding me?"

"You're not even on duty," Clint pointed out.

Zielinski gave him a hard stare. "Wardell, please. I *need* to do this."

Clint hesitated. The argument was pointless, only serving to waste time. Besides, disobeying the chief at this stage of the game was essentially a misdemeanor in a field full of felonies. "Fine. I'll call his wife. You head over to his girlfriend's condo. If either of us spots him, call. Keep an eye on him, and only ask for help from patrol if you have to."

Zielinski nodded gravely. He turned and headed out the door.

Clint reached for his phone.

Chapter 47

Farrell let the question hang in the air for as long as he dared.

"Captain?" Durand asked. "What's the answer? Who was your target with the Anti-Crime Team?"

He saw the trap she'd prepared for him. It was carefully constructed, with facts and inferences, witnesses, and suspicious behaviors. He knew that if he took a step forward, he'd spring that trap, and then things really would be over.

I let down everyone. The department, certainly. And Jun Yang. She hadn't deserved the lousy mission he handed her. Gary Stone, too. He paid for Farrell's mistakes with his life. Of course, he'd been letting down Clint since their partnership began, and now he was on the verge of letting down his chief of police, too.

If he stepped forward and sprung Durand's trap, there would not only be a consent decree slapped on the police department, but Farrell doubted she and her team would even leave as planned. They'd burrow in and keep investigating, calling back to Washington, D.C. for reinforcements. Neither he nor Clint would bring down Garrett, and who knew what the feds might do. They might finish the job for them, but he was willing to bet it was just as likely they'd lionize the dirty cop, especially if he was willing to talk. A rogue captain was a better catch than a dirty patrol officer.

Farrell knew Garrett was dirty, but how much could he and Clint *prove*?

More than that, how important was it that they, the Spokane Police Department, clean up their own dirty linen?

He thought everything depended on it.

Durand was staring at him with an expression that was equal parts intelligence, frustration, and regret. He didn't bother trying to decipher the reason for those sentiments. A more overwhelming thought settled into his mind with finality.

My career is over.

And I am destroyed.

"Captain?" Durand repeated.

A sorrowful calmness came over him in that moment. He realized what he had to do. He couldn't give her anything that led to suspecting Tyler Garrett. No matter what, she and her team had to leave as planned. That would give the chief and Clint a chance to bring Garrett in themselves.

"I was targeting hippos," Farrell said, surprised at how steady his voice sounded. Just a few minutes ago, he'd felt like he could have collapsed from weariness, vomited, or even wept. Now, he was resigned.

Durand's face scrunched in confusion. "I'm sorry…hippos?"

"High-profile offenders," Farrell explained. "HPOs. Hippos is the street jargon."

Durand pressed her lips together in momentary frustration. "I wasn't asking about the mission of your team. I'm talking about your ulterior motive."

"I didn't have one."

Durand leaned forward. "Jun Yang was put on that team to be a rat. That means you thought there was something there to watch. Now, I don't think it was Gary Stone. He seemed like too much of a straight arrow. It may have been Ray Zielinski, who's had plenty of IA trouble. But I don't know why you'd need a spy for that. You could just have Internal Affairs investigate openly, which they were doing anyway." She sat back in her chair and crossed her arms. "That leaves Tyler Garrett."

"You know what I think?" Farrell said. "I think you want to see corruption so badly that you're looking for monsters under the bed."

"Really? Then explain Yang to me."

Farrell shrugged. "I shouldn't need to, but I will. You've

been investigating police departments for how long?"

"Eleven years," Durand said. "What's your point?"

"I'm sure you've seen plenty of other specialty units or directed teams, just like ACT. You know the risk for noble cause corruption that exists in that scenario. Cops start out fudging events a little bit to make a good arrest on a bad guy and that leads to—"

"You don't have to educate me on noble cause corruption. I taught that block of instruction at Quantico for three semesters."

"Okay. Then you'll understand my thinking. Jun Yang was an officer who had already shown absolute integrity, even in the face of a difficult situation. She turned in several classmates who cheated at the academy."

"I know about this, too."

"Do you know how hard that is? Especially for a recruit?"

"They cheated. It should be easy."

"Easy?" Farrell made a dismissive sound with his lips. "If you've got ice water running through your veins, maybe. For most people, it's a hard thing to do. But she did it. And so I knew she'd do it again, if anything hinky started to happen on that team."

"That's the reason?" Durand's expression was skeptical.

"Yes. It helped that being a rookie, she didn't have any deep connections with anyone here yet that might muddy the waters for her. And it helped that she had a military background and was more mature than our average twenty-one-year-old rookie. But her integrity was the biggest piece." Farrell gave Durand a long stare. "Ms. Durand, Jun Yang wasn't my spy. She was my safety valve."

Durand sat quietly, soaking in his words. Farrell waited. He was fairly certain what was coming next. He wasn't disappointed.

"To your knowledge," Durand asked, her tone formal, "was Officer Gary Stone involved in anything illegal, immoral, or corrupt?"

"Of course not."

"Same for Jun Yang?"

"Pure integrity from her."

"What about Ray Zielinski?"

Farrell sighed. "Lately, it seems like he has fallen out of the unlucky tree and is hitting every bad decision branch on the way to the ground. But I think he's stumbling into his mistakes, not searching for them. He's not a malicious person."

"And Tyler Garrett?"

Farrell gritted his teeth. His stomach pitched a little when he spoke, but he made himself say the words.

"Officer Garrett is a fine officer," he said.

Durand watched him for a few moments longer. The frustration in her expression had faded, leaving the intelligence and regret to take up the slack. "I wonder, Captain Farrell, if these answers are ones you'd want read back to you during a full-fledged investigation."

"Are you coming back for one?"

Durand didn't reply. She considered Farrell for several moments, then appeared to make a decision. She stood, pushing her chair in. "My team and I are leaving for Washington, D.C. in a few hours, Captain. I'll make my recommendation and Justice will make a determination regarding further action. But no matter what happens, I believe that one way or another, you'll have some decisions to answer for."

Farrell's gaze was steady when he answered her. "Don't we all?"

A flash of sadness seemed to pass over Durand's features, then was gone. He wondered for a moment what it was she had to answer for. He had a crazy thought that he should ask her, even offer to commiserate. But before he could speak, she turned and left the conference room without another word, leaving him to his fate.

Chapter 48

"Grandma left thirty minutes ago," Royal Harjo said. "He's in there alone."

Tyler Garrett stood next to the sun-faded green Ford F-150 and kept his eyes on the front of the little house. Harjo sat in the driver's seat with the window rolled down.

Even though he was there to deal with Earl Ellis, his mind was clouded with thoughts of Angie and the kids.

Why was he thinking about them now? He shook his head to get rid of their images.

Harjo smoked a brown cigarette. When he exhaled, he blew the smoke through the side of his mouth, away from Garrett and into the cab of his truck.

Garrett rested an elbow in the open car window. "You sure he didn't leave out the back?"

"If he did, then he's on foot. Earl seems a man to take his ride with him." Royal pointed to a red Lincoln Corsair further up the street. "Especially a fine one like that."

The car was new. He would never have spotted Ellis in it.

"Go through the alley," Garrett said. "If he comes out, take him."

"As in…"

Garrett eyed the man behind the steering wheel. "As in drop him."

Harjo blew out a stream of smoke. "Got it."

The truck pulled away and drove toward the opposite end of the block. When it turned and disappeared around the corner, Garrett strolled casually toward Aurelia Ellis's house. His eyes swept the neighborhood. Nobody moved.

A car drove toward him. It was an older car, a Nissan Maxima, and loud rock music boomed from it. He turned his head away as the car passed. It continued out of the neighborhood.

He turned in front of the grandmother's house and ascended the steps to the front door. Discreetly, he pulled his gun from underneath his shirt and held it against his stomach. Then he stood off to the side of the door, a habit from being in uniform, and knocked.

It wasn't loud. He didn't want to draw too much attention from anyone not in the house.

He scanned the neighborhood again. A cat ran from one yard to the next in chase of something Garrett couldn't see.

He waited a few moments then knocked again. This time a little softer.

Another few seconds passed before the door opened slightly.

Due to where Garrett stood, though, he couldn't see who was behind the door and they couldn't see him.

The wait seemed forever for the door to either open further or close.

When it began to slowly shut, Garrett swung his leg around and kicked the door. It banged back into someone. There was a clunk as something fell to the floor.

Garrett charged into the house with his gun extended.

"Don't," he said and closed the door.

Earl Ellis was bent at the knees and reaching for a gun on the floor. He slowly straightened and lifted his hands in the air. Garrett removed his burner phone and placed a call. When it was answered, he said, "Come in the back."

"Who's with you?" Ellis asked.

He ignored the question and jerked his head toward the open room behind him. "Let's go in the living room."

"C'mon, G, you know—"

Garrett grabbed Ellis by the shirt and yanked him into the living room. Ellis stumbled, tripped over the coffee table, and fell into a floral-printed couch with an afghan draped over its back.

"Where've you been, Earl?"

Ellis rolled over to his back and lifted his hands again. "Around."

When Garrett lifted his gun, Ellis turned his head and closed his eyes.

"The hell does that mean?" Garrett asked. "Around?"

"I had to get out."

"You're not making sense, Earl."

There was a knock at the back door.

"Stand up," Garrett ordered.

Ellis clumsily got to his feet. Garrett grabbed him by the back of the shirt then pushed him toward the kitchen. He knew there were possible weapons in this room for Ellis to grab—knives, mallets, and pans—and he remained a couple steps back for that reason. If Ellis made any move he didn't like, he would end the man and move on.

Without being told, Ellis unlocked the rear door and moved out of the way to allow Harjo to enter. As he did, Ellis's eyes locked onto the revolver in the hand of the latest arrival.

"Earl," Harjo said flatly.

Ellis glanced back to Garrett. "Come on, G. It doesn't have to come to this."

Garrett tucked his gun in the back of his pants. "Then tell me why you left."

"Because," Ellis said. His eyes darted from Garrett to Harjo and back. "There was this detective."

"Which one?"

"Brother who thinks he's Virgil Tibbs."

Royal Harjo said, "Who?"

But Garrett knew exactly who Earl Ellis meant. His lip curled. "Wardell Clint."

"Guy stopped me after the…" Ellis glanced to Harjo. "The thing we did."

"What did he say?" Garrett asked.

Ellis turned his palms upward. "He knows what we did."

"He *thinks* he knows," Garrett said as he crossed his arms. "What did you tell him?"

"Nothing, man. That's why I left. So he couldn't press me."

"You could have called me about this. Instead, you went radio silent."

Ellis glanced to the gun in Harjo's hand. "I was afraid."

"Weak," Harjo muttered.

"Screw you, man!" Ellis shouted. "You don't know anything."

"You weren't afraid, Earl. What was the real reason?"

Ellis bowed his head. "I was afraid. I'm not lying."

"Of Clint?"

He shook his head. "Of you, man. Of you."

Garrett cocked his head. "You've got nothing to fear as long as you're straight with me."

"What we did to Strayer…" Ellis said.

"Leon?" Harjo asked. His brow furrowed.

"We set him up, G. Like a lamb for the slaughter."

Harjo glanced to Garrett. "Wait. You set up that cop?"

Garrett shrugged.

"If you could do something like that to a cop," Ellis said, "what could you do to me?"

"The detective," Garrett said, "the one you said you left town for, he was watching this house."

Ellis froze.

"Did he talk with your grandma?"

"He did."

"Is that why you came home?"

"No."

"Then why come back if you knew they were watching?"

Ellis shrugged. "She raised me and she's alone now. She needs some help."

Garrett scratched the side of his face. "You come home and suddenly the detective stops watching the house. Strange coincidence, don't you think?" Garrett glanced to Harjo. "What do you think that means?"

Harjo grunted. "He talked. Now, they got what they wanted, so they no longer got to watch his crib."

"That's not what happened," Ellis said. "I swear!"

"I don't know," Garrett said. "But I'm inclined to agree with you, Royal. Shoot him."

Harjo extended his gun, but before he could fire, Ellis yelled, "Wait!"

Garrett said, "Hold on."

Ellis held his hands in front of him as if they would somehow ward off an incoming bullet. "The detective! He took me to the station."

"Clint did?"

Ellis nodded. "I didn't say anything. I swear. He wanted me to, but I refused. You gotta believe me. He let me go. He had to. He had no other choice."

"But now he knows you're in town. He'll keep after you. You should have stayed gone."

Ellis glanced between the two men. "I'll leave again. He'll never find me. I swear—"

Garrett waved at Harjo and the gun fired. The boom echoed in the small house.

Earl Ellis grabbed his belly and moaned. He dropped to a single knee before collapsing to the floor. While Harjo moved in for a second shot, Garrett left the kitchen and returned to the entryway of the house. A second shot was fired as he returned.

"He used to be a good man," Harjo said as he stood over the fallen Ellis.

"Used to be," Garrett agreed.

Harjo knelt and pressed a couple fingers to Ellis's neck. "I can't believe you guys set up Leon to get a cop." When Harjo stood, he faced Garrett with a smile of disbelief. "That's a baller move."

His smiled melted as Tyler Garrett shot him twice in the chest with Earl Ellis's gun—the one Ellis had dropped in the entryway.

Royal Harjo dropped his gun, stumbled backwards a few steps before falling into a sitting position against a set of cabinets.

Garrett wiped his prints from the gun and stuck it in the limp hand of Ellis. He fired one more shot to ensure that some gunshot residue would be on the dead man's hand. Then he checked Harjo's pockets, found the burner phone he was using, and exited out the back door.

As he hurried out of the alley, thoughts of Angie and the kids again flooded his mind.

"Can I come in?"

"What for?" Angie asked.

Garrett cocked his head to pop a crick in his neck. "To see the kids."

After leaving Earl Ellis, he'd driven directly to his former home. The images of Angie and the kids seemed to plague him now. Was it some sort of guilt trip he was on? If so, it had never happened to him before.

"They're not home," Angie said. "Besides, it's not your day."

"Not my day," Garrett muttered. "No lie."

Angie leaned against the door. "Have you been drinking?"

"What? *No.*"

"Then what's wrong?"

Garrett shrugged. "Been thinking about you and the kids."

She remained quiet as he shuffled back and forth on the front steps.

He glanced around. "Can I come in for a bit? Maybe talk?"

"It's not a good idea."

"Why not?"

"Because I've moved on. You have, too. You've got a girlfriend."

"But I still…I love you. And the kids."

She sighed with frustration. "I know that in your own weird way you love me. The kids, too. But that's not why I left. I've already told you this."

He shook his head. "But we could—"

"I don't feel safe around you. No amount of love is going to change that."

She stepped back and started to close the door. He held up a hand to stop it from shutting.

"We never even tried," Garrett said.

"I did, Ty. You never even noticed how much I tried. That was part of the problem. Now, remove your hand from the door."

He stayed there for a moment.

"If you want to cry on someone's shoulder, go home to you know who. Remove your hand from the door."

"Angie."

"If you don't, I'll call the police."

His mouth hung open. "You would?"

She shrugged. "You're not respecting our boundaries."

"But I haven't done anything."

Her eyes flicked to his hand on her front door.

Garrett dropped his hand then.

He stayed on the steps long enough to hear the deadbolt lock.

Chapter 49

"Ms. Berg?" Clint spoke into the phone receiver. "Did you hear my question?"

Angela Berg was quiet on the other end of the line. Then she asked, "Why are you calling me? I told you—"

"Have you seen Garrett?" Clint repeated.

"No. Why?"

"It's all coming to a head," Clint told her. "Today. Now."

Angela made a sound that Clint couldn't quite interpret. He pressed on.

"You've told me since the beginning that all you care about is protecting your kids. Is that true?"

"Of course, it is."

"Then you know there's only one way to do that now, right?"

She fell silent. Clint waited, his limbs humming with nervous energy. He wanted to be in his car, going after Garrett. But he knew this would be important later.

Finally, Angela said, "Yes. Okay. If you need me to come in and talk with you, I will."

"I'll be in touch," Clint said, and hung up.

He left the detectives' bullpen, walking past Marty Hill's unoccupied desk. If he had to guess, the detective was probably already at the prosecutor's office, securing an arrest warrant for Garrett. If he followed his stated plan, his next stop would be the chief's office. That didn't worry him. Baumgartner would handle that. Clint had a single-minded purpose now.

Find and arrest Garrett.

He made it out of the building without having to speak to anyone. When he reached his Impala, he slid behind the wheel and started the engine. He waited the nine seconds required for his police radio to boot up and his Bluetooth to connect. When it had, he called Zielinski.

"Not at the wife's," he told him. He put the car in gear and started driving out of the parking area.

"Could she be lying?"

Clint considered. "I doubt it. She booted his ass, remember?"

"All right. I'm a couple blocks from the girlfriend's condo."

"When you get there, park—" A beeping sound interrupted him. He glanced down to see he had an incoming call. He immediately recognized Angela Berg's number. "Hold on," he told Zielinski, and switched over. "This is Clint."

"How'd you know?" she asked him. "How'd you know he'd come here?"

Clint's eyes narrowed. Had she lied to him before? "He was there?"

"Just now. Barely a minute after you called me."

"Is he still there?"

"No, he's gone. I called you right away."

"What did he want?"

"To see the kids. And maybe me, too, I think." She paused, her tone thoughtful. "Something was off about him."

"Something has *always* been off about him," Clint said. "Most people just can't see it."

"Maybe so."

Her voice sounded sad to Clint, but he couldn't be certain. "Do you know where he went?"

"No."

"Thank you, Angela," Clint said. He hung up, switching back to Zielinski. "You there?"

"I'm here and I'm outside the condo."

Clint told him what Angela had said.

Zielinski let out a low whistle. "You know what it sounds like, right?"

"That he's getting ready to run."

"Yep. One last goodbye to the kiddos and he's gonzo. That was his intention, at least."

"Wait for me at the building entrance. We'll go up togeth—" He stopped suddenly and turned up the police radio.

"What is it?"

"Shhh. Listen."

Normally, the hum and rhythm of the patrol radio was something Clint only listened to passively. But he'd heard an elevated tone in the dispatcher's voice, and as he listened to the details of the call for service, he understood why.

"—turned from the grocery store to find two men shot to death in her kitchen. She states one is her grandson, Earl James Ellis, a thirty-one-year-old black male who is in locally with drug charges. Complainant does not recognize the other individual, though she stated he appears to be Native American. She saw at least two guns and is unsure if anyone else in the home." The dispatcher paused for a moment, then continued. "Complainant is standing by on her neighbor's porch. All units exercise caution."

Clint turned down the radio.

"Are you kidding me?" Zielinski said over the phone. "That had to be Garrett, right?"

Clint didn't bother answering. His mind clicked through possibilities. There was no way Garrett would return to Tiana Kennedy's condo now. She was a luxury he couldn't afford. He had to be planning an escape. Where to? Another state? Canada?

"You want to me to pull off here and head over to the Ellis house?" Zielinski asked.

Clint frowned. "Why? Garrett's not there."

"I just thought—"

"That scene is static now. Let patrol and the detectives handle it. We need to find Garrett before he leaves town."

Zielinski sighed. "This may not be New York, but it's a big town. Where are we supposed to look?"

Clint smiled grimly. For the first time that day, he felt a small sense of satisfaction. All of those many long nights he spent trailing Garrett were finally going to pay off. He knew the man's haunts.

"I have an idea," he said.

Chapter 50

Chief Robert Baumgartner sat as his desk, staring out the window at the uninspiring view of the juvenile courts building and the employee parking lot. He had spent more than a few lonely moments in his office, contemplating difficult choices, but nothing had ever prepared him for this.

Tyler Garrett.

He didn't even want to delve into the psychology of a man like that. All he could do at this point was contemplate the repercussions of everything he now knew. Garrett was what DOJ would doubtlessly call a "bad actor." They'd be right, too, if making an understatement. But Garrett was a single man. No matter how corrupt, he didn't represent the other three hundred plus officers on the Spokane Police Department. *His* department was clean. Even Farrell's colossal mistakes were made in pursuit of a noble cause. It was a case of noble cause corruption, still in its purest form.

It didn't matter, though. What mattered was that DOJ wasn't finished with them. If there hadn't been enough information to merit a consent decree before, there would be once Garrett was caught and arrested. Maybe he could somehow manage to convince Justice to proceed with a technical assistance letter instead, but he doubted it. The odds weren't great before the Garrett revelation, but now?

No. A consent decree was coming.

He had to accept that. Not only accept it but embrace it. Take the good from it and try to mitigate the pain. That was the reality he faced.

Of course, I might not survive. Sikes might use this as an opportunity to do what he's been aching to do for years—fire me.

"Let him," Baumgartner muttered.

A knock came at his door.

"Later!" he hollered.

There was a silence, and then another knock.

"I said, *later!*"

The door cracked open. Detective Marty Hill peered in. "Chief?"

"Are you deaf?" Baumgartner rumbled. "I said I'm busy."

Hill nodded in understanding. "I know. But trust me—you're going to want to hear this. Nothing is more important."

Baumgartner almost snapped back *Wanna bet?* but stopped himself. Instead, he motioned to the chair in front of his desk.

Hill lumbered in, closing the door behind himself. He sat and fixed Baumgartner with a steely gaze. "Chief, I don't know how to say this other than to just say it. I have an arrest warrant for Tyler Garrett."

Baumgartner stared at him in astonishment.

Hill misunderstood the reason for the expression on his face. "I know, it's a shock, but let me tell you how I got here."

Baumgartner listened with rapt, surprised attention as Hill detailed his investigation into the Ocampo quadruple homicide, Clint's odd behavior at the scene, as well as his interest in the Anti-Crime Team. Then he dropped the bombshell about the bullet match, Clint's trip to Liberty Lake, and the shakily drawn circle Nona Henry had made around Garrett's photograph.

"I've been to the prosecutor already," Hill said. "I know I should have come here first, but I also knew that time was a factor. I have the warrant, so we can notify patrol and scramble SWAT—"

The chief raised his hand, stopping Hill. "Marty, I need you to stand down."

It was Hill's turn to be surprised. "Sir?"

"I found out most of what you've told me less than an

hour ago," Baumgartner explained. "I put things in motion to deal with it. I need you to wait for that to run its course."

Hill looked hesitant and uncomfortable. "Chief, I…"

"I'm not covering anything up, Marty," Baumgartner assured him. "Don't worry. But we need to make this arrest before anyone else hears about it. There are other factors in play here."

Hill stared at him, his expression thoughtful. "You mean DOJ," he stated.

"For one, yes." Baumgartner shifted forward, resting his arms on the top of his desk. "Once Garrett is in custody, you bring your case forward. Hell, if he isn't in custody in the next few hours, we might as well make it public. But until then, we've got a shot at cleaning up our own mess, and that matters for something."

Hill didn't answer. Baumgartner let him sit and think. He knew he had the authority to order what he wanted done, but he also knew that he'd have no recourse if Hill refused. He couldn't discipline a whistleblower, even if he wanted to.

Another knock came at the door. Before he could answer, it opened halfway. Marilyn stood in the doorway. "Chief, there's been a double homicide in East Central."

He almost sighed. When it rained, it poured. "Domestic?" he asked. "Gangs?"

"I'm not sure, but one of the victims has a drug record." She glanced down at the note in her hand. "Earl Ellis."

He heard a sharp intake of breath from Hill and looked over for an explanation.

"It's in Clint's file," Hill said. "His notes are all in some kind of code, but some of the paperwork is official records. Ellis was one of those, and he was near the front of the file."

Baumgartner nodded to Marilyn, dismissing her. When she'd closed the door, he said, "Marty, I need you on that scene."

Hill hesitated again. Finally, he said, "All right. I trust you, Chief."

"Thank you."

Hill got up to leave.

As the detective neared the door, Baumgartner said, "Call me directly if you need anything."

Hill nodded without looking back and left the office.

There goes a good man. Probably one of the best, but he believed that most of his officers were cut from that same cloth. Now, it was his duty to do right by them. Leadership was easy when the seas were calm. The real test came when it was time to ride out the storm.

Baumgartner stood and began pacing the length of his office. His hip caught a corner of his small conference table. The chief grunted. The pain was sharp but faded almost immediately. Frustrated, he pushed the entire table, chairs and all, to the side, leaving the path between the door and his desk wide open. Then he started walking again, back and forth.

Maybe I should call Clint for an update.

He knew that was a bad idea. He'd sent his man into battle. Now he had to wait for him to fight it. No one gets anything done with a boss looking over his shoulder, asking for updates.

Garrett was the immediate problem, but he'd made his decision on how to deal with that. There was nothing more he could do, at least for now. The gamble he took made his stomach tighten, but he still believed it was the right call. If there was any son of a bitch who could catch Garrett, it was Wardell Clint.

He was confident that he'd survive this wave.

But there was still an entire storm to contend with, each swell coming hard on the heels of the previous. He needed a plan. He couldn't just expect to grab onto the wheel and career across the waves. Passively standing by and waiting for DOJ to dictate terms would be the equivalent of that. He had to be proactive, steer into the waves, and mitigate their crashing power.

How?

He sat again and drummed his fingers on his desk. He

forced himself to forget the Garrett situation for the moment and look ahead. He needed to bring all his knowledge and experience to bear. A consent decree was coming. What could he do to steer into that?

Externally, there were a few things he could accomplish in short order. Ratchet up community programs and involvement. Bring back the citizen's academy, for one. It was expensive but transformative for most who attended. He could get the same effect on a smaller scale by increasing the number of citizen ride-alongs.

What else?

Expand the Public Information Officer program somehow? Some of the local media was neutral or even friendly, and maybe he could sway some opinions with those who took a more negative stance.

All good ideas, and fairly easy to put in place. But they were expensive and took time to bear fruit.

More than that, none of them were a blockbuster move, which is what he needed.

He considered asking for a community oversight board. Something like that would be tricky. The action could be construed by some as an admission that he didn't have control over a corrupt department and was asking for help. Officers would resent it as well. They already had Internal Affairs and anyone with a cell phone questioning their every move.

He'd take heat from the other side, too. Skeptics would say that he planned to stuff the seats with supporters.

He'd have to walk a thin line. Make it clear that he was inviting oversight for the peace of mind of the people, not because he was concerned. There'd have to be some naysayers on the board. But who?

Baumgartner grimaced.

Sam Gallico would be perfect.

Sure, the former SPD sergeant was a constant critic. He'd never believe there wasn't corruption within the department. But putting him on the board would make it clear

Baumgartner was serious. And hopefully Gallico seeing corruption in every innocuous action would wear thin with the other members and most of the public. In fact, Gallico would be a better choice than a more moderate critic for precisely that reason, and the image of transparency he'd get for selecting such a vocal opponent was an added benefit.

Baumgartner grabbed a notepad and jotted a few notes on it. The concentration steadied his nerves. He glanced at his watch when he finished writing. Clint still had some time left.

He turned back to his own problem.

What about within the department, internally? He knew he could hold things together and provide the leadership the department would need. That wasn't arrogance, just honest self-assessment. Like any other job, experience counted. Being chief was something he'd gotten good at in his long tenure.

But he wouldn't be in that position forever. Depending on what DOJ or the mayor did, he could end up out on his ass within a year. Barring that, he planned to retire someday. There had to be a succession plan.

Maybe it's time to bring back the vacant assistant chief position.

The position had been sitting there in the budget, unfilled since he became chief. The salary savings went toward an extra officer on the street with some left over for training and equipment. But he realized that was a luxury he could no longer afford. He had to fill the position, for two reasons.

The first was to make a not-so-subtle statement to the department, the public, and city hall as to who he believed should follow him as chief. He couldn't name his own successor, but he sure could stack the odds in that person's favor.

The second reason to fill the position was to prepare that person to be capable of taking over. The nuances of sitting in the big chair were different than any other role in the police department. They took a while to learn and longer to master, and much hinged on a leader successfully doing both.

He had always imagined that person would be Tom Farrell. Farrell had followed him up the ladder, always one rung behind, for their entire careers. He'd confided in the captain and asked his advice. In a way, he'd been Baumgartner's unspoken but demonstrated choice. When he retired, unless a mayor decided to go outside the department for his successor, Farrell would have been the obvious choice.

No longer.

Baumgartner sighed.

You should have trusted me, Tom.

He knew now how he had to proceed. He saw it all clearly. The moves, the sacrifice, the way forward. He knew what he had to do in order to ride out this storm.

Chapter 51

Zielinski parked more than a block away from the zombie house. It was the second one he'd checked from the short list of addresses Clint had given him. The first had been empty and secured all the way around.

Despite the time of day, Zielinski strove for the patrol objective of silent and invisible deployment. He kept mostly out of sight as he approached the house. He scanned the street for people walking, cars passing, and those vehicles parked along the street.

He squatted behind a tree a half block away from the target house. His thigh bumped against the butt of the .38 secured in his ankle holster. He wished he'd thought to bring field glasses, but when he left his house that morning, he had no idea he might need them. All he thought was in store for him was a lame interview with a fed.

From behind the tree, he carefully took in the entire scene. At first, everything looked normal. Just another lower-middle-class neighborhood with a foreclosed house mid-block.

Then he spotted the Lincoln Nautilus.

By itself, the vehicle wasn't out of place. But when he saw the slouching silhouette in the driver's seat, he knew who it was.

Garrett.

Clint had been right.

He's doing the same thing I am. Making sure the house is safe before he goes in to get his...what? Stash of drugs or money or whatever so he can run, probably?

Zielinski lifted his phone and dialed Clint. As soon as the detective picked up, Zielinski said, "He's here."

"Which one?"

Zielinski gave him the address. "He's still in the car."

"He's a careful bastard," Clint said. "I'll be there in three."

Zielinski broke the connection and slid his phone back into his pocket. He shifted his stance, as his legs were already cramping.

Three minutes. In three minutes, all of this would be over. A journey that began for him at Garrett's shooting two years ago was finally going to end. His arms and legs buzzed with excitement, the sensation traveling out to his hands and feet. He took some deep breaths to control the adrenaline flowing through him.

He glanced at his watch, waiting.

A minute passed.

Zielinski stood slowly, his joints popping as he did so. He pressed himself against the bark of the tree, careful to remain shielded behind it. If Garrett saw him and drove off, he could easily be six blocks away before Zielinski made it back to his car.

He took three more deep breaths. Long in, and long out.

Another thirty seconds.

Garrett's car door opened.

A spike of adrenaline shot through Zielinski, making his fingers tremble. He watched carefully, barely peeking around the tree. Garrett looked around casually, then started walking in the opposite direction of the house.

What the hell?

Zielinski wondered for a second if he'd been made. But if that were the case, Garrett would have sped off in his vehicle. He wouldn't get out and walk.

His question was answered as soon as Garrett reached the end of the block. He made a left, strolled to the alley, and turned into it.

Of course, Zielinski realized. He was going to enter the zombie house from the rear. Safer that way.

He considered waiting for Clint. That was the safest route

for him. But what if Garrett retrieved his money from the house and got back into his car? Then they'd be faced with a vehicle pursuit. Not only was that dangerous for them, but even more so for the public. He couldn't let that happen.

If he comes back toward the car, I'll confront him.

He waited another two seconds, watching Garrett's shape appear and reappear in the alley as he walked behind the house on the end of the block. Then another thought occurred to him.

If Garrett gets into that house, he has the tactical advantage. The man used to be SWAT, so he would know how to exploit that advantage. Their best option was to take him in the open.

My best option, he thought.

And before he could think about it any further, he was already running.

He was surprised at how quickly he made it across the street. His tennis shoes barely made a sound on the asphalt. Even his own breath was muted. When he turned into the alley, he saw Garrett's back as he walked almost two houses ahead of him. Like a bull, Zielinski lowered his head and charged, hoping to remain undetected for as long as he could. The reassuring weight of his .38 on his ankle made his gait slightly lopsided, but he didn't care. He stared at the back of Garrett's head and ran.

He made it to within fifteen feet before Garrett seemed to sense something. He stiffened and turned. When he saw Zielinski bearing down on him, his eyes flew wide. He pawed at the small of his back, but before he could grab the gun Zielinski suspected was there, the veteran officer plowed into him.

The two of them crumpled to the ground in a heap. Zielinski threw a right hand up toward Garrett's head, connecting with a shoulder as Garrett started to roll away. Zielinski lunged for Garrett's throat, but the man was already out of reach. Garrett scrambled to his feet, and Zielinski struggled to follow. He was still on one knee when Garrett reached behind his back again.

Zielinski sprang forward, forcing Garrett to change tactics. He raised his hands to deflect the first two punches Zielinski threw. His fists thudded into Garrett's forearms. Zielinski shifted his weight and threw a left hook, looping it behind Garrett's guard and catching him on the cheek.

The force of the blow sent Garrett staggering to the side. His arms wavered.

Zielinski lumbered forward.

Quick as a snake, Garrett lashed out with a foot, snapping a kick into Zielinski's groin. The blow caught him flush in the balls, and he stumbled, grunting in pain.

Garrett didn't stop. He waded in, raining punches at Zielinski's head and gut. The veteran blocked as many as he could, battling through sickening pain that slowed his reactions. One of Garrett's jabs caught Zielinski square in the nose. A momentary flash of white light filled his vision. His knees buckled.

Another blow crashed into his jaw. His head whiplashed to the right. Now black patches swam in his field of view. He felt his arms drop lower, and he struggled to remain alert.

The next attack struck him in the back of the head, and he fell forward. The patches of darkness broadened, and he almost lost consciousness. He groaned in pain.

"Get up, Ray," Garrett snarled. "Get up, you old drunk."

Zielinski pushed himself to his knees, but the effort proved to be too much. He collapsed onto his side and rolled onto his back. He blinked rapidly, trying to clear his vision. Above him, Garrett stood with his hands in a fighting position. Hatred and contempt twisted his features. He shook his head and lowered his hands, reaching behind his back again.

This is it.

"Hey, you two! Knock that off!"

Zielinski barely registered the frail but insistent voice of an old woman in the distance, but Garrett's eyes snapped to the left. Zielinski considered lunging at him again, but his limbs wouldn't obey. He turned his own gaze to follow Garrett's. He saw an elderly white woman on her raised patio in the nearby backyard. She wore a purple housecoat and held an oxygen tank on wheels in one hand and a cordless phone in the other.

"I'm calling the cops!" she hollered, raising the phone in the air, and then pulling it back to her face to dial.

Garrett glanced down at Zielinski. He stepped forward and delivered another short kick, this one catching Zielinski in the lower rib cage. Zielinski curled up into a ball, groaning, his head swimming.

And then Garrett was gone.

Chapter 52

Tyler Garrett smacked the steering wheel several times as he drove. He then wrapped his hands around the wheel and shook himself.

"You son of a bitch!" he shouted.

He slowed when he came to an intersection marked with four stop signs. Not seeing another car approaching from any direction, he disregarded the red octagon and accelerated.

"The hell do you think you are, Ray?" Garrett yelled into the rearview mirror. "You're lucky I didn't shoot you in your stupid face."

He blew through an uncontrolled intersection, barely missing a Volkswagen Beetle with a young woman behind the wheel.

"That old lady saved your life, Ray," Garrett hollered. "You realize that?"

He was about to shout again when a troubling thought occurred to him.

How the hell did Zielinski know where to find me?

Garrett's mind raced. Had Zielinski been following him all day? It was unlikely because he'd been careful and watched for a tail.

No, it was more likely that Clint had trailed him at some point and found the zombie house he used. If that was true, how many more did they know about?

Garrett glanced into the rearview mirror again. "Shit!"

Another uncontrolled intersection and another narrowly missed collision. This time it was a black Honda with duct tape over its front quarter panel.

He accelerated.

If Clint knew about the zombie houses, Garrett wondered

if the detective knew why he visited them. Probably not, as he'd found his stashes remained untouched in most of these houses.

Garrett made a hard right at Diamond and a quick left into an alley. He was traveling too fast for the condition of the roadway. It was full of ruts and potholes. His car bounced severely. When he arrived at his destination, he yanked the wheel and pulled into the small, designated area behind the old house.

He would have preferred to have parked at the end of the block and walk in, but there was no more time.

When the vehicle finally stopped, he jumped out and ran toward the back of the vacant house. He wasn't worried if any of the neighbors saw him. With barely a pause, he kicked the back door in. He ran to the living room and dropped to his knees near a floor vent. He popped off a vent cover, reached his arm down the cylindrical tube until it flattened out, then pulled out a stack of bills several inches thick.

A terrible thought hit him at this moment as he looked at all that money.

He had never planned to run. He didn't know where to go. He had no travel documents at the ready.

Once he collected enough cash, what was he supposed to do?

Garrett tossed the cash into the middle of the hardwood floor. Then he hurried to the opposite side of the room. Again, he fell to his knees, popped another vent cover, and retrieved a second stack of bills. Without hesitation, he tossed the bills toward the first stack.

Running to Canada flashed through his mind, but that was a bad idea. They checked IDs when going in either direction. They would surely put his name into a watch database now. Maybe he should go to a city where he wouldn't stand out so much, where there weren't so many pale faces.

Garrett ran into the first bedroom and dropped to his knees. He paused for a second as he thought he heard something. Carefully, he pulled his gun from the back of his pants. The noise was no longer there. He set his gun down and popped the vent cover off. He shoved his hand down the tube and grasped a stack of bills.

After he pulled them out, he didn't even bother looking at them. He tossed the stack in the middle of the living room. Two rooms down. One to go.

Maybe he could run to Mexico. All he would have to do is get across the border. There had to be plenty of spots to do that.

In the last room, he dropped to his knees and laid his gun on the hardwood floor next to him. He pried the vent cover free and shoved his arm down the tube. As he did so, his fingers pushed the money deeper into the tube. He frantically reached for the stack of money, but he couldn't get a purchase on it.

"Damn it," he muttered.

He yanked his hand out, grabbed his gun, and wriggled it down the tube. It took some work to get it around the bend but once he did, he carefully used the barrel to press down on the money and drag it toward him. Once it moved enough that he thought he could grab it, he pulled his hand out.

But now the gun was stuck.

"Damn," he whispered again. His fist rattled around the tube, but he couldn't get the gun free. "How the hell…"

He let go of the gun then and it clanked into a resting spot. He grasped it from a different angle, and it came out without much difficulty then. Garrett shoved his arm back into the tube, grabbed the stack of bills, and pulled it out.

A grin creased his face. He picked up the gun in his left hand—his non-firing hand—and moved toward the living room.

This haul here was close to thirty thousand. All he would need would be a couple more houses and he'd have enough to run. At least, that's what he thought was needed whenever he considered the unlikely acting of running. He wished he had given this more thought. Running had never seemed an option to him.

When he knelt to pick up the money from the living room floor, he realized he wasn't alone.

In the kitchen, partially hidden behind the wall was Wardell Clint. The detective's gun extended in Garrett's direction. If there was ever a time for the weird dude to smile, it would have been now.

Instead, Clint watched him coolly.

Immediately, Garrett understood his disadvantage. He was in the open of the living room. There was no easy cover to take and nothing to conceal him. His gun was in his weak hand and his right hand was full of cash.

There was no time for a plan, Garrett decided. He would have to react to the detective's play and look for an opening. He might as well start the game.

"What took you so long, Ward?"

"Drop it," Clint commanded.

Chapter 53

Clint kept his gun pointed at Garrett, who made no move to obey his order. Garrett held the gun loosely in his left which he was sure was his weak hand, but Clint remained diligent. All officers trained to shoot with the off-hand, and on SWAT, they were religious about it. He doubted Garrett was anywhere near the same proficiency as with his shooting hand, but at this range, it might not matter.

"I said to drop it," Clint repeated.

"No," Garrett replied, his voice dropping to a husky whisper. "I don't think so."

"Do it now."

"Or what, Ward? You'll shoot me?" Garrett shook his head. "Nah, that's not you. You might love the idea of putting a bullet in me, but you couldn't live with yourself if it wasn't a justified shooting. We both know that."

Clint kept his gaze on Garrett's eyes, but his peripheral vision focused on the hand holding the gun. "You think after all the rules I've broken to get a case on you that I won't hesitate to put you down?"

"If that was true, you would have shot me already." Garrett gave him a confident smile. Sweat streamed down from his temples. "How'd you find me, Ward?"

Clint said nothing. He moved around the edge of the wall and stepped a little closer to Garrett. He ignored the man's attempts to distract him.

"Did you just *guess*?" Garrett asked.

Clint hadn't. He'd arrived on Decatur in time to find Zielinski staggering out of the alley and to see Garrett's vehicle careening down the street, already two blocks away. Once Zielinski got into his Impala, Clint had given chase, keeping Garrett in sight until he got a sense of his direction. Zielinski stammered out a long, confused rambling but he was able to gather that Garrett hadn't managed to make it into the house. That meant he still needed money. And there were only so many places he could go for that.

He laid back, letting Garrett's speeding vehicle get out of sight. When Zielinski protested that Garrett was slipping away, Clint ignored him. The longer he stayed visible behind Garrett, the more of a chance the man would spot him. Clint didn't want a vehicle pursuit. Not only was his Impala no match for the much bigger engine in Garrett's rig, but the public danger of a pursuit was off the charts.

Based on Garrett's direction, there were only two likely zombie houses he could be heading toward. Clint took an alternate route, speeding to the first one. He saw no car outside. Clint didn't stop, knowing that Garrett had gone to the other house. When he arrived, he saw Garrett's vehicle in the alley, parked askew.

"Stay here," he ordered Zielinski.

"No," the veteran cop argued, still half in a stupor. He reached for the door handle.

Clint grabbed his collar and jerked him close. "You're in bad shape, Ray. You're a liability. Stay here and if I'm not the one that comes out of that back door, you know what to do."

Zielinski stared back at him, his dull and shaken eyes barely registering Clint's words. After a moment, he nodded.

Clint got out of the car and slipped into the house.

"I think you guessed," Garrett said now, watching Clint edge toward him.

"You don't have enough time to try that move," Clint told him.

Garrett smiled. "What move?"

"The one you're thinking about."

Garrett let a sly smile play on his lips. "You read minds now, Honey Badger?"

"Even factoring action versus reaction, you can't make it,"

Clint continued, ignoring the taunt. "I have every advantage. I'm expecting it. I have my weapon trained on you, center mass. And it's your weak hand. You don't stand a chance."

Garrett looked down at the gun in his hand and then at Clint. "Then why do you look so worried, Ward?"

"Put it down. You're under arrest."

Those last words seemed to anger Garrett. His eyes flashed and his jaw set. "I already told you no." He shrugged. "You say I can't shoot you before you shoot me. Okay, fine. But I say you won't shoot me unless I point this gun at you. That sounds like a stalemate to me."

"It's a stalemate I'll eventually win, when more cops show up," Clint told him.

Garrett considered, then shrugged again. "If you called any. Which I don't think you did. Otherwise, why did you have that old drunk Ray Zielinski checking houses?" Garrett chuckled, though it sounded forced to Clint. "Face it, you can't win."

Clint didn't answer. He shuffled a little closer. He now stood two strides away from Garrett. He kept his gun pointed straight at the man's chest while he stared directly into his eyes. "I *will* win," he told Garrett.

Garrett laughed, but Clint heard the strain in it. "That's not how this goes."

"It only goes one of two ways, and you know it."

"Oh, I do?"

"Yes. If we stand here for much longer," Clint said, "more cops show up. At that point, you'll surrender. I put you in cuffs, so I win."

"Or?"

Clint took a precise half-step forward. He settled into a solid stance, his knees bent, his joints loose. "Or you get stupid with that gun, and I pull this trigger. I put you in the ground, so I win." He curled his lip in contempt. "Either way, *you* don't get to decide."

Garrett fell silent. His eyes lost their mocking light and became flat. Clint knew the man was thinking over what he'd just said. It would either make him angry and force his hand or cause him to despair and surrender.

"You don't get to win," Garrett said to him fiercely, baring his teeth.

"I've already won."

The world slowed suddenly. Clint heard the sound of footsteps and the door swinging open behind him. He didn't take his eyes from Garrett's. He saw the man's recognition in a nanosecond and knew the intruder was Zielinski, barreling in through the front door instead of staying in the car like he'd been told.

Garrett exercised magnificent motor control. He barely jumped at the sudden commotion, and once he identified its source, his eyes flicked back to Clint.

He dropped the money in his right hand.

The falling bundle caught Clint's eyes, but he forced himself to ignore it.

Garrett's left hand shifted, and the gun swung upward.

Something was off in the way Garrett moved, but Clint didn't have time to process it. He began to depress the trigger of his Glock, ready to drill Garrett in the chest with three quick rounds. Hoping he could stop at just three.

Then, at the last moment, he realized what he was seeing by how Garrett's body moved, and he let up on the trigger before the gun barked in his hands.

Meanwhile, Garrett jammed the muzzle under his own chin. He brought his now empty right hand in to join his left and support the pistol.

Tyler Garrett closed his eyes.

Clint let his Glock fall from his hand. In one fluid motion, he shuffled forward, reaching for Garrett. His right hand found Garrett's wrist and he twisted it outward. The barrel tilted slightly to that side. At the same time, he slammed the knife edge of his left hand onto Garrett's clavicle. The force of the blow drove Garrett's shoulder back, and shifted the barrel a little more, even as it boomed and spewed smoke and flame toward the ceiling.

Garrett cried out in pain and rage. His head jerked back as a bloody furrow appeared along the side of his face, creasing his cheek from jaw to temple. Warm blood freckled lightly onto Clint's face, but he ignored it. He swiftly brought his left hand to Garrett's gun hand, completing the levering motion to take Garrett to the ground. Still yelling, Garrett landed hard on his back, grunting as he hit. Clint pivoted and stepped over Garrett's outstretched arm, applying a twisting pressure until he felt and heard a pop.

Garrett screamed in agony.

The gun clattered to the floor.

Clint used his toe to flick the weapon. It skittered across the wooden floor toward a dumbfounded Zielinski, who stood holding his .38 in his hands.

Garrett screamed again, all of it primal pain and rage.

Clint reversed his direction, quickly working Garrett onto his stomach. The man bucked and struggled, but Clint maintained control of his arm. Coupled with the pain from the dislocated shoulder and possibly his elbow, too, Garrett was unable to stop Clint from handcuffing first one wrist and then the other.

Garrett's chest heaved as he bellowed in pain. He cursed Clint, calling him every horrible name he could summon, but Clint didn't respond. His knee pinned Garrett to the wooden floor in that abandoned zombie house as he waited for the man to scream himself out. While he endured Garrett's cries, he looked over at Zielinski, who was still standing at the door, stunned at what he'd seen.

Clint got Zielinski's attention. He raised his finger straight up and twirled it a few times, then pointed at Garrett. Zielinski took his meaning.

Call for a patrol car.

Zielinski stepped out onto the porch, pulling his phone from his pocket.

Garrett slowly stopped shouting, gulping in his breath and letting it out in huge, racking exhales that sounded almost like sobs.

Clint waited until he heard sirens in the distance before he leaned down closer to Garrett. "You hear that?" he asked.

"Screw you," Garrett growled back, then winced in pain.

"That's justice coming," Clint said. "The beginning of it, anyway. The rest of it is you in prison for the rest of your natural life."

"I'll kill you!"

Clint patted Garrett's good shoulder. "You had your chance. But that's not how this goes." He smiled a little as he threw Garrett's own words back at him. "You don't get to be a hero anymore," he told him. "Everyone is going to know who you really are."

Garrett didn't say anything to that. He kept breathing in painful fits and starts. Zielinski stepped back inside and gave Clint a nod. Clint nodded back, keeping Garrett pinned to the floor. Together, all three of them listened to the sirens, and waited.

Chapter 54

"Does it grate you that they booked us on the redeye?" Danielle Watson asked.

Esteban Curado shrugged. "Why's it matter?"

"Because we could have spent the night here and flown out early in the morning."

"And lose your whole day?" Curado asked. "This way we sleep on the flight and wake up at home. The day will be ours."

"It's a four-hour flight, Steve. We lose three hours due to time zones. Plus, we have a layover in Minneapolis. Not like you're going to get much sleep there."

"Esteban," Curado joked. "You know I prefer Esteban."

Édelie Durand listened to her team banter behind her with only partial attention. They were waiting in the Delta Airlines baggage check at Spokane International Airport. Every minute or so they moved one spot forward. She was unsure if this line was supposed to qualify the airport as busy, but she was pleased there was only a handful of people in front of them. This was about to be her third flight of the day—the first couple being the early morning visit to and from Seattle—and she was tired of airports.

She had called Roland prior to leaving the police department. It was a stilted call, though. He coughed most of the time. Durand asked how he was feeling, and he deflected her concerns by asking how the investigation "out there" was going. She loved the man, but it was clear when he didn't want to talk about his feelings or his condition. In those instances, he would avoid her questions or shut down the conversation. Since Durand didn't want that to happen, she told him what they learned.

When she was finished, he asked, "Shouldn't you stay? Sounds like there's some unfinished business."

She hesitated before saying, "I want to come home."

"The way you tell it," Roland said, "that department needs help. Maybe you need to be out there for a full investigation."

Durand shook her head even though her husband couldn't see her. It almost sounded like he *wanted* her to stay in Spokane.

"If you have to, Lee..." He was the only person to have ever called her that nickname. "I understand. What you do is important."

She whispered, "I need to come home."

"Then come home, baby. I miss you."

Durand wondered how much new sick time she had accrued over the past few weeks. She'd already used up her vacation days for the year along with the few personal days she was given. Then she burned through her sick time taking care of Roland. Now, the only time available would be the new days she accrued. The overtime she'd gotten on this trip coupled with that sick time might get her a few days, maybe even a week with her husband. After that, if she wanted more time, it would be unpaid.

She made up her mind then to do just that. She'd deal with the financial and career repercussions later. Once Roland got better, he could help her figure their way out of any quagmire.

The line ahead of them moved and Durand stepped forward.

"We should be staying," Watson said flatly.

The way she said it grated Durand. She glanced over her shoulder to her subordinate.

"I'm just saying," Watson said as her eyes widened.

"Would we have that authority?" Curado asked.

Watson clucked her tongue as Durand turned forward.

She'd had her fill of these two. They were good investigators and good people, but she wanted to go home and be with her husband. His cough sounded worse. He was probably doing too much without her around.

"I mean," Curado said, "do we have the authority to change our flights and hotel reservations? We did our job, right? We've been out, reviewed files, conducted interviews—"

"And learned this place needs oversight."

"We don't know that," Curado said.

"Edie," Watson said. "Edie, what do you think?"

Durand glanced over her shoulder. "We write our report and have it ready for Monday. As Esteban said, we did our job." Her voice was harder than she expected, but she didn't apologize for it. There were more important things than this job.

"But we're here now," Watson said. "Everything we've learned…What you heard today, Edie, that's enough for us to stay and dig further."

When she didn't respond, Watson pleaded, "Edie—"

"Enough," Durand snapped and turned around. "Give it a rest."

Watson leaned back, clearly hurt by her supervisor's sharp tone.

Durand knew she'd gone too far. She reached out and gently wrapped her hand around Watson's upper arm. "I appreciate your enthusiasm, Dani. I do. But I need to get home."

Watson studied her face. "Is everything okay?"

Curado asked, "What's going on, Edie? Anything we can help with?"

"I'm fine," Durand said. "Everything's fine." Her next words were delivered in a staccato fashion. "I just need to go home."

The younger woman lowered her eyes and nodded. Curado glanced away.

Durand turned around and stepped forward. The team was next to the check-in associate.

In a moment, Curado asked, "Are you twittering now?"

Watson chuckled. "I use it to keep up with the latest news...*Dad*."

"What's going on in the world?"

"Says here that the president is lashing out against Switzerland."

"For what? They refuse to send the best chocolates?"

A spot at the counter opened, and a pale-skinned woman with platinum blond hair waved. "Next!" she called.

Durand grabbed the handle of her bag and muttered, "We're up."

She walked to the end of the counter. The ticket clerk stepped behind her computer and asked, "Checking bags? Or do you need to check in also?"

"Checking bags," Durand said and hefted her bag onto the scale.

From behind her, Watson mumbled in astonishment. "No way."

"What?" Curado asked.

"ID, please." The clerk said as she took Durand's already offered driver's license. "Where are you headed?"

"Washington," Durand said, then belatedly added, "D.C."

The woman behind the counter smiled. "Two Washingtons is confusing, isn't it?"

"Edie," Watson said as she tapped her supervisor's shoulder.

Durand faced her.

Watson held up her cell phone with its screen turned outward. "SPD just arrested Tyler Garrett."

She leaned in to read the news alert.

"For murder," Watson said.

Durand's shoulders slumped slightly. Thoughts of love, duty, and regret raced through her mind.

"Does it say who he murdered?" Curado asked.

"It doesn't," Watson said. "The department is going to hold a briefing later."

Durand's gaze shifted to her subordinates who now watched her keenly. What she did in this moment mattered, not only in the eyes of the department, but in their eyes. They were still at the beginning of their careers and had years to grow and mature within Justice. How she responded would forever impact them.

Would she be a leader to emulate or to eschew?

She knew what Roland would tell her.

Édelie Durand turned back to the counter. She pulled out her identification wallet and showed it to the clerk behind the counter. The woman's eyes widened. They widened further when Watson and Curado showed theirs as well.

"There's been a change of plans," Durand said. "We need to shift our flights."

EPILOGUE

I am not the law,
but I represent justice so far as my feeble powers go.
—Arthur Conan Doyle's Sherlock Holmes, "The Adventure
of the Three Gables"

Chapter 55

Captain Tom Farrell stared down at the white cardboard box in front of him, half full with all his possessions. He'd walked around his office twice now and was surprised at how few items were truly his. Almost everything belonged to the department, and so he left it for the next occupant of this room. He'd turned in his badge, his gun, his uniform, his keys, his ID card, everything that marked him as a police captain. Sergeant Ragland had collected every police-issue item, officiously marking each off his list as he went. Farrell could tell he enjoyed the task. Then he'd handed Farrell the empty box and escorted him here.

This room was the last thing. It wasn't his anymore, either.

Baumgartner had allowed him to retire, at least. His career was destroyed, and he had lost more than just his job. He'd lost his legacy. His name was forever sullied. That had been the cost of his actions.

Was it worth it?

That was what the chief asked him when Farrell showed him his retirement papers. He'd asked without rancor, his tone genuinely curious, so Farrell told him the truth.

"I don't know."

Three days ago, it had briefly felt worth it when he watched Detective Wardell Clint march a bloody-faced Garrett into the jail. In that moment, if Baumgartner had asked him if it was worth it, he might have said yes. But the chief had remained as silent as he had himself, and Garrett had turned his head, looking away from both of them.

Now, though? With his career gone? Was it worth it now?

He thought perhaps yes. If he had lost his pension, had

hurt Karen's future that way, then he believed it would have been a resounding no. But Robert Baumgartner was old school, a pragmatist who believed in honor. When he gave Farrell his medicine straight—retire or be fired—he told him as much.

"I know why you did it, Tom. I know what your intentions were," he'd said. "But you messed up too badly to ever come back from this."

Baumgartner was right. He was lucky to be leaving via retirement, his name in shambles. Of course, he was still at risk for anything the Department of Justice might decide to throw at him. And who knew what civil suits might come out of this debacle. He still had a long road ahead of him.

But it would be as a civilian, not a police officer.

Farrell stared down at the photograph on the top of his personal items in the box. It was his academy class, taken decades ago now. His own smiling face, utterly naïve, gazed up at him, full of hope, promise, determination. Ashamed, Farrell reached into the box and turned the frame facedown.

A knock came at his door. He looked up sharply. He'd been hoping to get his things and slip out of the station. The few eyes that had lighted on him today either held pity or contempt, and he had no desire for either.

Captain Dana Hatcher stood in the doorway, eyeing him expectantly. "Bad time? I can come back."

Farrell pointed to the white cardboard box. "I won't be here."

She followed his gesture. Her face fell. "Oh." She looked back at him. "I'm sorry, Tom."

He considered her. He'd thought she had come by to gloat, or to get a look at the corpse of his career, but he saw genuine sympathy in her.

"Thanks," he said.

"I...I wish I had known," she said. "Maybe I could have helped. Instead of...what happened."

"It wasn't your fault."

"I know, but...I *am* sorry."

Farrell nodded. He reached for the cardboard top to the box and fitted it on. He gave Hatcher a slight lift of his chin to say farewell and headed out the door.

"Good luck," she said after him.

As he walked out of his office and away from mahogany row, he tried to keep his head high. But when one of the crime analysts rounded the corner near the chief's office, he averted his eyes as they passed in the hallway. Neither of them spoke.

Farrell decided he didn't want to go out through the foyer of the Public Safety Building. Everyone from cops to lawyers and clerks to civilians to criminals would see him, carrying his white box of shame. He didn't want to endure their stares or hear them murmur as he walked past. He decided to use the west doors to exit the building. He didn't have his ID card, but the employee entrance only required one to enter, not to leave.

Thank the fire marshal for small favors.

He turned around and headed back down the hallway. His mind was curiously quiet, as if he were clinically observing his own final moments inside a police station. Even his shame seemed to step to the sidelines.

Then a thought struck him. Right now, his actions were scandalous, but everyone knew what he'd done. He'd helped orchestrate Garrett's downfall. Yes, it had been Clint who brought the man in, but he had been a part of that. But as the years passed, would people lose that distinction? Would his fall from grace become lumped in with Garrett's, melted together into one scandalous event?

Farrell passed the Investigative Division and reached the west doors. He turned sideways and depressed the push bar with his hip to open the door. Warm summer air greeted him when he stepped outside. He headed to his personal vehicle, wondering if he was going to be remembered as the dirty captain who was forced to retire as part of the Garrett affair.

He hoped not.

But he thought so.

Chapter 56

"He just…he looked so devastated," Captain Hatcher said.

Chief Baumgartner pursed his lips. "I imagine he was."

"It must have been difficult for you," Hatcher said. "To fire him."

"I didn't fire him. He retired."

"Of course. That's what I meant."

Baumgartner leaned forward. "Then, Dana, *that's what you need to say.*"

The intensity of his words seemed to surprise her. He realized she had no idea what was coming or why he'd called her to his office today.

"You're right," she managed. "Thank you."

Tom Farrell had departed only yesterday, but Baumgartner knew he couldn't wait to put things into motion. The Department of Justice wasn't known for its agility, but he still didn't expect it to be long before he received formal notice that a consent decree was coming. Lou, his so-called football friend from high school who now worked at Justice, had reached out to let him know that it was almost a certainty. Baumgartner wondered if Durand was behind that notification, too, just like she'd orchestrated the tip that she and her team were on their way.

Once the decree was in place, his decision-making authority would be severely curtailed. He needed to put his plan into effect quickly so that it would already be in place when any sort of freeze occurred.

Hatcher was a central part of that plan.

"I'm promoting you to assistant chief," he told her. "Effective tomorrow."

Her eyes widened in surprise. "I thought that position was

dead."

"No, only hibernating until I thought the time was right. Now is that time."

Hatcher processed the news. He could see she was both pleased and confused, and perhaps even a little suspicious.

Good. I need your optimism, but I need you to be suspicious, too. It's the only way you'll survive.

"Can I ask why?" she asked.

"A consent decree is almost certainly coming in the wake of Garrett's arrest," Baumgartner said. "I may be a casualty of that process, whether I get canned right away, or down the road. There needs to be a successor in place, with time to get up to speed."

"But why me?"

Baumgartner fixed her with a speculative look. "Why do you think?"

"Tell me it's not because I'm a woman," she said. "Because if that's why…"

"If that's why, you don't want it?"

Hatcher paused. "I didn't say that."

Baumgartner smiled slightly. "Well, it's not, so you can relax. But if you're going to be my number two, we need to be able to be honest with each other, agreed?"

"Agreed."

"Then the truth is, the woman part doesn't hurt. The optics are good, and Lord knows we need some good optics these days."

Tyler Garrett and his wounded face had become the image of the police department, and he wanted to change that. Swiftly.

"But the biggest reason is that you're a good leader, Dana. And I think you can be a good chief someday. I don't get to name my successor, but I can try to rig the game in your favor as much as possible when the time comes. At the very least, you'll get some time as the interim chief, and a fair shot at the job."

"When the time comes?"

Baumgartner shrugged. "Whenever that is. Tomorrow, or five years from now."

"Is there a catch?" she asked. "There's always a catch in politics."

"I suppose there is. I'll admit to being a little selfish here. I've given most of my life to this department. I want to leave it in good hands. By making you the AC, I know you'll get the experience to do the job. Because we'll be working closely, I'll be able to pass on what I know, what I've learned."

"Mentor me?"

"Call it what you will." She had it right, though. Steering the department through the consent decree was his immediate concern, but that didn't mean he wasn't concerned about his legacy. If things went as he hoped, *she* would be his legacy.

She nodded, understanding. "This is a political move."

Baumgartner almost smiled again. Of course, it was political.

Promoting Hatcher threw up a little bit of a shield where DOJ was concerned. They might urge Sikes to fire him, but it would look bad to fire Hatcher, too, without even giving her an opportunity. As a captain, she wouldn't be afforded that, but as assistant chief? She had a claim.

Having her in the second chair might also blunt Councilwoman Margaret Patterson's attacks on him. Since a chief and an assistant chief were considered as one office, any slings and arrows she flung toward Baumgartner would strike her friend, too. The only alternative for Patterson was to claim Hatcher was only a figurehead. That wasn't a viable option because it undermined Hatcher, something Patterson would want to avoid. He suspected that the councilwoman would be forced to adjust the nature and intensity of her criticism. With a little work, maybe she could even be turned into an ally.

The biggest checkmate this move provided was with the mayor, though. Baumgartner had no doubt Sikes was biding his time, waiting for his first viable opportunity to fire him.

He'd said as much. The Garrett arrest hadn't given him quite enough, since it had been his own people who brought in the dirty cop. But a consent decree would provide sufficient ammunition for the mayor to send him packing.

He could still do so, but Baumgartner doubted it. If he left, that would make Hatcher the interim chief by default. Sikes would have to respect that or risk the terrible look of canning the first female chief in the department's history without even affording her a fair chance to prove herself. But if he left her in office, even as an interim, he'd have to deal with the fact that his greatest political rival, Margaret Patterson, was closely allied with his police chief. Sikes would never allow that. He'd see all these political nuances before he acted, like waiting chess moves, and eventually recognize that his strongest play was to stick with Baumgartner, at least for a while longer.

"You still haven't told me the catch," Hatcher said.

"The catch is simple," he told her. "You have to commit. This is an all-in proposition. There are no half measures. Can you do that?"

"Yes."

"I'm serious, Dana. It means you have to fully embrace executive leadership. It's a completely different sphere. You don't get to be a three-stripe captain anymore, you follow?"

She frowned. "That's unfair. I care about my people."

"I know. It's one of your strengths. But every strength is also a weakness. You have to learn how to serve them in the role you are in now. You're not a sergeant, holding their hand. Not a captain, either. You'll be a chief, and that is something altogether different. There are difficult choices to make and your every action has significant consequences for people. You have to be able to do the right thing for the greater good, even it if it is the hardest thing."

"Like forcing a longtime friend to retire?"

"Yes," he agreed. "Or leveraging a friendship with a city councilmember. Can you do that?"

Hatcher didn't hesitate. "If it is for the good of the

department or the public, absolutely."

Baumgartner heard the sincerity and the resolution in her tone. He was glad to hear that because she was going to need it.

"Plenty of departments have survived a consent decree," he said. "Many have come out the other side better for it. But everything depends on leadership, especially on the chief." He gave her a knowing look. "And the assistant chief. We have to show a united front to DOJ and to our own people."

"I understand."

"Can I count on you, Dana?"

Hatcher sat up straight in her chair and met his gaze. "Yes, Chief. I'm in."

Chapter 57

Ray Zielinski sat at a table in the corner of the Starbucks. He remembered the last time he'd been at this coffee house. He'd met Dana Hatcher—Assistant Chief Hatcher now, as of three weeks ago—for coffee and conversation, something they'd been doing since they were both patrol officers. She'd moved up the ladder and he'd stayed on patrol, grinding it out. Then, in the last two years, she jumped from lieutenant to the office next to the chief's, and he'd landed in a world of hurt.

Assistant chief. Talk about going over to the dark side.

He sipped at his coffee, glad for the constancy of it. He always got the same thing at Starbucks, and it always tasted the same way. There wasn't much in life with that kind of consistency. Wives filed for divorce, kids grew distant, and friends stopped calling…or got promoted to assistant chief. But his Pike brew tasted like a damn Pike brew, every time.

Dale Thomas, the union president, hustled through the door. He didn't bother with the line of customers waiting to order coffee, making his way directly to Zielinski.

I guess he's not staying long.

The truth was, he didn't know where he stood with the union anymore. When Internal Affairs completed the investigation into the complaints against him, Chief Baumgartner took very little time to consider before firing him. Any rhythm he had hoped for when it came to Hatcher lobbying on his behalf either never materialized or didn't have an impact. It took her all of a few weeks wearing a star on her collar to hang him out to dry. To be fair, he supposed the looming potential of a consent decree from DOJ influenced the chief's decision, too. But he thought firing him was a harsh response. A suspension would have been fair, but to flat out fire a guy with *his* time on the job? And after his role in helping bring Garrett in? It seemed like there was a lack of appreciation and one of the things he was hoping to discuss with Thomas today was some sort of an appeal to get himself reinstated.

Thomas pulled out a chair and plopped into it. He was breathing a little heavily, and his collar and armpits of his shirt were ringed with sweat.

"Get you a coffee?" Zielinski asked.

"In this heat?"

"They have iced."

Thomas shook his head. "I don't have a lot of time. This DOJ stuff is heating up."

Zielinski scowled. "Well, sorry to bother you with my wrongful termination."

Thomas didn't react, except to raise his eyebrows slightly. "Wrongful?"

"Yeah," Zielinski said, his anger bubbling. He'd been paying union dues for his entire career, and those dues paid this guy's salary. So why was he always too busy for him?

Thomas loosened his tie. "Ray, I think we're going to need to have a reality check discussion here today."

Zielinski thought so, too. Thomas was supposed to represent him. Not do it half-assed, and not bail on him. "So do I," he said.

"Let's start with the good news. I just came from the county prosecutor's office. They are declining to pursue any criminal charges against you."

Relief flooded him. That *was* good news. While his second encounter with Darold Barden fell into a gray area, he'd been worried about how the prosecutor interpreted their first encounter. He'd heard from Thomas that they had discussed whether it qualified as a burglary, which was a felony. The prospect of a felony criminal charge after all he'd been through had been weighing heavily on him.

"Their decision will almost certainly help if Barden or

Sanita sue you civilly," Thomas said, "but that will be something for you to discuss with your attorney."

Zielinski did a double take. "My attorney? *You're* my attorney."

Thomas shook his head. "No. I am the union president, who happens to be a lawyer by trade. I will continue to represent you in one matter and one matter only, and that is where your employment is concerned."

"So you'll get me reinstated but I'm on my own for anything else?" Zielinski asked in disbelief. "Are you serious?"

"Your defense is your own responsibility, yes. And reinstatement isn't an option, Ray. We won't be appealing the termination."

"Not appealing…what the hell?"

"There are no grounds, and we can't risk a frivolous appeal that damages our credibility."

"*Frivolous?*"

"We'll be arguing for the city to pay out your remaining vacation days and sick time, and we'll negotiate with the Department of Retirement Systems regarding your pension, but that's the end of it."

Zielinski sat back in his chair, spreading his arms wide. "I don't get it. I'm the good guy here, Dale. Garrett was the bad guy, not me."

Thomas looked at him for a long while. Then he said, "Garrett is in jail, awaiting trial. In addition to a nasty crease on his face that wasn't there before, it's my understanding he's looking at life imprisonment if convicted. So I think the system is humming along where he's concerned."

"Maybe so, but it's broken for me."

Thomas leaned forward, peering at him closely. "Do you *really* think that, Ray?"

"Of course."

"Wow." Thomas sat back. "Well, I don't know what to say. Wait, I suppose I do. Outside of representing your employment interests, let me provide you with my final services as your union representative, okay?"

Zielinski shook his head. *Worthless. The man is worthless.*

"Most of your IA stuff was pretty minor," Thomas said. "Letters of reprimand, maybe a day or two suspension. Even failing to report that collision wouldn't have gotten you fired. But when you forced your way into Barden's house and assaulted him? That's a first-degree burglary, whether the prosecutor elects to charge you or not. That alone was enough for Baumgartner to fire you, DOJ or not. But then you barge into Sanita's apartment and arrest the guy? Don't you know when to quit?"

Zielinski glared at him but said nothing.

"Sorry," Thomas said sarcastically. "Asked and answered. But let's be clear: when you went into Barden's apartment that first time, flashing your badge, you didn't just commit burglary. You did it under the color of authority. That's a civil rights violation. Now, I'm not supposed to tell you this, but here it is anyway. The only reason the prosecutor passed on charging you is because she knows DOJ is going to hit you federally. You're going to be charged with a civil rights violation, so it isn't worth the time and expense for the DA to move on this."

Zielinski's mouth fell open. He struggled to process what Thomas was telling him. Federal charges? How could that be?

"You didn't do yourself any favors with your interview when DOJ was here, either," Thomas told him.

An image of Danielle Watson flashed in his mind. "Is she the one charging me?" he asked mechanically.

"No, but I'm sure she passed on her findings."

"Dale, I don't…how can this be happening?"

Thomas pressed his lips together. "You did this to yourself, Ray. You need to own it."

Zielinski felt his eyes grow hot with tears. He clenched his jaw. "I'm a good guy," he said hoarsely. "What about Garrett? What about what I did there?"

"Wardell Clint arrested Tyler Garrett," Thomas said

evenly.

"I was *there*," Zielinski insisted. "I fought with him in that alley, I—"

"Ray, none of that matters. What matters is what else you did, and now you have to answer for it. I suggest you find yourself a good attorney and prepare your case."

Zielinski shook his head in disbelief. "What's going to happen to me?"

"I couldn't say. Your attorney—"

"Come on, Dale, just give me an idea!" Zielinski shouted. Several patrons glanced over, some surprised, others irritated.

Thomas wasn't moved by the outburst. "I think you should expect to do some time."

"Time?"

"Incarceration," Thomas specified.

"Oh, man," Zielinski muttered. "Are you kidding me?"

"No." Thomas spoke in a flat voice, not sympathetic at all. "I think you're going to find yourself behind bars, Ray. Your best hope now is that it's at the jail and not prison."

Zielinski shook his head at the thought. "No. That…that can't be."

The two men sat without speaking for a short time. The hum of conversation and the clatter of the baristas working filled Zielinski's ears, and he focused on that. The rest was too big, too foreign for him to consider. It didn't seem possible to him. It wasn't supposed to work out this way.

Finally, Thomas broke the silence. "I've done all I can for you, Ray. Good luck."

Thomas waited a second for a response. When there wasn't one, he got up and walked away, leaving Zielinski alone at the table, trying to make sense of the wreckage of his life.

Chapter 58

Édelie Durand folded the shirt and placed it on the couch.

She was folding her second load of laundry. The third and final load was in the dryer now.

There were plenty of chores for her to catch up on. She'd let many things fall behind over the past year. When Roland's illness progressively got worse, they quit doing house projects. In home ownership, maintenance items quickly add up when ignored.

House projects weren't the only thing that got ignored. Relationships with friends. Church activities. The list was long.

Durand grabbed a T-shirt and folded it. She carefully laid it onto the pile.

But the distractions couldn't all be attributed to taking care of Roland. In the first part of the year, there were work trips to Tulsa, Shreveport, Cincinnati, and Spokane. All of them were for different reasons and of various lengths, but it was the final one—Spokane—that she resented. That wasn't true, she decided.

She resented them all. It was Spokane she hated.

Durand grabbed a pair of Roland's pants. She deftly folded them and put them on the edge of the couch.

When news broke about Tyler Garrett's arrest, her team walked out of the airport. The department's travel agency was closed by that time of day, so Durand rented a new car. She called the hotel and got three rooms for another few days. She wasn't sure how long they would be.

At the department, they couldn't even get close to Garrett. He was taken directly to jail and booked for the murder of four gang members. Afterward, she and her team attempted to put together the pieces of what had occurred, but no one was happy to see them arrive back at the department.

Chief Baumgartner wouldn't interact with them while the biggest incident in his career was occurring. Therefore, he assigned Captain Hatcher to provide assistance.

Hatcher herself seemed overwhelmed by the fallout surrounding Garrett's arrest so she tasked Sergeant Kelly Ragland with watching over the DOJ team until she had a handle on things.

Unfortunately for the captain, she didn't understand that was like throwing Brer Rabbit into the Briar Patch. Without Union President Dale Thomas around, Ragland turned into the biggest leaker since Deep Throat.

Initially, they found a quiet spot in the chaplain's office, but once Ragland got going, Danielle Watson realized it was best to get him away from the department. She suggested a walk across the street to O'Donnell's Irish Pub. Ragland seemed absolutely thrilled by the idea, especially since the Justice Department was buying.

"You know what I heard?" Ragland asked. "He tried to kill himself."

"Garrett?" Esteban Curado asked.

"That's right," Ragland said after a sip of beer. "But that crazy bastard Clint saved him from doing it."

"Lucky for Garrett," Curado said.

Ragland smacked the table. "He still blew his own ear off, though. Creased his face good, too."

"You saw it?" Watson asked.

"No, but I heard about it. It's supposed to be nasty."

The bit about the ear ended up not being true, but most of Ragland's scuttlebutt proved valuable.

"And Ray Zielinski," Ragland said after another hoist of his beer. "I never thought much of the man, but he sure came through when it really mattered."

Curado leaned forward. "Yeah? How was that?"

"He was Clint's ace in the hole," the sergeant said with a laugh. "He's actually the guy who found Garrett. Can you believe that? Got himself into a real donnybrook with Garrett in an alley somewhere. That guy," Ragland said with a shake of his head, "I'm gonna have to apologize the next time I see him."

Watson cocked her head. "Isn't Zielinski suspended?"

Ragland thought about it for a moment. Then he shook his head and laughed. "That poor guy doesn't know how to stay out of trouble, does he?"

Durand folded another pair of Roland's pants and stacked them with the others.

When the doorbell rang, she walked reluctantly to the door. She opened it to find two white men in jeans and T-shirts politely smiling at her. The older man took off his baseball hat and clutched it to his chest. He smacked his younger counterpart in the arm and that man quickly removed his hat, too.

"We're here for the bed," the older man reluctantly said.

Durand pulled the door fully open. "It's over there."

In the middle of the room sat an adjustable bed. It had been stripped of its sheets. Months ago, the couch and chairs had been pushed to the outside walls to make room for it.

The two men hurried in. Before they began, they both glanced sheepishly at her.

She didn't envy their work. When they delivered a bed, they were the harbingers of death. When they later retrieved it, they were like ghouls, whisking away the final memories of a loved one.

It took them twenty minutes to disassemble the bed and carry it out. When they were finished, the older man came back and said, "We're finished."

Durand nodded at him.

"I'm sorry," he said then hurried back to their truck.

She shut the door and returned to her folding.

Roland had died before she made it home. Even if she would have left when originally scheduled, she would never have seen him again.

She hated Spokane for that. Had they run their department

in an honorable fashion, she and her team would never have been sent out there. She would never have heard of Chief Baumgartner, Captain Farrell, or Tyler Garrett. Those men had robbed her of the final moments of her husband's life.

The report her team drafted was damning. The offenses they listed were overwhelming: officers committing murders, officers dealing drugs, officers committing crimes under the color of authority. On top of that, a clandestine investigation was led by a well-respected captain. It didn't take much to get the Justice Department to authorize a consent decree investigation.

Durand wanted to be a part of the returning team, but her supervisor declined her request. It was obvious she could no longer be unbiased.

Instead, the department authorized her family leave to grieve the loss of her husband.

What good was this extra time now? She should have taken time before Roland was gone, but he told her to continue working. It was true that she didn't argue hard enough to stay at home with him. No one wants to see the love of their life wither away before them.

Instead, she pretended to be strong while he slowly died alone.

She gently folded another pair of Roland's pants. When the dryer beeped, she would collect that last and final load. Later in the afternoon, the Salvation Army was coming by to pick up his clothes.

Durand pushed the stacked clothes aside to clear a spot for her to sit on the couch that was pressed against the far wall. The pants and shirts teetered briefly before she caught them and repositioned them. Then she dropped onto the sofa.

Staring into the emptiness of the room left behind by the missing bed, she didn't feel like crying. She didn't feel like yelling, either. In fact, she didn't feel like much of anything.

Édelie Durand leaned her head against the back of the couch and stared at the ceiling.

Chapter 59

Clint arrived at the homicide scene before Jody did. By the time she pulled up in the evidence truck, he'd already done his walk around the outer perimeter, sketching the external layout. He waited for her before proceeding into the inner perimeter, as per protocol. The man inside was reportedly seated at his dining room table, a plate of food in front of him and a bullet hole in the center of his forehead. He wasn't going anywhere.

Jody parked, greeted him, and retrieved her camera. As she waddled ahead of him, rapidly snapping pictures with her customary ease, he commented, "Any day now, huh?"

She grunted, looking through the lens and pressing the button. "Not soon enough. Pregnancy sucks, Wardell. I'm telling you."

"I can imagine."

"No, you can't. You have no idea. If men had to do this, the species would die out."

He didn't argue, partially because she was nine months pregnant, and partially because he thought she might have a salient point.

They worked their way inside the crime scene until they finally reached the dining room. The fading odor of steak and potatoes still hung in the air. It wasn't a pleasant smell, but Clint had to admit it was better than what they would have encountered if the body had sat at that dinner table for a few days before they received the call. In this case, the call came from the man's own wife. She hadn't confessed exactly, but her comments had been vague enough that Clint already knew what his first line of investigation would be. He'd already ordered her detained and her hands bagged so that a gunshot residue test could be conducted.

The man sat at the head of the small table. His body was mostly upright in the chair, leaning straight backward. His head dangled over the back of the chair as if he were staring up at the ceiling. Brain matter and blood hung from the shattered remains of the back of his skull and pooled on the floor beneath him. More blood spatter adorned the wall behind him. Jody took a multitude of shots of that while Clint examined the victim without touching him.

"Can you get a shot of this?" he asked her.

"Just a sec." She took another round of pictures of the blood spatter, then returned to his side. "I already got the overall and a close-up."

"Can you take an extreme of the entrance wound? You see that scoring?"

Jody nodded. "Contact wound?"

"I believe so." Whoever had shot this man had put the end of the barrel to his forehead and pulled the trigger. The burning powder and the heat from the barrel created a black, burnt circle around the outside of the entrance wound.

Jody took several shots, then continued her sweep of the room.

"Hey guys," came a voice from the doorway.

Clint looked up to see Marty Hill. He gave him a terse nod and went back to visually scanning the victim.

"Hey, Marty," Jody said. "You on this?"

"Lieutenant Flowers sent me to help. Where are we at?"

"He's dead," Clint said.

Jody and Marty exchanged a look.

"I'm going to get some overalls of the other rooms in the house," Jody said. "I'll be back in five."

"All right," Hill said.

Clint didn't reply. He knew it was likely he and Marty would never be on friendly terms again, and he accepted that. Bringing Tyler Garrett to justice had meant everything to him, and he had accomplished his goal. He'd accrued evidence, done surveillance, broken rules, and found a way to tie it all up in a neat bow that the prosecutors were able to use at trial, which was expedited by all parties. Clint knew why the prosecutor wanted to speed things up—that always worked to their advantage. But why Garrett and his lawyers pushed for a speedy trial was a mystery to him, unless it was as simple as them believing they would win.

They didn't.

Clint sat at trial each day next to the prosecutor and heard one damning piece of evidence after another presented against Garrett. Then he got up on the witness stand and testified, putting the nails in the man's coffin. Usually, when Clint testified, he followed the protocol of looking at the prosecuting attorney while the question was being asked and turning to the jury to answer it. It was a simple tactic, and it helped overcome the naturally stilted delivery in his testimony.

But at Garrett's trial, Clint listened to the question while looking at Garrett. He answered the question while looking at Garrett. And he waited for the next question still looking at Garrett. He looked the man in the eyes, just as he had in that zombie house living room. He looked past the ugly injury that creased his face, and past the posturing expression he wore for the jury. He peered into what he could only think of as the man's soul, and all he saw there was darkness.

When the jury came back with a conviction, Garrett had the poor form to look surprised, and then affronted. For his part, Clint felt a sense of satisfaction miles beyond any other case he'd ever worked. Garrett had dirtied the badge, and Clint had brought him down. It had been two years of difficult work, and a great amount of risk. He'd suffered losses, and Marty Hill's friendship was a casualty, but in the end, it was worth it.

He'd do it again.

It might mean for cold relations with many of his colleagues for the rest of his career, but he could still be professional and work a case with anyone Lieutenant Flowers assigned.

Hill moved a little closer to where Clint stood. "Hey, Wardell?"

"Hmmm?"

"Can we talk for a second?"

Clint looked up. "About what?"

Hill hesitated, seeming to gather his thoughts. When he spoke, he did so with a sincere tone. "First, I have to say that I'm still a little mad about what happened, if I'm being honest. But I've been thinking about it and reading all the reports. The more I do both, the more I think I understand why you did what you did."

Clint stared at him. "All right."

"I'm not saying it was cool. You should have brought me into the loop." Hill frowned. "But I realize you didn't do what you did to be malicious or to screw up my case. I understand what you were working toward."

"Okay."

Hill chewed on the inside of his mouth. "I don't know if you're sorry for doing what you did—"

"I'm not."

"—but I'm sorry for blowing up at you. What I called you was mean, and it's not what I really think of you."

"All right."

Hill stared at him, expectantly. When Clint didn't speak, Hill asked, "Is there anything you want to say to me about this situation?"

Clint considered the question. He realized Hill was trying to mend fences, and he was mildly surprised at his own reaction at the effort. For most of his life, he hadn't cared what anyone thought of him. He focused on the task at hand. But he realized that there were a few people whose opinion he actually *did* care about. He supposed that made them friends.

He thought for a moment, then answered, "I'm glad you understand the full ramifications of that investigation now. That's good."

Hill took in his words, then shook his head, a hint of a

smile on his lips. "I guess that'll have to do."

Clint looked back to the victim, working his jaw and saying nothing.

"I get it, Wardell," Hill said gently. "Keep trying."

The two of them were silent for a few moments. Then Clint turned back to Marty. "Can you give me your opinion on something?"

"Sure."

Clint pointed to the victim's forehead. "What do you think about this entry wound?"

Hill walked over. He shined his LED flashlight onto the dead man's forehead and bent to look closely. After a moment, a warm smile broke across his face. He suppressed it before straightening up to answer Clint.

"That," Hill said, "looks like a contact wound to me."

"Yeah," Clint answered. "Me, too."

Chapter 60

Tyler Garrett sat on the edge of his bed.

This isn't so bad.

Today was his first day at the state penitentiary in Walla Walla. Up until now, he'd been housed in the Spokane County Jail. After his conviction and sentencing was complete, he was transferred here.

The in-processing was quick and efficient. No one asked him any questions beyond the basics—food allergies, medical needs, that sort of thing—before he was whisked to the quartermaster. He was given a white uniform and told to change.

When he was done, he was just a number in the system.

Garrett leaned back, put his hands behind his head, and lifted his feet to the wall.

His room contained a single bunk, a sink, and a toilet. He wasn't going to have to share with another inmate. This was done due to his law enforcement background. That was fine with him, but he wouldn't have cared if they roomed him with another man. It would have been an opportunity to have another soldier.

But he was fine being alone. It would give him time to think and make plans.

He knew he could survive in here. Better than that, he could thrive in here.

Garrett had the skills to create a network of men through manipulation, intimidation, and (if need be) negotiation. He wasn't afraid of the others inside these walls and he was less concerned with those guarding it.

It was all about learning how a system functioned then inserting one's self into it. He just needed to pay attention for a bit, see who did what, who was aligned with who, and begin to move the pieces around the board. Same as the department. Same as the street.

He stood, walked over to the sink, and ran some water. When it didn't get any warmer, he splashed some of it onto his face. He dried off with the front of his shirt.

There was no mirror for him to see himself, so his fingers touched the jagged scar across his cheek.

That was a moment of weakness.

Instead of putting the gun under my chin, I should have surrendered.

It would have been the same result as what he had now. Except no scar, and Clint wouldn't have dislocated his shoulder.

At least he got to kick Ray Zielinski's ass before it all went down.

Garrett chuckled to himself.

When he sat on the bunk again, his mind drifted back to his court case.

Angie and the kids never came to the trial. He didn't expect them to. Tiana came every day, though. When the verdict was read, she wailed in anguish.

His attorney, Pamela Wei, had suggested a speedy trial. She wanted to push the department and the prosecuting attorney into court. Her argument was that it gave them less time to prepare. She hoped to catch them flat-footed. Garrett agreed with the strategy. It didn't work, though, and he was found guilty.

For the Ocampo murders *only*.

He pretended to be shocked and outraged after the verdict was read, but as the trial went along, he realized the jury was going to find him guilty. It should have been obvious to him. He was a black cop on trial in Spokane, Washington. The outcome was almost guaranteed before he stepped into the courtroom. Wei had even told him to prepare himself that such a thing was a possibility.

Now, they were playing the long game and it was

important to steel one's mind for it.

Even though he lost this case, he won by learning just how much the department really had on him—which wasn't much.

The department didn't charge him with Butch Talbott's murder. Probably because they knew it was committed in self-defense. Charging him would have been a loser's bet.

And they had no way to prove he was involved in Justin Pomeroy's.

Wardell Clint may have suspected Garrett of orchestrating Gary Stone's murder, but the man couldn't prove it. The only way he could tie it to Garrett was Earl Ellis. That lead was dead now, which meant that that conspiracy would remain forever unproven.

The murders of Sonya Meyer and Ezekiel "Skunk" Hetzel were never even mentioned, which meant Clint and his team had nothing to connect them to him. Therefore, those murders would only be connected to Garrett in one of Wardell Clint's conspiracies.

He believed that everyone would want to connect all sorts of murders or crimes to him. The more the merrier. Let them believe he was the devil because if they believed he committed all sorts of crimes, then they couldn't prove any of them. It would clog up their thinking and blind them to what was important.

After his sentencing—he'd been given life—Wei immediately got to work on his appeal. She rightfully argued that the bulk of the case against him was based on circumstantial evidence. The only witness to put him at the scene of the Ocampo murders was an elderly woman—Nona Henry. She looked ill on the stand, and Wei suspected she wouldn't be around come appeal time.

The heart of the prosecutor's case rested on two pieces of evidence.

The first was a bullet match from a gun they never found. They couldn't prove it was Garrett's gun, anyway.

The second was a picture of Tyler Garrett with Nona

Henry's circle around his face.

Clint built a hell of a case with the little he had, but time would be in Garrett's favor. Not only did he believe this, so did his attorney.

The delivery slot on his door clanged opened, and a cardboard tray was inserted. On it was a sandwich and a carton of milk. Nothing else.

Garrett yelled, "Hey guard!" and stood.

"Yeah?"

He bent over the tray to look through the delivery slot but could only see the duty belt around the guard's waist.

"When do I get into gen-pop?" *General population.* Where the rest of the inmates were. He needed to start learning the system and networking. That was crucial.

"You're in solitary, man." The guard's voice was deep and hard.

"Yeah, I know," Garrett said, "but it's only temporary, right?"

The guard laughed. "You're in there for life, player. You're never getting anywhere near gen-pop, ever."

Garrett's face fell.

"But you'll get an hour outside tomorrow," the guard said. The delivery door slammed shut with a clang.

Garrett took his tray back to his bed and opened the sandwich. Peanut butter. He crinkled his nose then shrugged.

He scooched across the bed until his back was against the wall. He stared at the wall across from him for a long while. At first, it seemed like it was closing in on him, but he brushed that thought away. He bit into the sandwich and glanced around while he chewed.

"This isn't so bad," he mumbled defiantly. "Not bad at all."

Acknowledgments

While this police procedural is based in a real city and mirrors reality in many ways, it is absolutely a work of fiction. The authors have taken a great many creative liberties in the interests of telling the story of this series. For instance, no characters are directly based on anyone, with the exception of some positive homages done with permission. No actual incidents are rendered here, either. Some police codes or procedures are slightly different than in reality. Additionally, the political structure and history of both city government and the police department has been modified for dramatic purposes. While we're certain that astute readers will notice those differences, we're equally confident they'll forgive the discrepancies.

The authors—both of whom have seen the world through civilian eyes and also worn the badge—hold what may be an unpopular opinion due to its lack of polarity. We believe that there is a deep and compelling need for police reform in the United States. The institution itself and its role in our society must change. But we also believe this is not an indictment of the thousands of men and women who toil honorably in law enforcement. Their dedication, bravery, hard work, and sacrifice stands as a stark counterpoint to those few who dishonor the profession, and for that matter, in contrast to a broken system itself.

These two views are not at all mutually exclusive. Holding them both does, however, prevent one from accepting a cleaner, more seductive narrative. Life is easier when things are clear-cut, when the choice is between good and evil, right and wrong. The truth is that things are rarely that simple. The truth is also that perspective plays a considerable role in how we see things.

We have tried to explore this grayness of our

contemporary existence through this four-book arc. Few would argue about whether or not Tyler Garrett is "a bad guy" (except for Garrett himself, of course). But what about Wardell Clint's actions? Or those of any of the other major characters in this series? Hardly anyone escapes these pages without some nobility *and* some dirt on them, and perspective matters.

Just like real life.

The authors would like to thank:

Chris Rhatigan, for some excellent editing.

Zach McCain, for nailing another cover.

Carla Warren, Judy Orchard, Bonnie Conway, Cheryl Counts, Dave Mather, Melanie Donaldson, Brad Hallock, John Emery, Ron Sarich, Candace Pringle, and Kristi Scalise, for reading this book early and giving invaluable feedback to make it better.

Marty Hill, for inspiring his namesake character.

Jerry Anderson, for the same.

Every reader who took this four-book journey with us. We will see you all further on up the road.

Colin Conway
Frank Zafiro
August 2020

About the Authors

COLIN CONWAY is the author of the 509 Crime Stories, a series of novels set in Eastern Washington with revolving lead characters. They are standalone tales and can be read in any order. He served in the US Army and later was an officer of the Spokane Police Department. He's a commercial real estate broker/investor, owned a laundromat, invested in a bar, and ran a karate school. Colin lives with his beautiful life partner, their three wonderful children, and a crazy, codependent Vizsla that rules their world. Find out more about him at his official website: **ColinConway.com**.

FRANK ZAFIRO was a police officer in Spokane, Washington, from 1993 to 2013. He retired as a captain. He is the author of numerous crime novels, including the River City novels, and hosts the podcast *Wrong Place, Write Crime*. He lives in Redmond, Oregon, with his wife Kristi, dogs Richie and Wiley, and a very self-assured cat named Pasta. He is an avid hockey fan and a tortured guitarist. You can keep up with Frank at **FrankZafiro.com**.